"From the Predators, I've Learned That a Man Takes What He Wants."

Brig's hand curved itself to the back of her neck, the rough skin of his fingers snaring strands of her auburn hair. Jordanna took a quick breath and lost it. His thumb traced the outline of her lips.

The hand at the back of her neck increased its pressure to lift her on tiptoe. Her hands slid over the slick material of his vest. Passion leaped between them like a living flame as he parted her lips and explored the intimate recesses of her mouth. Desire quivered through her, warm and golden, a shaft of sunshine lighting her soul.

Together they blazed a trail of golden fire across the mountains. They searched for a game trophy—the biggest prize remained the elusive possession of their own hearts—a treasure which would be their glory . . . or their destruction!

Books by Janet Dailey

Ride the Thunder
The Rogue
Touch the Wind

Published by POCKET BOOKS

Janet Dailey

Ride the Thunder

PUBLISHED BY POCKET BOOKS NEW YORK

Another *Original* publication of POCKET BOOKS

 POCKET BOOKS, a Simon & Schuster division of
GULF & WESTERN CORPORATION
1230 Avenue of the Americas, New York, N.Y. 10020

Copyright © 1980 by Janet Dailey

ISBN: 0-671-83604-8

First Pocket Books printing July, 1980

10 9 8 7 6 5 4 3 2 1

POCKET and colophon are trademarks of Simon & Schuster.

Printed in the U.S.A.

Ride the Thunder

Prologue

THE LARGE DEN was paneled with rich walnut wood. Sunlight filtered through the sheer curtains over the windowed door opening onto the rooftop of the penthouse apartment. The walls gleamed with a natural luster. Few books lined the shelves which ran floor to ceiling in one corner of the room. The volumes it contained were devoted to weapons and hunting and were worn from frequent handling. Mostly the shelves held souvenirs and photographs of a hunter posed beside his kill. A mounted wolverine prowled an upper shelf while a lacquered coiled rattler threatened the unwary from its shelf nearer the floor.

The trophy heads of deer, moose, and elk, hanging on the walls, were interspersed with the more exotic breeds of rhino, wildebeest, and gazelle. A mounted bobcat stalked the hearth of the plain brick fireplace; its prey, the Chinese pheasant on the other side. Atop the mantel, twin ivory tusks from a rogue elephant formed an arc for a golden eagle, mounted with its wings spread, protecting the lifeless gray squirrel in its

1

talons. On the floor, in front of the fireplace, was the shaggy brown hide of a grizzly, its beady eyes and bared teeth frozen in silent menace.

An expensive and solidly built gun cabinet sat against one wall. The metal barrels of the weaponry gleamed from careful oiling, but the wooden stocks showed the wear of use. A massive desk had no litter of paperwork on its top, only more photographs and mementos from successful hunts.

A pair of twin sofas covered with blond leather faced each other across the bearskin rug. Seated on one was a gangly fourteen-year-old boy dressed in a sky-blue sweater and darker blue trousers. His long, delicate fingers were busily cleaning the bore of a rifle. A lock of dark, nearly black hair had fallen across his forehead as he bent to his task. There was a quality of perfection about his sensitive features, as if drawn by an artist. Long, thickly curling lashes outlined a pair of velvet brown eyes that were earnestly concentrating on the rifle.

Seated opposite him on the other sofa, a twelve-year-old girl was similarly engaged in cleaning a lighter weight weapon. There, the resemblance ended. Her coltish figure was clad in crisp blue jeans and an over-sized gray sweatshirt. Her long hair fell in a single copper braid down the front of her shoulder. When it interfered with her task, she flipped it behind her in a gesture of impatience. Fresh and eager, her features glowed with vitality. Only the curve of her lips exhibited the vulnerability and sensitivity that stamped her brother's handsome face. Her hazel eyes were heavily flecked with green that could flash and sparkle in anger or excitement, or become dark and troubled like the sea.

From a high-backed armchair that had been covered in brown leather and worn to a tan shade, a man silently supervised the pair. He absently rubbed a cloth over the wooden stock of the Winchester in his lap, a gesture that was both affectionate and respectful. His rifle was already cleaned after its recent use. Long years of experience had enabled him to finish before the pair he was watching.

A briar pipe was clamped between his teeth, its bowl dead although the aromatic blend of tobacco lingered in the air. Dressed in a bush jacket and brown pants, he looked the part of the hunter. His dark brown hair had an auburn hue. Distinguished tufts of gray were appearing at the temples. Virilely handsome, he possessed an air of remoteness. Over the years, he had attained such a control over his emotions that little of what he was thinking or feeling was visible in his chiseled face or dark brown eyes.

From beyond the closed door of the den came the sound of another door opening and closing. Instantly the young girl's head came up, a viridescent shimmer of excitement lighting her eyes. The rifle and cleaning tools were swiftly cast aside as she jumped to her feet.

"That must be Mother. Wait until I tell her the news!"

"Jordanna, wait." By the time the man had taken the pipe from his mouth to call to her, she had darted from the room. The corners of his mouth tightened briefly as he set his pipe on the tobacco stand beside his chair. Without any display of haste, he rose and walked to the gun cabinet. After locking his rifle inside, he turned and met the look of anticipation in his son's eyes. "You finish cleaning your rifle, Kit. I'll inspect it before it's returned to the case." A smile accompanied the firm order.

"Yes, Dad." The teen-aged boy returned his attention to the task without any show of unwillingness or resentment, as his father left the room.

Moving from the strictly masculine den to the chandeliers and brocade of the living room was almost a cultural shock. A plush carpet in the palest shade of muted green covered the floor of the spacious room. Paintings of Italian masters, both originals and expensive prints, adorned the off-white walls in a variety of heavy gilt frames. A full-size sofa was covered in a blue brocade with a faint gold design. Crystal and brass lamps resting on Italian-style tables flanked the sofa, while a long coffee table of pecan stood in front of it. Matching love seats in the same fragile green as the carpet faced each other in front of a white marble fireplace. The monochromatic theme of pale green was repeated in the velvet draperies and their heavily swagged valances. Vases filled with freshly cut flowers were scattered about the room, the flowers all varigated shades of pink.

In the center of all this studied elegance stood a raven-haired woman, a ravishingly beautiful creature of cool sophistication. A uniformed maid waited at her side, a sable coat draped over her arm, while the woman gracefully removed the black kid gloves she wore.

"Thank you, Tessa." As she handed the gloves to the maid, her cultured voice made a polite dismissal; she had no further need for the maid's services.

The maid quietly left the room, as the copper-haired girl came rushing in. "Guess what?" she challenged her mother with breathless excitement.

"What on earth are you doing in those wretched clothes, Jordanna?" A pair of jade green eyes skimmed the girl's attire with open distaste. Her own winter-beige suit was cut in the latest style, all accessories painstakingly coordinated for the best effect. "I thought I told Tessa to throw them out. You have a closet full of beautiful outfits that I've bought you. It's time you stopped looking like a common little hoyden."

"We've been target practicing." The criticism sailed over the young girl's head. "Dad says I can go hunting with him next weekend when he takes Kit," Jordanna announced with unabashed joy.

A shocked stillness claimed the lovely alabaster features, to be slowly replaced by a building anger. "You're talking nonsense."

"No, I'm not," Jordanna insisted. "Dad said he would take me. Honestly, he did." Sharp-eyed, she caught the movement in her side vision and turned. "If you don't believe me, you can ask him. You said you'd take me, didn't you, Dad?" she appealed to the man entering the living room.

"Yes, I did," he admitted, the even look of his brown eyes meeting the green fire of his wife's gaze.

"Jordanna is a young girl, Fletcher. It's bad enough that you have to take Christopher on this bloody test of manhood without dragging my daughter along to witness it!"

"But I want to go," Jordanna protested.

"You shut up and keep out of this!" Her mother whirled on the girl, barely controlling the fury that trembled through her. "This is between your father and me."

"Livvie, you are over-reacting, as usual." The dryly issued statement provided more fuel for an already blazing temper.

"Over-reacting?!!" The girl was forgotten as the woman glared at the man facing her. Long, manicured nails were dug into the soft palms of her hands. "That's your favorite accusation, isn't it? Olivia, you are being too emotional." Sarcastically she mimed his previous comment.

"You are," Fletcher Smith stated, the calm tenor of his voice never fluctuating. "Look at you. You're trembling like a leaf."

"What do you expect me to do?" she cried in frustration. "My daughter comes up to me and announces she's going hunting with you next weekend. She is my child, too, Fletcher! I believe I'm entitled to have a say in this matter. My permission is required, too."

"I would have discussed it with you, but you are so rarely around. You have such a busy calendar of engagements whenever I'm home." His comment held an underlying hint of condemnation.

"Which is seldom!" Olivia Smith retorted. "And when you are here, you spend two-thirds of your time in that room with your stuffed animal heads and your damned guns! Hunting may be your life, but it isn't mine!"

"Isn't it?" The firmly chiseled mouth quirked in cynical humor. "You do quite well at stalking the male gender of the two-legged species, I've heard. You seem to be as adept at collecting trophies as I."

"Why don't you come straight to the point, Fletcher?" Her embittered challenge was cold with anger. "Do you want to know how many lovers I've had?"

The taut line of his jaw seemed to become sculpted in bronze. His gaze ran pointedly over Jordanna's whitened face. "If you intend to pursue this topic, Livvie, may I suggest that you wait until after Jordanna has left the room? Considering your supposed concern for the unpleasantries she might be exposed to in her formative years, you can hardly disagree."

A shaky, bitter laugh came from his wife. "You are good at making me look like a bitch, aren't you, Fletcher?" she murmured. Rounding her green eyes to hold back the stinging tears, she looked at her daughter. "Go to your room, Jordanna."

Instead the girl turned to her father and wrapped her arms around his middle to hug him tightly. "I'm sorry, Daddy," she choked on a sob. "I didn't mean for her to get mad at you."

"It's all right, Jordanna." He held her for a comforting instant then straightened the braid of her red hair so it rested along her spine. Unwinding her arms from around him, he set her firmly away. "You run along now."

"Please don't let her make me stay home next weekend," she begged him. "I want to go with you."

"I know," he nodded and gave her a gentle shove out of the room. "Run along."

Slow, dejected strides carried her from the room. Her obedience lasted until she reached the concealment of the hallway. There, she stopped and flattened herself to the wall to listen, wanting to hear the outcome, yet hating the bitter arguing that seemed to hurt her more than it hurt them.

"Jordanna isn't going with you," her mother declared. "It's bad enough that you are taking Christopher. He's such a fine, sensitive boy. When are you going to realize that you can't force him to grow up to be just like you?"

"Considering the way you have pampered him, it will be a miracle if he ever grows up. Most boys his age have already been hunting," he argued. "I've waited until now because you have kept saying he was too young. Kit wants to go. Stop smothering him with your love and let him grow, Livvie."

"Christopher doesn't want to go. If he says he does, then it's only because he knows it's what you want to hear."

"You are wrong." He didn't raise his voice or alter its even pitch. "Some of his friends at school have been deer-hunting and told him all about it. Kit is excited about going."

"He doesn't realize that you actually expect him to kill a deer. He feels things, Fletcher. He could never kill a poor, defenseless animal in cold blood. You get a thrill out of it."

"When are you going to stop equating hunting with murder?" he demanded.

"When you stop trying to mold my son into what you believe a man should be!" she retorted angrily. "I should have stopped you when you bought Christopher his first gun."

"Rifle," he corrected automatically.

"Rifle. Gun. What's the difference? You convinced me to let him keep it. I stood by while you taught him how to use it. How you ever managed to talk me into letting Jordanna learn to shoot is something I'll never understand. You always get your way, Fletcher. I even agreed to let you take Christopher hunting. But not Jordanna. I won't let her go with you."

"Both of them want to go. I want them to go. I don't get to see them that often. If they aren't in school, then I'm gone somewhere. I want some time for us to be a family, to share things together."

"Then stay home! Stop traipsing all over the world!" Olivia Smith shouted in frustration. "I'm not asking for myself anymore, but for the children. Stop this senseless hunting of yours."

"It's what I enjoy. There are few pleasures left to me," he stated.

"That's a dig at me, I suppose. Have I made your life miserable Fletcher? I hope so, because mine has been hell since I married you!"

"Liv, why do we have to argue? Why can't we discuss this rationally?" He tiredly ran his hand over the graying hair above his ear.

"Why can't you give up hunting?"

"You don't know anything about hunting. You think it's a sport of killing. It's the thrill of the chase, Livvie. It's pitting your skills and knowledge against another. It's the hunt, not the kill. Come with us next weekend and find out for yourself."

"After all these years that I've stayed home alone, you are finally asking me to come with you. It's too late." Her husky voice throbbed with emotion. "You have never been here when I've needed you, Fletcher. You've been off on some safari or in some godforsaken place where I couldn't reach you. You have shut me out. Is it any wonder that I've turned to others? Yet you blame me for it. Now you expect me to go with you when you haven't made a single concession to me."

"What do you think this apartment is? I hate New York. This is where you want to live, not me. It isn't a fit place to raise children, not that you give a damn. All you care about is shopping and parties and the theater." For the first time, there was a thread of angry exasperation in his voice. "I don't understand why you are so upset that I want to take Jordanna and Kit both with me next weekend. You would have a whole two days to spend with whomever your latest lover is!"

"What a pity I didn't think of that!" she laughed, but it was a brittle, false sound.

"Damn you, Livvie!" He crushed her stiff shoulders in his grip as if he wanted to shake her. "You are my wife."

She held herself rigid in his arms, not yielding to his attempted domination or his angry declaration. "I stopped loving you a long time ago, Fletcher." Slowly, she was released as Fletcher Smith collected himself, to regard her again with his former composure. It was Olivia who turned away. "As for Jordanna, you can take her with you next weekend. A couple of days to myself just might be what I need. You've won, Fletcher—but then, you always do."

"I give you my word, Livvie, that she won't do any shooting. She'll just tag along with Kit and me. That's all," he stated.

Jordanna had her answer. She was going on the hunting trip after all. But she couldn't find any elation at the news. Tears were streaming down her face. There was a sickening lump churning about in her stomach as she slowly made her way down the hallway to her room.

The first light of dawn was beginning to filter into the Vermont woods. The air was still and quiet except for the twitter of birds in the treetops. A man, a boy, and a young girl were stationed next to a fallen tree. The man was crouched, not moving, his rifle nestled in the crook of his arm, the muzzle pointed away from the children. The boy was sitting on his knees, the barrel of his rifle resting on the dead trunk of the tree. Dressed in a brand new hunting jacket of red plaid, he watched the deer trail that wound closely past their hiding position.

The girl was sitting cross-legged on the ground, her hands shoved deep in the pockets of her parka and the collar turned up around her neck. A white wool scarf was wound around her head, covering most of her copper-red hair, and knotted at the throat. It was chilly in the dawn hours of the autumn day, but Jordanna was afraid to shiver. She was afraid to blink. Her father's instructions had been very precise. They mustn't move or make a single sound. He had scouted the area before the hunting season had opened and assured them a big whitetail buck would come by this very spot.

Very carefully and quietly, Kit sat back on his heels and without turning his head, slid a questioning glance at his father. The anxiety of waiting was written on his face. Fletcher Smith gave him an encouraging smile and, with a movement of his eyes, directed his son's attention to the trail.

Jordanna saw Kit's eyes light up with excitement. She followed the direction of his gaze, but found nothing. She stared until her eyes hurt, then remembered her father's admonition to keep her gaze moving. Seconds later, she saw a flicker of movement, concentrated on it, and recognized the object. It was a doe, a small, delicate-looking creature no higher than the belt buckle on her father's pants.

Despite the carpet of dead leaves and the heavy underbrush, the doe didn't make a sound as it walked cautiously along the trail toward them. That doe was followed by two more does and a small fawn. Jordanna barely stopped herself from breathing in sharply. Her mouth opened in awe but not a sound came out. Her dancing eyes met the glance from her father. He winked his understanding of the enchantment of the wild creatures parading past. Kit's grin echoed her excitement. This sight alone was worth enduring the cold and the discomfort of cramped muscles.

The does disappeared up the deer trail, working their way to a higher elevation. Still, the trio maintained their silent vigil. The female deer weren't the object of their hunt. They were waiting for the antlered head that heralded a buck. More minutes dragged by and the anxiety mounted again.

Fletcher Smith lightly rested his hand on his son's shoulder. Where once there had been nothing but trees and brush stood a seven-point buck. Its head was turned to study the trail behind it, testing the motionless air. With a one-finger signal, Fletcher indicated for his son to wait until the deer was in closer range. Jordanna's heart was pounding so loudly that she was sure the deer could hear it. With a twitch of its white tail, it started forward—proud, majestic, and wary. Not even a leaf rustled beneath its hooves.

When the buck was within easy range, the hand tightened on Kit's shoulder. Remembering the hours of practice, he took aim and squeezed the trigger. At the same moment the rifle was fired, the buck took a bounding leap toward a nearby thicket. Kit jumped up.

"I got him! I hit him, didn't I, Dad?" His positive statement dwindled into uncertainty. The deer was nowhere in sight.

"You hit him," his father assured him. "But you should have led him a bit more. You hit him in the stomach."

"I was watching all the time and I didn't see that," Jordanna declared in amazement. "How do you know where Kit shot him?"

"By the sound of the bullet when it hit," he explained. "It makes different sounds when it strikes different parts of the body. After a while you learn to recognize the difference."

"Man, that was really something," Kit declared, at least partly satisfied with the accuracy of his shooting. "It was just like the guys said in school. He was a big buck, wasn't he, Dad?"

"He was good size, very respectable for your first," Fletcher agreed with qualification and smiled broadly. "I wish your mother could see you now. She was so positive you wouldn't like hunting."

"It's great!" His pride of accomplishment was overflowing into his excitement. "Come on, Dad. Let's go get my deer."

Fletcher Smith allowed himself to be hurried to the deer trail by his eager son. Jordanna lagged behind. Her father's comment about their mother had brought back unwanted memories. With an effort, Jordanna shrugged the vague sadness aside.

A tell-tale splatter of blood marked the trail of the wounded animal. They followed it to the thicket. The sound of something thrashing in the dead brush brought them to a halt. Fletcher pointed in the direction of the sound and the trio hurried cautiously toward it.

The whitetail buck lay in a small clearing on the other side of the thicket, unable to rise. Blood stained its hide and the ground beneath it. Its head was lifted and turned toward their approach. They all stopped at the sight of the expressive brown eyes looking at them.

"You'll have to shoot it, Kit," Fletcher stated. "If you leave it like that, it will take a long time for it to die." He gave the teen-ager a gentle push toward the deer. Under the regard of those gentle brown eyes, Kit shook his head in refusal. "You have to put him out of his misery. Look at his eyes, boy. Can't you see the forgiveness?"

Kit stared, his face whitening under the silent blessing. The rifle slipped from his hand as he turned and ran, tripping and stumbling over the twigs and underbrush. Fletcher Smith took a step after him, his hand outstretched.

"Don't worry, Dad." Jordanna had already reached down to pick up the rifle. As she spoke, she turned and aimed it at the fallen deer. "I'll do it." The trigger was squeezed and the shot rang out before he could react. "He's dead now," she said simply and quietly. Lifting her gaze to her father's face, she tried to offer some comfort. "Kit didn't understand."

His hand seemed to be trembling as it gripped her shoulder and pulled her into his arms. He hugged her tightly for a moment, then drew a deep, shuddering breath. He smiled down at her, a flood of warmth and tenderness spilling from his eyes.

"You've always been my little girl, haven't you, Jordanna?" he said.

"Always," she agreed. There was a special closeness between them. Mutual understanding and mutual needs fulfilled.

"Do you want to help me dress out this deer?" Fletcher drew a knife from its sheath. "It would be foolish to leave it lying here."

"Sure, I'll help," Jordanna agreed.

"You don't think you'll feel queasy? It's alright if you do," he added.

"No. What do you want me to do?"

Kit was sitting in the back seat of the enclosed jeep when they returned to where they had parked. Fletcher said nothing as he secured the dressed buck to the rack atop the vehicle. Along the trail, he had caught the tell-tale odor where Kit had lost his early morning break-fast. One look at his ashen face was proof enough that he wasn't feeling much better now.

Once they were back on the main road, he glanced in the rear-view mirror to meet the haunted eyes of his son. "It's alright, Kit. You don't have to apologize or feel guilty for the way you behaved. It was the first time you've ever been exposed to anything like that. It's bound to be something of a trauma. The next time we go hunting, it will be easier."

"I don't want to go hunting any more," Kit stated flatly.

"I'm sure you feel that way now," Fletcher agreed patiently. "But you'll change your mind later on."

"No, I won't."

Fletcher didn't pursue the argument as he returned his attention to the traffic on the highway. Jordanna saw the dispirited light that dulled his brown eyes. She glanced over her shoulder at her brother.

"I brought your rifle, Kit. Here." She started to hand it over the seat to him.

"You can have it, Jordanna. I don't want it." He turned to stare out the window at the scenery racing by.

"But it was a present," she protested. "Dad gave it to you. You just can't . . ." Her father's silencing hand rested on her arm. Jordanna faced the front and he patted her arm in approval.

PART ONE

THE MEETING

Chapter I

THE BIG BUCKSKIN horse trotted across the high meadow with a free-swinging stride. Its golden coat was shaggy with winter hair. Its warm, moist breath formed clouds, twin spirals coming from its nostrils. The horse mouthed the metal bar, jangling the bit against its teeth. The leather saddle creaked beneath the weight of the horse's rider, blunted spurs jingling on his boots.

He was a tall man with a rangy build that deceptively hid solidly muscled flesh. Relaxed in the saddle, he rode in a partly slouched position. Yet every movement of the horse was transmitted to him through the reins and the bunching muscles beneath the saddle. Beneath the indolent posture was a keen alertness.

His boots were dusty and dirty and worn down at the heels. The metal of his spurs had become dull with time. The faded but still serviceable Levis that covered the long length of his legs were patched at the knees and on the seat. A heavy suede jacket lined with sheepskin hung down to his hips, a slit at the back for easier riding. The hands holding the reins were gloved, the leather worn smooth from much usage. The collar of his jacket was turned up against the breeze blowing down from the high mountains. A dusty felt Stetson was pulled low on his head. Dark coffee-colored hair grew thickly, its length curling into the collar of his jacket.

Hours in the sun had browned the planes and hollows of his face to a bronze hue. A full mustache grew above his mouth, a neatly trimmed brush of dark brown. His eyes were brown, a dry and dusty shade. The sun had creased permanent lines that feathered out from the corners of his eyes. His thick, dark brows had a natural arch to them. Strength, sureness, and stamina were etched in his features. He was a man others would go out of their way to avoid irritating. If the situation demanded it, he could be ruthless. Other times, simply hard with a trace of cynicism.

His keen eyes spotted something thirty feet to the right. With a twist of his wrist, Brig McCord reined the buckskin toward it. As the horse drew close, he slowed it to a walk. The spring grass of the mountain meadow swished against the buckskin's black legs. Where the trees grew down to the meadow's edge, patches of snow could still cling to their shadows, the remants of the last blizzard to hit Idaho in the spring.

The horse stopped of its own accord, snorting and tossing its head at the object near its feet. As the buckskin shifted sideways, Brig saw the skeletal remains of a calf, the bones partially covered by its red hide.

"Damn!" he swore softly at the sight. How many did that make? He'd lost count.

He looked away, his hard gaze sliding to the patches of snow. That spring blizzard had come at the worst possible time—calving time. He'd be lucky if forty percent of his spring calf crop had survived. One average year—that was all he had needed to get his head above water. Instead, he was going to be lucky if he didn't lose the ranch. If he'd had some insurance . . .

"Hell, I couldn't afford the premium!" Brig inter-

rupted that thought with a soft curse. Jabbing a spur
in the horse's ribs, he reined it away from the carcass
the scavengers had already picked clean. The horse
bounded into a canter and snorted a disgruntled sound.
It fell into a tireless, ground-eating lope that it could
maintain for miles. A complete survey of the losses
couldn't be made at that pace and Brig slowed his
mount to a striding trot.

Two more calves were found. The carcass of a
third was in the woods, dragged there by a scavenging
predator. With each calf, Brig's mind worked harder
to find a solution to his problems. At a cold mountain
stream fed by the snow run-offs, Brig stopped his horse
to let it drink. His gaze lifted to the mountains. Maybe
if the sheep market would hold together, as well as
Jocko's flock, he could recoup some of his cattle losses.
The trend wasn't good.

His gaze roved back to the meadow and the rocky
escarpment rising on one side. A movement caught his
eye. He focused on it. Grazing near the base of the
rocks was a large, heavy-bodied animal. When it lifted
its head, Brig saw the massive curling horns hugging
close to its head then winging out to the sides.

"A bighorn sheep," he murmured. "I wonder what
it's doing at this elevation."

The buckskin shook his head sideways as if replying
to the question. The leather and metal of the bridle
rattled together. In a flash, the big ram took to the
rocks, showing the distinctive white circle on its rump.
Amidst the clatter of hooves striking stone, it scrambled
to the safety of higher ground where its sure-footed
swiftness gave it the advantage over predators.

Brig watched until the wild sheep was out of sight,
then walked his horse through the mountain stream.
There had been a trophy pair of horns on that bighorn
ram, a full curl or better. But he wasn't interested in
such things. He killed a couple of elk a year for meat,
and a deer now and then for variety. Two years ago, a
marauding black bear had ended up hanging on the
wall in the ranch house. Shooting that ram for its

horns wasn't reason enough for Brig. He'd seen and done enough killing in his life that he found no sport in it.

Funny, he hadn't thought about those times in years, Brig realized. They belonged to another lifetime. This wild Idaho country had a way of fading memories. Either that or the fact that he was on the wrong side of thirty.

The buckskin had been wandering along without direction. A low-hanging branch took a swipe at his Stetson and Brig ducked at the last minute. He halted his mount and looked around. One corner of his mouth curled into his mustache. It had been ten years since he'd done more than pass through this area looking for cattle . . . before that, almost thirty years.

Taking a minute to orient himself, Brig kneed his mount to the right, where a tangled mass of undergrowth formed a dark mound about a hundred yards away. The trees were dense. The horse's hooves made little sound on the thick carpet of pine needles. Hugging close to the horse's black mane, Brig avoided the low branches that tried to sweep him off the saddle. When he reached the dark mass, encroaching on a small clearing, he dismounted and looped the reins over the buckskin's head to lead it while he walked closer. The horse pricked its ears at the overgrown mound, snorting nervously and testing the air.

Beneath the tangling vines and bushes was the rusted hulk of a fuselage, all that remained of the private plane that had crashed here. Brig had been nine that summer. His gaze strayed to the tumble of small rocks on the far side of the clearing, rocks he had carried to cover the graves of his parents, who had been killed instantly in the crash. He had buried them himself, so that the animals would quit eating their bodies. Using the limb of a tree, he had scraped and dug two shallow graves in the rocky soil and mounded them with rocks.

Tipping his head back, Brig looked up. The branches of the trees formed a roof, a leaky roof that permitted dappling rays of sunlight in. It had been almost as thick then, hiding the wreckage from the search planes. And a little boy was a mighty small object when viewed from two thousand feet above the ground.

It had been more than a week after the crash before the first plane had flown over. There had been several after that in the next three days, then none. Brig tried to remember the small, starving boy that had followed a bear around one whole day, eating what the bear ate. But he couldn't remember how he had survived, what he had eaten, or how he had kept warm on the cold mountain nights.

For two months he'd lived here, alone, learning the laws of survival from the hardest teacher of all—nature. Then he'd stumbled into a shepherd's camp, an uncle of Jocko—the man who looked after his flock of sheep now. He'd spent two weeks with the shepherd, who couldn't leave his flock untended to return a small boy to civilization. In those two weeks, he had learned much about herding sheep and the shepherd's simple philosophy. Then the rancher had come, bringing the shepherd's supplies and taking the small boy back.

His unerring directions had brought the authorities to the crash site. Brig lowered his head to look at the rusted body of the aircraft, half-hidden by the weeds. The radio equipment, instruments, and all parts that were salvageable had been removed. His parents were no longer buried in the graves he'd dug for them. Their bodies had been exhumed and flown back East for a proper burial, and he'd gone to live with his grandfather, Sanger. But he'd never forgotten this place, this wild and free land.

When he'd finally come back fourteen years ago, at the age of twenty-four, he'd felt that he was coming home. He'd bought the section of land where his ranch house now stood and leased this federal graze . . . and struggled to make it pay. It had been rough. Most of the time he'd been lucky to break even. Then two bad years in a row had been followed by this spring blizzard that practically wiped out his calf crop. If the future had looked bleak before, it was nothing compared to what he faced now.

Turning to the horse, Brig gripped the saddlehorn and swung aboard. He paused for a moment in the clearing, then rode back through the trees to the meadow. Wildflowers spilled over the high mountain valley, bobbing their heads in the nippy breeze. Before he'd lose all this, he'd eat a little pride and go to the Sanger's for a loan.

A dozen head of Hereford cattle looked up as the shaggy-coated buckskin carried its rider toward them. Brig began hazing them toward the ranch headquarters. Maybe after the spring roundup was done, the calves branded and castrated, and the yearling bulls dehorned, he'd find out things were not as bad as they seemed now. He doubted it. Grim-faced, he rode on.

Tired and thirsty after the long drive from the ranch to town on a graded track that didn't deserve the term road, Brig parked his four-wheel-drive pickup in front of a building where an unlighted neon sign in the window advertised Coors. His dusty brown eyes lingered on the suitcase sitting on the seat beside him, his mouth tightening into a thin line.

With a yank of the handle, he pushed the truck door open and stepped out. He glanced around, separating the tourists on the sidewalk from the townfolk of Salmon. As he walked to the entrance of the bar, he knocked the dust from his hat and brushed at his clothes. They'd been clean when he started out this morning.

The interior of the bar was dark after the brilliance of a July sun. Brig paused inside the door to let his eyes adjust to the gloom. The juke box in the corner was playing a country song about a man who kissed an angel every morning. Tables and chairs were scattered around the room, empty of customers. Two men were sitting on stools, leaning their elbows on the carved oak counter bar. They gave him a sidelong look and resumed their conversation.

Brig walked to the far end of the long bar and slid onto a stool, resting a boot on the brass foot rail. There was no one behind the bar although there were sounds coming from the back room. Pushing his hat to the back of his head, he shook a cigarette from the pack in his shirt pocket. Without removing the match from its book, he snapped it against the sandpaper-rough strip. There was no breeze but he cupped the flame to his cigarette from habit.

Centered in the shelves of liquor behind the bar was a clock with a slowly rotating series of advertisements on one side. With each quarter turn, a new advertisement slid into place. Brig read the ads for the local funeral home and the bank. As the one for the insurance company fell into the slot, a woman emerged from the back room carrying a half-dozen bottles of liquor to restock the shelves.

Her hair was bleached to a brassy shade of blonde. Blue eye shadow coated her lids above a heavy line of black eyeliner and lashes matted with mascara. The excessive use of make-up gave her a hard look, but it didn't cover up the vulnerable softness of her red-painted lips or the open honesty of her blue eyes . . . or the wrinkles collecting around them. Her full figure was edging toward the plump side. The plain white blouse she wore was unbuttoned to expose the cleavage of her abundantly round breasts. The black straight skirt was stretched like a second skin across her hips, defying the strength of the stitching. The effect was crudely suggestive. Brig felt the stirring in his loins from an abstinence forced on him by the endless demands of the spring ranchwork—and the knowledge that the woman was good in bed.

Intent on her task, the brassy blonde didn't see him sitting at the dimly lit corner of the counter. "Hello, Trudie," Brig spoke to draw her attention.

She stopped and turned abruptly. Her widened eyes found him in the shadows, her look of surprise changing to one of delighted recognition. Then it became masked slightly with an attitude of coyness that bordered on provocative.

"Well, well, well. The old lobo wolf has finally come down out of the mountains," she declared and hurriedly set the liquor bottles on the work counter behind the bar. "I was beginning to think you had moved on to parts unknown."

"And leave my favorite girl behind? I wouldn't do that, Trudie." His gaze was deliberately suggestive, running over her figure with a lusting look.

"Favorite girl? Hah!" she laughed aside that remark, but it started a warm glow of pleasure that spread through her expression. "What'll ya have, Brig?"

"Beer."

"On tap?" At his affirmative nod, she drew him a glass, letting a head form on the pale gold liquid.

"How's tricks?" Brig sipped at the beer and wiped the foam from his mustache with the back of his hand.

"Not bad since the tourists hit town for the summer float trips on the 'River of No Return.' " Her emphasis made fun of the phrase. She changed the subject then. "I suppose you're in town to pick up supplies. What's this—your last stop before heading back to the ranch?"

"This is my first stop. I sent Tandy Barnes in last week for a month's supplies," he explained, referring to his wrangler and all-around ranch hand.

"What brought you to town then?" A puzzled frown followed the lines already stamped in her forehead. Immediately she added, "And don't say 'me,' because I won't buy that."

"I'm headin' into Idaho Falls to catch a plane for New York." He swirled the beer in his glass and watched the dissipating foam. For all the indifference in his tone, there was a flat, dry look to his eyes.

"New York? What for?" Trudie breathed out a soft, incredulous laugh. "Most of the ranchers around here can't afford a glass of beer and you're taking a vacation."

"I can't afford this either. It isn't a vacation. It's a

business trip," Brig corrected in a brisk voice. His mouth quirked in an expression of cynicism. "I've gotta visit a rich cousin and see if I can't collect on a few favors."

"A rich cousin?"

"Yeah." He drained the beer from the glass and set it down. Picking up the cigarette burning in the ashtray, he let it dangle from his mouth, squinting one-eyed against the smoke. Standing, he reached in his pocket. "How much do I owe you for the beer?"

"It's on the house." She waved aside his attempt to pay and lowered her voice to add, "Everything's always on the house. You know that, Brig."

"Thanks." A faint smile softened the usually hard line of his mouth.

Brig was aware of her meaning. Every town, no matter how small, had its quota of local drunks and a whore or two, whether the respectable, church-going folk wanted to admit it or not. Trudie fell in the latter category. Except for the first time, he'd never had to pay for her services, so he'd gradually stopped regarding her in that light these last ten years. She was a warm, giving woman, who supplemented her income with the highest paying part-time job she could find. She wasn't a hard-core professional. Those were the kind he regarded with contempt.

"Have another beer." Trudie was pouring him one before he could refuse. With a faint shrug of his shoulders, Brig sat back down on the stool.

The blonde walked to the work counter where she'd left the new bottles of liquor. "That was really some winter. It hit everybody hard." From under the counter, she pulled out a set of wooden steps and took two of the bottles, tucking one under her arm. "Jake Phelps was in last month and said he ran out of hay in March."

"I had plenty of hay. That May blizzard hit me right at calving time." The first beer Brig had downed to quench his parched throat. This second one, he nursed along. "I lost almost two-thirds of the calf crop."

"Oh no, Brig." She glanced over her shoulder and gave him a commiserating look.

"As you said, it hit everybody hard," he said diffidently.

Crushing his cigarette in the ashtray, he watched her climb the two steps and rest a knee on the counter to reach a high shelf on the wall behind the bar. The tight black skirt rode up to her thigh on one side. His attention began to dwell on her heart-shaped bottom and the shapely curve of her legs. Again he felt that stirring hardness growing inside of him.

It was a full second before Brig realized Trudie had partially turned to look at him. Boldly he lifted his gaze. Something seemed to catch fire in her eyes. He noticed the way her breasts strained against the material of her blouse as she took a breath and appeared to hold it. Then she was climbing down the two steps.

"This trip to New York," she said, turning to face him once more, a soft, breathless quality to her voice, "is it necessary for you to leave right away?"

"There's nothing to be gained by postponing it."

"Not even until tomorrow?" Without giving him a chance to respond, she glanced at the two men farther down the bar. "Do you guys want anything else?"

The two men looked up from the figuring they were doing on a paper napkin. One shook his head and the other said, "No."

"I'm going in the back room for some supplies. If anyone comes in, holler, will you?"

"Sure."

Her blue eyes made a silent appeal to Brig as she asked, "Would you help me bring out a keg of beer?"

For an answer, Brig straightened his length from the bar stool and walked behind the counter. Trudie led the way through the door into the backroom, pausing to close it after Brig. She had positioned herself so he would have to brush against her as he went by. He felt the faint tremor in her body at the contact and smelled the cloying fragrance of some cheap cologne. Picking up her silent message, Brig could hear the thudding of his own heart. After a long winter in isolation, his desires were easy to arouse.

"The keg is over there." She pointed to a far corner of the dimly lit room and took a step in that direction.

His fingers circled her elbows to halt her. "To hell with the keg, Trudie."

He allowed her a second to resist, although he knew she wouldn't, then turned her into his arms. He had forgotten how short she was as his head came down to claim the red lips already parting to receive his kiss.

His blood ran hot as she molded her amply rounded curves against him. Her firm, round breasts were making an imprint against his flesh, a pair of hard buttons pressing through his shirt. He heard her moan and felt her eager hands clinging to his neck. Her tongue made a wet circle of his lips, then probed his mouth. Her show of aggression unleashed a fragment of savagery in his character. Brig reclaimed the dominant role, bruising her lips with his kisses, until the strain on his neck became too much and he lifted his head to ease it. His breathing was heavy with passion. Trudie was quivering. Her trembling fingers separated the buttons of his shirt from the material, then slipped inside against his flesh and curled into the rough hairs on his chest.

"You don't have to leave today, Brig," she whispered in an aching voice. "Tomorrow is soon enough. I'll be through here in a couple of hours."

Her lips pressed moist kisses on his chest, her warm breath heating flesh already burning. The room was cool, but Brig felt perspiration beading on his skin. His hands were making random forays over her shoulders, waist and back, then pressing her hips harder against his thighs. He ached with a need that threatened to consume him.

When Trudie lifted her head, he took one look at her soft red lips and covered them with a groan.

"Please stay, Brig," she begged under his demanding mouth. "It's been so long."

"I don't believe that," he mumbled with harsh skepticism and tried to silence her needless words. He was beyond the point of caring who had gone before.

"No, with you it's different, Brig," Trudie protested. "It's special. I . . . You know it is."

"Yes, yes, I know," he agreed impatiently.

Her token resistance ended and she seemed to melt against him. "Make love to me, Brig. Do it to me now," she pleaded and began fumbling with the rest of the buttons of his shirt.

Her tight-fitting clothes were unwanted obstacles. He had barely managed to tug her skirt up around her hips when a voice from out front called, "Trudie! You've got a customer!"

She stiffened in his arms and Brig ordered, "Ignore it."

"No." She struggled against his iron hold. "They'll just send someone back here to look for me. Let me go, Brig. Please."

Swearing a savage string of oaths under his breath, he released her and took a step away. He was laboring under the weight of primitive forces that weren't so easily controlled once they had been aroused. Trudie was hastily adjusting her clothes and nervously smoothing her hair into place. She cast one apologetic glance in his direction before hurrying to the door.

He couldn't walk back out there, not yet, not with this hard bone straining against the denim of his pants. Brig cursed again and wiped the perspiration from his chin. The back of his hands came away with a red lipstick smear. Pulling his handkerchief from his back pocket, he wiped his mouth and hand, then jammed it back.

It was several minutes before he felt sufficiently composed to return to the bar. Locating the keg of beer, he hoisted it onto his shoulder and walked to the door. Trudie gave him an apprehensive but adoring look as he entered.

"Where do you want this?"

"You can set it right there for now." She indicated an empty place under the counter near the beer taps. After setting it down, Brig walked around the counter to his stall and the nearly full glass of beer. "That's probably flat," she said. "I'll get you a fresh one."

"Don't bother." A beer wouldn't satisfy the kind of thirst he had. Brig started toward the front door.

"Where are you going?" Trudie hurried out from behind the bar to catch him.

"For a walk." He knew he sounded curt and unfeeling. It hadn't exactly been her fault. But he was still all twisted into knots and as testy as a grizzly out of hibernation.

"Will you be back?" She searched his shuttered expression for some clue to the answer.

"I don't know." He shouldn't have stopped in the first place. He would have been thirty miles closer to Idaho Falls if he hadn't, and that much closer to New York, where fourteen years of work would either be saved or finally lost. At the moment, the importance of that had waned under the potency of baser needs. Trudie took hold of his hand and something hard dug into the center of his work-calloused palm. "Dammit, Trudie!" Brig cursed her for making demands that couldn't be satisfied now.

"It's my house key," she identified the object he had thought was her fingernails. "It's the only one I have. Will you wait for me there? I'll be off work soon."

His fingers closed around the key to make a fist. With a curt nod of agreement, Brig started again for the door. This time Trudie didn't stop him. Outside he paused to take a deep breath. The air was fresh and clean. He wondered if he had taken the key because he truly wanted to be with Trudie or because he wanted to postpone the trip to New York. Releasing a sigh, Brig decided it was a combination of both.

*   *   *

Reaching over, Brig flicked the ashes from the tip of his cigarette into the ashtray on the bedstand. Blonde curls tickled the underside of his chin and he smoothed them against the head nestled on his chest. Then his hand returned to the curve of Trudie's bare waist. Trudie let her fingers explore the flatness of his stomach and follow the dark hairs upward from his belly-button to the scattered cloud of them on his chest. She traced the white scar on his left shoulder, where no hair grew.

"Why haven't you ever married, Brig?" Her voice was thoughtful as her stubby fingers continued to caress his skin.

Women, he thought with absent annoyance; why do they always have to talk after they make love? He'd much rather smoke his cigarette in silence than listen to her murmurings. Containing a sigh, he roused himself sufficiently to answer.

"I'm content with my own company, I guess." He took a drag on his cigarette and let twin trails of smoke curl into his nose.

"Haven't you ever been in love?"

"I guess not." Not since he had discovered that he loved a woman more before he got her into bed than he did afterwards.

"You told me once that you used to be a mercenary. Was that true?" she asked curiously, changing the subject.

A frown briefly knitted his forehead. Had he told her that? Those years were something he rarely discussed with anyone. He considered denying it, but he wasn't ashamed of what he'd done.

"Yes, it's true," Brig admitted.

"Why?"

"Why is it true?" A pillow was propping his head up. He smiled at the brassy mop of curls, finding her question a little on the peculiar side.

"No, silly!" Trudie laughed and looked up at him. There was little makeup left on her face. He had kissed most of it off and the rest had rubbed off on the sheets. She looked older without it, easily his age, but more attractive in a plain sort of way. "Why did you become a mercenary?"

"I don't know. I suppose I fancied myself as some kind of soldier of fortune." It had all been too long ago for him to remember what his motives might have been at the time. And it didn't concern him now.

"But surely your family . . ." she began.

"My parents are dead." But Brig didn't tell her the circumstances of their death or his survival of the crash that had taken their lives. "My grandfather raised me—or tried. We never got along. I was too wild and rebellious and he was too strict. By the time I was fifteen, I'd run away from home seven times. At seventeen, I enlisted and did a tour of Southeast Asia —Nam, Cambodia, Laos. When I came back, nothing had changed. My grandfather still lived in a world that worshipped two gods—money and business— where a man is judged by the number of digits in his bank account and the influential people he knows, not how he got it or what kind of man he is." He stubbed out the cigarette in the ashtray, exhaling a last stream of smoke.

"But why did you become a mercenary?" Trudie lifted herself on one elbow to see his face better. His expression told her little.

The calloused tip of his finger traced a light curve from one side of her jaw, under her chin, and slicing across her throat to the other side. "Because I knew how to kill quickly and silently. I was proficient with almost every weapon that was manufactured at the time and could teach others how to use them." Brig paused at the leap of fear in her eyes, the twinge of mistrust, and wished he'd kept his mouth shut. "It was all I knew when I got out of the service. It was what I did best. When someone offered to pay me a lot of money to do it, I took it."

"Is that why you did it? For the money?"

"I thought that was why at the time," he admitted. "But I was probably trying to get back at my grandfather. He was livid when I told him what I was going to do. As far as he was concerned, mercenaries were the scum of the earth. It didn't matter to him that the men who worked for him were little more than that. They went across the country setting up his little discount chain stores and driving local merchants out of business. He hired respectable mercenaries, but he couldn't stand the thought of his grandson becoming one. He made a fortune and ruined a lot of good people along the way."

His voice became hard with remembered bitterness. While some had admired his grandfather's business acumen and others had envied his wealth, Brig had only felt disgust for the man whose given name he bore—Brigham Sanger, founder of Sanger Discount Stores.

"Brig?" Trudie's voice was hesitant. She was a little bit frightened by the cold look that had hardened his features.

His eyes softened as they refocused on her face. Something like a smile touched his mouth, curving the corners into his mustache.

"My grandfather is probably the reason I kept hiring out to fight on the losing side. I was always backing the little guy, trying to even out the odds."

"Wh . . . Where did you work?" Almost in spite of herself, she was fascinated by his past, repelled yet attracted.

"Central America, Africa, South America. I moved around a lot. You've got to remember that I wasn't very good at picking a winner so the wars rarely lasted long. Either that or the money gave out, which meant I wasn't paid and there wasn't cash to buy ammunition or guns . . . or food." Brig didn't go into details about comrades killed, food that wasn't fit to eat but had been consumed anyway because there was nothing else, or sleeping on the ground with no protection against the elements. And he didn't talk about the soldiers that fell under the bead of his gun.

"Why did you quit? You must have been young at

the time." She stopped making any attempt to hide her curiosity as she scooted into a more comfortable position to listen to his answer.

The sheet was draped around her hips. The heavy globes of her breasts drooped against her ribcage, the large rosy-crested centers swaying as she moved. Brig was momentarily distracted from her question. His hand reached out to caress the nearest breast.

"There was an ambush. My patrol was caught in the middle of it. I remember a bullet tearing into my shoulder and then yelling at everyone to take cover. Then everything went black," he said. "When I came to, there was a butchering doctor standing beside me. He had a scalpel and a pair of forceps in his hands. He was going to dig the bullet out of me. I was lying on the ground underneath a piece of canvas strung up as a lean-to. Flies were everywhere. This doctor jammed a bullet between my teeth and told me to bite it. The makeshift hospital didn't have any anesthesia. When he started probing and cutting into me, I realized that I didn't want their damned money or their war. Before I blacked out again, I swore if I lived through the so-called surgery, I was going to get the hell out of there. My life was worth more than the money they were paying me."

"And did you?"

"Did I live through it? No, I died," Brig mocked the question.

"I meant, did you quit after that?" Trudie elaborated.

"Yes. As soon as I could move, I headed for the States . . . and ultimately here. End of story." He started to pull her back into his arms and begin a more intimate exploration of her heavy breasts.

But Trudie wasn't satisfied and she laid a rigid arm against him to maintain distance. "When you came back, did you see your grandfather again?"

"No. He'd had a massive coronary. They buried him a month before I returned." He took hold of the hand on his chest straining to keep them apart and lifted it to his mouth. He kissed the tips of her fingers and slowly worked his way to the palm, licking the sensitive hollow with the tip of his tongue. He heard the tiny gasp of arousal she tried to conceal.

"What about his business?" She let herself be pulled down. "His money?"

"He left it all to another grandson, my cousin." Which wasn't precisely the truth, but Brig was tired of the questions. And the answer to that one wasn't any of her business.

"The cousin you are going to New York to see?" she persisted.

"The very same."

Brig rolled her onto her back. The most effective way to silence her endless questions seemed to be with a kiss. While he ravished her lips, he felt the resistance ebb from her. Cupping the weight of one breast in his hand, he teased its peak into hardness with his thumb. His knee forced its way between her legs to spread them apart.

As his mouth followed the curve of her cheek to her neck, Trudie whispered in his ear, "You are a horny bastard, Brig McCord." Her voice was reluctant in its demand for satisfaction. He laughed softly at her loving insult.

Chapter II

THE NOISE. HE'D forgotten the noise of a big city. The stream of traffic was a constant hum, punctuated by horns and whistles for a taxi. Voices with a variety of accents and languages seemed to drum into his ears. The heat was stifling after the coolness of the mountains. The sun beat down and the miles of concrete streets and buildings baked in its reflected warmth. The air was foul with the smell of gasoline fumes and automobile exhausts. Not even the hog dogs and sausages from the push cart at the corner had an appetizing aroma.

Bending down, Brig looked inside the open window of the cab. The driver was slowly and painstakingly counting out his change, fumbling through pockets and producing money from each one. It was an old ploy to try to increase his tip by wearing out the patience of the passenger waiting for his change.

"It's your time you're wasting, friend," Brig dryly informed the cab driver. "I've got all day." The last bill magically joined the others and the wiry man passed him his money. "Thanks."

As he stepped onto the sidewalk, the cab pulled away from the curb, forcing its way into the traffic. Brig paused to look up at the building towering in front of him. The main office of Sanger Corporation occupied the entire twenty-third floor.

"We grow them tall in New York, cowboy," some wise-cracking pedestrian remarked.

His dusty gaze flicked to the young man already laughing over the comment with his companion. Brig noticed the curious glances his white straw Stetson, brown boots, and western-cut leisure suit of forest green were receiving from the passersby. He would have drawn less attention if he'd been wearing a long, flowing robe of a sheik, he thought cynically.

Entering the building, he walked to the elevators. A pair of doors slid open as a bell dinged and an "up" arrow was lit. Brig stepped inside and pushed the floor button. More passengers entered, two young women among them. Brig removed his hat as everyone shifted to allow more room. A young brunette stood beside him, giving him the eye. She didn't look old enough to be out of school, but Brig suspected she was probably twenty. They all looked so young to him any more. He could remember when girls of twenty looked old. A sign of age, he thought wryly, and his lips twitched in amusement beneath the dark broom of his thick mustache.

"Are you from Texas?" the girl asked with a look that was certainly not sizing up his home state. She was as short as Trudie, the top of her head barely reaching his shoulder.

"Idaho."

"Idaho?" The girl repeated. Brig could tell by her puzzled expression that she had no idea where it was. A surge of disgust swept through him. Didn't anybody in New York realize there were forty-nine other states out there? The dumb broad probably thought Idaho was a potato.

The elevator hummed to a stop and the doors slid silently open. "Excuse me. This is my floor." He pushed his way past the girl, who was startled by his abrupt behavior.

Habit returned the hat to his head once he was out of the elevator. Glass doors were emblazoned with gold and black letters that spelled out "Sanger Discount Stores," below that "Corporate Headquarters." Brig felt the tightening in his gut, a sensation he hadn't been conscious of feeling since his guerrilla days. His jaw hardened, flexing a muscle in his sun-browned cheek. A deadly calm settled over him.

With long, unhurried strides, he walked to the glass doors of the main reception area and pushed them open. A very attractive black woman sat behind a large desk. Her appearance was one of efficiency, embellished with smooth sophistication. Her eyes were softly brown, and sharply intelligent. The smile she gave him was polite and nothing more.

"May I help you?" Her voice had a husky, soothing quality that was very easy on the ear.

The hat came off again as he towered in front of her desk. "Max Sanger, please." Brig clipped out the request.

Her eyes made a quick assessing sweep of him, an eyebrow arching briefly in hesitation. "The President of the company?"

"The very same." The dryness of humor was in his look. Obviously, he didn't fit the required standard of people who asked to see the President of the firm.

"Do you have an appointment?"

"No."

"I'm sorry. Mr. Sanger is a very busy man. He doesn't see anyone without an appointment. I'll connect you with his secretary if you like, and she can acquaint you with his schedule and when he might be available to see you."

He was very politely receiving the brush-off. Brig smiled, but it was a cold expression. He tapped the brim of his hat on her desk phone. "You call Max and tell him Brig McCord is here. He'll see me."

Without waiting for a response, Brig turned away from the desk and walked across the width of the reception area with its potted plants, ultra-modern furniture of glass and chrome, and lush pile carpeting. He stopped at the window overlooking midtown Manhattan and the glimpse of green to the north that was Central Park. His stance was a slightly wide-legged one of command, a hand negligently thrust in the pocket of his pants. Holding his hat by the crease in the crown, he tapped it against his thigh in vague impatience.

Behind him, he heard the receptionist pick up the receiver. A few seconds later, she was speaking softly to someone, her low murmur making the words unintelligible.

"Mr. McCord?" At her questioning voice, Brig made a half-turn to give her a sidelong look. She held the receiver in her hand, the mouthpiece covered. "His secretary informs me that Mr. Sanger is in a meeting. He left word to hold all calls. Would you like to speak to her?"

After a negative movement of his head, Brig said calmly, "Tell her to take him my message."

"I'll tell her." She looked skeptical, but complied. As the minutes ticked by, Brig returned his attention to the haze and dust hanging around the tops of the skyscrapers. At the click of the telephone, he sent a glance over his shoulder. There was a new look of respect in the attractive features of the black receptionist. "Mr. Sanger will be right out, sir."

"Thank you." His lip curled in cynicism. Nothing had changed since his grandfather's time. A man was still judged by who jumped when he called. Brig didn't turn from the window until he heard the sound of footsteps in the corridor.

The man walking toward him had a smile fixed on his face. For all the naturalness of its expression, it didn't reach his cool, blue eyes. Dressed in a dark vested suit and color-coordinated shirt and tie, he had the slender build of a dancer. Brig didn't need to see the lining of the suit jacket to know that it was hand-tailored by the best in the business. The only changes fourteen years had made in his cousin was the distinguished sprinkling of gray in his black, curling hair. Max was ten or eleven years older, approaching fifty. His appearance was smoothly polished to project the proper image. Brig caught a whiff of a manly cologne and couldn't help comparing it to the pungent odor of a skunk.

"Brig!" Max Sanger's voice sounded genuinely delighted to see him, but Brig knew better. "My God, man! How long has it been?"

"Fourteen years." His hand was gripped by smooth fingers while another hand clasped his forearm to demonstrate affection. Brig was conscious of his calloused palms. "A nice, firm handshake, Max," he observed with arid coolness. "Just the way the old man taught."

An uneasiness flickered in the blue eyes, but it was quickly masked as his cousin laughed. "You haven't changed, Brig. You're still the cynic." He clamped a hand on Brig's shoulder in a further attempt to establish a camaraderie that had never existed between them. "Why didn't you let me know you were coming? I couldn't believe it when my secretary told me you were here."

"A tactic held over from my mercenary days—never give advance warning before you strike."

His cousin abandoned his pretense of friendliness, his arm dropping to his side. "I'm not your enemy, Brig," he stated.

Brig feigned a mild surprise. "Did I say you were?"

With a thinning mouth, Max Sanger made a sweep of the reception area and suggested, "Why don't we go to my office where we can have some privacy?"

"By all means," Brig agreed and followed a half-step behind, as his cousin led the way down the corridor. At the far end was a set of double doors. Max opened one and waited for Brig to precede him. His secretary glanced up as they entered, her gaze swinging curiously to Brig. She was an older woman, starched and pinched.

"Hold all my calls, Agnes," Max ordered. Another set of doors led into an inner office.

It was a massive room, occupying a corner of the building. Large windows lined two walls. A large hardwood desk sat diagonally in the corner with an executive-style leather chair behind it. Along with two stuffed armchairs, there were a long sofa and coffee table as well as a wet bar. Brig walked to the window to look at the view.

"Impressive," he murmured with a trace of sarcasm. "But it was designed to be, wasn't it?" No comment was forthcoming from Max Sanger as he sat down and let his slender build become enfolded in the plush chair behind the desk. He swiveled toward Brig, leaning back to regard him through narrowed blue eyes. Brig reached in his shirt pocket for the pack of cigarettes. His hand stayed there for an instant. "Do you mind if I smoke?"

"It wouldn't stop you if I did." Max moved the heavy copper ashtray on his desk to the side closest to Brig. "Why don't you come to the point, Brig? This isn't a social call. You aren't trying to re-establish family ties. Just exactly why are you here?"

One-handed, he lit the match and touched the flame to his cigarette. "Maybe, as a major stockholder, I came by to see how the company is doing." He exhaled a thin stream of smoke.

"The company doesn't mean shit to you!" Max scoffed at that possibility.

"You're right," Brig agreed with a crooked smile. "I'm calling in my markers."

"I don't have any of yours." Max rocked the chair forward, whitening a bit. "You know what the provisions were in the old man's will. Unless you work for the company, you are entitled to zero."

"And you know I could have contested that."

"It was your choice. And you decided not to," his cousin retorted. "You didn't want any of his 'ill-gotten' gains. You already had your blood money, money you'd earned yourself."

"You wouldn't be sitting in that chair if I hadn't stepped aside," Brig reminded him coldly. "You wouldn't even be there if I hadn't given you proxy to vote my shares. I'm not here to take that chair away from you. The company is yours. But you owe me, Max."

Max looked prepared to argue. Instead he issued a tight-lipped demand, "Tell me what you want."

"I need a loan." It was a grudging admission. "Twenty thousand."

Amusement flashed across his cousin's face. He hesitated for an instant, then opened the center drawer of his desk. Pulling out a folder, he tossed it onto the desk in front of Brig. It was marked "confidential."

"Read it." Max gestured toward the folder and leaned back in his chair, resting his elbows on the sides and tapping his fingers against each other.

Brig hesitated, then picked it up. It was a financial statement prepared by a firm of certified accountants, complete with a balance sheet, profit and loss statement, a list of assets and liabilities, long term and short term. Brig gave the first two pages a cursory glance of identification. When the figures began to sink in, he studied the report more closely. A sinking sensation began in his stomach. He shot a hard look at the man behind the desk. His cousin's initial expression of amused satisfaction had given way to one of grim resignation.

"It's the latest audit, delivered yesterday," Max stated. "I can keep it under wraps for a couple of months, maybe more. This company doesn't have twenty thousand dollars, Brig."

"With you as President, I should be surprised the company hasn't gone bankrupt before this." He dropped the report on the desk, fighting the anger and frustration that was welling inside. "How did it happen?"

"The profits started dropping off from the stores.

You know the kind of shape the country's economy has been in. I tried to diversify and made a couple bad investments."

"A couple? It took more than a couple to get the company into that condition." Anger, contempt, and disgust all mixed together in Brig's response. "You should be sued for gross mismanagement."

"Dammit, Brig!" Max came to his feet in angry self-defense.

"Forget it. I won't be the one to sue you. I take it no one else has seen this report?"

"No one."

"Then I haven't seen it either. All I want is my twenty thousand," Brig stated. "I don't care whether I get it from the company or you personally. And don't try to convince me that you haven't sucked off a fortune, because I know you better." The desperation of his own personal situation brought an extra edge of harshness to his voice. He was fighting for his life.

Max appeared to squirm in his chair. He could no longer meet the desert-brown eyes. "I haven't got it either," he admitted after a long pause. "Everything I have, and everything I could beg, borrow, or steal, is wrapped up in a land development project in California. Condominiums. I can't get it off the ground."

A cold rage spilled over Brig. He wanted to grab Max by the shirt front and smash his fist into those handsome features until they were a bloody pulp. Before the urge for violence could overwhelm him, Brig walked stiffly to the window. He'd been a fool to come here, a fool to hold out hope that he'd receive any assistance from his cousin. Maybe he could talk to his banker again. Maybe if he sold all his stock cows and the sheep . . . but what would he do for income the following year? He was trapped between a rock and a hard place.

"Why did you need the twenty thousand, Brig?" Max's voice was quiet and respectful, as if he were aware the wrong tone would rile a sleeping wolf.

"I need the cash. My balance sheet looks a helluva

lot better than yours, but it so happens that I'm land and cattle poor," he admitted. "I've been in some fights before. And I haven't counted myself out of this one yet." Turning from the window, he started for the doors. There wasn't any more reason to stay.

"Where are you going?"

"Back to my hotel so I can check out and catch the first plane back to Idaho." Brig didn't look back. He still didn't trust himself to keep his hands off his cousin. His grip started to wring the neck of the door-knob.

"Wait," Max said. "Maybe we could work a deal where both of us could get some money."

"In the first place, Max, I wouldn't like the smell of any deal you'd make. And in the second place, I don't work with anyone who forces me to look over my shoulder for fear of getting knifed in the back." He yanked the door open.

Max hurried to catch up with him as Brig strode out of the outer office into the corridor. "It's almost noon. Let's have lunch. It won't hurt you to hear me out," he argued.

"You'll be wasting your time."

"It's my time."

"And mine," Brig countered. "You can tell me your little scheme during the cab ride to my hotel."

Max didn't like the terms, but he was smart enough not to press for more. There'd never been any love lost between them. From the time Brig had moved in with their grandfather, Max had resented him, almost hated him. Brig had always been the favorite grandson, the hand-picked heir to the Sanger throne, even though Max was the elder. It would have all gone to Brig, if he'd met the conditions of his grandfather's will. Max had taken over by default. Now he was in deep trouble, but there might be a way out with Brig's help. And it almost gagged him to admit it.

Outside the building, Brig walked to the corner to hail a cab. "You'll never get one at this hour," Max informed him with the smugness of a New Yorker.

Brig paid no attention to him as he emitted a piercing whistle through his teeth. A cab switched lanes amidst a blare of horns and squealing brakes to stop at the curb in front of them.

Brig opened the rear door for him. "That was always your problem, Max. Nobody ever jumped when you whistled." Pure hatred smoldered in the fiery look Max sent him before climbing into the cab. Brig folded his long frame and slid into the seat beside him. "The Hilton," He leaned forward to tell the cabbie, then settled back in the seat. "You'd better start talking, Max. You don't have much time."

"You came to me for twenty thousand, you arrogant bastard!" Max fumed through clenched teeth. "If you think I'm going to crawl on my knees and kiss your ass so I can have a few minutes of your precious time to tell you how you can get it, you're wrong."

"Am I? You were always very good at doing it with the old man," he baited, amused by the impotence of his cousin's anger, because Brig knew it was all hot air. "Do you want to talk or trade insults?" He smiled as he watched Max struggle to collect himself.

"It's simple," he began in a stiff voice. "I have someone who might be interested in buying the company. I've been trying to sell him my stock, but it wouldn't give his management firm control unless they had your proxy. According to the will, you can't sell your stock to anyone except a family member unless it's a total buy-out of the company or a merger. I think I can talk them into a buy-out."

"The poor sucker hasn't seen the latest audit, has he?" Brig guessed.

"I told you I just got it!" Max snapped. "It doesn't matter anyway. The guy is looking for a tax write-off. He's got more money than God."

"If he has, then he didn't get it by being a fool. All he has to do is wait a couple of months and he can pick up the company for a song through the bankruptcy courts."

"Yeah, well, that doesn't do you or me any good, does it?!" he flared, in sarcastic challenge. "The annual company audit isn't due until the end of October. I ran this one early, because . . . I didn't think it was in that bad a shape yet. So what do you think?"

"I think it smells of misrepresentation," Brig declared in a disgusted breath. "I've never cheated a man in my life. And I'm not going to start for a lousy twenty grand." The cab swung into the circle in front of the hotel and stopped near the revolving doors. Brig leaned forward and handed him a bill. "Keep the change." As he stepped from the cab, Max climbed out the other side.

"You're always so damned righteous, McCord!" he snarled as he followed him through the revolving door, walking swiftly to keep up with Brig's longer strides. "You're a hypocrite. That's what you are. I haven't forgotten that you used to get paid to kill people."

"Governments paid me to fight," Brig corrected in a savage underbreath and stopped at the cashier's desk.

"I'm . . . *asking* you," Max hesitated over the verb, then emphasized it, "to at least think over what I've said. The man has got the money and he's interested. He . . ." He stopped, staring down the wide foyer that ran the length of the hotel's ground floor. "There he is now." He pointed. "The tall man with the gray hair standing outside the restaurant."

Disinterestedly, Brig let his gaze follow his cousin's discreetly pointing finger. He saw the man, but it was the woman with him that caught his eye. She had a long, leggy look although she was a few inches shorter than the man she was with. Her hair was auburn, a brown that seemed to catch fire in the light shining from overhead. There was an animal earthiness about her, a latent sensuality. She was a fascinating creature —young, yet with an air of maturity. His blood warmed at the sight of her. In fact, there was a certain ripeness about her that asked to be picked. Brig felt an urge to do the harvesting.

His gaze strayed to the man. There was easily thirty years difference in their ages, if there was a day. Physically the man looked fit and virile. There was something vaguely distinguished about his presence, an aura probably described as charismatic. Nothing was wrong with his health. Or his appetite, Brig decided, as he saw the man take some money from his pocket and slip it in the woman's hand.

His attitude toward the attractive brunette began to harden. When she lightly kissed the older man, his eyes darkened sardonically. With a wave, she hurried toward the far exit with long, graceful strides. Near the door, Brig saw her pause to put the money in her purse—and probably to count it too, he thought cynically.

"Come on." Max took hold of his elbow to steer him forward. "I'll introduce you to him." Brig started to draw back, but the man had already seen them and lifted a hand in greeting. "Hello, Fletcher. This is a surprise seeing you here," Max declared as they met midway.

"I could say the same for you, too, Max." The man made no explanations as to why he was at the hotel. Brig wasn't surprised. Few men of any worth went around bragging about the girl they'd just laid in a hotel room upstairs. "What brings you here?"

"Brig is staying here. He just flew in from the West to discuss some company business. Let me introduce you. Fletcher, this is my cousin, Brig McCord," Max said, then reversed it. "This is Fletcher Smith. Most people know him from the articles in the sporting magazines about his big game hunting, but I know him as a businessman extraordinaire."

Brig thought the praise by Max was a bit too obvious. Fletcher Smith seemed indifferent to the description of himself as he clasped Brig's hand in a firm handshake.

"It's a pleasure, Mr. McCord." The calm, relatively unlined features on the sun-bronzed face held the look of a man who had learned the wisdom of patience and persistence, two essential qualities for a successful hunter. "Were you in California? Max has told me a lot about the project he has there."

"No. I'm from Idaho," Brig corrected, wanting no connection with his cousin's development.

"Brig has a ranch there," Max hurried to explain. "I have his proxy to vote his stock in the company, but we generally discuss the issues beforehand."

"Where in Idaho is your ranch located?"

Brig couldn't help noticing the way Fletcher Smith was ignoring his cousin's attempts to bring the company and its shares of stock into the conversation. The man was shrewd. Max would never fool him for long.

"In the mountains near the Middle Fork of the Salmon River," he answered.

"That's a primitive area," he nodded as if he'd already located the area on a map he kept in his head. "It must be good hunting."

Brig shrugged and avoided a direct comment. "I usually kill two elk a year for meat."

"I like elk venison myself." The man smiled in agreement.

"Isn't that something? Brig has a cattle ranch and he eats elk." Max forced a laugh. "He has to come all the way to New York on company business to have beef. Which reminds me—Brig and I were just going to have some lunch. Would you like to join us, Fletcher?"

The older man hesitated, glancing at Brig before he made up his mind. "I'll have some coffee with you," he accepted.

"I don't care for any lunch, Max," Brig stated.

"Jet lag," Max explained to Fletcher with a laugh, and shot a furious look at Brig. "You and Fletcher can have coffee and I'll eat."

"We'll let him gain the pounds," Fletcher smiled and turned to walk to the restaurant. Glancing sideways at Brig, he remarked, "I heard you had a severe winter this year." He started walking.

A glint of admiration entered Brig's eyes. The man

was quite a hunter, luring his quarry on. And he was the hunter's quarry. If he was going to reply to that comment from Fletcher, he had to walk with him. Fletcher looked back and read in Brig's expression that his game had been discovered. He grinned and stopped. Max glanced from one to the other in total puzzlement.

Brig started walking. "It was a bad winter," he admitted. "Parts of the rest of the country were hit pretty hard, too." This time they were on equal terms.

"How did the wild game come through it?" inquired Fletcher.

"They always do better than the cattle. Deer, elk, and sheep will dig through the snow for forage. A cow will stand and starve even if there's only four inches of snow covering the grass."

Brig wasn't sure why he had agreed to the lunch invitation. He should be checking out of the hotel and catching a cab to the airport. But this cagey hunter appeared to be an interesting man. In the span of a few minutes, his curiosity had been aroused. What was an hour or two? Brig sized the man up again as they entered the restaurant and were shown to a table.

Fletcher Smith was as tall as he was, an inch or two over six feet. His build was heavier, thicker and broader, but Brig wasn't deceived by the bulk. The man was solid. There wasn't any fat on his bones, only muscle. His hair was metal gray, whiter at the temples, but it had once been brown. He was loose and relaxed, yet possessing a hunter's reflexes. Their timing might have slowed, but Brig suspected it was still faster than most men's. Brig noticed the bulge in the inside chest pocket of the man's suit—a glass case, which meant his eyesight was going. Fletcher Smith had reached the crest of his prime and begun the downward slide. The man knew it. That probably explained the young auburn-haired woman. He had been trying to show he still had what it took, reproving his manhood.

While the waiter was pouring their coffee, Brig

watched the way Fletcher's brown eyes centered on his cousin, as if focusing on a target. "I haven't seen you at our apartment for a long time, Max."

"I was out of town or had other engagements recently and had to refuse several of your invitations." Max smiled blandly as he opened the menu. "I guess your wife stopped inviting me."

"We're having a small party tomorrow evening. Why don't you come?" Fletcher suggested.

"I'd like that," Max nodded. But his acceptance hadn't been eager. In fact, Brig noticed that he had hesitated.

"It isn't a black tie affair, just an informal get-together. He glanced at Brig. "Naturally, you are invited, too, Mr. McCord."

"I'm flying back to Idaho. Thanks, anyway," he refused.

"You said your ranch was located near the Middle Fork of the Salmon? That's isolated country." Fletcher sipped his coffee, looking at Brig over the rim of the china cup.

"It is, but I like it that way. It suits me."

"A tribe of Indians called the Sheepeaters lived in that area before the white man came," he remarked.

"They were called Sheepeaters for the obvious reason that wild sheep were the mainstay of their diet, but they were more commonly known as the Shoshone Indians." Brig smiled to himself. His knowledge was being tested and he wondered what this game of wits was all about.

"Have you seen any bighorn sheep in the area?"

"Some. They keep pretty much to the high country."

"Any that were trophy size?"

Brig remembered the ram he had seen in the spring, but he didn't mention it. "It depends on what your definition of trophy size is."

"The horns should be a full curl or better. After that it depends on the circumference of the horns and the spread of the tips." Fletcher leaned back in his chair, regarding Brig with a steady look. A wry smile touched his mouth. "You know how it is. A hunter is always planning his next hunt. I've been talking to an outfitter in the Bitterroots about setting up a hunt in his part of the country for a bighorn."

"It sounds exciting," Max tried to participate in the conversation.

"The Rocky Mountain Bighorn is the only big game trophy that has eluded me in all my years of hunting. I've successfully hunted the Stone Sheep in British Columbia and the Dall in Alaska, but I have yet to get a Bighorn." There was a haunting grimness in the determined expression.

"What are you trying for—a grand slam in sheep?" Brig's gaze held a dusty, dry look of contempt. He'd heard of rich sportsmen resorting to any method, legal or not, to obtain trophies of all four North American sheep—the Dall, the Stone, the Rocky Mountain Bighorn, and the Desert Bighorn.

Amusement glittered in Fletcher Smith's eyes. "That's a dilettante's goal. No self-respecting hunter cares about getting his ticket punched. The thrill is in the hunt. A hunter is like a fisherman. He'd be out there doing it even if the big one got away every time, because he loves the sport," he stated, then sobered. "This may be my last chance at a bighorn. I may be too old when my turn comes around again. This time I'm going to give it everything I've got to bring one back. If I don't, I'll know I tried."

There was a lull in the conversation as the waiter took Max's order. Brig's coffee was lukewarm and he drained the cup. He leaned sideways in his chair, resting an elbow on the table and thoughtfully rubbing the soft broom of his mustache.

Brig realized he had guessed right. Fletcher was conscious of his advancing years and had started to grab for the pleasures of life before they passed him by for good, whether it was a young, beautiful woman or the thrill of a hunt. He couldn't condemn the man for it, because he couldn't be sure he wouldn't act the same way in fifteen years. But who the hell could know?

"Is yours strictly a cattle ranch or do you have sheep, too?" Fletcher asked after the waiter had left.

"Both."

"Domestic sheep are the most dangerous enemies of the bighorns," Fletcher remarked. "They not only graze on his feeding grounds, but the domestic sheep carry diseases they have become immune to and transmit them to the wild ones."

"The old, bitter argument between the rancher and the hunter." Brig laughed without making a sound.

"A rancher can wipe out an entire herd of bighorn with the disease transmitted by his flock of sheep. A hunter is looking for the trophy animal, if he isn't taking it for meat. Trophy size horns only belong to the old rams, the ones nature and the mountains would be killing anyway," Fletcher pointed out.

"I've heard that argument. But all species on earth have to mutate, adapt, and grow stronger with the changing times. It's the law of survival, nature's law. My sheep carry diseases nature put here. If they didn't transmit them to the bighorns, something else would. The bighorns will acquire immunity or they will become extinct. That is nature's law, not man's."

"Then you don't believe in preserving a species?" Fletcher challenged.

A smile played with the edges of his mouth, deepening the corners. "Personally, I thank God that we didn't have any zealous conservationists back in the cavemen days running around yelling 'Save the dinosaur!' Can you imagine if we had a couple hundred of them in some sanctuary now where man would have to recreate its habitat and food supply as closely as possible? All creatures have a lifespan. So do all species. Man might become extinct someday. By his hand or nature's, it's one and the same thing," he concluded.

"Man believes he can save the world," Fletcher said with a bemused smile. "You're saying he'll be lucky if he can save himself. That is a rather profound philosophy." He took a deep breath and released it as a sigh. "It's probably closer to the truth than any of us cares to admit."

"The laws of nature often seem brutal and harsh because it's only the fittest that survive." Brig lit a cigarette and tossed the match in the ashtray.

"Ah, but it's the arrogance of man to believe he is above nature," Fletcher murmured. The waiter arrived to place Max's lunch in front of him. "I hope our slightly morbid conversation didn't dull your appetite, Max."

"Not at all. It was very enlightening." He shook out his napkin and placed it on his lap. "Brig is something of an expert on surviving through personal experience. When he was nine years old, he spent almost three months alone in the wilderness after his parents were killed in a plane crash. Later he saw action in Southeast Asia." Max hesitated, as if intending to say more, then changed his mind. "And you are something of an expert on nature with all your hunting experiences, Fletcher. You know all about the predator and the prey, and the changing conditions that have produced the decline in big game animals. The two of you figuratively stand on opposite sides of the fence, one the hunter and the other the rancher. You are the harsh romanticist and Brig is the cold realist."

"You are very observant, Max. Sometimes I underestimate you." There was a faint narrowing of Fletcher's gaze. "You've done some hunting yourself, haven't you?"

"I have, but it was a long time ago. Certainly nothing on the scale that you've done," Max insisted modestly.

"We should go hunting sometime, you and I." Fletcher spoke as the thought occurred to him.

"It sounds good," Max agreed and laughed, "as long as you let me know far enough in advance so I can get in shape for tramping through the woods."

Tapping his cigarette on the rim of the ashtray, Brig

realized that in many respects his cousin was an intelligent man, aware of his limitations and capable of exploiting his assets. What was the flaw in his character that prevented Max from being a success? Was it because he was willing to use any means to get what he wanted or because he always wanted what was someone else's?

"You never did give me a direct answer about the game prospects in your area, McCord," Fletcher reminded him.

"For bighorn?" Brig raised an eyebrow in query.

"Yes."

"I've seen some," he admitted.

"Trophy size?"

"It's possible the ones I saw could qualify." Brig took a drag on his cigarette and squinted at the smoke that curled into his eyes.

"Has it been hunted much?"

"Not in the area that I'm familiar with." He shook his head. "The sheep are far back in the wild, high country. They aren't easy to get to, even with a packstring. It's hard getting in and hard getting out."

"Have you ever done any guiding, or considered it?" Fletcher studied him thoughtfully.

"Nope."

"What would you say if I told you I'd like to hire you to guide and outfit a hunting trip for me?" he smiled complacently as he asked the question.

"Why would you want me?" Brig tipped his head to a wary angle. "I haven't any experience. Besides you're already making arrangements with an outfitter in the Bitterroots."

"From all the information I've received, the bighorn sheep in his area and in Montana are young. Which means my chances of finding a ram with trophy size horns are next to nil. From the little you've told me about your area, I'd say my chances are better there. You are familiar with the landmarks and terrain. You own a ranch, which means you have access to good mountain horses for a packstring. As for your lack of experience," Fletcher paused, "you strike me as a man who would make certain that if you took someone's money, he would receive what he paid for."

"I've heard about guides who have planes to haze sheep toward the hunters," Brig remarked.

"That's illegal."

"You know that. And I know that. But some hunters want a ram real bad." A thin trail of smoke punctuated his drawling statement that was half challenge.

"If I get a ram, it will be strictly by the books, with nothing underhanded or illegal involved." He traced the outline of his spoon on the tablecloth. "I'll make it worth your while, McCord. Money is no obstacle for me. I'll pay you three hundred . . . four hundred dollars a day."

Brig sucked in his breath and tried to conceal his shock at the figures. "Getting in, getting out, plus the hunting time, it could take twenty days." He'd already done the multiplication in his head and knew the sum would be a sizable portion of what he needed.

"That's about average, depending on the weather," Fletcher agreed, a complacent gleam in his eye at Brig's barely disguised reaction. "There will be two of us going. Naturally that price is per person."

He swore silently. That amounted to more than half the money he needed. Killing an animal for meat—for food to survive—was one thing. But killing it for a pair of horns to hang on a wall in some den went against the grain.

"If the pair of horns goes over forty inches, there'll be a ten-thousand-dollar bonus in it for you." Fletcher sweetened the pot.

Damn! He felt as if his guts were being torn apart as he was pulled in two different directions. "I know what that country is like. I can't guarantee you'll even come in range of a ram that size. It would be an arduous trek in some of the roughest country you've ever seen." At that elevation where the bighorns roamed, the air was thin. Even the mildest climb would have the heart pounding like a locomotive. "I don't know whether or not you're in condition for that kind of trip." It would be a strain on him and Fletcher was more than fifteen years older than he was. Brig didn't pull any punches letting the man know it.

"I'll worry about whether or not I can take it." His voice hardened. "I don't for one minute think it's going to be a joy ride. All I expect from you is to completely outfit the hunt and guide me back in there where the sheep are. I'll carry my own gun and do my own shooting. Whether I hit or miss will be my problem. Yours is to show me the target. Is it a deal?"

"I'll have to think it over," Brig said in a taut voice. Hell! What was there to think over? He needed the money. But he refused to override his own request for time.

"Think it over," Fletcher agreed. "You can let me know what your decision is tomorrow night at the party."

"That isn't much time," Brig protested.

"I haven't got much time. The season opens the first of September and runs through the third week in October. I have to make my plans now. I can't leave it until the last minute."

"Stay over until Saturday morning, Brig," Max inserted. "You don't have any pressing reason to go back to Idaho today, do you?"

"No." He made the admission grudgingly. He'd thought there would be paperwork involved in connection with the loan from Sanger. He'd made his return reservations for Saturday and wasn't expected back until then.

"In that case," Fletcher pushed his chair back from the table and stood up, "I'll see you tomorrow night, anywhere between eight and nine. You, too, Max."

"We'll be there," Max assured him.

An unreadable expression flickered across Fletcher's chiseled face. "I'm counting on it." His glance encompassed both of them. Fletcher signaled the waiter for the check. Max started to protest, but he was waved into silence. "I'll take care of it," Fletcher insisted as he asked the waiter what the total was and handed him a bill. "Keep the change."

"Thanks for lunch, Fletcher," Max expressed polite gratitude as the man moved away from the table.

"Don't mention it."

Brig said nothing, not a thank you and not a good-bye, as the man walked out of the restaurant. He had the feeling he'd just been bought, and he didn't like the taste it had left in his mouth.

"You really fell into a sweet deal this time, Brig," Max declared with a wry shake of his head.

"Shut up, Max," he growled and crushed his cigarette butt in the ashtray.

"What did I say?" He looked startled by the snarling reply. "Fletcher's going to pay you the money you need, with a little left over."

"I haven't said I'll take it yet." Irritable and restless, Brig rested his arms on the table and swirled the coffee dregs in his cup, staring at the dark grounds.

"You'll be a fool if you don't. You've always been stubborn, Brig, but I didn't think you were a fool," his cousin mocked.

"Well, maybe I am." He took a drink of water to wash away the bitter taste in his mouth. He set the glass down with a thump and pushed away from the table.

"Where are you going?"

"For a walk." He had to think.

Not until he was outside the hotel did Brig slow his stride. He began walking the streets, following Fifty-fourth, down Madison, back over to Fifth Avenue. Finally the baking heat of the July sun drove him into a dingy, air-conditioned bar on one of the side streets. He sat at a table in a dark corner and nursed his way through a couple of beers.

A hard-faced hooker with the map of the world on her face sidled up to him. "Want some company, cowboy?"

Brig glanced up. Her dull blue eyes didn't have any of the tenderness of Trudie's. He stood up and tossed some change on the table. "Honey, when I do, you'll be the last to know," he drawled.

She called him a few choice names as he walked out of the bar. The heat hit him like the blast from a steel furnace. It reminded him of the oppressive steaming jungles of Central America. Except here, he was surrounded by concrete instead of teeming plant life. Removing the lightweight jacket of his leisure suit, Brig swung it over his shoulder and started back to the hotel.

A few minutes before five, he stopped at the desk for his key then walked to the elevators. Perspiration had plastered his shirt to his back. His skin prickled with the heat as he waited for the elevator. The doors opened and Max stepped out. Brig's eyebrows shot up in momentary surprise, his alert gaze catching the furtive movement as Max slipped a room key into his jacket pocket.

"Hello, Max. I didn't expect to find you still here at the hotel," Brig commented dryly, stepping to one side as the elevator was emptied of passengers.

"I had an appointment." The defensive response was as revealing as the cloying perfume that had attached itself to his clothes.

A sarcastic sneer curled his mouth. "You're still the ladies man, huh, Max?" At the moment, Brig didn't like anybody very much. Max took the brunt of his displeasure at the world in general. "Who was it? That gorgeous black receptionist you've got working for you? I'm sure you're taking the precaution of leaving the hotel separately." Even as he made the accusation, he knew it hadn't been the receptionist. Brig remembered the clean fragrance that had scented her skin.

Max stiffened, a little white beneath his tan. "I don't owe you any explanation."

"You're right. You don't. But you should do something about the way you smell before you go back to the office. It's worse than the perfume counter at a department store."

The elevator doors were about to close. Ignoring the flush creeping into Max's face, Brig moved past him into the elevator. On the ride up, he removed his hat and wiped out the sweatband with his handkerchief. A cool shower was uppermost on his mind.

Unlocking the door, Brig stepped into the room. The drapes were closed and the room was dark. Tossing his jacket on the chair, he walked over to pull them open. Sunlight fell on the blue coverlet of the bed. He grimaced in distaste at the room, a carbon copy of a thousand others in the building.

Chapter III

HUMMING TO HERSELF, Jordanna walked down the apartment's corridor. She shifted the heavy, bulky package in her arms to a more comfortable position. It was wrapped in shimmering silver-green foil with a bright emerald green bow that kept tickling her chin.

Inside the box was one of those modern art sculptures that didn't resemble anything. As far as Jordanna was concerned, they were strictly conversation pieces, but her brother loved such pieces. They were expensive, too. She wouldn't have had enough money if she hadn't persuaded her father to chip in on the gift during lunch. After the argument last week, she hoped Kit would accept the present as a peace offering, even if it came in the guise of a house-warming present.

She sighed at the thought of their argument. She couldn't even remember what had started it. It was supposed to be natural for a brother and sister to quarrel, but she felt they argued more than was healthy. Her problem was the quickness of her temper, all the fault of her dark red hair. And there wasn't any closeness between them. She and Kit were too different, their interests too divergent. They were at opposite ends of a spectrum, their opinions colored by different viewpoints.

Her searching gaze located his apartment number on a door. Jordanna stopped in front of it and juggled the package to push the doorbell. She heard the muffled buzz it made and waited.

As the door opened, she smiled and said, "Surprise," but the smile faded at the sight of the strange man standing in the opening instead of her brother.

Recognition flashed in his eyes. "Hello, you must be Jordanna."

"Y . . . Yes," she faltered, staring at the sandy-haired man. "I was looking for my brother."

"Christopher isn't here right now. I'm sorry he didn't say what time he'd be back. Was he expecting you?" He was good-looking in a clean-cut way, young, in his middle twenties.

"No. I just dropped by to bring him this housewarming present for his new apartment." Jordanna indicated the bulky gift in her arms and tipped her head to one side to study him with a straightforward boldness. "Who are you?"

"I'm Mike Patterson." There was a wary alertness in his returning look. "Hasn't Christopher mentioned me?"

Jordanna had become accustomed to people calling her brother by his given name. She and her father were the only ones that still used his nickname of Kit.

"No, he hasn't," she admitted openly. "Should I know who you are? I'm sorry, but Kit doesn't talk to me very much about his girls or his friends."

"I see." A smooth mask seemed to slide over his expression. "I've moved in with Christopher to share the expenses on the apartment."

"I didn't know." Jordanna shrugged her ignorance aside with a casual laugh. "I haven't talked to Kit in more than a week." The gift was growing heavier by the minute, despite the strength in her slender arms. "Do you mind if I come in?"

"Sure." He reacted swiftly, as if suddenly remembering his manners, and opened the door wide to admit her. He stepped forward, offering, "Let me carry that for you."

"No. That's okay. I can manage it," she insisted. He moved out of her way and Jordanna entered the apartment. "You can set it on the coffee table," he told her.

Stooping, she carefully placed it on the glass-topped table and straightened to look around the room. "This is nice." As she pivoted to face her brother's friend, her dark hair whirled about her shoulders, flaming with red highlights. "I haven't seen it since Kit furnished it," Jordanna explained. "Personally I prefer something more traditional and homey than all this modern chrome and glass, but Kit likes it. Do you?"

"Yes." He smiled and his eyes had the same indulgent look that Kit so often gave her.

It irritated Jordanna. It made her feel like a child instead of a grown woman of twenty-four. Turning away, she held her temper. Her eyes, green flecks glittering in hazel pupils, fixed on the luxuriant potted tree by the window.

"That's a beautiful rubber plant. It must be your contribution to the apartment," she guessed.

"It is," Mike Patterson admitted. "How did you know?"

"It was easy," Jordanna laughed in a warm, throaty sound. "Kit isn't good with plants—or anything that has to do with nature as far as that goes."

"Can I get you anything?" Mike offered. "Coffee or a Coke? Or maybe you'd like a drink. I fix a mean margarita."

"No, thanks," she glanced at the thin gold watch on her wrist. "I'd better be going."

"You're welcome to wait for Christopher." He seemed worried that his actions had given her the impression she should leave.

"As you said, Kit didn't say when he'd be back," Jordanna reminded him. "And, my parents will be expecting me." She moved toward the door with smooth, graceful strides.

"He'll be sorry he missed you."

She shrugged at that. Maybe if he had forgiven her, he would be. "Tell him I stopped and . . ." She opened the door and paused, ". . . I hope he likes the present. It was nice meeting you, Mike."

"Same here."

The shoulder strap of her purse slipped as she swung the door closed. Jordanna adjusted it and retraced her route down the long corridor.

A half-hour later, Jordanna opened the door into the formal entryway of her parents' penthouse apartment. The maid was arranging a bouquet of pink roses on the elaborate baroque rosewood table that occupied the center of the foyer.

"Hello, Tessa. The flowers look beautiful, as usual." Jordanna paused to admire the arrangement. "Are my parents back yet?"

"Your mother returned an hour ago. She's in her room resting before dinner," the maid replied, still smiling from the compliment of her floral skills. Her wand-slim figure didn't show her age, but her shyly drawn features were etched with wrinkles.

"Thanks." Jordanna started toward the den, then turned, continuing to walk backwards as she asked, "Dinner is at eight?"

"Yes."

She glanced at her watch. "I guess I'll have plenty of time. Mother is such a stickler about changing for dinner." She wrinkled her nose in disdain for a custom she felt was needless.

Skirting the living room with its Louis XIV furniture, upholstered in pale green silk damask, and Baccarat crystal chandeliers, she walked directly to the den. She knocked once and walked in. Her father was sitting in his favorite chair, its brown leather worn soft and faded to tan. A magazine was lying open on his lap. His grayed head was resting against the high back. A dead pipe was clamped between his teeth. The weary look was wiped from his face as he smiled.

"Hello, Dad." Her gliding walk carried Jordanna to his chair, where she bent to kiss his smoothly shaven cheek. She had seen the tiredness in his expression, but knew better than to mention it. Straightening, she suggested, "I'm going to have a Scotch. Can I fix you one?"

"Please." Fletcher Smith took the pipe from between his teeth and knocked the ashes from the bowl into the ashtray.

A crystal decanter of Scotch sat on a tray atop his desk, along with a matching set of four glasses. Jordanna filled two of them, not bothering with ice since they had both acquired a taste for Scotch served at room temperature. Her gaze strayed around the room. The decor in the rest of the apartment changed at her mother's whim, but this den always remained the same. The only alterations were additions of new trophies on the wall. The latest was a pronghorn antelope that she had downed.

"Did you stop by to see Kit?" He took the drink she handed him.

"Mmm." Jordanna swallowed the sip she had taken and walked to the nearest sofa, curling her long legs beneath her on the cushions. "Yes."

"What did he think of the present?"

"He wasn't there. I didn't want to wait until he came back so I left the gift." She took another sip of the liquor and glanced at her father over the rim of the glass. "He's sharing the apartment. Did you know that?"

"No." Fletcher set his glass on the tobacco stand and began filling his pipe.

"Well, he is. I met his roommate today. His name is Mike Patterson. He seemed nice. The two of them

are really going to turn that place into a bachelor pad."
Jordanna leaned back against the cushions and studied
the liquid swirling in her glass, caused by the circular
motion of her hand. "Kit is really serious about living
on what he earns, isn't he? I mean, there he is—
having someone else move in to share the expenses
of the apartment."

"He seems to be serious." He held a lighter flame to
the bowl and puffed out smoky clouds. "From now on,
you had better check first to be sure Kit is there before
you go to his apartment."

"Why?" Jordanna lifted her head from the back
cushion to frown at her father. "Just because he's
sharing his apartment with someone? Mike looked like
a nice clean-cut guy. He isn't likely to attack me or
anything."

"No. That isn't what I meant." He sounded angry
and her frown returned. "I simply believe we should
respect Kit's desire for privacy and not drop in on
him without calling in advance."

"I suppose you're right." she conceded and watched
him closely through her lashes. She saw him turn his
head away and close his eyes in an expression of pain
before he rubbed his forehead. "What's the matter,
Dad? A headache?"

Startled by the question, he looked up and opened
his mouth as if to deny it. "Yes, I guess so," he
nodded.

Her gaze strayed to the magazine opened on his
lap. Uncurling her legs, Jordanna rose and walked
over to his chair. She set her glass beside his on the
stand and moved behind his chair to massage his
temples.

"Better?" she asked.

"Much," he murmured and relaxed under the manip-
ulation of her fingers.

"If you would quit being so vain and stop reading
without these . . ." Jordanna tapped the glass case
inside his jacket pocket, ". . . you wouldn't strain

your eyes and get headaches." She shifted her attention to knead the taut muscles in his neck.

"I'd find some other excuse to get one of these rubdowns," he told her and she could hear the teasing smile in his voice.

"You are spoiled," Jordanna accused.

"Thanks to you," he replied, vaguely serious. Jordanna knew it was a veiled reference to her mother's lack of interest in his health or him.

"What have you been doing all afternoon?" She quickly changed the subject.

"After you left, I had coffee with Max Sanger and . . ." A knock at the door interrupted his answer. "Yes?" The maid, Tessa, stepped inside.

"There's a telephone call for you, Mr. Smith. It's your attorney, Mr. Blackburn."

"Thank you, Tessa. I'll take the call in here." He rose from his chair while the maid quietly withdrew.

"It sounds like business," Jordanna remarked and picked up her drink to walk to the door. "I'll leave you to your dull and dreary legal conversation while I clean up for dinner."

"A fine friend you are," Fletcher mocked, "deserting me in the face of boredom."

Vibrant, deep-throated laughter was Jordanna's only response to his jesting reproach before she slipped out the door into the hall. It wasn't until later, when she was in the bath, that she thought about what he'd said and agreed with his conclusion. They were friends, the very closest of friends, a relationship that was stronger and deeper than just father and daughter.

There were only two place settings at the table when Jordanna entered the living room that evening. She hesitated in front of the French Empire dining table, the black pleats of her long skirt swaying with her uncertain motion. Her gaze skipped over the crystal chandelier suspended above the table and the richly carved Victorian china cabinet against the one wall.

Flanking the cabinet was a pair of rose acacia onyx pedestals with matching turquoise Sevres urns sitting atop them.

As Jordanna turned, her mother appeared in the archway wearing a long mandarin-style gown of peacock blue. The color cast blue highlights on her raven-black hair, piled atop her head, and accented the cat-green of her eyes. Her gaze ran over Jordanna's simple white silk blouse and long black skirt in a dismissive fashion.

"Your father won't be joining us this evening," she announced in explanation of the two settings at the table. "There was some legal business, documents to be signed or something." Her vagueness about the reason for his absence revealed the inattention she had paid when she had been informed. "So it will be just the two of us."

"How cozy." Jordanna murmured and sat down in the Chippendale chair to her mother's right.

The mixing and blending of different periods and furniture styles was one of her mother's favorite projects. The only thing that ever remained predominant in the decor of the apartment was the color green, like the draperies in the dining room; the velvet material then was moss green, with valances and gold tassel trim.

Seconds after they were seated, Tessa entered to serve the soup. "Will you be going out this evening, Jordanna?" her mother inquired.

"No." She dipped her spoon into the soup and cast a sidelong look at the still very striking-looking woman. "Will you?" The softly voiced question bordered on a taunt.

"No. Tomorrow is going to be a busy day with all the preparations for the party in the evening so I'm having an early night." Olivia Smith returned with implacable ease. "Perhaps you could help me tomorrow?"

"Of course," Jordanna agreed.

Their conversation through the rest of the meal's courses continued in the same stilted fashion, like two cats warily circling each other. Jordanna felt the strain of it as she reacted and responded to a variety of subjects her mother introduced.

"We'll have our coffee in the living room, Tessa," Olivia requested when the maid entered to clear the dessert dishes. She rose from the table and Jordanna followed her into the living room. Her mother was so slender and petite that Jordanna always felt like a gangly schoolgirl walking beside her, except that she knew her willowy stature was equally graceful and attractive. "I'm relieved to discover you are still capable of intelligently discussing politics, the theater, and a variety of literary subjects, Jordanna."

"You are forgetting, Livvie, that while you are reading the condensed versions of novels, I am reading the unabridged editions." She had ceased referring to her as 'Mother' a long time ago.

Her jibe was smoothly deflected. "I truly enjoyed our conversation. It was such a pleasant change," her mother remarked. "I am usually bored to tears listening to you and your father talking about hunting."

"Perhaps if you contributed something to those conversations, the topic would be changed," Jordanna suggested, knowing her mother's exclusion from the discussions were self-imposed. "Daddy and I would be happy to talk about something else."

"Daddy and I." Something seemed to snap inside the green-eyed brunette. "It's always 'Daddy and I.' You are with him so much it's a wonder *you* don't want to marry him!" she laughed caustically.

The delicate thread that had held Jordanna's temper in check broke. She wasn't even conscious of turning or striking. Not until she felt the flat of her palm connect with her mother's rouged cheek was she aware of what she'd done. By then, she was trembling with rage.

"That was an ugly thing to say!" Jordanna's voice was loud and harsh. "Dad and I share the same interests. We like each other. I love my father and you make it sound like some incestuous thing! Why? Or

are you simply jealous because I've succeeded in forming an attachment to one person? That's it, isn't it?"
she accused. "One man isn't enough to satisfy you."

Blinded by her white-hot anger, Jordanna didn't see
the hand that struck at her. The stinging blow turned
her head and brought tears to her eyes. She widened
her eyes to keep them at bay and looked back at her
mother, proud and coldly defiant.

"Don't you ever speak to me like that," Olivia ordered in a voice that shook.

"I was twelve years old when I finally realized that
all of your male friends were really your lovers. I
know it's something that no one is ever supposed to
mention. It's the family secret, the skeleton in the
closet," Jordanna said with contempt. "But we all
know—Kit, Dad, myself, Tessa, and all the servants,
probably all of our friends, too. I'll never understand
why you treat Dad the way you do, or why he keeps
on letting you hurt him!"

"There are two sides to everything, Jordanna." The
dark-haired woman had regained her composure. Her
expressionless features resembled smooth, fine-boned
china, except for the livid red mark on her cheek. Her
jade-stone gaze swept past Jordanna. "Bring the coffee
in, Tessa, and stop looking so shocked." There was a
degree of weariness in her dry tone. "You've witnessed
our little family squabbles before."

"Yes, Ma'am." The uniformed maid minced her way
forward as if walking on eggshells, and set the coffee
service on a gold-leafed table. She hovered beside it.
"Will that be all?"

"Yes." With a dismissive flick of her ringed fingers,
Olivia waved her from the room, an order that was
obeyed with alacrity. Sitting on a damask seat cushion,
she began pouring the coffee. "It would be a novelty if
you ever considered the situation from my side, Jordanna."

"You've painted yourself as a martyr for so long,
Livvie, that you are finally beginning to believe in
your own image."

"You have no conception of loneliness." She handed Jordanna a fragile cup and saucer in a delicate rose pattern. "At least Christopher understands."

"He was always your favorite," she stated without jealousy. "From the time I can remember, you've doted on him. You wrapped Kit around your finger and used him to get back at Dad. You knew how much he wanted a son and you turned Kit against him. Every father dreams of teaching his boy to hunt and fish, telling him about life and training him to take over the family business."

"Is that what you've been doing all this time, Jordanna? Trying to play the role of a son to your father?" Olivia challenged in a saccharin voice.

"No." She abruptly set the cup and saucer on the table. She didn't trust it in her hands. The urge to hurl the steaming contents on her mother was too great. She had given way to her temper earlier and had resolved not to do it again. "I am not trying to be like a son. I am a woman. I look like one; I act like one; and I think like one. Simply because I enjoy sports and hunting doesn't make me less of a woman. I am not his surrogate son. I am his friend, one of the few he has, thanks to the way you've cuckolded him in front of the others."

As Jordanna started to cross the room, her mother demanded, "Where are you going?"

"To my room," she answered, not skipping a step. "The atmosphere in here has become sickening."

"Do you understand what I meant earlier, Jordanna?" The question followed her. "I'm always being left alone."

The emptiness of her room offered cold comfort. The aftermath of such scenes was always the same. Her nerves were stretched taut, tying her stomach into knots of tension. Jordanna paced back and forth across the Oriental rug of beige, green, and blue, like a caged tigress.

Stripping out of her skirt, she changed into a pair of red satin pants and tied a designer scarf around her waist. She slipped the gold chain of her miniature shoulder purse onto her arm, bolted from the room and out of the apartment.

It was sticky outside, the pavement holding the day's heat to mix with the night's humidity. The door man hailed her a cab. She slipped him a tip as she climbed into the rear seat. Jordanna gave the driver the address of a club she frequented when she was in New York and leaned back in the seat to nibble at a fingernail.

Alone, she hovered inside the club entrance. The music was loud and the pulsating lights were confusing. The place was crowded, the din grating on her nerves. Jordanna wished she hadn't come, but since she was already there, she started toward the bar.

Before she could reach her destination, she was invited to join a group that could loosely be described as friends, the regular bunch that frequented the club. Jordanna knew most of them at the two tables. She returned their greetings, missing the introductions of the two she didn't know in the noise of music, voices, and laughter.

Someone bought her a drink. It momentarily soothed her nerve ends. She drank more, seeking a release from the tension that had her so on edge. Jordanna danced, laughed, and didn't object when someone flirted with her, yet she couldn't shake the feeling of alienation. It was this, more than anything, that prompted her to leave after she had been there little more than an hour.

Her announced departure brought several offers to escort her home, but Jordanna refused, knowing an acceptance would mean taking the long way home. She hadn't reached the age of twenty-four without discovering that her desire was as easily aroused as her temper. She didn't even have to like the man she was kissing to derive a measure of satisfaction from the experience. All she had to do was close her eyes. But sooner or later, she had to open them and she rarely liked what she saw.

It wasn't the answer for her loneliness; nor would it solve her problems. Men's arms only offered temporary forgetfulness and she craved something more. An empty bedroom looked better than empty passion. Outside the club, she flagged down a taxi cab and rode home alone.

Chapter IV

JORDANNA SCOOPED SOME caviar onto a cracker and slipped it into her mouth. The caterer watched as she licked a few globules of the expensive roe from her finger. "It's very good."

"Would you care for another sample?" he inquired blandly.

"Mmm, no thank you." Unperturbed by his vague irritation, she wandered out of the kitchen into the main rooms of the apartment where other members of the catering staff were busily preparing for the party. Jordanna heard voices in the living room. One of them sounded like her brother's.

". . . seem to be going smoothly for the party to-night." She caught the last half of Kit's statement.

"Yes, they are," her mother replied. "I missed your help. It's all so much easier when there are two people organizing things."

"I'm sure you managed quite adequately without me."

"I really don't know what kind of party this is going

to be," her mother sighed. "Your father invited some of *his* friends . . ." There would have been more to the comment, but Olivia glanced up to see Jordanna appear in the archway.

"Don't let me interrupt you, Livvie," she mocked the sudden silence, the shimmering green flecks of her hazel gaze locking with the jeweled brilliance of her mother's.

"Hello, Jordanna," her brother inserted his greeting into the exchange.

"Hello, Kit." Her gaze softened as it shifted to her brother. "I stopped by to see you yesterday."

Tall and lithe, Kit had his mother's rich black hair and his father's dark eyes, outlined by long and thick, curling lashes. His features were chiseled in classic lines. Maturity had hardened the sensitivity in his mouth and eyes, overshadowing it with a certain air of cynicism. He was a handsome man, as close to perfect as Jordanna had ever seen.

"I came back to the apartment a half an hour after you had left," he said.

A rustle of tissue paper drew Jordanna's gaze to the hallway. Tessa was walking by with a shaded plastic garment bag draped over her arm. The hem of an emerald green gown peeked out of the bottom.

"What's that? A new dress for the party, Livvie?" Jordanna's tone was caustic. Her mother had a closet full of gowns that hadn't been worn more than twice.

"Yes. A Christopher original designed especially for me for the party tonight," was the quick retort. "I thought you were in your room getting ready for the party, Jordanna."

"There's plenty of time," she shrugged. "It doesn't take me as long as it takes you." That wasn't true. Jordanna looked at the features that had been nipped and tucked by skilled hands into an ageless face.

As Olivia bristled, Kit laid a quieting hand on her shoulder. "Why don't you lie down and rest, Mother? I know you want to be at your best for the party this evening. I'll see that the caterers have everything ready," he promised. "You've had a long afternoon with all the preparations. You deserve some quiet before the party starts."

"Yes." Gentleness beamed in the look Olivia gave her son. "That is an excellent suggestion. Thank you, Christopher."

With tightening lips, Jordanna watched her sweep from the room, all regal grace and pride. Glancing back at her brother, she shook her head in wry confusion.

"You are always pampering her, shielding her like a child from any hint of unpleasantness. Why? She's a grown woman—with claws."

"You have no compassion, Jordanna."

"I have no compassion?!!" She nearly lost her temper. She struggled to control it, then vented her bottled fury at the fates. "Why can't we exchange ten words without getting into an argument, Kit?"

"We are two different people." He was calm. He always seemed to be calm. "No matter how much we care about each other, we can't get along. When will you realize that our parents have the same problem?"

He was asking too much of her to equate their situation with her parents. She turned away to walk from the room. "I don't have time to discuss it with you. I have to bathe and change before the party."

After a long soak in the luxuriant bubble bath, Jordanna stepped from the sunken tub and toweled her skin dry. Her short terry cloth robe was hanging on a hook behind the door. She wrapped it around herself and tied the sash. Walking to the dressing alcove, she pulled the pins that held her hair piled atop her head and shook it free. As she picked up the jar of cream to moisturize her face, there was a knock on her bedroom door.

"Who is it?" Jordanna called out.

"It's me," her brother answered. "Do you mind if I come in?"

After a second's hesitation, she replied, "Come in."

The door to her bedroom opened and closed. She heard his footsteps on the parquet floor as he crossed the room to the open door of the Italian marble bath. She smoothed the cream onto her face and gently massaged it in. Christopher stopped in the doorway, leaning a shoulder against the frame. She glanced at his reflection in the mirror, afraid that he might intend to resume the argument they had begun in the living room.

"I wanted to thank you for the present," he said.

Her mouth relaxed into a smile. "You're welcome. I hope you liked it."

"I did. It has an honored place on the coffee table."

"I like what you've done wtih the apartment." Jordanna picked up an eyebrow brush and began stroking the natural sweep of auburn brows. "What does Mike do?"

"He's an engineer for a high-rise construction firm." His dark eyes watched her. He appeared to be waiting for another question.

Jordanna searched for something to say. "He seemed like a nice guy," she offered.

"He is." Christopher paused again, but not as long. "How long before you and Dad leave on another hunting expedition?"

"I don't know for sure. We've drawn a permit for bighorns in Idaho. The season opens in September. Dad mentioned something about doing some sport fishing in August, but he's been working out at the Club to get in shape for the bighorn hunt."

"Have you ever thought about settling down?" The look in his dark eyes was intent, almost anxious in its seriousness. "Quit flying all over the world killing dumb animals and build a life for yourself, maybe?"

"Just because you have been bitten by the bug to build a nest of your own doesn't mean I have, or will." Jordanna glanced at his reflection with amusement and reached for the jar of make-up base. "I enjoy what I'm doing, which, by the way, isn't killing. It's hunting."

"Mere semantics. The end result is the same, a dead

animal." The corners of his mouth were pulled down by a grim expression of disdain, black lights glittering in his eyes.

Jordanna attempted a patient explanation in defense of her position. "If there weren't hunters in this country, the wild game would overpopulate. They would do endless damage to the agricultural crops, take away valuable grazing land, and ultimately starve to death. Their numbers have to be controlled. Hunting is a much more merciful way than hunger or disease."

"I concede the necessity, but what I don't understand is how you can enjoy it."

"I like roughing it. I like being outdoors—away from everything and everyone. It's fascinating to see wild animals in their natural habitat, instead of in some zoo. Have you ever seen an eagle soar on the mountain currents? Or watched a fawn gamboling at a dawn hour in some dew-studded glade? That's the beauty of a hunt. The thrill comes from pitting your skills against an animal whose senses are twice or three times as keen as yours and a hundred times more wary."

"Hear! Hear!" Christopher clapped when she finished, teasing laughter dancing in his eyes.

"Stop it." Jordanna flashed him an exasperated look.

"Alright," he agreed. "We'll change the subject. Who is your escort for the party tonight?"

"I don't have one." She blended the beige and brown shadow on her eyelids and reached for a brown pencil.

"Why not?" A thickly drawn black brow arched in surprise. "You usually have a stream of beaus to choose from."

"I've decided to swear off men. One promiscuous member of the family is enough. I have no intention of competing with Livvie for the dubious honor." Her tone was acid and dry.

"Dammit, Jordanna." Christopher straightened, his expression darkening with anger. "When are you going to let up on her?"

"When are you going to stop leaping to her defense?" Jordanna countered just as swiftly. "We both know all about her many lovers. It's past history—past, present, and future. She'll never change. I have stopped expecting that. My only point is that I'm not going to follow in her footsteps."

"Who said you would?" He followed the question without giving her a chance to answer. "I know you've had some empty relationships, but your choice of partners has left something to be desired. You can't walk around in that body and pretend that you don't have needs and desires."

"I can control them," she stated decisively.

"That isn't your problem."

"Oh?" she challenged. "Since you seem to know so much, what is my problem?"

"You seem to think sex has something to do with shame. Maybe that's why you've been indiscriminate about your choice of men in the past. Sex is a beautiful experience, Jordanna, when it's shared with someone you care about. There's no shame afterwards, only a pleasant afterglow."

"My, my," she mocked the vehemence of his answer. "Maybe I should follow you out on a date and take notes."

Christopher whitened, his features drawn into taut lines. "Perhaps you'll better understand what I mean if I compare it with hunting. You don't waste your time with an inferior member of the species. You keep looking until you find the best representative of the breed—one with stamina, heart, and looks. I believe your term is trophy class." He paused, his composure slowly returning to calmness. "Everyone has a mate, Jordanna. You'll never find yours if you stop looking. And denying your own sexuality will only bring you misery."

Unable to meet his reflected gaze in the mirror, Jordanna studied the rolled brush tip of her mascara wand. His comparison made sense but it conflicted with her own resolutions. The silence that followed his words finally made her lift her gaze, but she saw only her reflection in the mirror. Her brother was no longer standing there. Startled, Jordanna turned. The soft crackling whisper of tissue paper came from the bedroom.

"Kit?" Curious, she stepped into the doorway.

His back was to her as he bent over an object lying on her bed. Jordanna couldn't see what it was with her brother standing in the way. At the sound of his name, he glanced over his shoulder and smiled absently.

"Come here. I have something for you."

Jordanna walked forward. "What is it?" she asked, an instant before her brother stripped away the protective plastic and turned to hold up a long black gown.

"I designed this for you."

The simplicity of the design caught her eye first. "It's beautiful." The bodice consisted of two straps, wide where they joined the high and broad waistband, tapering to narrow bands over the shoulder, and even slimmer strips of the cloth down the back. "It's daring," Jordanna observed with a half-laugh.

"It's perfect for you," he insisted. "It will show off the ideal symmetry of your figure and your beautiful skin. The flare of the skirt will permit that strong and graceful movement that is unique to you. And I prefer the word 'provocative' to daring."

"But I've never worn black before," she offered the hesitant protest. It had always seemed her mother's color.

"It will bring out the fiery highlights of your hair. Trust me," her brother urged. "You will be beautiful in this. And it's time you wore something that brings out that earthy quality that sets you apart from other women."

She sent him a glittering look that was both sharp and amused. "Is this all part of accepting my own sexuality, Kit?"

"It's a step," he conceded smoothly. "Will you wear it tonight?"

"Yes." Then Jordana remembered, "You designed a dress for Liv to wear tonight. We are being used, aren't we? We're modeling clothes you designed. Livvie will show off your look for the mature beauty, and I will portray the femme fatale of the young jetsetter. You're hoping to drum up some business among the party guests," she accused, but without malice.

A wry, cynical expression touched his handsome face as he shrugged. "It's done all the time." He moved toward the door. "I'd better check on the caterers."

Jordanna watched him leave, not moving until the door to her bedroom had closed. She couldn't shake the feeling that she really didn't know her brother at all. The confused sigh that whispered through the room belonged to her.

Taking her time, she finished applying her makeup before returning to the bedroom to dress. The sheer simplicity of the black gown made it stunning. Made of a stretchable jersey, the bodice followed the contours of her breasts, the low cleavage revealing the swelling sides that formed the valley between them. The waistline was snug, compressing her ribs and relaxing to flow over her hips.

The black sheen of the material was a perfect contrast to show off her ivory-smooth shoulders, while accenting the scarlet lights in her hair. Jordanna left it loose, lifting the hair away from her face with a pair of combs. She limited her jewelry to a pair of earrings, plain gold studs polished to a high gloss.

When she ventured into the hall, there was still a quarter of an hour before the guests were due to arrive. Instead of going to the main section of the apartment, Jordanna turned toward the master suite where her parents had adjoining room, to see if her father was ready.

The door to her mother's room stood ajar. As Jordanna started to walk past, she heard her father's voice come from within. She stopped, not intending to eavesdrop but only to wait for her father to come out of the room.

"That's a beautiful gown you're wearing, Olivia," her father commented. "It intensifies that fascinating green of your eyes. It's new, isn't it?" His words were complimenting, yet there was a sarcastic tone to his voice. Lately, it was always there when he addressed his wife.

"Yes, it is. Christopher designed it," her mother announced with a challenging lilt.

"Ahh, yes, my son the dress designer," Fletcher declared with a wealth of bitter contempt.

Shock rippled through Jordanna. She had known there was a chasm between her father and her brother, but she hadn't realized her father regarded him with such derision. She had been aware of his disapproval, but not this.

"That's enough, Fletcher." Her mother's defense was immediate. "Christopher is a gifted designer. He will be famous someday."

"God help us all when he is."

"Be honest for once, Fletcher. You are only thinking of yourself and what others will say about you," Olivia retorted. "You are concerned that it will reflect badly on you, that perhaps your own manliness will be questioned."

"Kit is what you made him," was the swift, angry reply.

"Yes, blame me," she taunted. "Everything is always my fault. I suppose I'm responsible for Jordanna turning into a gun-toting adventuress. I'm sure you'll deny you had anything to do with it."

"Leave Jordanna out of this!" her father snapped. "She's a woman. No one would mistake her for anything else. Even when she's carrying a rifle, she's all woman."

There was a sound of something being slammed onto a table top. "Why did you come in here, Fletcher? Was it just to start a quarrel before the party?" Olivia demanded. "You aren't going to spoil my evening because I'm not going to let you!"

"Why? Is this evening special? Have you invited your current lover?" He was arrogantly sarcastic. "Is it anyone I know? I hope you introduce me to him."

"If I did, what would you do?" Olivia challenged. "Do you think you might challenge him to a fight? Or would you look the other way and pretend you didn't know he's my lover?" Her mockery of him was deliberately cruel. Even Jordanna flinched at it.

"Who is it, Livvie?" Her father's voice rumbled in a low, ominous threat.

"A man. A very special man. When he holds me, I actually forget that you even exist, Fletcher. It's an extraordinarily pleasant sensation."

The bitterness had accumulated to gargantuan proportions over the years of their marriage, until it was too high to be surmounted, too deep to be subverted, and too wide to be bridged. The ugliness was more than Jordanna could stomach. She retreated to her room and closed the door.

As a child, their venomous arguments had made her physically ill. They were no easier to take at twenty-four. Jordanna had no idea how long she had been sitting on the edge of her bed, hugging her arms around her stomach. There was a knock at her door, but she didn't hear it.

The door opened. "Jordanna?" Her brother walked in and paused. "The guests are arriving. Aren't you coming?" She glanced up, looking at him but not seeing him. A furrow formed between his dark brows as he walked toward her. "What's the matter?"

"Why don't they destroy each other and be done with it? Why do they keep tearing each other to pieces bit by bit? At Jordanna's tortured questions, Christopher breathed in deeply, held it, and released it in a weary sigh. "She taunts him with her lovers, Kit. She brags about them as if they were trophies. Why doesn't she leave him?"

"Do you think she hasn't tried?" he murmured.

Her eyes widened. "But . . ." she began in confusion.

"Dad won't give her a divorce, Jordanna," he stated. "God knows you and I might have had a more pleasant childhood if he had, but . . ." There wasn't any need to finish the rest. "You can't let their problems become your burden, Jordanna. Come on." He extended a hand toward her. "No one will ever see that gown if you stay in this room." His mouth quirked into a coaxing smile. Jordanna hesitated, then placed her hand in his. As a child, she could hide in her room; but she was an adult and life went on.

Chapter V

MAX WAS WAITING in the lobby as Brig stepped out of the elevator. Brig didn't bother with the pleasantries of a meeting. His glance encompassed his cousin and the area immediately around him.

"Where's your wife? Aren't you taking her to the party?" Brig was irritable and he was taking it out on Max. Dressed in a tan suit and tie, he'd left his hat in the hotel room. He felt naked without it, but less conspicuous.

"Charlotte and I got a divorce five years ago, shortly after the kids were grown. I thought you knew." Max started toward the entrance. "We'll catch a cab outside."

"I suppose she finally got tired of you stepping out on her all the time." Brig was aware he was picking on Max, deliberately baiting him, and using him as a scapegoat for the decision that was eating him raw inside. But he couldn't seem to stop himself. "I have often wondered if the only way you get any thrill out of sex is by doing it behind someone's back."

"Anyone else but me would punch you in the nose, Brig." Max held his temper, even though his neck was reddening.

"Anyone else would try," he agreed with a taunting smile. "I'm surprised you haven't remarried, Max."

"As a matter of fact, there is someone I'm serious about, but I'm not about to talk to you about her and subject her name to your insulting comments!" Outside the revolving doors, Max signaled the doorman for a cab. One was immediately waved to the curb and the two men climbed into the back seat. "Have you decided what your answer to Fletcher is going to be?"

"Yes." A muscle flexed along Brig's jaw.

"Are you going to keep it a secret?" Max sent him a sideways glance that seemed to know he'd found the jugular vein.

"I'm going to guide and outfit his hunt."

Smugness was written in the deepening corners of Max's mouth and in the glinting depths of his blue eyes. "It's reassuring to know that everyone has a price, Brig—especially you."

Bile clawed at his throat. "But I didn't have to sell out to you, Max," Brig reminded him. "I don't have to become involved in your underhanded scheme to dump the company on some rich sucker before it goes down the tube."

"But I can still sell my stock. And Fletcher is still interested in it. Even if he loses on the deal, he'll never miss the money."

Brig eyed him. "You hate Smith, don't you?"

Max Sanger avoided his gaze. "He has something I want."

"Like the old man, you're going to get it if you have to lie, cheat, or steal to do it." Contempt riddled his voice.

"I'm going to have my chance. I'm not going under."

Guys like Max usually didn't, Brig thought. It was the honest, hard-working men who lost everything they'd worked all their lives to get. It wasn't fair. But life generally wasn't. Look at himself. He had compromised his principles to save the ranch. Maybe he despised Max so much because he saw in him a magnification of one of his own flaws. He'd heard it said that the faults you find with others are the ones you find in yourself.

The taxi stopped at the address Max had given him. Brig climbed out and waited on the sidewalk. "What floor?" he asked when Max joined him.

"Top floor penthouse, what else?"

Brig wondered why he had come. Why hadn't he simply telephoned? He wasn't in the mood for any damned party. Any details could have been settled by phone. But it was too late. He was here, committed to a course of action. Maybe this was Fletcher Smith's way of making him jump at his whistle. That prospect didn't set well with Brig.

The party was in full swing when they reached the top floor. The ornately carved door couldn't muffle all the sounds of laughter and voices coming from within. Max pushed the doorbell. Within seconds, the door was opened by a man in the black uniformed attire of a butler. Max gave him their names which were discreetly checked against a list before they were ushered through the foyer into the living room.

A mass of people were already crowded into the room, sitting, standing, talking, laughing, eating, and drinking. A waiter appeared at Brig's elbow and offered champagne from the trayful of glasses he carried. The last time Brig had drunk champagne, he had been living on his grandfather's estate. He took a glass and Max ordered a martini. Brig sipped at the sparkling wine. An eyebrow arched in surprise.

"You like the champagne, Mr. McCord?" Fletcher Smith paused in front of him, smiling faintly.

"It's excellent." Brig studied his glass, noting the color and the natural effervescence.

"You speak as a man who knows." Fletcher regarded him with a sideways tilt of his head.

"My grandfather prided himself on being able to distinguish between a fine wine and one that was merely acceptable. He didn't believe in settling for the latter if he could have the former. Wine-tasting was a part of my education. My grandfather considered it essential knowledge." One corner of his mouth curved into his dark mustache. "I regarded it as a means of getting drunk."

"Obviously you acquired some expertise," Fletcher remarked.

"Some people are experts at setting up dominos." Brig shrugged away the idea that knowing the difference between a good wine and a bad one was worth anything but snob value.

"I'm glad you could come to the party, Mr. McCord," Fletcher offered his hand in a greeting that had been postponed until that moment. He turned to Max. "I knew you would be here, Max, but I wasn't so positive that your cousin would come."

"Weren't you?" Brig was still in that irritable mood that put a biting edge to his voice. "You know you made me an offer that I couldn't refuse, if you'll pardon the cliché."

"Did I?" Brown eyes widened in false surprise. "I hope that means you aren't going to refuse."

"I'm not. I'm accepting your offer," Brig admitted a trifle stiffly.

"Good." Fletcher reached inside his jacket and pulled an envelope from his pocket. He handed it to Brig. "Here's a deposit and a generalized statement of the terms we discussed. You can contact me within a week or so after you've settled on a convenient date. In the meantime, maybe I can talk Max into coming along."

Brig didn't bother to open the envelope as he slipped it inside his jacket pocket. Irritation simmered through him. Why had he come to this party? It hadn't been necessary unless the man wanted to gloat over his moment of triumph.

"This hunt sounds fascinating," Max remarked. "I've never been West before." Immediately he qualified that. "I have been to California, naturally, and skiing in Aspen several times, but every luxury imaginable is there. The trip you're planning seems to be a tremendous challenge. Maybe I could come hunting with you this time."

"You don't have a permit. Max. It's too late to get one." Fletcher quietly studied him.

"I'm not really interested in hunting nearly as much as I am in going on the trip," he countered. Brig guessed why his cousin wanted to go. There would be two, possibly three weeks for Max to convince Fletcher Smith to buy his stock. He would have a captive audience for his sales pitch.

"The mountains would kill you, Max," Brig stated. The man was in no shape for such a grueling trek into the high sheep country.

"It's almost two months away. I have time to get ready for it." Max appeared unconcerned by Brig's warning as he glanced at Fletcher. "As a matter of fact, we could work out together at the club."

"That's true. I hadn't thought of that," Fletcher agreed and smiled. "I can't think of any reason why you couldn't come along for the ride, can you, McCord?"

"I can think of a couple," Brig replied in a grim, flat tone.

"Don't worry, cousin. I'll pay my share," Max laughed as if Brig had been making a joke.

"Excuse me a moment, would you?" Fletcher requested. "My wife is over there. I'd like you to meet her. I'll see if she can spare a few moments."

As he moved away into the crowd, Brig darted an irritated look at the man beside him. "You aren't going on this trip, Max."

"The man just invited me. You heard what he said." He rocked back on his heels in satisfaction. His curling black hair glinted with silver in the light of the chandelier overhead.

"I'm not going to be a party to your schemes," Brig warned. "If you try to come along, I'll give him back his money and he can find somebody else to take him."

"No, you won't. You need that money." His glance mocked the impotence of Brig's threat.

Brig swore silently because he knew it was true, but he tried to bluff it out. "But I don't need you. My agreement with Fletcher Smith was for a party of two hunters and I'll make him stick with it."

"You try to mess this up for me, Brig, and I'll queer your deal with Fletcher. And if you think I can't, just try it," Max challenged. "I've got nothing to lose. But you do. You'd be smart to remember that."

Could Max create enough mistrust to make Fletcher back out? Brig didn't know, and he couldn't risk finding out. It was salt on an already sore wound.

"If you come, Max, you'll pay. And I'll want it in cash the day you arrive. There won't be any credit."

"Aren't you worried that my money might be tainted?" he taunted.

"I know it is. But I'm not throwing away good money to feed you or provide you with transportation and a place to sleep." Brig was in a corner but he could still snarl. "You go ahead and make your pitch to Smith, but don't mention my name or try to include me even distantly in any of your dealings."

"We understand each other." Max's agreement was smooth and self-satisfied.

"And you'd better be in shape for this trip, because if you fall behind, I'll leave you. That's big country. I may not be able to find you again." The champagne had gone flat. Brig handed the half-full glass to a passing waiter and ordered a Scotch on the rocks. He needed something stronger.

"You won't lose me unless you lose Fletcher." Max sipped at his martini, covering his next words with the glass. "Speak of the devil, here he comes now with his wife."

Brig glanced in the direction Max was looking and saw the tall gray-haired man escorting a petite brunette through the throng of guests. She was a striking woman with vivid green eyes, their color intensified by the emerald green gown she was wearing. It took Brig a second to realize that the black hair had once been natural, but now its ebony sheen was achieved by the skillful application of dye. He missed seeing the character lines in her face. Her skin was too smooth. The tightness of her perfectly bowed lips suggested acrimony. She was pushing fifty, but clinging desperately to a youthful appearance. Brig wondered what it cost her to maintain that trim figure.

As they approached, he noticed that she never once glanced at her husband. She appeared indifferent to the guiding hand at her elbow. There was none of the close rapport he had seen between the married couples of his ranching friends. Something in the crisp tension between them made him suspect their marriage had been made in hell.

Her green eyes gave their undivided attention to Max. Something glinted in their depths, barely veiled, hinting at a secret. A cat focusing in on its prey, Brig thought. He glanced sideways at his cousin. Max appeared to preen slightly, but he would do that at the approach of any halfway attractive woman. When the husband and wife stopped in front of them, Brig studied Mrs. Smith with a lazy interest that concealed his astuteness.

"I believe you and Max are already acquainted, Livvie," Fletcher Smith stated politely.

"Yes, we are," she admitted and offered her hand to Max. "I'm so glad you were able to come, Max. How are you?"

"Much better now that I've seen you again, Livvie." He was all smooth, urbane charm. "You look even more beautiful than when I saw you last."

"You are still the flatterer, Max." She laughed, but Brig saw the faint rosy blush that seemed to make her glow with a fresh radiance. He marveled at the gullibility of older women. Or maybe it was desperation. "And I love you for it."

"If only I could believe that," Max countered with mock regret. Glancing sideways, he said, "I'd like you to meet my cousin, Brig McCord. This is Olivia Smith."

"How do you do, Mrs. Smith." He felt her fingers hesitate against the roughness of his hand. Brig doubted that she'd ever come in contact with callouses before.

"It's Livvie to my friends," she corrected, not showing in any other way her rejection of his touch.

He could have made a suave reply to equal anything from Max, but his days of posturing and bowing had ended many years ago. Brig merely inclined his head in mute acknowledgement. He wasn't interested in impressing her.

Now that Max had completed the introductions, Fletcher spoke. "McCord has agreed to act as guide on my hunt for bighorn sheep this fall, Livvie."

"Oh?" She couldn't have looked less interested in the announcement.

"Yes, he owns a ranch in Idaho," her husband elaborated.

"How interesting." She smiled politely at Brig.

He wasn't surprised by her lack of enthusiasm. She was a green-eyed cat who reclined on velvet cushions and drank cream from a sterling silver bowl. He was struck again by the mismatch of the pair, a big game hunter and a sophisticated cosmopolitan.

"It's wild, beautiful country where McCord has his ranch. When we were talking about the hunt the other day, Max became so fascinated that he's decided he'd like to go with us."

Her green gaze swung in sharp surprise to Max. "I didn't realize you liked to hunt."

"It isn't the hunting," Max insisted. "Fletcher and Brig's description of the trip makes it sound like an adventure. I've been thinking about taking a vacation. Out there, I can't be reached by telephone. I'm intrigued by the idea. Of course, it will mean Fletcher and I will have to spend a great deal of time together so I can get in shape."

"Do you think it's wise?" she asked.

"If you are implying that I might have a heart at-

tack trying to get in shape, that isn't very flattering."
Max laughed and Brig frowned narrowly. He didn't
think Olivia Smith was implying that at all and he
wondered why he had that impression. "You're making me feel old."

"You'll never be that, Max." Olivia denied the possibility with a quick smile. The waiter returned with
Brig's Scotch and paused to murmur something to the
hostess. "Please excuse me." She took her leave from
them.

Someone came up who knew Max. Brig suffered
through the introductions and the exchange of pleasantries, then left his cousin, pretending an interest in the
buffet table set in the dining room. He sampled a few
of the finger-sized canapes and found an empty corner.
Leaning a shoulder against the wall, he nursed his drink
and listened to the idle chatter going on around him.
It was all so familiar, the fine wines, the exotic deli-
cacies, the expensively dressed guests, and the super-
ficial conversations—like something out of a recurring
dream. Except that it wasn't out of a dream; it was out
of his past.

The air was tainted with the smell of tobacco
smoke. A heavyset man near him was puffing on a
cigar, sending noxious clouds of smoke into the room.
The voices and laughter ran together to make a senseless din, snatches of sentences stringing together to
make a confused jumble of conversations.

His gaze shifted back to the living room where his
cousin was locked in a conversation with the man who
had joined him. If he'd made a different decision, Brig
knew he could have been in Max's position, the head
of a national corporation, wearing hand-tailored suits,
driving an expensive car, vacationing in Europe, and
living in a penthouse apartment. If he'd been running
the Sanger Corporation, Brig doubted it would have
suffered the reversals it had in his cousin's hands. Or
was that a mark of his own conceit? Look at the mess
he was in at the ranch.

Hell! Brig took a hefty swallow of the Scotch and grimaced at the taste. Swirling the glass in his hand, he rattled the cubes against the sides. His impatient gaze made an inspecting sweep of the two expensively furnished rooms in his view. It was a sharp contrast to the log ranch house he and Tandy Barnes had built with their own two hands. All of this could have been his, Brig realized. And it was a relief to discover he didn't want it.

As he raised the glass to his mouth to take another drink, he saw the auburn-haired woman framed by the dining room arch. The glass remained poised a half-inch from his mouth. For a stunned instant, Brig couldn't believe it was the same woman, the one he'd seen with Fletcher Smith at the hotel. But it was. He lowered the glass and leveled his steady gaze at her. She had actually come to this party given by her lover and his wife. One look at her smooth, proud carriage and Brig realized she was the type that could be that bold.

His gaze made a wayward sweep of her from head to toe. The black gown was sexy without being vulgar. It definitely revealed more of her figure than the blouse and pants she'd been wearing the other day. Her shape was flawless, neither overly rounded nor overly slender. Her breasts would nicely fill the palms of his hands. Brig was aware of a tingling itch in the hollows of his hand to do just that. Lord knew the plunging front of the gown invited such a wish. He lifted his gaze to her chestnut hair, shot with red fire. Its color reminded him of a spirited sorrel horse he owned.

A movement attracted his attention to the young man at her side. Tall and dark-haired, with Apollonian looks, the man reminded Brig of someone, but he didn't take the time to puzzle it out. His mind was registering the fact that the woman hadn't come alone, but with an escort. Brig wondered at that. Who had chosen the man, Fletcher Smith or the woman?

The question had barely formed when an attractive

blonde joined the pair. Effusive and gushing, the blonde had obviously made liberal use of the bar. After briefly greeting the auburn-haired girl, she ignored her to devote her attention to the man, clinging to his arm and pressing against him. Brig watched the indulgent, yet indifferent way the man regarded the blonde's attentions. His mouth suddenly twisted into a smile as Brig realized the redhead couldn't have a safer escort. Her handsome companion wasn't interested in the female sex.

Downing the contents of his glass, Brig straightened from the wall, intent on refilling it at the bar on the near side of the dining room. As he started forward, he saw his hostess approaching him.

"Has Max deserted you?" Olivia Smith inquired in a voice of cultured honey.

"He's in the living room talking to some of his friends."

Her green eyes noticed the empty glass in his hand. "Would you care for another drink, Mr. McCord?"

"I was just on my way to the bar," he admitted.

She motioned to a waiter wandering through the scattered groups and took the glass from Brig's hand to give it to him. "Another drink for this gentleman," she ordered and glanced inquiringly at Brig.

"Scotch on the rocks."

The waiter nodded at his answer and walked toward the bar. "How long will you be in New York, Mr. McCord?" Olivia Smith was standing close to him. The cloying fragrance of her perfume was nearly overpowering.

"I'm leaving in the morning." Brig lit a cigarette to fill his nose and lungs with the smell of tobacco smoke.

"So soon? How long have you been here?" The questions were polite, a dutiful attempt to make conversation with a guest.

"Two days." Brig was no more interested in talking to her than she was in talking to him. The waiter returned with his drink and offered an escape. "I won't keep you, Mrs. Smith. I know it's a hostess' duty to circulate among her guests."

"Let me introduce you to the Fennimore's." She curled a hand inside his elbow and Brig was obliged to accompany her or be needlessly rude.

A flash of green caught Jordanna's eye. The only woman at the party wearing that distinctive shade was her mother. Shut out of the one-sided conversation Alisha Van Dyke was having with her brother, Jordanna let her restless gaze seek the emerald gown.

Her mother was talking to a dark-haired man in a tan suit. Jordanna didn't recognize him. Vaguely curious, she ran her gaze over his hawk-like profile. Tall and lean as a winter wolf, he was wide and deep in the shoulders and narrow at the hips. His face was tanned by the sun, a neatly trimmed mustache shadowed his mouth. His hair was the rich color of dark chocolate. Thick and indifferent to any current style, it shaped his head and formed short sideburns. Despite his casual stance, there was something about his rangy build that suggested coiled readiness.

The thought struck Jordanna that it wouldn't be wise to cross that man. He would make a dangerous enemy —strong, powerful, and sure of himself. There wasn't a man in the room that could be a match for him, unless it was her father.

Her brother nudged her with his elbow. Turning, Jordanna glanced at him. His dark eyes pleaded to be rescued from the blonde hanging on his arm.

"Kit, be a dear brother and fetch me a drink?" Jordanna asked, her hazel eyes twinkling.

"Of course," he agreed and smiled politely at the blonde as he unwound her hand from around his arm. "Excuse me, Alisha."

When Christopher returned with her drink, the blonde had left. Together, Jordanna and her brother began mingling with the other guests, stopping to chat with various clustered groups until they were finally separated.

Drifting away from two couples arguing the aesthetics of modern art, Jordanna wandered into the living room. The banal conversations she could overhear didn't interest her. A few feet ahead of her, she saw her father politely withdrawing from a circle of guests. The expression of concealed boredom on his face matched her own mood. Approaching him from behind, she touched his elbow.

In a pseudo-cultured voice, she remarked, "Papa, have you seen the latest exhibition at the gallery?"

He pivoted, arching a peppered-gray eyebrow at her before a smile curved his mouth as he realized she was mocking the conversations around them. "As a matter of fact, I haven't. Tell me about it."

Jordanna laughed briefly, then sighed. "It's a pity we aren't guests. We could leave."

"Isn't it?" Fletcher Smith agreed. His gaze swept the room. "We seem to be a minority. Nobody else seems inclined to leave. I think it's more crowded than the last party. Apparently, the party is a success. That should please your mother."

"Yes."

At his reference to her mother, Jordanna automatically glanced to the corner of the room where the raven-haired woman was talking to an older, well-dressed man. Slender and attractive, he had curly hair, its darkness well peppered with gray. The man looked vaguely familiar, but she couldn't recall his name. His charm was evident in the way her mother was basking in the glow of his attention. She glanced out of the corner of her eye at her father. His mouth had thinned into a hard line, his gaze also focused on the woman who was his wife. Jordanna felt his pain and bitterness, and sought to distract his thoughts.

"I'd love ten minutes of peace and quiet," she said. "Who would know if we slipped away for a little while?"

His downward glance was indulgent. "No one. Where do you have in mind?"

"The den." It was his favorite place, unburdened by the opulence of the rest of the apartment. It was Jordanna's, too.

"All right," he agreed with a half-smile. As they started toward the hallway to slip unobtrusively away from the party, Fletcher stopped. "Wait a minute. Here comes Sam Brookfield. I want to have a quick word with him." He pressed a key in her hand. "I locked the door so no one would get some stupid notion to mess around with the gun cabinet. You go ahead. I'll join you in a few minutes."

"Don't be long," she urged as he left her side to speak to the tall, spare man in glasses walking toward them.

"You honestly own a ranch—with horses and cows and everything?" The brunette gave Brig a skeptical, sideways look. She was an attractive woman, recently divorced, she had informed him, but Brig suspected her looks would vanish when the makeup was cleansed from her face.

"Yes, I do." His gaze wandered to the hallway where he had seen the redhead disappear after briefly meeting Fletcher. Perhaps she had left.

"You don't look like a cowboy, except for the mustache maybe," the brunette was saying.

"The next time I'll wear spurs and a ten-gallon hat," Brig replied with a biting dryness that was meant to silence, but the woman laughed.

"What sign are you? I'm a Taurus."

"Sagittarius." Brig hoped it was an incompatible sign.

"That's too bad." She made a moue of disappointment, then brightened. "Do you know your ascending sign?"

"Nope. 'Fraid not." He smiled, but the expression didn't reach the dusky brown of his eyes.

"I don't know if you can believe horoscopes anyway," she shrugged. "My ex-husband and I were supposed to be very compatible, but we fought all the time."

"It happens." Brig didn't want to hear the messy details of their divorce.

A rich, throaty laugh attracted his attention. Olivia Smith was standing off to one side with Max. His cousin was weaving a charmed spell over the woman and she was loving every enchanted second of it. When they'd first arrived at the party, Brig had gained the impression it had been a considerable time since Max had seen Fletcher's wife. Now, they were acting as if it had been yesterday. Brig wondered if the two of them were having an affair, and dismissed the idea just as quickly. Not even Max would have the gall to romance a man's wife while he was trying to get his money. He glanced to where he'd last seen Fletcher, but he wasn't there. Brig wondered if he had disappeared into the hallway where the redhead had gone. But he didn't have time to dwell on that thought.

"I said, do you know the Fitzpatricks?" the brunette repeated the question he had missed the first time.

"No."

"They are having a party tomorrow night. It should be fun. Would you like to go with me?"

"I can't. I'm flying back to my ranch tomorrow." Brig was glad of the excuse.

"Oh." The woman was trying to hide her disappointment. "When will you be coming back to New York?"

"It's been fourteen years since I was here last. With any luck, it will be another fourteen." There was only ice left in his glass and it was melting. "Excuse me while I get a refill."

The brunette didn't protest and Brig suspected that she knew he wouldn't be coming back. That edginess was back on his nerves. In the dining room, he handed the bartender his glass and asked for a fresh drink. It was his third, not counting the champagne, but he hadn't felt the affects of the first yet.

He wandered over to the buffet table, but nothing looked appetizing. Three men were standing in the corner of the room. Brig heard one of them mention something about stalking and paused to listen in. One man was bragging about an elk he had dropped instantly with a single shot a hundred and fifty yards away. A second man followed that story with one of his own, adding ten yards and changing the elk to a running antelope. Brig moved on, wondering why they never mentioned all the shots that missed.

Chapter VI

THERE WAS A light rap on the door. Jordanna rose from the sofa to answer it, skirting the bearskin rug in front of the fireplace. Before turning the knob to unlock the door, she asked, "Who is it?"

"It's me," her father answered in a low voice.

She let him in, smiling a welcome. "You made it."

"It's quiet in here," Fletcher remarked as the door was closed and locked to shut out the party and its noise.

"Wonderfully so." Jordanna walked to the center of the room, pausing in front of the open jaws of the grizzly bear rug. "Would you like a drink?"

"No." He sat down in his favorite armchair and leaned his head against the back rest. A muffled burst of laughter filtered through the thickly insulated walls into the room. A weary, disgruntled look passed over his face.

"You look tired, Dad," she observed with wary concern and smoothed out the folds of her long skirt as she sat down on the sofa.

"No, just old." Fletcher smiled crookedly at his reply.

Jordanna didn't smile. "You wouldn't be saying that —you wouldn't be thinking that if you hadn't argued with Livvie before the party."

"How did you know about that?"

"Just a guess." It was wiser not to admit she had been accidentally eavesdropping. Her mother caused him enough grief without him knowing that she had witnessed it.

"After all this time, the odds were in your favor that your guess would be right." It was the closest her father had ever come to openly admitting his marital problems. The rift between himself and his wife was something he had never discussed with her or her brother. It was a forbidden topic and he didn't break the taboo by pursuing it. "Why don't you put on some soft music? Maybe we can drown out the party," he suggested.

Jordanna walked to the bookshelf, where a stereo tape deck was enclosed in the wood. Selecting an instrumental tape, she slid it into the slot and turned the volume low. She returned to the sofa and relaxed against the cushions. Her father closed his eyes to listen to the dulcet strains.

She thought he'd fallen asleep, but when the tape started repeating itself, he opened his eyes and pushed himself out of the chair. As he straightened his jacket, he felt something inside his pocket. Frowning, he took out a slim jewelry case. He glanced at Jordanna with a smile of chagrin.

"I meant to give you this before the party and forgot," he said.

"What is it?" Rising from her reclining position on the sofa, she snagged a hook of her gown on a pillow. It came unfastened. "Damn," Jordanna swore softly in irritation. "Will you fasten this for me, Dad?" She walked to the front of the desk where he was standing.

*　　*　　*

The walls were beginning to close in on him. The staleness of the air was almost suffocating. Brig glanced around at the chattering people who seemed indifferent to the noise they were making. A cool, fresh draft unexpectedly blew over him and he looked for the source. The sheer panels of the dining room drapes were moving gently. Behind them, he saw a set of latticed glass doors evidently leading onto a roof garden.

Slipping through them, Brig escaped outside. The sounds of the party followed him, muffled now, and mingled with the traffic sounds from the streets far below. The city lights were too brilliant for the stars to be seen. But at least he had the feeling of space, room to move and breathe.

Fancy wrought-iron deck furniture and potted plants adorned the rooftop. Brig ignored the invitations of the cushioned seats and walked to the parapet. A couple followed his route of escape, the girl giggling. Not wanting company, Brig faded into the shadows and moved quietly around the corner of the rooftop to a more secluded site.

Light streamed through another set of glass doors, laying a square of light on the astro-turfed roof. Only absently curious, Brig glanced inside. It was a den —Fletcher's trophy room judging by the mounted game heads on the wall. At that moment, he saw the gray-haired man walk to the desk and turn. His behavior suggested someone was in the room with him. Before Brig could hazard a guess, the auburn-haired woman in the black gown came into view. She turned her back to Fletcher so he could fasten her gown.

Brig's mouth quirked cynically. If he had any question why they'd snuck away from the party separately, he had his answer now. Brig studied the creamy smoothness of her shoulder blades and the rippling line of her spine. Fletcher took something from a jewel case and fastened it around her neck. She appeared delighted by the gift of a necklace and thanked Fletcher with a quick kiss. Brig thought she was such a consummate actress that she belonged on stage.

"It's beautiful, Dad." Jordanna held the jade pendant, carved in the shape of a cross, in her hand, the stone cool against her palm. "But what's the occasion? My birthday isn't for another six months yet."

"Does it have to be your birthday before I can buy my own daughter a present?" he asked. "I saw it and thought of you, so I bought it."

"I like it. Thank you." He'd never done anything like this before that Jordanna could remember. She was surprised, a little puzzled, and very pleased.

"I'm going back to the party. Are you coming?" Fletcher started toward the door.

She didn't feel like going back yet. "No, I'm going to stay for a while."

"I'll lock the door so you won't be disturbed. Be sure it's locked when you leave," he added.

"I will," Jordanna promised.

After he had walked out and closed the door, she turned away from it. Fingering the pale green pendant, she smiled faintly at the present that was prompted only by affection. She was facing the latticed doors leading to the rooftop garden. A light flared, the size of a match flame. Jordanna stiffened at the sight of a tall figure standing outside. It moved forward and the door handle turned. Jordanna recognized the man entering the den as the stranger she had seen talking to her mother.

"How long have you been there?" Her tone was faintly accusing. She didn't like the idea that he had been spying. It was an invasion of privacy to be watched, even if she had been unaware of it at the time.

A thick, dark brow lifted in mockery of her tone. "Not long." His voice was pitched low, with a faint drawl to it. "If it was privacy you were seeking," he reached for the drapery cord and pulled it, swinging the heavy drapes closed, "you should have closed the curtains."

"If I had suspected anyone was out there, I would have." It was a quick retort, but there was no sharpness to it.

"Didn't anyone tell you? There's a party going on. People are everywhere." His arm moved in a half-arc. In his hand, he held a drink that had gone to water, a cigarette burned between his fingers. "Although I must admit you have found yourself a quiet niche away from the noise and the crowd."

"It's peaceful here," Jordanna agreed and wondered why she didn't order him to leave. The truth was, she found him fascinating.

Studying him across the width of a room amidst a party had not prepared her for the impact of a face-to-face meeting. The look in his brown eyes was as dry and searing as any desert wind. The handsome lines of his face had been weathered into toughness. His dark mustache shadowed a mouth that was hard. There was a dangerous virility about him that was exciting as well as alarming. But most of all, it was the sensation of power that captivated her, an indefatigable strength that went to the very marrow of his bones.

Adjectives were difficult to find. Jordanna threw out *worldly*. She sensed he knew everything the way an animal does, born with the cunning and instinct to survive. *Experienced* didn't fit him either, although she was positive he had escaped many a trap and had increased his knowledge from it. In that suit and tie, he looked comfortable and at ease, yet it was an artful camouflage that reflected an ability to adapt to his surroundings. Sheep's clothing on a sagacious wolf, the last of his kind.

Jordanna was released from his gaze as he swept the room with a glance. "This is quite a display of trophies." He wandered over to the mounted head of a javelina, ivory tusks gleaming from open jaws. Jordanna could have claimed it as her kill, but she doubted that he would be impressed.

"Yes, it is." She heard the thread of breathlessness in her voice, but she doubted that he had. It was startling to discover how profoundly disturbed she was by his presence.

He turned from the wall and started to loosen his tie, then glanced at her. "Do you mind?"

Jordanna suspected that it didn't matter one way or the other if she did. "No. Go ahead." She lifted an indifferent hand and watched him tug the knot loose and stuff the tie in a suit pocket. He unfastened the top two buttons of his shirt. A trembling weakness shook her knees. Determined to conquer this reaction, she walked to the decanter of Scotch on the desk and splashed some of it into a crystal tumbler.

"There isn't any ice," Jordanna warned him.

"May I?" He held out his glass.

"That's alright. There's some in my glass." Cubes clinked against the sides as if to prove it.

Jordanna took the glass from him, avoiding contact with his fingers without knowing why. "Strong or weak?" The decanter was posed above his glass in her hand.

"Strong."

She poured a liberal amount of Scotch onto the melting cubes of ice and set the decanter down, re-stopping it. Picking up a glass in each hand, she turned and found him standing directly in front of her. A shiver of anticipation danced over her skin at the lazy, sensual look in his gaze. Jordanna stood eye-level with his mouth, a rather disconcerting fact to discover at such close quarters. His suit jacket had been discarded. There was only the white of his shirt.

"Your drink," she prompted, extending the hand that held his glass.

He reached, but the object wasn't the glass. His fingers closed around the jade cross, nestled in the valley between her breasts. Instead of lifting it for a closer examination, he left it there where the cup of his hand could rest on the swelling curves of her breasts. His action was insolent, but indignation was difficult to summon when an entirely different kind of flame was heating her skin.

"Carved jade. It's very beautiful . . . and expensive."
He lifted his gaze to her face and Jordanna returned
his steady look.

"Yes, it is." She succeeded in keeping her voice
calm and firm. "Would you mind removing your hand
and taking this glass?"

His gaze roamed slowly over her face, as if he were
making up his mind. "I think I do mind." He sounded
bemused.

It was a challenge, a glove thrown down. Jordanna
realized that she was being dared to pick it up.

"If you don't remove your hand, I will be forced
to pour this drink on your head," she threatened
calmly and seriously.

"Don't do it." The statement sounded more like an
ominous threat than hers had. His fingers slid up the
gold chain, closing it together and twisting it into a
tight circle just below her chin.

The movement had been purely instinctive. The gold
chain was thin and strong. Brig realized that one more
twist and it would serve as an adequate garrote. As it
was, it was achieving his objective of holding her
immobile without struggling. He noticed the fine gold
links stretched across her neck and was careful not
to exert any more pressure that might mar her skin.

Damn, she had beautiful skin. Could the rest of her
body be as ivory smooth as what he saw? Brig didn't
blame Fletcher for making her his private stock, his
mistress and lover. He hadn't expected her flawless
beauty to stand up under close scrutiny.

He glanced into her eyes. She was wary, unsure of
him, but she wasn't frightened. She had courage . . .
and her own brand of strength. Brig thought of the
other women he'd bedded in the last twenty years
and knew this one was more woman than he'd ever
known. But he knew what she was and was irritated
by the knowledge.

His gaze slid to her lips and he knew he had to
taste them. His mouth covered them. They were cool

to his touch, not warmed by the kisses that had come before his. But they were soft, so very soft. Brig let go of the gold chain and cupped his hand against her throat to hold her head motionless.

The jade cross slid back to its nesting ground in the shadowy cleavage as the chain was released. Jordanna felt its coolness once more against her warm flesh. She didn't resist the grip that firmly encircled her throat. She was passive under his kiss, but the gentle persuasions of his mouth were gradually dissolving that passivity. The soft bristles of his mustache teased her skin while his warm, male lips courted hers, exploring every curve and hollow with ease and sureness. The pulsepoint in her neck was pounding against his finger, betraying the rapid beat of her heart. Of their own free will, her lips began to cling to his.

Slowly he lifted his head. Her eyes were wide and faintly puzzled. In their look was a veiled question Jordanna was too proud to ask. His face held no expression. Without saying a word, he took the glasses from her hands and set them on the desk.

When he faced her again, he made no attempt to take her into his arms, nor did he put any distance between them. That was her option. She was being given the opportunity to leave before she was seduced by him. But Jordanna was all the more firmly intrigued by this stranger, who was like no man she'd ever met.

His hand reached out to stroke the mahogany sheen of her hair where it was pulled back from her face by a comb. "You have beautiful hair." It was a simple observation, not a compliment meant to flatter.

A response wasn't necessary and Jordanna made none. She continued to regard him with a steady look, although her heart was racing madly. His hands settled on either side of her neck to pull her closer, then moved to slide the straps of her gown from her shoulders and lightly caress her arms. Her lashes fluttered down. His touch reminded her of the pleasing roughness of a cat's tongue.

His breath was warm against her lips an instant before his mouth covered them in a long, drugging kiss. Slipping free of the gown's shoulder straps, her hands explored the flexible steel bands rippling along his upper arms. She was aware of her breasts swelling to fill the large hands that cupped them in their palms. She tasted the Scotch on his tongue and the nicotine on his lips, and savored the male flavor of him.

A thumb drew lazy circles around the rosy peak of her breast, hardening it into an erotic button. The weakness that had attacked her legs earlier returned with triple force. Jordanna swayed against him and he obligingly molded her to the supporting frame of his body. The heat emanating from his hard flesh spread quickly through hers, its warmth ennervating.

Leaving a trail of golden fire, his mouth followed the slanting curve of her jaw to the hollow below her ear, down the smooth column of her neck all the way to the base of her throat. Her head was tipped back to allow him greater access to whatever area pleased him while Jordanna trembled with quaking desire.

This hot, languorous passion was something she had never experienced before. It produced an ever-changing array of sensations, like the slowly turning magic of a kaleidoscope. Each time her skin tingled under his caress she wanted to stop the moment and hold it forever, but the heady male smell of him would crowd the sensation out with its intoxicating force, or she would taste the lazy fire of his kiss, forgetting all else until another sensation overwhelmed her.

Shaping her hips to the thrust of his, she tried to ease the throbbing ache that was slowly consuming her. His hands were at the back of her waist. Jordanna felt the slackening of the material around her middle as the zipper was pulled silently down. Then the strength that she had previously only suspected he possessed was revealed to her as he lifted her out of the gown and its slip, exerting no more effort than he would picking up a child. Just as easily, he shifted her into

the cradle of his arms. Jordanna heard her shoes hit
the floor, but she wasn't conscious of kicking them off.
Locking her arms around the tanned column of his
neck, she met the frankly desirous light in his eyes.
She neither shied from it, nor brazenly returned it.
It was all much simpler than that. There was no need
for role-playing, not the virgin nor the temptress.

Carrying her to the fireplace, he stood her on the
bearskin rug. As his arms withdrew their support from
her, Jordanna sank to her knees before stretching to
lie on her side, partially elevated by an arm. The
shaggy fur of the bear hide brushed her naked skin,
heightening already sensitive nerve ends. The animal
skin made a primitive mattress, but one that met their
needs.

She watched as he undressed. He shed his clothes
with unhurried ease, making the moment feel natural
and untainted. When he came to join her, Jordanna
felt the quickening rush of blood surge through her
veins. As the heat of his body seared her length, her
hands came in contact with the solid flesh of his
muscled shoulders and back. While his hard kiss
plundered the yielding softness of her mouth, his
skillful hands manipulated response from every area
he touched.

A tightening low in her stomach twisted her into a
coiled knot of need. Whimpering sounds were coming
from her throat, but he ignored her silent pleas to
release the unbearable tension within. No one had ever
made love to her like this before—taking it slow as
if they had all the time in the world.

In a gradual dawning of discovery, Jordanna realized
he expected more from her than just to be a receptacle
for his satisfaction. He wanted her to give in return
—to give of herself. No man had ever asked this of
her before. This casual demand for a commitment
was frightening, but not nearly as terrifying as the
black emptiness that threatened to swallow her if she
refused.

Her responses were tentative at first, gaining confi-

dence from his expertly sensual encouragement. She
was drawn into a whirlpool of raging desire. When
his weight settled on her, she thought she would drown
in the eddying rapture. Instead she was lifted higher
and higher until the world seemed to explode in a
dazzling display of lights that illuminated every corner
of her being.

When the fiery lovestorm passed, tiny beads of perspiration dampened her skin. Jordanna waited for the
shadows to crowd in, but they couldn't darken the
moment. The edges of her mouth deepened slightly to
reflect an inner smile. A roughened hand smoothed
her cheek and pushed away the tendrils of hair clinging to her damp skin. Her eyes were soft and wondrous
as she opened them to gaze at the man silently studying her. The strong, lean features wore a bemused
look. Bending his head, he let his mouth linger on her
lips for a warm instant.

"How long has it been since you made love for the
sheer pleasure of it?" His voice was low, faintly drawling in its curiosity.

"I . . ." How could she say "never" "I . . . I
don't know."

Something grim flickered across his expression. Jordanna wondered why her answer had displeased him.
She had admitted how very special she had felt in his
arms. Most men would have been puffing up with
conceit if a woman told them that.

Laughter and loud voices from the party suddenly
intruded into the moment. He gave her a crooked
smile of regret, an expression with no emotion behind
it, and rolled away from her. Her body felt cool without the warmth of him beside her.

"It's time we were rejoining the party." His clipped
explanation hung in the air as he began to dress.

"Yes," Jordanna agreed, but couldn't shake the
confusion his strange attitude had caused.

It haunted her as she stepped into the black gown
and pulled the straps over her shoulders. Drawing
the material snugly around her waist, she raised the

zipper, but the hook at the top defied her fingers. She walked over to him. His shirt was tucked into his pants and he was buttoning the front. She turned her back to him.

"Would you fasten this for me, please?" When her request was met with silence, Jordanna glanced questioningly over her shoulder. His hands were on his shirt front, halted in the act of buttoning the shirt. At her glance, he moved to fasten the hook, his gaze cynical and hard.

"You're having your share of trouble with it tonight, aren't you?" There was something taunting in his remark as his fingers brushed against her spine.

A frown drew her brows together until Jordanna remembered she had needed her father's assistance earlier when he must have been outside on the rooftop patio. She had forgotten that.

Someone tried the door to the den. The attempt was immediately followed by a knock. "Jordanna? Are you in there?"

She recognized her brother's voice. "Yes, Kit." The hook was fastened and his touch was withdrawn from the sensitive skin of her backbone. "Thank you," she murmured but he had already turned away. Before her brother could knock again, Jordanna hurried to the door, nervously running a hand over the sides of her hair.

When she finally opened the door, Christopher's face wore a frowning smile of bemused concern. "I've been looking all over for you," he began and stopped as he looked beyond her.

"Excuse me." A low voice said and Jordanna turned to find the tall, dark-haired stranger behind her. His suit jacket was suspended from the hook of his finger, and swung over his shoulder. His bronzed features were devoid of expression as he met her look. "Thanks for sharing the peace and quiet . . . and the Scotch." He lifted the glass in his hand before inclining his head in a mocking gesture and brushing his way past them into the hall.

"Who was that?" her brother asked.

She was jolted by the realization that she didn't know his name. A bubble of hysterical laughter rose in her throat. What would her brother say if she told him she had just made love to a total stranger with glorious abandon? What was more absurd, not five hours ago she had declared she was swearing off men! Had she taken leave of her senses? If she had, Jordanna hoped it wouldn't be the only such experience. The way she felt had to be what Kit had been talking about. All this warm, wonderful confusion lingering inside had to be a sensation that would be repeated. She wished she could tell her brother how right he had been, but their relationship wasn't close enough.

"A guest," Jordanna finally answered his question. "We never got around to introductions." They had met on an elemental level where names had been superfluous . . . until this moment.

"Dad said you were in here."

"I've been . . . relaxing," she said, in case her appearance needed explaining.

His dark gaze skimmed her face. "You look rested . . . and refreshed, considerably less tense than you did earlier," he admitted, but his eyes seemed to probe.

Jordanna didn't want to be examined that closely. It was all too new. "I guess I'd better be rejoining the party before I'm accused of being rude," she declared with a mock grimace, but her brother didn't move out of her way.

A teasing light danced in his eyes. "You'd better put your shoes on first."

At his remark, her bare toes curled into the carpet. A self-conscious warmth flooded her skin as she laughed and turned away. "I wish I didn't have to wear them."

Brig abandoned his drink on the first table he came to. A grim kind of anger was simmering in his veins. What had started out as a tasting kiss had become a hunger he couldn't control. Not only had his appetite been satiated, but he'd also had the satisfaction of knowing she had enjoyed her experience. He could still feel the smooth softness of her body against him, the sensation lingering. Damn, but she had been a helluva woman when her wall of inhibitions had finally crumbled. He had been surprised by the invisible barrier and determined to have all of her or none.

Someone jostled his shoulder, snapping the thread of his reverie. Brig glanced around the crowded room. On the far side, he saw Fletcher Smith and turned in the opposite direction, hating himself for doing it. Max was standing twenty feet away, part of a clustered group.

A growing self-disgust welled inside Brig. Earlier he had viewed his cousin's flirtation with Olivia Smith with searing contempt. He had been derisive of a man who would take another man's money and his woman. But he had done just that.

Long, impatient strides carried him back to Max. "I'm leaving," Brig announced curtly.

"So soon?" his cousin frowned.

"Tell Smith I'll be in touch." Brig started toward the foyer.

"You can tell him yourself. He's standing right over there," Max declared.

But Brig didn't respond. He was already halfway to the door. He didn't like himself very much at the moment—nor what he'd done, nor the fact that he had derived so much pleasure from doing it.

When Jordanna returned to the party with her brother, she looked for the stranger, but there was no sign of him. After nearly an hour of discreet searching, she finally admitted he had left. His identity was a mystery to her, one she wanted to solve. She wanted to see him again, to discover if the wild wonder of him had been only an illusion.

The next day, a janitorial company came to the apartment to clean up after the party. The living room was being vacuumed and Jordanna wandered into the dining room where her mother was supervising the storing of personal silver bowls and flatware.

"Livvie," Jordanna began her question hesitantly, wanting to sound only mildly interested, "last night at the party, who was that man I saw you talking with?"

Her mother stiffened, her swift glance sharp and wary. "I spoke to everyone who attended. You'll have to be more specific than that, Jordanna."

The curt response was concealing something else. Guilt? A shock wave rocked Jordanna. What if that man had been one of her mother's lovers. The possibility twisted her stomach into a churning mass of revulsion.

"Never mind." She didn't want to find out who he was anymore. It was better if she didn't know. She hurriedly retreated from the room, leaving her mother staring after her in confusion.

Alone, Jordanna kept trying to convince herself that he hadn't been her mother's type. But what did she know of the kind of man her mother found attractive? It wasn't possible, she kept insisting. But the question remained no matter how much she tried to ignore it.

Chapter VII

As JORDANNA PUSHED open the door leading from the fire stairs to the top floor, her brother stepped out of the elevator. Perspiration flowed freely over her face, curling wisps of wet hair clinging to her temples and forehead. The rest of her long hair was pulled to the nape of her neck and secured by a circular, combed holder. Dressed in a forest green jogging suit with cream yellow stripes, she was puffing heavily.

Christopher stopped. "What's wrong with the elevators?" he mocked. "Or are you naturally so energetic?"

"I rode the elevator halfway up and took the stairs the rest of the way," she said breathlessly and halted to rest her hands on her hips. She blew the stale air from her aching lungs and flexed the cramping muscles in her legs. "I've been out jogging," Jordanna panted, trying to stay limber.

"So I guessed," he inserted dryly.

"I've got to get into shape for the mountains," she explained between gasping breaths.

"Another hunting trip?" Christopher took the key she handed him and unlocked the apartment door.

Jordanna nodded. "We're leaving the second week in September—another three weeks." She entered the apartment ahead of him, still struggling to catch her breath.

"Where are you going this time?" He closed the door and returned her key. Jordanna dropped it in the slashed pocket of her jacket, and mopped the perspiration from her neck with the sleeve.

"Idaho. Somewhere around the Salmon River, I guess. Some rancher named McCord is guiding us back into the sheep country." She continued to pace the living room to keep from getting stiff. "Dad has made all the arrangements."

Fletcher always handled the details of planning a hunt. Normally Jordanna had more interest in the arrangements he made and discussed them with him, but not this time. She couldn't concentrate on anything. The memory of that July party and the man she'd made love to that night kept crowding into her thoughts. She had never mentioned him again after that one, abortive attempt the next day. She wanted to forget him, but she couldn't forget the way he had made her feel.

At first she had tried to recapture the emotion with other partners. Their kisses hadn't lived up to her expectations and Jordanna had backed out of their embraces because they demanded nothing from her but submission. She had experienced something more fulfilling and she wanted to find it again. Not even the ache of frustration could make her settle for less.

"How long will you be leaving Mother alone this time? Three weeks? A month?" Her brother's questions were vaguely angry.

Jordanna's temper was always easily aroused, but lately it didn't take much provocation to rile it. "Probably three weeks. But she won't be alone," Jordanna snapped. "You'll be here. And, whoever she's sleeping with now." A sharp pain stabbed at the thought of who it might be.

"You can't resist an opportunity to put her down, can you?" he accused. His mouth was pressed into a tight line of control, but the flashing darkness of his eyes betrayed his anger. "You use her mistakes to rationalize away any guilt for leaving her behind, while you and Dad go off alone to some forgotten corner of the earth."

"It so happens that we aren't going alone this time," she retorted. The breath was back in her lungs and they were operating normally as the blood flowed hotly through her veins.

Her statement made Christopher momentarily forget his anger. "You aren't? Since when? Dad never takes anyone hunting with him except you and a guide."

"This time Dad is taking a friend. He isn't going to hunt, he's just tagging along on the trip."

He eyed her skeptically. "Who is going with you?"

"A friend of Dad's. His name is Max Sanger." Jordanna didn't know the man all that well. Her father included her on his hunting trips, but she was excluded from activities involving male friends. His evenings out were strictly his own. Jordanna didn't participate in them.

"Max Sanger?" Her brother appeared stunned by her answer. "Are you positive?"

"If you don't believe me, ask Dad."

"I will." His handsome features were set in an expression of grim purpose. That surprised Jordanna. "Where is he? In the den?"

"I imagine." There was a trace of haughty unconcern in her shrug. But when her brother strode off for the den, curiosity impelled her to follow him.

The door to the den was already standing open when Jordanna rounded the corner of the hallway. Her brother was inside, issuing a clipped greeting to his father. "Hello, Dad."

"What are you doing here, Kit? I don't recall asking to see you." At the bitter scorn in her father's voice,

Jordanna slowed to a halt short of the doorway. She'd never heard her father speak to Kit with such contempt before. It shocked her.

"I wasn't aware that I needed an invitation," her brother countered in a hard, flat voice.

"What do you want? If you're here looking for your mother, I have no idea where she is. Ask Tessa." There was a rustle of papers being shuffled.

"At the moment, I want to talk to you," Christopher stated.

"We haven't anything left to say to each other. And I'm busy with some reports."

Jordanna knew her father had resented the way Kit had rejected his financial support and moved out in favor of making it on his own, but she never realized how embittered he had become toward his own son.

"Jordanna tells me you are leaving on a hunting trip soon," her brother continued.

"Since when have you been interested in any of my hunting trips?" her father snapped.

Disbelief that it was actually her father speaking like that, despite the fact that it was his voice, carried Jordanna into the doorway. He was seated behind his desk. His expression was filled with a derision that made her flinch.

"Jordanna also mentioned that you aren't going alone this time." Her brother had tipped his head to one side, a hint of challenge in the angle.

"That's right." Her father removed his glasses and leaned back in the swivel armchair. As he did, he noticed Jordanna standing in the doorway. Immediately his attitude changed to one of aloof interest.

"She said Max Sanger is coming with you. Is that right?"

"Max has scheduled his trip to coincide with ours," he admitted, his gaze narrowing faintly. "He isn't going hunting. He's just taking a vacation in the mountains."

"But why is he going with you?"

"I believe McCord, the rancher who will be serving

as our guide, is related to Max, his cousin or something. I imagine that had something to do with his decision to come with us," her father explained with reasonable logic. "Plus, I've expressed an interest in some stock he is considering selling, as well as a land development project he's started in California. I think he wants to discuss the possibility in more detail."

"But you don't mix business and hunting," Christopher accused.

"So I've told him, but Max remains to be convinced." Fletcher Smith smiled with mild amusement.

"Why are you letting him come with you when you've always objected to others accompanying you in the past?" There was a doubt still needing to be put to rest before her brother was convinced that her father didn't have some other ulterior motive.

"I have objected to other hunters," Fletcher qualified the statement. "Because it meant sharing the skills of a guide. Max is simply coming along for the adventure of the trip."

"In that case," Christopher paused, still wary, although Jordanna couldn't understand why, "you wouldn't object if I came along?"

His gray head lifted slightly in a gesture of surprise. "This is still a hunting party, Kit. The purpose is to shoot a bighorn ram. It isn't a trip for the squeamish or the faint-hearted." He studied the slender man facing the desk. "You've never expressed an interest in coming before. Why now, Kit?"

"I reject your sport, not you. Whatever else you may think about me, I am a man. I won't faint at the sight of blood," Christopher assured him with dry humor. "I want to go with you, Dad."

Fletcher Smith sat forward in his chair. A shudder seemed to quake through him. He looked suddenly very old and tired . . . and vulnerable. His brown eyes were haunted with love as he gazed at the young man.

"You don't know how many times I've wanted to hear you say that, son." His voice shook, revealing how much he had been moved by Kit's last statement. "Why haven't you? Why did you wait until now?"

"Because . . . this is one trip I have to take." Her brother seemed to choose the words of his answer with care. "May I come with you?"

"Yes." A wide smile beamed from her father's face, making him look young and invincible again. His sparkling gaze swung to her. "How about you, Jordanna? Do you think you can put up with your brother for three solid weeks?"

"I doubt it." But there was a faint smile on her lips. She could see how pleased, how proud her father was that Kit wanted to come with them. No matter how angry Kit could make her, she was grateful and happy that he had taken this step to heal the break with their father. "But I guess I'll survive the experience."

It was nearly dusk. The distant peaks were catching the first flames of sunset. Tugging the gloves from his fingers, Brig walked toward the rough log house. There was no buoyancy to his stride. His steps betrayed his bone-weary tiredness as the spurs jingled on his boots. A dusty, matted cow dog trotted at his heels.

He'd been pushing himself hard, harder than he would have pushed anyone else these past weeks. The last cutting of hay was up and he could only hope it was enough to get him through the coming winter. He'd ridden up to the high camp where Jocko was grazing the sheep to take him supplies.

Lifting his gaze to the sky, he remembered the shepherd's warning that the mountain creatures were preparing for an early winter. It had been a clear blue day. How long could he leave the cattle in the lush grasses of the high valleys before he'd have to bring them down to the winter pastures close to the ranch house? He had hoped to gain part of September, but with this hunting expedition and now Jocko's warning, he couldn't risk it.

Impatiently, Brig slapped his gloves against his thighs. The herd would have to come down next week. The mottled cow dog left his side to trot over and flop in the shade of a tree. Brig's smiling glance resembled a tired grimace.

"That's what I'd like to do, Sam," he told the dog. Its tail hit the ground once in response to its name.

Gripping the wooden hand rail, Brig climbed the steps to the back entrance of the two-story log structure. He removed his straw Stetson as he entered the door and hung it on a wooden peg. A short, stocky man in blue jeans and a plaid shirt was standing in front of the kitchen stove, stirring the contents of a pot. Barrel-chested with narrow hips, he glanced at Brig when he entered.

"How's Jocko?" he asked.

"Fine." Brig walked directly to the sink and turned on the faucets to wash up.

Tandy Barnes had been with him since he'd started the ranch and had become accustomed to abrupt answers from his boss. He'd often joked that Brig didn't waste five words when one would do. Brig rubbed cold water on his face and neck in an attempt to revive his tired senses, then lathered his hands with soap.

"He's starting the flock down," Brig added. "We'll be going after the cattle next week." Rinsing his hands, he reached for the towel and turned around. "Where's Frank?"

"Repairing that pack saddle," Tandy replied. "Toss me that towel."

Brig wadded the hand towel and threw it to him. Tandy used it as a holder to take a tray of biscuits from the oven. "What's for supper?" Brig asked.

"Stew and biscuits."

"Again?" Brig snapped.

"Don't bitch at me about the food," Tandy warned. "Anytime you don't like the menu, you can do something about it. I didn't hire on as a cook."

"If you had, I would have fired you ten years ago." Brig breathed in disgust.

"Ring the bell and get Frank in here so we can eat

this while it's hot." The stocky cowboy began slopping spoonfuls of the stew onto the plates he had stacked on the stove.

Walking to the back door, Brig held it ajar and stepped out to pull the rope of the dinner bell mounted on the side of the house. Its clang rang out across the yard. He didn't wait to see the figure emerging from the barn as he stepped back inside and closed the door.

Tandy handed him a plate mounded with venison stew and three biscuits balanced precariously on the edge. Brig carried it to the table, kicking out an old wooden chair with the back of his boot. A small stack of mail sat on the table. Brig scooped up a spoonful of stew and chewed it while he leafed through the envelopes. One carried a New York City postmark. He laid his silverware down and opened it. Tandy carried two plates of food to the table. Pulling a chair out for himself, he set the second plate in front of a third chair.

"Who's the letter from?" Tandy stretched his neck to get a peek at the contents. His dark hair was thinning, and silvered with gray. A bald spot at the back of his head was partially hidden by the hair he had slicked back to cover it.

Brig ignored the question as he continued to read the contents. His mouth tightened into a harder and harder line. When he'd finished the letter, he wadded the paper into a crumpled ball and breathed out an irritated sigh.

"What's it say?" Tandy frowned.

"It's from Smith." There was a wealth of restrained and savage anger in his voice. "There'll be another non-hunting member on the trip. His son is coming along. Is this going to be a sight-seeing excursion or a hunting trip?" he demanded.

When he hadn't been beating himself into the ground with ranchwork these last two months, he'd been scouting the high country, studying the land, locating the bighorn herds and defining their range. Fletcher Smith had been right. If Brig was going to take his money for a hunt, he was going to do everything he could to insure Smith got his money's worth. But this hunt for a trophy ram seemed to be turning into something else—first with Max being invited along, and now Smith's son.

"For two bits, I'd tell him to find somebody else," Brig grumbled.

There was so much that still had to be done. The extra supplies had to be brought in from town. All the gear, pack-saddles, halters, bridles, riding saddles, had to be in first-class condition as well as the riding horses and packstring. All the ranchwork had to be caught up to the point where one man could handle it for the three weeks Brig would be gone. Tandy was coming with him to serve as the wrangler. Jocko would be the cook. Frank Savidge would be left in charge.

"But you said you needed money, so how can you tell him to find somebody else?" Tandy wanted to know.

"I know what I said." Brig took another bite of the stew, but it tasted like chalk. He dropped the spoon onto the plate. "If there is any of this left after tonight, throw it out."

"Aren't you going to eat it?" Tandy demanded.

"Have I got a choice?" he jeered and picked up the spoon.

The back door opened and Frank Savidge entered the kitchen in time to catch Brig's words. "What's the matter?"

Frank was a burly mountain of a man, lantern-jawed with sandy brown hair. He was a beer-drinking, fist-brawling good ole boy who had been fired from every outfit within a hundred miles. His problem was he didn't respect any man if he could whip him, whether it was his boss or his buddy. He'd worked for Brig the last five years.

Tandy darted a resentful glance at Brig before he answered Frank's question. "Ahh, he's just acting like a wolf with his tail caught in a crack. I'll be glad when his disposition improves."

"It'll probably coincide with an improvement in the cooking," Brig retorted.

"Stew?!!" Frank glared at the plate on the table.

"That's it! That's the last time I'm cookin' supper!" Tandy declared.

No one argued. The conversation ended as the three men ate the meal in silence. The balled piece of paper beside Brig's plate was a mocking reminder of events he wanted to forget. His irritation wasn't caused by the increased size of the hunting party and the changes in accommodations it presented. His wish to cancel the agreement to guide the hunt had nothing to do with that. It was the prospect of facing Fletcher Smith and taking the man's money after making love to his mistress. Jordanna. Damn, but he wanted to forget her name. He wanted to forget her.

Brig slammed the door on the pickup and glanced at the supplies loaded in the back. Ignoring the fact that he should be on the road back to the ranch, he walked up the broken concrete path that had once been a sidewalk and knocked on the door. The small house was old and badly in need of paint. The landlord had told Trudie that if he painted it, he'd have to raise the rent.

The door was opened and his gaze swung from the peeling paint on the sides of the house to the blonde woman behind the screen door. "Brig?" Her startled voice betrayed her surprise. She immediately became flustered, a hand rushing to fluff her hair and touch her naked lips.

"Can I come in?" He felt hard and cold, but the stone ache inside him drove him on.

"Of course." She unlatched the screen door to let him in and clutched the front of her housecoat. "I must look a sight. Grab a beer from the refrigerator while I put on some make-up."

His hand caught her wrist. "Don't bother." Brig pulled her into his arms and crushed the lips beneath his. He hated the dry feel of them when his mouth ached for the touch of a soft pair.

He picked her up and carried her across the small living room and down the narrow hall. The bedroom door was closed and he kicked it open with his boot. The bed wasn't made and clothes were scattered on the floor. When he set her down, Trudie hurried to pick them up.

"I'm sorry," she apologized for the mess. "I wasn't expecting anyone."

"Forget them." He had already unbuttoned his shirt and was pulling the tails out of his waistband. Her subservient attitude grated when in his mind was a memory of pride with a touch of arrogance. "And take off that robe."

His head touched the pillow for an instant. He felt worse than he had before. The frustration of wanting was clawing at his guts despite the physical gratification of lust. It ate at him. Brig swung his long legs to the floor and reached for his pants.

"Who is she?" Trudie pulled the sheet over the nakedness, a tremor of hurt in her voice.

"Who is who?" Brig feigned cold ignorance.

"You were trying to pretend I was some other woman," she accused softly without anger.

"I don't know what you're talking about." He shrugged into his shirt and tucked it inside the waistband of his Levi's.

"Brig, this isn't the first time it's happened," she chided him for treating her like an ignorant child. "After we made love, you used to lay in bed with me and we'd talk. Lately, you . . . well, you're out of bed almost before it's over."

"I have to get back to the ranch."

"Sure." She didn't believe him.

"Dammit! If you don't like it, . . ." Brig pivoted, the rage fading at the gently forgiving look on her face. He closed his mouth, a muscle leaping in his jaw as he contained the frustration that made him lash out at whoever was near.

"I never said that, Brig," Trudie murmured. "But we've known each other a long time. I didn't think we had to lie to each other. There is someone else. You know it doesn't matter to me."

"You have a vivid imagination." His mouth smiled but his eyes were cold. He'd get that she-bitch out of his system if it was the last thing he did. "I've got to leave," Brig stated and reached for his hat on the dresser. "Take care, Trudie." He bent over the bed and kissed her.

Halfway to the front door, he discovered his hand was wiping the feel of her lips from his mouth. He hadn't accomplished anything by stopping here. Yanking open the screen door, he pushed it out of his way, letting it swing shut with a bang as he walked out.

His long, swift strides slowed at the sight of Jake Phelps coming up the walk. Jake owned a ranch near the Montana border. At fifty, he'd never been married, a road Brig was headed down. He was a short man with a pock-marked face and a beer belly. The snowy white hat on his head hid his baldness. Brig's gaze ran over the western suit and string tie. His jowlly cheeks had been shaved so close they were almost raw. Brig could smell the spicy shaving lotion from three feet away. Jake's face reddened under Brig's narrowed look.

"What brings you here, McCord?" he blustered.

The rancher was slicked up to a go a-courtin'. The only things missing were a bouquet of flowers in his hand and a box of candy under his arm. Brig glanced back toward the house and smiled cynically.

"The same thing that brought you here, Jake," he replied.

The man began to puff up like a bullfrog. "I don't like them kind of references to . . ."

"Save your breath, Jake," Brig interrupted. "I won't be back."

"What do you mean?" The rancher frowned uncertainly.

"Trudie is a nice girl. She deserves someone who will treat her decent." And not use her as a pounding board for his frustrations, he thought to himself.

Brig left the short man standing on the cracked and broken sidewalk with his mouth open. He didn't look back as he climbed behind the wheel of his pickup and backed away from the house into the street.

The image of an auburn-haired woman with green-speckled eyes kept dancing in his head. Her memory was becoming an obsession with him. He'd dream about her at night and wake up hurting. He'd ride through a mountain meadow and catch the tantalizing scent of her amidst a patch of wildflowers. Watching a sunset, he'd remember the way her brown hair caught fire in the light.

"Jordanna." Brig said the name aloud and wanted to tear out his tongue. He cursed savagely at the memory that had destroyed his peace of mind. He had walked away from Trudie without a twinge of regret. Why couldn't he walk away from the memory of a night two months old?

But it lived with him. He could hear her voice and feel her soft, alabaster skin. He could taste her mouth and smell the wild sweetness of her skin. Most of all, he could see the smooth, proud lines of her body lying on that bearskin rug.

Brig stepped on the accelerator and the pickup shot forward, but he couldn't outrace the visions in his mind.

PART TWO
THE HUNT

Chapter VIII

"This is as far as we go," Tandy Barnes announced as he set the brake and switched off the ignition. "We're here."

Jordanna moved stiffly, cramped and sore from the bouncing, jarring ride over the dirt road. She looked out the windows of the high-mounted four-wheel-drive vehicle, but she couldn't see a sign of a building. The bulk of yesterday had been spent flying, in and out of airports, changing planes, and finally arriving in Idaho. The short, stocky driver had met them at the airport and taken them to a hotel to spend the night, advising them the drive to the ranch should only be taken during the daylight hours. After traversing that road, Jordanna could understand why. It would have been suicide in the dark.

"Where is here? I don't see the ranch." As soon as she had said it, Jordanna realized it had been a mistake. The driver was giving her a look that said he expected a female to complain.

"It's on the other side of the river. We have to go the rest of the way on foot. There's only a pack bridge across it," he explained with the patience of a man who knew a woman would disapprove of such primitive conditions. "Like I been tellin' you, we're pretty well isolated here. We're a working ranch so don't expect luxury accommodations."

"I believe you mentioned that before, Mr. Barnes." Jordanna smiled tightly, irritated by his patronizing attitude.

Ever since she had stepped off the plane with her father, brother, and Max Sanger, and this squatty, short-legged cowboy had come forward to meet them, she had been subjected to all kinds of warnings about how rough it was going to be. Although Tandy never said it, his meaning was obvious—a woman didn't have any business in a hunting party.

Granted, she probably hadn't made the best impression. She had been wearing an ochre traveling suit that looked like something out of the pages of Vogue, which it was, but it was the most comfortable set of clothing she had for traveling. He had taken one look at the slender brown heels of her shoes, the jeweled brooch on her scarf, the earrings dangling from her earlobes, plus the suit, and labeled her a foolish female. Jordanna hadn't been able to change his opinion. She had the feeling he would have regarded her more favorably if she'd arrived wearing blue jeans and a sloppy sweater, and no make-up.

Opening the door, she jumped lightly to the ground. Today she had worn slacks, a thick sweater over her blouse, and sensible flat shoes, but Tandy Barnes continued to give her sideways looks of disapproval. Jordanna was used to such skepticism. Eventually she would overcome it. Her father had often teased her that she wouldn't have any problem if she were skinny and ugly.

But men, especially the rugged outdoor types, didn't expect young beautiful women to like their kind of life. Women like that were supposed to be interested in fashion and jewels and candlelight dinners instead of campfire fare, insects, and insulated underwear. Whenever she looked like she was enjoying the discomfort, they would laugh and say that she was being a "good sport" about it. There were times when it was impossible to win and Jordanna had learned to stop trying to batter down their prejudices and ignore them so she could enjoy herself.

The sound of rushing water turned her gaze to the river sprouting in rocky ground beyond the pines. A worn stone and dirt path wound through the trees toward the shimmering water visible through the limbs. It was the Middle Fork of the Salmon River. Its white-water rapids, alternating with deep pools, carved out a gorge in the rocky terrain.

On the other side of the river gorge, mountains rose. The conical shapes of pine trees dotted their slopes. But Jordanna could see no sign of the ranch buildings Tandy Barnes had claimed were on the other side. Rugged peaks made jagged points on the horizon, snow-capped and wild.

"Its beautiful country, isn't it?" Christopher was standing near her, his hands on his hips, his dark head tilted back to see the tops of the mountains.

"Beautiful," she agreed and turned to follow his gaze to the east.

Bare granite mountains stabbed the sky with a multitude of rocky spires and jutting ridges. The forbidding peaks loomed above them with rugged grandeur, majestic and awesome. An osprey floated on the mountain currents, following the snaking river.

"Those are the Bighorn Crags." Jordanna had oriented herself with an area map and identified the mountain range.

"Is that where we'll be going?" He studied the wild terrain with an apprehensive look.

"No. We'll hunt west of the river, as I understand it," she answered. "In the Idaho Primitive Area, where no motorized vehicles are allowed unless they belong to private ranchers in the area."

"I can't imagine living out here." Her brother shook his head at the thought. "It's so lonely."

Lonely? Jordanna looked around again. Somehow she wouldn't have used that word to describe it. It was isolated, yes. Few people would stop by for a visit or a cup of coffee. But she had known times when she had felt the loneliest and was surrounded by people. Lonely was a state of mind, not a place.

"It takes a special breed to live out here and not go stark-raving mad," he smiled wryly and turned from the scene.

"You may be right."

"I'll tell you one thing," Christopher said, "compared to those mountains," he gestured behind him to the Bighorn Crags, "the other side looks tame."

"Don't be fooled, Kit," Jordanna warned. "They are wild. One day in that terrain and you're going to discover muscles you didn't know you had."

"Have you been here before?" He looked surprised by her knowledge.

"Not here. But Dad and I have hunted in the Canadian Rockies for Stone Sheep and in Alaska for Dall. It can be a demanding country, it takes all the strength you have and forces you to dig deep for more. It's amazing sometimes when you think you can't go another step, you wind up pushing yourself another mile or more. It's been said if you flattened all the mountains in Idaho, you'd have a state bigger than Texas." She grinned.

"I can believe it," her brother laughed.

"That's enough sight-seeing," her father called. "Come on and give us a hand."

Their gear was being unloaded from the back of the all-road vehicle. Her father and Tandy Barnes were doing all the work while Max Sanger stood to one side supervising. Jordanna glanced at the slender man, surprised that he was talking about his company. That's all he'd done since they'd left New York.

"Do you suppose Max is going to expect us to carry his things?" she muttered to her brother. His dark eyes narrowed on the man, then immediately slashed to their father. "I wish Dad would buy his stock, or whatever it is he's trying to sell him. Maybe he'd change his mind about the trip."

"That's what I keep wishing," Christopher agreed with a strangely sober expression.

"Here." Her father held out her rifle scabbard, its excellently crafted leather showing signs of use. It had protected the rifle inside on many a hunting trip. Jordanna took it from him and slung it behind her back. Her personal saddlebags were draped over her shoulder, along with the cases for the spotting scope and binoculars. The dufflebags were unloaded from the back and separated to go to their owners. As Jordanna reached for hers, Tandy grabbed it first.

"I'll carry it for you," he offered in a gentlemanly fashion.

A small suitcase containing clothes she wouldn't be taking into the mountains was already in one of her hands. He obviously felt she couldn't be expected to carry more.

"I carry my own gear, Mr. Barnes. Thank you." Determination was in her smile as she reached out and took the dufflebag from his grip.

Max hadn't been pushing people aside to claim his things, but when he heard Jordanna refuse the cowboy's assistance, he came forward to pick up his. Jordanna noticed it and her lips curved into a dry smile of amusement.

Tandy Barnes continued to eye her hesitantly, as if expecting her to collapse any minute under the load. Her father glanced up from his sorting and noticed the cowboy's hesitation. His gaze swung to Jordanna and back to the man.

"Don't worry, Tandy," he said, already on first-name basis with the man who would be the wrangler for the packstring. "She's tougher than she looks."

"Maybe." As he scratched the back of his head, his hat tipped forward, revealing a balding patch in his dark hair. Tandy Barnes had admitted to Christopher to being forty-six, but Jordanna suspected he'd left six years off somewhere. His squat, barrel frame looked fit enough for a man half his age. He pushed his hat back on his head and pulled the front low on his forehead. Glancing in the back of the wagon, he announced, "That looks like it's everything." There were only two items left to be carried and he picked them up. "You folks travel light."

It was a compliment, noting their experience at packing back into the mountains, where only the essentials were taken. Jordanna met her father's glance. The sizing-up process was always the same between hunter and outfitter.

Leading the way, Tandy Barnes started down the path to the river, and they followed single file, with Fletcher Smith bringing up the read behind Max. The pack bridge across the river was substantial, although its narrow width gave it a deceptively flimsy appearance. Upstream, the water tumbled over large boulders and sawtooth rocks. The steep granite walls of the gorge echoed the roar of white water. Below the bridge, the river slowed to turbulent eddies before dumping into a deep placid pool where the banks widened downstream. There, a white sandbar jutted into the water to form a short, wide beach.

"I'd hate to fall off this bridge," Max commented behind Jordanna. She glanced over her shoulder. He had paused to look down at the water below. She knew how hypnotic those spinning whirlpools could be and the uncanny sensation they created of pulling a person down. "Are you sure it can hold all of us at the same time?"

"I'm sure." Her father nudged the man's shoulder with his dufflebag.

Christopher had stopped at the sound of the conversation. "Is everything all right back there?" he called.

"It's fine. We're coming," Fletcher answered as Max walked cautiously forward.

Tandy waited on the other side until they were all

across the bridge. Jordanna paused beside him to look downstream. "The Middle Fork is protected under the Wild and Scenic River Act, isn't it?" At his nod, she asked, "The Salmon River is north of here, isn't it?"

"North and east is the way the current flows."

"Why is it called the 'River of No Return'?" An absent frown creased her brother's forehead.

"Because it was so wild and rough, there was only one way to go—downstream. 'Course now they got power boats and jet boats that can make the return trip," he explained.

Fletcher Smith joined their semicircle. "Lewis and Clark tried to navigate it and turned back. They named it the Lewis River. The Indians called it the Big Fish Water because of the salmon that swam up to spawn."

"We catch salmon here during their spawning run. There's a fish ladder way upstream by Dagger Falls," Tandy told them. "There's steelhead, cutthroat, rainbow and Dolly Varden in the river, too. Frank caught quite a batch of Chinook salmon the other week. If we're lucky, Jocko will cook it for supper tonight."

"The Middle Fork is a major spawning ground for the salmon, isn't it?" her father asked.

"Yup. If you want to try your hand at fishin' later this afternoon, this is a good spot." Tandy pointed to the sandbar.

"I might do that."

"Let's get this gear to the house so you folks can settle in." The cowboy shifted the case he carried. His gaze briefly touched Jordanna before he started on.

The path was wider on this side of the river. It curved around a solid granite boulder that rose twenty feet above them. The first glimpse of the ranch came when they rounded the rock. A wide meadow spread out before them, thickly tufted with brown grass. A stand of aspens shimmered gold from an autumn frost. Their white bark contrasted with the darker green of the pine trees on the distant mountain slopes.

Scattered across the rolling pasture, a herd of Hereford cattle grazed. Farther away, Jordanna saw a flock of sheep and heard their bleating calls, muted by the scuffling sound of their own footsteps. The air was fresh and clear, lightly scented with pine and hay. Beyond, the rugged mountains blended in with the pastoral scene.

Turning her gaze from the view, Jordanna saw the ranch buildings on the near side of the meadow. A log barn loomed tall, surrounded by a corral where more than a dozen horses were held. Tall mounds of hay were fenced with the same wood poles as the corral, winter forage for the livestock when the snows were deep. Jordanna recognized a smaller log building as a smokehouse.

The ranch house was nestled near the granite rocks that formed the gorge on the riverside. It, too, was constructed of logs, a compact, two-story building. The front porch was designed from rough hewn logs, in varying sizes for the railings, posts, and beams.

Tandy's boots thumped on the porch steps and floor as he walked to the front door. He held it open for the rest of them. Jordanna walked into a small living area dominated by a black wood-burning stove. A set of stairs rose into a ceiling well to the second floor.

There was a sofa and a couple of worn-looking armchairs. A desk was against one wall, its top cluttered with papers, and a crude chair sat before it. The walls themselves were bare of pictures. The only ornamentation was the tanned hide of a black bear, hanging on one wall. There was a shelf of books and a card table and chairs. A worn deck of cards was on the table, spread out in a game of solitaire that the player had lost and left.

"Just set your gear down anywhere." Tandy followed Fletcher to be the last one entering the house.

"We might as well take it to our rooms," her father stated.

"Well . . ." he hesitated and glanced at Jordanna. "I don't exactly know how Brig was going to arrange that. You'd better wait until he comes."

"Where is McCord?" Her father glanced around.

"I thought Brig would be here," Max added.

"He'll be here directly," Tandy promised. "There's always coffee on the stove. Would anyone like a cup?" Christopher was the only one who refused. Tandy walked to a door half-hidden behind the staircase and disappeared through it.

By the time they had stacked their gear in a neat pile near the front door, he was back carrying three unmatched mugs steaming with hot coffee. He was followed by another man. The second man was as tall as Tandy, but his slight build gave the impression he was smaller. Hatless, his thick, dark hair was shading to gray. Although his swarthy complexion gave his lean features a foreign look, his dark eyes held untold gentleness. In one hand, he carried a mug of coffee and in the other, a plate of donuts.

"This is Jocko Morales." Tandy introduced the man. "He's the best cook around when you can drag him away from his sheep."

He was a shepherd. Somehow, Jordanna felt that explained the quality of gentleness she had observed in his face. *"Buenos dias."* The lilting Spanish greeting was directed to all of them. "Welcome." The accompanying English phrase held only a trace of an accent.

While Tandy passed out the coffee mugs to the others, the shepherd walked to Jordanna to give her the mug he carried and offer her a donut. She could see he was not a young man, but the years sat easily on his shoulders.

"Thank you, Senor Morales." She took one of the donuts.

"Please. It is Jocko," he corrected graciously.

"Thank you, Jocko." Jordanna smiled. It was very easy to smile when she was looking into such gentle dark eyes. It was also easy to ask him questions without feeling that it might be considered prying. "Are you from Mexico?"

"My family is from Spain. I am Basque." There

was pride in the statement. With a nodding smile, he turned to offer the plate of donuts to her father.

"Would anyone like sugar or milk for their coffee?" Tandy asked.

"Sugar," Max requested.

Biting into the moist and airy donut, Jordanna glanced at her father. His look mirrored her own. If the donut was an example of Jocko's ability, he was going to be an excellent cook on the trip. A good cook was a vital ingredient on a hunt.

From outside came the drum of hoofbeats. Eating her donut, Jordanna wandered to the front window, one of the few in the log house. Two riders were approaching at a canter. One of them was a big, heavy-set man. There was something aggressive about the way he sat the bay horse, as if he expected people to get out of his way. Jordanna suspected he was something of a bully and wondered if he was the rancher McCord.

She licked the frosting from her fingers and glanced at the second rider astride a big buckskin. Relaxed, almost slouching in the saddle, he appeared to be an extension of the horse. The width of his shoulders was accented by the insulated black vest he wore over a faded plaid shirt. As he turned his head to say something to the other rider, craggy features that had been shadowed by the wide brim of his hat were exposed.

Her stomach did a somersault. It couldn't be! Jordanna stared in disbelief, certain her eyes were playing tricks on her. It was just the mustache that made him resemble the man from the party, her shocked mind insisted. It was a mistake she had made before. Besides, what would he be doing here?

The riders reined their horses to a halt in front of the porch. The big man riding the bay stayed in the saddle. Jordanna watched the second man dismount with a lobo-like grace that erased the last doubt. She felt shattered, raw, exposed, and rooted to the floor at the sight of him. He handed the reins of this horse to the other rider, who immediately started toward the barn while the mustached man mounted the porch steps.

"Take care of my horse." Brig flipped the reins to Frank.

"Tell Jocko not to let them dudes eat all the donuts. My mouth's been watering for some of them all day." Leading the buckskin, the big man kicked his horse into a trot toward the barn.

His gaze flicked upwards to the roof of the two-story house as long, unhurried strides carried him to the porch. Dudes. Brig hoped they were prepared for some cramped accommodations tonight. A bunkhouse had seemed a needless building. Frank, Tandy, and Jocko, when he was at the ranch, all shared Brig's living quarters. They used the two bedrooms upstairs, while his was on the first floor. Tonight they'd be bunking on the floor of the living room so Fletcher Smith and his group could have the bedrooms. Frank had done considerable grumbling about that.

His spurs jingled to the accompanying thud of his boots on the steps. A grimness settled over his features as he reached to open the door. He couldn't put off meeting Fletcher Smith any longer. Brig fought down the irritability that gnawed at him and walked into the house.

His gaze glanced over Jocko and Tandy to seek the iron-haired man a few feet from them. Brig forced a tight smile onto his mouth and pulled off a leather glove to shake hands with the hunter.

"Hello, Fletcher. I'm sorry I wasn't able to meet you. Tandy looked after you all right, I hope." He felt the strong grip of the older man.

"Fine. He explained that work here at the ranch kept you from meeting us," Fletcher assured him.

"Hello, Brig."

His gaze swung around to his cousin standing near the door. "Max." He nodded a curt acknowledgement of his cousin's presence and noticed the gear stacked beside him. "Tandy, give them a hand carrying their stuff upstairs." Brig turned to the stocky cowboy as he gave the order.

An uncertain look flashed across Tandy's expression. He glanced uneasily at Brig. "I didn't know exactly how you were going to work it so I thought I'd better wait until you got here to show them where they were going to sleep tonight."

Annoyed, Brig suppressed the urge to snap an impatient remark. He had made the sleeping arrangements plain. The hunters would double up in the rooms upstairs. But he wasn't about to rebuke Tandy in front of Fletcher. He could chew him out later when they were alone.

As he turned back to Fletcher, his gaze started an arc to encompass all members of the hunting party. When it touched the tall young man with the black hair and dark eyes, it hesitated in surprised recognition. It flashed through Brig's mind that he might be the reason for Tandy's uncertainty about the sleeping quarters.

Out of the corner of his eye, he caught a glint of red. Sunlight streaming through the window had set fire to the brown hair of the woman standing by it. The sight of her hit him like a hard blow to the stomach. For a second, Brig couldn't move, breathe, or think.

Desire seared through his veins, burning him up in a white-hot heat. It wasn't a mirage. Jordanna was actually standing there, in the flesh—in beautiful, soft, alabaster flesh. The look in her hazel-green eyes said she recognized him, too, and remembered. He wanted to groan with aching relief that she was finally here to put an end to his torturous obsession. His need was so great he wanted to strip the clothes from her and take her where she stood, then carry her to his bedroom and not come out for a week. Even then, he wasn't sure if it would be long enough.

Before he could obey the urge, someone moved and made Brig aware of the others in the room. Then it struck him, why she was here and who had brought her. The hot flames burning through him turned to rage.

His head jerked to Fletcher in savage accusal. "What's she doing here?" The man was asking too much from him. The thought of her being under the same roof and sleeping in another man's arms was more than Brig could tolerate.

Startled by the violence in the question, Fletcher frowned at him in confusion. "Who? Jordanna?"

"Yes! Jordanna." The words were dragged through his clenched teeth. Never in his life had he actually wanted to kill a man, but Brig ached now to circle Fletcher's throat and strangle him with his bare hands. He turned away before he was overwhelmed by the urge to kill. "The hunt is off!"

"What?" Her father's voice held confusion. "What are you talking about, McCord? We made an agreement."

Shaken by the discovery that the stranger was Brig McCord, the rancher who was going to serve as guide for their hunting trip, Jordanna could only stare. He remembered her. She had seen it in his eyes when he'd first noticed her. Now he looked as unfeeling as stone, hard and cold.

"There was nothing in the agreement about a woman!" His withering gaze flashed to Tandy Barnes. "Why did you bring her?"

"What else was I supposed to do?" Tandy defended himself. "You never said anything about a woman, but how was I supposed to know you didn't know she was coming?"

"McCord, I'm sorry if I forgot to mention Jordanna," her father apologized with a helpless shrug. "It wasn't intentional. Jordanna always goes hunting with me."

"That's your problem," Brig retorted and sent a glowering look at Jordanna. "I didn't make any arrangements to accommodate a woman. We don't have the facilities. The hunt's canceled."

"But we've come all this way," her father protested. "It's too late for me to try to get someone else."

"You should have thought of that sooner. I'll see that you get your money back. Tandy. Jocko." He turned to the two dumbstruck ranch hands. "Help . . ."

"This is nonsense!" Fletcher interrupted with a burst of impatience. "Just because Jordanna happens to be a woman, she doesn't require any special facilities. She's prepared to rough it right along with the rest of us. She always has."

"I don't give a damn what she's done or where she's hunted with you in the past!" Brig pivoted to point a threatening finger at her father. "I'm not taking a woman on what is supposed to be a hunting trip. Now if you want to send her back to New York, fine."

"No!" Jordanna found her voice. "Nobody is sending me back to New York."

Cold brown eyes met her defiant look. "You're going—either alone or with the rest of them. But I don't want you here."

His flat statement of rejection chilled her. It seemed impossible that this was the same man who had made her feel so warm and good inside when he'd made love to her. Maybe she hadn't really felt like that. Maybe it had all been an illusion.

"McCord, you agreed to take a hunting party up into the high country for bighorns," her father reminded him stiffly.

"A hunting party? Is that what you call this?" Brig jeered, looking contemptuously around the room. "All I see is one hunter. And I'm not so sure about you any more!"

"I have nothing to do with Max being included," Fletcher retorted. "He invited himself along. As for my son, Kit—granted, he won't be doing any hunting."

"Your son?"

Jordanna saw her father whiten with anger at the amused and scornful look Brig McCord cast in her brother's direction. Family loyalty made her bristle, too. He had no reason to look at Kit that way.

"Jordanna, on the other hand," her father continued as if pretending he hadn't heard the derogatory tone Brig had used in reference to his son, "will be hunting. I told you in New York that this would probably be my last chance at a trophy bighorn. I'm going to have it. You aren't going to back out on our agreement."

"Let's get this straight, Fletcher. You may consider this little group to be a serious hunting party, but you and I have different definitions. I don't consider it serious when you drag along a woman for your own amusement."

Jordanna's mouth opened and closed in wordless shock. He couldn't mean what he was implying. Her gaze flew to her father.

"He thinks I'm your mistress," she gasped in outrage.

"What?!" He stared at Brig: "My God, Jordanna is my daughter!"

"That's a likely story," Brig scoffed in icy mockery. "But more believable than if you claimed she was your niece."

"It's the truth, Brig," Max inserted. "Jordanna is Fletcher's daughter. Didn't you know that?"

His cousin's unexpected support of her father's claim caused a flicker of uncertainty to cross Brig McCord's expression. Jordanna was subjected to his piercing scrutiny. She was hurt and indignant that he could continue to question her identity.

It was becoming evident that he had believed she was her father's mistress when he'd met her in the den at the party. But why? With vivid clarity, she remembered his comment about fastening the hook on her gown after they had made love. He'd seen her father fix it earlier and had presumed that his reason had been the same. The fact that he hadn't known Fletcher was her father didn't lessen Jordanna's sense of outrage. Brig had believed her to be some kind of whore. He had amused himself with her, not caring who she was or even bothering to ask her name.

Incensed by the discovery, Jordanna crossed the room to stand in front of him. Fiery green lights were shooting from her eyes. "How dare you insult me like that?" Her voice was low and trembling with burning anger. "You bastard." She slapped him hard, too angry to feel the stinging numbness in the palm of her hand.

Her wrist was clamped by the iron shackle of his grip and she strained to free it. The white mark on his tanned cheek was slowly turning red. Jordanna's only regret was that she hadn't hit him harder. The blazing darkness in his gaze didn't intimidate her.

An arm came between them as her brother stepped in to separate them. "Let her go, McCord," he ordered in a calm voice.

Christopher's intervention prompted Tandy Barnes to step forward and place a restraining hand on Brig's shoulder. "Back off, Brig." He walked softly with his words. "The lady didn't mean anything by it."

An eyebrow lifted in cold, arrogant mockery. "I think she did." Brig released her wrist and stepped away.

"I hope we've straightened out this misunderstanding, McCord," her father stated. "I'm sorry Jordanna lost her temper like that, but . . . under the circumstance, I think it was forgivable."

"You could be right." Brig rubbed his cheek but was not prepared to completely agree.

"As for myself, I can't help but feel complimented by your mistake." Fletcher Smith smiled with faint wryness. "It's flattering to think a woman as lovely as my daughter could be interested in me."

"For enough money, there are some people who can pretend an interest in anything," he retorted.

"Speaking of money, I hope you're going to change your mind about the hunt now that you know who Jordanna is. We both have our heart set on getting a trophy bighorn."

"She is your daughter." Brig took a deep breath as if he wasn't quite convinced it was true.

"Do you want me to show you my passport?" Jordanna challenged. "Would that convince you? Or how about a copy of my birth certificate?"

"How serious are you about hunting?" he ignored her caustic questions.

"Didn't Jordanna show you her trophies mounted in the den?" Kit's question revealed that he remembered Brig as being the man in the den with his sister the night of the party. "Most of them in there are Dad's, but a few of them are hers."

"No, she didn't." Brig studied her with a cold, hard stare.

Jordanna had always considered brown eyes to be warm and luminous, but his weren't. They were stone-brown, hard and flat. There was a dry quality to them, like a desert rock. It wasn't easy to withstand their scrutiny, but Jordanna didn't let her gaze waver.

"Your concern that we aren't serious about hunting is unnecessary," her father stated. "My daughter is as dedicated to the sport as I am."

He didn't take his eyes from her. "She'll be nothing but trouble."

"If I didn't think that she had the strength and stamina to make this hunt, she wouldn't be here. Nothing is going to stand in my way of getting a trophy ram, not even Jordanna. She learned a long time ago that she receives no concession for being a female. Her sex doesn't entitle her to special treatment, or special accommodations."

"Hunting isn't a sport restricted only to males." Jordanna's voice was low and challenging. "As a matter of fact, in the predatory animal world, it's the female who does the bulk of the hunting. The African lion, the supposed 'King of the Beasts,' does very little. It is the lioness that makes the kill to feed the pride of lions."

The atmosphere was thick. Jordanna left the invisible bombardment of tension along her nerve ends. Brig McCord continued to stare at her for another full second; then he turned to the two men who worked for him.

"Take their gear up to the room, all except for Miss Smith's. Put hers in my bedroom." The command was issued in a low, rumbling voice that would tolerate no discussion. In spite of her anger, her senses leaped at the assignment of her sleeping quarters. Jordanna received a brief, sardonic glance. The elaboration he added was for her benefit, although he addressed it to his men. "I'll be bunking in here on the floor with you."

"Then you are going to honor your agreement?" Fletcher Smith insisted on an answer more clear-cut than the implication of Brig's orders.

Brig started for the door that led to the kitchen, impatiently throwing the answer over his shoulder. "Yes, you'll have your damned hunt." He yanked the door open and strode through the opening, slamming the door shut behind him in a way that betrayed the inner violence of his emotions.

Chapter IX

SHAKEN BY THE encounter with the man she hadn't expected to find here in the wilds of Idaho, Jordanna turned to her father. She had argued with him for the hunt to take place as planned, but the prospect of spending two or three weeks with Brig McCord, considering his low opinion of her, was too daunting. As she opened her mouth to object, her father gave her a stern, silencing look. Any discussion would take place when they were alone, not with others listening in. Jordanna held her silence, trying to contain the upheaval of emotions.

Stiffly she walked to where the two ranch hands were separating the gear. "These are mine." She identified the items belonging to her.

As Jordanna picked up the small suitcase, the Basque shepherd gathered up the rest of her things. "I will show you where you will sleep, Miss Smith," he said with an ingratiating nod of his head.

Her father, brother, and Max followed Tandy up the stairs while she crossed the living room with Jocko toward the plain wooden door. It opened into a bed-room. The monastic interior contained a dresser, a crude chair, a nightstand, and a bed covered with a heavy quilt. The bed was wider than a single, yet a few inches short of being a double. The austerity of the room seemed to match the man who slept in it. Jordanna had envisioned lying again with him too many times in the past not to be disturbed by the prospect of sleeping in his bed. It was agitating to discover the thought of his caresses still had the ability to arouse her, even when she was angered by his attitude.

The shepherd noticed the thinning of her lips and guessed the cause. "You must make allowances for Brig's harshness, Miss Smith," he said in his softly accented voice. "We do not have much contact with women of your breeding. He has, perhaps, forgotten how to treat someone like you."

"I doubt if he will thank you for making apologies for his behavior, Jocko." Jordanna breathed out a silent sniff.

He overlooked her reply to inquire, "Your accommodations are satisfactory?"

"Yes." She had to agree. The shepherd wouldn't understand her objections to the choice of sleeping quarters.

"If you wish for anything, I will be in the kitchen." With a faint nod, he moved toward the door.

"Thank you."

After he'd left the room, Jordanna remained standing in the same place. The sheer masculinity of the room was overpowering. She felt its effect in the shallow quality of her breathing and the racing skip of her heartbeat. Her gaze strayed to the bed that could snugly sleep two and she pivoted from the sight of it. Jordanna discovered she was rubbing her wrist, where his hand had been, the sensation lingering. Her fingernails dug into the palms of her hands to fight the sharp ache inside.

She heard footsteps on the stairs and left the room through the open doorway as her father descended the steps ahead of the other men. She walked swiftly to the base of the stairs to meet him. The troubled darkness of her hazel eyes relayed a silent message of concern and misgivings.

"I want to talk to you, Dad," Jordanna requested, in a voice husky with urgency.

He appeared momentarily impatient at her demand, but he paused at the foot of the stairs to ask Tandy, "Is there someplace where we can check-fire our rifles?"

"You can test them out back."

"We'll need something for targets. Paper plates will be fine, or tin cans."

"I'll find something," Tandy promised and started for the kitchen. "I'll meet you outside, in back of the house."

"Max, would you mind going back upstairs after my rifle?" Fletcher glanced at the curly-haired man standing on the second step.

"I don't mind," Max assured him and turned to mount the stairs.

"What's the matter, Jordanna?" It was her brother who asked the question.

"This situation is intolerable." She addressed the answer to her father. "You know what it's like to live day-in and day-out on the trail, Dad, and how nerve-wracking it can be if you aren't compatible with the people along on the hunt. The . . . rancher's attitude toward me is going to make it impossible for all of us." She kept her voice low so it wouldn't carry to the other rooms.

"You are exaggerating," Fletcher insisted with an indulgent smile that refused to take her seriously. "So he did make a mistake about your relationship to me," he shrugged his lack of concern over that. "There's no need for you to take it as a personal insult. Where is your sense of humor, Jordanna?"

"I'm just supposed to laugh it off, is that it?" She was angry, because there were memories she could not laugh away.

"It would certainly ease the tension around here if you pretended it was a joke," he reasoned.

"I can't stretch my imagination that far." The retort trembled from her lips, the turmoil inside surfacing in her words.

"What happened that night at the party?" Christopher frowned. "Did he make a pass at you?"

"You could say that," Jordanna admitted with a bitterly soft laugh. She turned to her father to accuse: "If only you had mentioned that Brig had been at the party . . . If I had suspected who he was before we had arrived . . ." Jordanna stopped.

It wouldn't have made any difference. If anything, she would have been more eager to meet again the man who had made such a profound impression on her. Now, faced with his low opinion of her, she wanted only to escape it.

"If McCord made a pass at you the last time you met, he obviously found you attractive." Her father didn't see why that should add to the difficulty of the present situation. "More than likely, he still does. Instead of losing your temper and making the misunderstanding worse, you should try a little charm, Jordanna. He's agreed to take you on the hunt. Now make him like it." Fletcher paused to absently murmur to himself, "In fact, it might make everything very easy."

"Easy?!"

He looked startled to discover he'd spoken the thought aloud, but hurriedly defended it. "Yes, easy. As you pointed out, the hunting trip could become uncomfortably tense if his resentment of your presence continues."

In agitation, Jordanna turned from her father. "Let's cancel the trip. We can find another reputable outfitter and guide to take us at the last minute if we pay them enough. Or we can go another time."

"No." His swift, decisive denial was followed immediately by a hand clamping on her arm. Rarely had Jordanna ever seen her father angry, but he was now.

His nostrils were flared and his mouth was pinched in a tight line. "We'll go now! And with McCord! I'll never have another set-up like this! I could never arrange anything this perfectly again!"

"What do you mean 'set-up'?" Christopher demanded. "What are you talking about, Dad?"

His head jerked to the dark piercing eyes of his son, as if he had forgotten Kit was there. Instantly Fletcher released Jordanna's arm, and the harsh lines of anger were wiped from his expression. Jordanna was puzzled by the swift change of mood that reminded her of a chameleon taking on protective coloring to hide himself from the enemy.

"I mean that I'll never have a better chance to get my trophy ram. McCord is guiding exclusively for me, taking me to an area that hasn't been heavily hunted and one that he's become thoroughly familiar with. The fact that he isn't a professional guide is in my favor this time. He won't be holding back a ram with trophy horns for any favorite client."

Jordanna glanced at her brother. He looked withdrawn and contemplative. She had the feeling she was being shut out from something important, but didn't know why she had that impression.

"But you weren't this upset when Brig wanted to cancel the hunt?" she remembered, using the rancher's given name with unconscious ease.

"He said that in the heat of the moment. I knew once he'd cooled off he would retract it, whether you were my daughter or my mistress."

Bewildered, Jordanna didn't understand how her father could have been so confident. She had believed completely that Brig had meant every word. Canceling the hunt hadn't simply been an empty threat.

"How did you know that?"

"Because I bought him. He'd already seen the downpayment and knew the color of my money." Her father sounded so cynical and calculating that Jordanna felt hurt.

"You bought him?" She was skeptical that Brig

McCord could be bought at any price. He was too self-possessed, too self-sufficient for that.

"Do you find that hard to believe?" Fletcher laughed at her in that stranger's voice. "The severe winter wiped him out. He was going to lose this place until I met him in July."

"But you couldn't have known that then?" Jordanna protested.

"I didn't. I had him investigated. After all, I wanted to be sure I was dealing with a reputable person," he defended his action. "I'm paying him top dollar for this hunt, plus a sizable bonus if I get my trophy ram. I bought him and McCord couldn't afford to tell me 'no sale.'"

"Why did you get so angry with me?"

"Because McCord is in my pocket. He'll make the hunt. I resented your suggestion that we should cancel. You are my daughter. But I won't cancel this hunt, not even for you, Jordanna."

"If it's so important for you to get this trophy ram," Christopher inserted, "why are you dragging around the dead weights of two non-hunters, Max and me?"

"How could I refuse your request to come hunting with me when I've waited so long to hear it, Kit?" Fletcher countered. "As for Max, I didn't invite him along. You'll have to speak to McCord about him. Until he proves to be a burden, I can't make a complaint. If and when he does, you can be sure I'll say something."

"Fletcher?" Max appeared at the head of the stairs. "I can't find your rifle. It isn't up here."

"It isn't?" Her father raised an eyebrow in surprise, then glanced toward the front door. A look of chagrin passed over his face. "You're right. It isn't. It's downstairs by the door. I'm sorry for sending you on a wild goose chase, Max."

"That's all right." Max started down the stairs.

"You'd better get your rifle, Jordanna. Tandy is waiting outside for us," her father reminded.

Entering the bedroom, Jordanna picked up the worn scabbard with her rifle inside and a box of ammunition. She returned to the living room and trailed behind her father and Max Sanger to walk with her brother. Outside, she lagged behind, eyeing her father with confusion and concern. Christopher fell back with her.

"I've never heard Dad talk like that, Kit," she admitted.

"He's probably never let you see that side of him before. You are daddy's little girl."

"What do you mean by that?"

"He has always shielded you from what he considers the unpleasantries of life. He's taken you all over the world, Jordanna, so your eyes would be dazzled by so many different sights that you wouldn't see what's in front of your nose." Sadness was mixed with his cynicism.

"Was that . . . really our father talking?"

"A man doesn't accumulate the wealth and power that he has without learning how to use and manipulate people for his personal benefit. Our father expects the best. He won't settle for less. And failure is something he won't tolerate. He'll fight it as savagely as any beast he's ever hunted. He won't give up . . . on anything. He'd cut out his own heart first."

"No." Jordanna rejected the image her brother had portrayed. He didn't argue, but his look said he felt sorry for her. "You don't know Dad as well as I do," she insisted.

Tandy was waiting for them by the woodshed in back of the house. "I've set up some paper plates to use as targets." He motioned toward the white circular objects tacked against a back cushion of hay, some eighty strides in the opposite direction of the pasture.

"That looks fine." Her father nodded his approval and glanced at Jordanna. "Do you want to go first?"

The rear screen door slammed. Jordanna didn't have to turn around to know Brig McCord had stepped outside. Some inner sense made her aware of his presence. He momentarily unsettled her and she gave a negative shake of her head.

"You go ahead, Dad," she insisted.

A built-in radar system seemed tuned to his approach. Jordanna made a project of unfastening the flap of her scabbard to remove her specially made .30–06 rifle. When Brig McCord entered her side vision, her nerves quivered, but she refused to acknowledge him with a look. Gripping the French walnut stock, she removed the rifle and handed the leather scabbard to her brother.

"Hello, McCord." Her father nodded and walked to within twenty-odd feet of an outcropping of granite rock. "We decided to check our rifles after the journey here and adjust our scopes." He glanced to Jordanna who was loading hers. "I'll take the plate on the right."

"Okay." Steadfastly, she avoided looking at the tall, broad-shouldered man to her left.

Her father's first shot hit the plate dead-center. The horses in the corral milled nervously in surprise at the sound. With an unhurried spacing of his shots, he emptied a round into the paper disc. The accuracy of his shots cut out a black bulls-eye in the center of the plate.

"Your turn." Fletcher stepped back to reload.

Jordanna moved to a spot parallel with her father. Lifting the rifle to her shoulder, she sighted the target through the scope. Conscious of the pair of hard brown eyes watching her, she steadied her arm. The first shot went wide of the center, betraying her nervousness, but the rest formed a cluster in the middle of the plate. Lowering the muzzle of the rifle, she glanced over her shoulder at Brig McCord. The haughtiness of challenge was in the tilt of her chin.

"Are you convinced I can shoot?"

He stood relaxed, his hands on his hips, his gaze directed at the paper target. Leisurely, the gaze swung to her. "I'm convinced you can hit a paper plate at eighty yards."

Seething, Jordanna realized she had invited that remark. She should have kept silent. She was angered by her own foolishness.

"That's a beautiful rifle," Max commented. "May I see it?"

"Sure." Turning her back on the target, she handed the rifle to him.

Max double-checked to make sure it wasn't loaded before running a caressing hand over the smooth wooden stock. "It's a beauty," he repeated absently. As he held it lengthwise in front of him, the muzzle of the rifle was accidentally pointed at Brig.

Jordanna saw the flash of anger thin his mouth as Brig took a sideways step forward out of the rifle's line. His hand grabbed the barrel and pointed the muzzle into the air.

"Hey! What the . . ." Max began in surprise, the rifle nearly jerked from his hand by Brig's sudden action.

"Don't ever point a gun at me," was the low, ominous warning.

"It isn't loaded. I checked," Max protested.

"I don't give a damn if it's unloaded, the safety's on, or it's disassembled!" Brig retorted. "Don't ever point a gun at me or you'll wish to God you hadn't!" He took it from him and thrust it back in Jordanna's hands. "And you should have more sense than to give your rifle to a rank amateur."

"I'm no amateur," Max bristled.

"Leave it be," Fletcher inserted, offering the advice to Max. "Why don't you go sit down on those rocks where you'll be out of the line of fire, Max?" He lifted his rifle to take aim on the target.

Hesitating for an instant, Max glared at the impassive facade of his cousin, then walked to the outcropping of rock. As he sat down on a jutting formation, Jordanna heard the warning whirr of a rattlesnake. She glimpsed the coiled snake within striking distance of Max's shoulder.

Simultaneously, Brig barked the order, "Don't move,

Max." Before her father could react, Brig had grabbed the rifle from his grasp. In one fluid move, he snapped it to his shoulder and fired. The snake's head exploded into fragments, leaving a writhing, twisting body on the rock.

White with shock, Max stared at the remains of the reptile. Disregarding Brig's instructions, he had straightened from the rock at the warning rattle. Only the swift reflexes of his cousin had saved him from being bitten by the snake.

"This is snake country," Brig announced. "Most of them will be in hibernation soon, especially in the higher elevations. But there might be more like this one, sunning itself on a rock enjoying the last warmth of Indian summer. Keep your eyes open. And look." His hard gaze centered on her father. "You should have seen it, Fletcher. You are supposed to be the hunter."

"I should have," he agreed.

"Better go to the house, Max, and have Jocko pour you a stiff shot of whiskey," Brig advised.

"I think I will," he agreed shakily and started toward the back entrance of the log building.

Brig watched him for an instant, then followed. Christopher hesitated, glancing from Jordanna to his father. Opening his mouth as if to say something, he changed his mind and walked after the other two.

Numbed by the swiftness of it all, Jordanna glanced at her father. "Where did he learn to handle a gun like that?"

Her father began unloading his rifle, changing his mind about doing more target practicing. Glancing sideways, he watched Tandy leave before answering her question.

"McCord was a professional soldier before he bought this ranch."

"A professional soldier?" She was surprised by the information. "Do you mean he was a career man in one of the services?"

"No. He was a mercenary, hired by various foreign governments."

Jordanna remembered that feeling of danger she had experienced the first time she'd met Brig. She thought of his coldness, his cynicism. A man who did that would have to be hard. In his own way, he was a predator.

"He saved Max's life. If he hadn't reacted so quickly, the snake would have struck him," she said.

"Yes." Her father seemed to consider that thoughtfully. "I'm a little surprised by that."

"Why?"

"The two of them may be cousins, but there is no love lost between them." At her questioning look, Fletcher explained, "According to the information the agency obtained, old man Sanger, the founder of the company, left the bulk of his estate to McCord with certain provisos. Brig refused to meet the conditions of the inheritance and Max obtained control of the company. However, if Max dies, the conditions no longer stand and Brig gets the company with no strings attached."

"Then . . ." The Sanger discount stores were a major chain, a multi-million dollar corporation. If Max were dead, Brig would have control of it, and all its money. ". . . he stands to gain a lot," Jordanna whispered.

"The company happens to be floundering at the moment, rather badly from what I've been able to uncover."

Jordanna felt almost relieved to hear it. "Is that the stock Max is trying to sell you?"

"Yes."

"If the company is going broke, why would you want to buy it? Why would you even consider it?"

"Because it has some solid foundations under it. With some financial backing and sound management at the top, it wouldn't be long until it was a giant again."

"Are you going to provide that financial backing?"

He didn't answer immediately as he met her frank gaze. When he did, he looked away. "I haven't decided." He slid his rifle back in its scabbard. "I doubt if I'll make up my mind until all the reports are in."

"But you are considering it?" she persisted.

"Yes. But my ultimate decision will depend on a variety of circumstances." He smiled suddenly, the absently thoughtful expression leaving his face. "End of business discussion. This is a hunting trip, remember?"

So many other things had crowded in, she had almost forgotten the objective of their trip. "I think I did." Jordanna laughed. The dancing lights in his brown eyes and the ready smile was so like the man she identified as her father, not the cold stranger she had glimpsed earlier.

"Let's go check our targets," he suggested. "You were wide of the mark on that first shot."

"A case of nerves," she admitted and fell in step with him to examine the paper plates.

"Because Brig McCord was watching you?"

"Yes." There was no need to lie. The man disturbed her—in many ways.

"Use a little charm," he repeated his earlier advice. "Be nice to him."

"Yes, Dad."

Chapter X

On the first step to the rear entrance of the house, Brig paused to glance at the father and daughter engaged in what appeared to be some earnest discussion. Daughter. He was still trying to take that relationship in.

The physical resemblance was vague, although it was conceivable that Fletcher's gray hair had once been auburn. The touch of green in her eyes could have been inherited from her mother. Brig remembered Olivia Smith's eyes had been a vivid shade of green. Instead of her mother's petiteness, Jordanna could have obtained her slender stature from her father.

The side view of her revealed the thrusting peaks of her breasts pushing at the knitted sweater. He felt the tightening in his groin and cursed himself for letting Fletcher talk him into going ahead with the hunting trip. At the time, he'd let himself believe he was capitulating because of the money. Now Brig wondered how much of a part the discovery Jordanna was Fletcher's daughter, not his mistress, had played in the decision. More than he was willing to admit, he suspected.

He'd committed himself to spending the next three weeks with her—and her father. How was he going to keep his hands off of her? Or should he even bother to try? She had been willing enough the last time. But there was her father—and her brother, and Max. On a trip like this, they would all be living on top of each other, five chaperones counting Jocko and Tandy. Would he be able to steal even five minutes alone with her? The mounting frustration made him clench his jaw. It was still tender where she had slapped him. Maybe she wouldn't want five minutes alone with him. By God, he'd make her want it! Brig resolved grimly. She hadn't possessed his mind these last months only to elude him in the flesh now.

"Mr. McCord?" A voice demanded his attention.

He lifted his unfocused gaze to the lithesome young man stopping in front of him.

"Yes?"

"I know rattlesnakes are poisonous, but are their bites fatal?" Christopher Smith questioned with an absent frown.

"Not as a rule."

"What do you mean?"

"It depends on the location of the bite, how much venom reaches the bloodstream, how quickly it's treated, and the general health of the victim. More people die from shock than from the poison."

"The location of the bite. If it was near the head, it could be potentially fatal," he persisted.

"It is possible." His gaze ran dryly over the dark-haired man, faintly amused by his apprehension. "But don't worry. We have serum for snake bite."

"So if Max had been bitten around the shoulder . . ."

"He wouldn't have died. We would have drained what venom we could immediately from the wound and given him a shot of serum. He'd have been quite ill for a few days probably, but since he doesn't have a bad heart or anything like that, it's highly unlikely he would have died." It was obvious the son wasn't the woodsman/hunter his father was. "Out here, we can't be sure how quickly we can get to a hospital or professional medical help, so we always have snake bite kits with us, complete with serum."

"I see." Christopher appeared relieved. "I suppose it's standard procedure, something most guides would do."

"That's right."

"I have one other question I'd like you to answer for me," he said with a long, thoughtful look.

"What is it?"

"Max isn't the outdoor type. He isn't cut out for this kind of a vacation."

"Neither are you," Brig countered.

"Not as a rule."

The youthful jaw hardened, the only indication he had heard the comment. "My point is—why did you invite him on this trip?"

"Why did *I* invite him?" Brig frowned in amusement. "You have things mixed up. Having Max come along wasn't my idea. Fletcher is the one who mentioned it first. You'll have to speak to him."

"I see." The handsome face looked very sober. "My mistake," Christopher shrugged.

"Anything else you wanted to know?"

"No, I guess not." Kit turned to take back the rifle scabbard. Brig climbed the wood steps to the back door. Max was sitting at the kitchen table, a glass in front of him. His color had returned to normal. Brig entered the kitchen. Ignoring the bottle of whiskey on the counter, he walked to the stove and poured himself a piping-hot cup of coffee. A drink would have been preferable. The trouble was, Brig doubted that he would stop until he'd drank himself senseless.

"How do you feel?" Brig walked to the table, sweeping Max with an appraising look.

"I'll make it."

"I warned you these mountains weren't anything

like the city." Pulling out a chair, Brig straddled it and rested his arms on the curved back, cradling the cup in his hands.

"You told me the mountains would kill me. I didn't realize it was a prophecy," Max declared. It was said as a joke but he couldn't seem to laugh at it.

"You didn't have to take Fletcher up on his invitation to go hunting with him. Or you could have waited for tamer country."

"I haven't got all the time in the world. I've got him all set up. I can't let him get away from me for three weeks to cool down when I've got him all warmed up."

"There isn't any other reason for you tagging along?" Brig eyed him with a cold, narrow look. He didn't like the thought that had been growing in his mind. It filled him with an ugly, mean feeling.

"I don't think I follow you." Max looked puzzled.

"Fletcher's daughter. You must have known she was coming with him." He knew his cousin fancied himself as a lady-killer. If Max put his slimy hands on Jordanna, Brig thought he would kill him. But he had to know. The wondering was worse than the knowing.

"Jordanna? You really put your foot into that one, Brig." Max laughed, taking delight in the mistake Brig had made. "Whatever gave you the idea that she was Fletcher's mistress? I wish I had kept my mouth shut and let you make a fool of yourself. You were doing such a great job of it."

"Appearances can be deceiving." He took a sip of the scalding coffee in his cup. It burned the bitter taste from his tongue, but it didn't improve his irritation at the unneeded reminder of the bungling mess he'd made earlier. "But I'm not deceived about you, Max. Was Jordanna an added incentive for you to make this trip? She is a looker. And you have never been the kind who didn't look without touching."

Max paused to consider both his answer and Brig's challenging expression. "I won't deny that I thought about it. She and Fletcher are as thick as thieves.

With her on my side I have a better chance of getting his support," he admitted. "However, she's as difficult to get close to as her father. She has the reputation of being a cold fish." At the upward sweep of Brig's thick brow, in silent question, Max elaborated. "From all I've heard, she's too inhibited despite her fiery looks. When she slapped you, that was probably the most emotional reaction she had ever displayed."

Brig knew better. The knowledge groaned inside of him, but he kept silent. Max was in a talkative mood. The brush with the snake and the shot of whiskey had loosened his tongue. Brig didn't interfere with its flapping.

"So while I considered it, there was too much risk of it back-firing. It doesn't make sense. Olivia is ten times the woman her daughter is. There isn't an inhibited bone in Olivia's body."

"Is that the voice of experience talking?"

"That is none of your business."

The back door opened and Tandy Barnes entered the kitchen. Brig looked sideways. "Where have you been?"

"Giving Frank and Jocko a hand with the generator." He walked to the sink to wash the grease from his hands.

"What was wrong with it?" Dismounting his chair, Brig walked to the stove to refill his cup.

"It was sputtering like it always does, but it's running smooth now." As he lathered his hands, the door opened and Jocko came in.

Brig looked beyond him. "Where's Frank?"

"He is outside yet."

Tandy grinned over his shoulder. "He got himself an eyeful of our guest. Poor Frank is putty in the hands of anything with curves."

Brig moved to the kitchen window to look out. The mountainous bulk of Frank Savidge was standing near Jordanna. His hat was in his hands. His mouth was opened in a panting grin as Jordanna smiled at him. Brig had seen dogs wear that same expression when they were trailing a bitch in heat.

Pivoting from the window, he flashed a hard look at the Basque. "Get Frank in here."

Jocko Morales walked to the back door and stepped outside to call the man. Tandy watched from the window, tee-heeing at the sight of the big cowboy bobbing and bowing in a caricature of courtly manners as he excused himself from Jordanna.

"I told you, Brig, to send Frank in town last week for an injection of three b's," Tandy joked, his eyes twinkling with humor, but Brig couldn't enter into the spirit of his fun.

"The three b's? What's that?" Max frowned.

"Booze, brawling, and broads. Not necessarily in that order." The stocky cowboy laughed. "Frank is addicted to all three."

The laughter was still dancing in his eyes when Frank walked in. "Did you want to see me?" A drunken look of joy was in the big man's expression.

"Wipe that grin off your face," Brig snapped impatiently.

The slack-jawed smile was erased. "What did you want?"

"I wanted you to quit making a fool of yourself by drooling all over our guest." He set his cup sharply on the table, angered because there wasn't a single part of him that didn't hunger for Jordanna.

Frank wasn't embarrassed by the comment. "Why didn't you tell me a woman was coming?"

"Because I didn't know."

"Let Tandy stay here at the ranch and take care of things. I want to go on the hunt."

"Forget it." The razor-sharp edge to Brig's voice kept Frank from continuing the discussion. He had heard the warning challenge and knew better than to call it.

"Why do you have all the dumb luck?" Frank grumbled at Tandy with envy.

" 'Cause it's my turn. You've been hoggin' it all, up 'til now," Tandy insisted.

"Me? You were the one who got to go to the airport to pick them up. You were with her for a whole day!" Frank protested. "Why, if you weren't an old man, I'd . . ."

"Old man?!" Tandy bristled.

"That's enough? Both of you?" Brig stepped between them. Damn, she was trouble . . . trouble for him and trouble for his men. "I give the orders around here. Tandy goes. And you stay, Frank. If you want to argue about it, do it with me. I made the arrangements and they are going to stand." He saw the measuring look Frank was giving him. "Don't forget, Frank," Brig warned. "I'll finish any fight you want to start."

"Hey, Frank, how about a cup of coffee?" Jocko offered.

The big man hesitated, then turned away, grumbling, "Yeah."

When the evening meal of salmon was over, Jocko insisted he needed no help in the kitchen and everyone wandered into the living room. Fletcher Smith wanted to look over the forestry maps of the area they would be hunting and Brig spread them out on the home-made coffee table. Max sat in a nearby armchair to listen in on their discussion. Christopher Smith took up Tandy's challenge to a game of cribbage. Since Jordanna stood beside her brother's chair to watch, Frank did, too.

Frank had virtually become her shadow, following her everywhere. Brig knew his gaze was guilty of following her movements and Frank was always near. The pairing reminded him of the beauty and the beast. Only Jordanna didn't seem to object as strongly as Brig did. It was jealousy, pure and simple. He wanted no man looking at her the way he did. It tested his control to keep from challenging Frank to leave her alone. Meanwhile, the frustration of watching and wanting mounted.

Fletcher asked him a question and Brig had to have him repeat it. With a force of will, he concentrated his gaze on the map, determined to conceal his preoccupation with the man's daughter. He replied intelligently to a few questions before his gaze strayed back to the table where Jordanna had been standing. He made a frantic sweep of the room without success, then Brig smelled her. She was standing behind the couch, looking over Fletcher's shoulder at the maps. Instead of being relieved to find her so close, Brig was angry, enraged. She was tying him in knots like he was some damned schoolboy.

"You study the maps, Fletcher." Brig rose from the couch. "I'm going to the kitchen to see if Jocko has any coffee left."

He didn't ask if anyone else would like a cup, as his long strides put distance between himself and the woman with the gleaming copper hair. A pot was on the stove and he poured himself a cup of coffee. Putting away the dishes, Jocko paused to study him.

"You are thinking about the trip tomorrow?"

"Yes," Brig lied.

"Sometimes, in order to live, we must do work that is not pleasant to us. My uncle was once a shepherd. Now he is an old man. His eyesight is fading and his legs are failing him. To earn money, he sweeps the floors in a saloon. He tells me he doesn't like looking through windows yellow with nicotine, at the mountains where he once walked."

"I know." Brig stared at the steam rising from the black liquid. He'd seen the old shepherd, whose camp he had stumbled into those many years ago when the plane had crashed and killed his parents. "I've told him that if he wants to sweep floors to earn a living, he's welcome to come here and do mine."

"But he won't leave his woman. That is a part of his life that is still good," Jocko smiled. "My aunt is not well. She needs to be close to the doctors. My uncle needs to be close to her." He set the iron skillet atop the stove and glanced at Brig. "I think it is not the trip that troubles you. It is the woman."

"What makes you think that?" Brig eyed him in cold challenge.

"Because my blood, and that of my ancestors, is hot like yours. But I think you have never met a woman that made you burn, eh?" His dark eyes danced with a roguish glint.

"You don't know what you're talking about." He took a swallow of coffee and swore when it scalded his tongue.

"You are a tough, hard man, but she makes you want to feel soft. I have told her that you had forgotten how to treat a woman like her."

"I suggest you mind your own business, Jocko."

The shepherd laughed. "She said you would not thank me for making your apologies." He picked up the coffee pot to see how full it was. "Does anyone else wish to have coffee?"

"I don't know. You'll have to ask them yourself." Brig emptied his cup into the sink and walked to the back door. "I'm going outside for some air."

At the bottom of the outside steps, he stopped to zip the insulated vest, warding off the chill of the mountain night. Moonlight carved a patch across the meadow floor. Clouds were gathering in the northwest. Stuffing his hands in the slashed pockets of the vest, Brig set out briskly toward the barn to check the corraled horses. He could see dark humps scattered across the meadow and knew them to be the cattle.

Inevitably, his steps turned back to the log house and the yellow lights shining from the window. When he mounted the porch steps to the house, Brig didn't go inside. He walked to the far, shadowed corner of the porch. Resting a boot on the railing, he lit a cigarette and gazed into the night.

When Brig had left the room, Jordanna had expected to feel relieved that those wolf-brown eyes were no longer watching her every move. Instead, she felt restless and edgy, deprived of something vital. She finished drinking the coffee Jocko had brought her.

"Would you like some more?" The ever-present Frank was eager to fetch her anything she wanted.

Like some dogs, he was so ugly he was cute. "No thanks," Jordanna refused.

"I'll take the cup for you then," he offered.

Jordanna gave him the empty mug to be returned to the kitchen. As his hulking frame moved away from her, she glanced around the room. Kit and Tandy were still locked in their cribbage game. Max had cornered her father again. Now Frank had disappeared into the kitchen where Jocko and Brig were. She was at loose ends. Unable to dispel this restless mood, she walked to the couch and touched her father's shoulder.

"I think I'll go outside and get some fresh air," she told him.

He patted her hand and nodded, then resumed his discussion with Max. No one seemed to pay any attention to her as she crossed the room and opened the front door. Jordanna stepped onto the porch and closed the door quietly behind her. The scrape of a boot sole on wood attracted her attention to the darkened corner of the porch. No longer than it took for her pulsebeat to rocket, Jordanna recognized the tall, broad-shouldered frame straightening at her appearance.

"I didn't know you were out here. I thought you were in the kitchen." Jordanna didn't want Brig to think she had come looking for him.

He remained in the shadows, not moving into the light cast from the window. "It's cool tonight. You might want a jacket."

She didn't feel the chill. Her blood was racing too hotly. She moved away from the door, her steps pulled in his direction. "This sweater is heavy enough. I just wanted some air. It was getting stuffy inside." Jordanna didn't want to explain about the restless mood that had so suddenly vanished. "You're not wearing a coat," she observed as his shape became more distinct.

"I'm used to the cold."

Behind Jordanna, the front door opened, momentarily bathing the porch with light. The angles and planes of Brig's face were carved in sharp relief. The thick black line of his mustache added to his ruggedly masculine appearance. Again she was the cynosure of those brown eyes. And Jordanna felt the force of his raw virility.

"There you are." It was Frank's voice. She turned, having briefly forgotten the light had come from the open door.

"Hello, Frank," she greeted him.

"Were you going to check on the horses, Frank?" Brig's low, drawling voice startled the big cowboy. He'd only had eyes for Jordanna and didn't see the dark form behind her.

"I just came out for some air."

"You can have it while you check the horses," Brig stated. Frank hesitated, then clumped off the porch to disappear into the shadowy darkness. "Beautiful women are one of Frank's greatest weaknesses."

"What is yours?" Jordanna turned back to him with a trace of challenge.

The question was ignored as she had anticipated it would be. "Cigarette?" He unzipped the top of his vest and reached in the shirt pocket for the pack.

Shaking one out, he offered it to her. Jordanna placed it between her lips and learned forward for the light. A breeze teased at the match flame. Brig cupped the fire protectively in his palm as he carried it to the tip of her cigarette. It was a full second after it was lit before he shook the match out, as if he'd been watching the way the flame had illuminated her face.

"Thank you," she murmured in a puff of smoke.

"Why are you here?"

"I told you." She felt shaky inside. She held her

wrist, afraid her hand might be trembling. "I wanted some fresh air."

"No. I meant, why did you come on this trip?"

"Believe me, I had no idea you would be here. It was just as much a surprise to me when I saw you," Jordanna insisted, moving to the porch rail.

"And if you had known?"

"It . . . wouldn't have made any difference."

"You're getting too old to play daddy's little girl. That's why he brings you along, isn't it, so he can have a worshipping audience to admire his prowess?"

"He doesn't need anyone to admire him," Jordanna flared. "I go hunting with him because I enjoy it as much as he does. I'm here to get a trophy bighorn."

"The idle rich. You just fly from place to place, hunting big game. Do you actually enjoy killing?" His head was tipped to one side, his features completely shadowed.

Tired of being defensive, she countered, "Do you?"

Turning, Brig flipped his cigarette into the air with his thumb and forefinger. The burning tip made a red arc in the darkness.

"I suppose Max has been talking about my sordid past." He sounded amused in a cold sort of way.

Jordanna was reluctant to admit she had gained the information from her father, or that he had obtained it from an investigative agency. Since Brig had offered her another source, she accepted it.

"Did you think he wouldn't?" she hedged.

"It was a long time ago." He looked out into the night, showing neither remorse nor regret for what he had been.

"It explains how you were able to react so quickly this afternoon when that snake struck at Max. You haven't lost your instincts."

"Man is a predator. He never entirely loses that instinct. In my case, it was honed to a fine edge. It was the only way to survive." Brig turned back to her and she felt the thrust of his gaze. "From the predators, I've learned that a man takes what he wants."

His hand curved itself to the back of her neck, the rough skin of his fingers snaring strands of her auburn hair. Jordanna took a quick breath and lost it as his other hand cupped her chin and lifted it. His thumb traced the outline of her lips, parting them to probe at the white barrier of her teeth. The tip of her tongue tasted the saltiness and abrasive texture of his calloused thumb.

"You aren't frightened of me—or what I was. Why?"

"Should I be?" Her voice was soft, a faint whispering sound.

"Most people are." His mouth was making a slow, unhurried descent and her heart was pounding.

"Most people are afraid of their own shadow," she murmured as she was being engulfed in his.

The hand at the back of her neck increased its pressure to lift her on tiptoe. Her hands slid over the slick material of his vest to wind around his neck, her fingers running through the thickness of his dark brown hair. Passion leaped between them like a living flame as he parted her lips and explored the intimate recesses of her mouth.

His hand slid from her throat to mold her back and hips to the unyielding contours of his length. Her senses remembered the musky smell of them, the heady taste of his tongue, and the hammering of his heart. Her raw, wild reaction to him was the same as before. Jordanna felt his hunger devouring her lips, tasting and eating them and arousing an insatiable appetite for his. They strained to satisfy each other. His hands slid underneath her sweater to stroke and mold the bare flesh of her shoulders and back, erotically kneading her skin. Jordanna shuddered at the waves of intense longing that broke over her.

The need was so profound, it became a physical pain. Jordanna twisted away from the possession of his mouth, trying to find some measure of control before she abandoned her pride. As Brig nibbled at the sensitive cord in her neck, desire quivered through her, warm and golden, a shaft of sunshine lighting her soul.

"Brig," she sighed his name, at last being able to identify the face that had haunted her.

He lifted his head to take a deep, shuddering breath. His hands glided from beneath her sweater, leaving the bare flesh he had heated, and moved to frame her face. His fingers trembled over her features.

In a wondrous mood, she studied the male face so close to hers. His lean features had been trained to permit few expressions to flit across its surface and to allow few emotions to be revealed. Lines crowfooted from the corners of his eyes and grooves were slashed into the sun-browned skin on either side of his mouth, disappearing into his mustache. It was a compelling face, confident of its ability and its masculinity. She turned her lips into the palm of his hand and kissed it.

The animal brilliance of his hard gaze lifted from her face to look beyond her into the dark. "Frank is coming back." His voice was husky in its impatience, as his hands left her face to settle on her shoulders.

Jordanna tipped her head to the side, listening intently. There were only night sounds. How could he have heard anything? Then she heard a crunching sound, very faint, footsteps on gravel.

"How could you hear him?" she whispered incredulously.

"This is my home ground. I know the sounds that belong and those that don't." Brig moved, creating space between them.

"Brig," Jordanna repeated his name. "Where did you get your name?"

"It's short for Brigham, after my Grandfather Sanger, but nobody ever uses it." His fingers tightened to dig into her flesh. Just as quickly, she was released and Brig was turning away. "You'd better go inside."

Jordanna stiffened in resistance. From the darkness, Frank Savidge emerged on the porch steps. The thud of his weight hit the first board. She gave him a sideways glance, resenting his intrusion. He was looking at Brig.

"The horses are all right."

"Good."

Frank paused on the porch, turning an expectant look to Jordanna. "Are you going inside?"

"Yes." She rubbed her arms, as if feeling a chill.

Frank walked to the door and opened it for her. Her glance ricocheted off the tall figure in the corner of the porch. His back was turned to her. Walking past the lantern-jawed cowboy, Jordanna entered the living room. Her father glanced up, noting the ranch hand who followed her in.

"Was it cool outside?" he asked.

Her hands were still crossed in front of her, clasping her elbows. "A bit." She hadn't noticed it until shortly before she came in.

The door had barely closed when it was opened again and Brig entered. Fletcher rose from the couch and glanced around the room.

"I don't know about the rest of you, but I'm going to turn in. We're having an early start in the morning."

"Two games apiece," her brother declared. "It's time to quit before I end up the loser." He pushed his chair from the card table where the cribbage board was sitting. "Enjoyed it, Tandy."

"Anytime."

"How about you, Jordanna?" Kit glanced her way. "Are you calling it a night, too?"

"Soon. When everyone's through with the bathroom, I thought I'd take a last bath. A tub is a luxury we aren't going to have once we are out in the mountains. I'm going to take advantage of it while I have the opportunity," she said.

"It's early for me to be going to sleep," Max said. "But it will feel earlier when I have to get up at dawn. So I guess I'll go to bed, too."

"Come on, Frank." Tandy folded the cribbage board closed. "Let's get our beds made up here. Brig?" His gaze swung to his employer in silent question of his intentions.

"I have some paperwork to do before I call it a night." Brig walked to the desk against the wall. He pulled out the chair and glanced over his shoulder at the others. "Good night."

Chapter XI

THE BATHROOM DOOR opened and closed. Brig remained hunched over his desk, not turning around or glancing over his shoulder at the sound of bare feet approaching the downstairs bedroom—his bedroom. Again there was the click of a door opening and closing.

Behind him, he heard Frank groan and whisper, "Have you ever seen a more beautiful woman in your life?"

His fingers gripped the pen until their tanned knuckles turned white. For the third time, he added the column of figures and came up with the third different answer. He tried again.

"She is very beautiful," Jocko agreed softly.

Brig combed his fingers through his hair and forced his eyes to concentrate on the numbers. The figures blurred into scratch marks. He had to start the addition all over again.

"The next time I take a bath, I'm going to wallow in that tub," Frank declared in a disturbed manner.

"Can't you just see her sitting in there, splashing the water?"

"That's enough, Frank." Brig couldn't take it any more. His voice was low and rough. He was tortured by the agony of having held her in his arms and being unable to do more than that.

His rumbling order was initially met with silence. But it didn't last long. "I can just see her soaping up her hands and rubbing that lather all over her breasts," Frank dreamed aloud.

A silent groan tore at his guts. Brig turned in his chair. "I said that's enough!" he snapped the warning at the bundled cowboy lying on the floor in his sleeping bag. "Turn off the light and go to sleep."

"What about you?" Frank challenged testily. "Ain't you going to bed?"

"Not until I get this paperwork done." As he turned back to the desk, Brig saw the sliver of light beneath the bedroom door. Jordanna wasn't in bed yet either. He tried to shut his mind to that fact.

"You can't see if we turn the light off," Frank protested.

"I have the desk lamp." Brig flipped the switch to light the bulb in the green shade. A click sent the rest of the living room into darkness.

"This floor is hard," Frank grumbled. "I sure can think of a bed I'd rather be sleeping in."

"Frank." The low growl from Brig was his final warning. It didn't matter that the cowboy didn't know what his evocative comments were doing to him. They had to stop.

"I'll shut up." Then he mumbled to himself, "But there ain't no harm in wishing."

The harm was in wanting until desire ate you up whole. Brig could have told him. Silence slowly settled into the room, broken only by the scratching of his penpoint on the paper and the restless rolling and tossing of Frank in his sleeping bag. Brig continued through the tally slip, checking off the earmarks of the calves he'd sold and noting the breeding heifers he'd kept.

He tried not to acknowledge how many times he glanced toward the sliver of light shining below the base of the bedroom door.

Tandy was snoring when Brig finally laid the pen down to rub the rough stubble of beard on his cheek. His hand slid to massage the tense muscles at the back of his neck. He arched his head back, aware of the sleeping sounds from his three ranch hands. Turning his head, his gaze was drawn to the magnet of light. It held him motionless, firing his blood with a rush.

Rising from the chair, he switched off the desk lamp and let his eyes adjust to the darkness; a total darkness, except for the crack of light. His gaze swung to where the staircase was located, his head tipped to a listening attitude. There was only silence from the second floor.

Long, panther-soft strides carried him to the door. If he was taking a risk, Brig didn't care. It was worth it for the chance to hold that soft, female shape against him, the one that had tortured him for so many nights.

He knocked lightly on the door. At first, there was only silence. Had she fallen asleep with the light on? He reached for the handle when he heard a low, throaty voice demand, "Who is it?" The female huskiness of the sound was like a caress.

"Brig." His own voice came from a low, deep place, vibrating from the disturbances going on within. "I left some things in my room."

He sensed the hesitation on the other side of the door. Interminable seconds passed before the knob turned and the door was swung open. The muscles constricted in his chest, paralyzing his lungs. Tall and vaguely regal, Jordanna stood to one side to admit him. A cranberry robe in some velvety material covered the whole of her body all the way to her toes. Its color and the lamplight shining from behind her brought out the red lights in her brown hair. The front of her robe was zipped all the way to her throat. The cuffs of the long sleeves hid her slender wrists.

It was crazy, but Brig didn't think she could have looked sexier if she had been standing naked before him. Her face was washed clean of make-up, but the classic lines of her cheekbone, nose and jaw and the fathomless depths of her unusual green-brown eyes didn't need any adornments.

Her hand fell away from the door and she moved farther into the room. She gestured toward a pile of gear near the wall. "I suppose that's what you want."

Brig stepped inside and closed the door. "You didn't have to wait up for me to get them. You could have set my things outside the door."

"Yes," she admitted with a natural candor that was neither bold nor brazen. Where was the mask of sophistication that rich and beautiful women like her usually possessed, Brig wondered? She pretended to be neither coy nor alluring. She confused him at the same time that she aroused him. The need for her, and her alone, pulsed through him like a drumbeat, growing steadily stronger.

"Why didn't you?" Brig slowly approached her.

"Because I wanted to speak to you . . . privately." The vague hesitation in her answer made her all the more feminine and all the more desirable. It suggested a vulnerability that he wanted to explore to the fullest.

"What about?" He stopped a foot in front of her, assaulted by her nearness. Her gaze was lifted to his face, her look open and unveiled. He saw in the glittering depths of her eyes the disturbance he was causing. Satisfaction momentarily calmed him.

"I'm sure you have formed the wrong impression —that I'm promiscuous. I'm not," she asserted in a voice that trembled with the need to convince him. "It isn't a habit of mine to let perfect strangers make love to me."

Her choice of adjectives amused him. "I'm not perfect." Tantalized by the proud lift of her chin, Brig reached out to trace its line.

"That isn't what I meant."

Brig felt her agitation and sensed that part of it was due to his touch. It filled him with an exhilarating sense of power. His hand caressed the slim column of

her neck. Her pulse was beating unevenly. His fingers
curved to follow the neckline of her robe, stopping
at the metal tab of the zipper. He ran it down to expose
the hollow of her throat, then further to reveal the
shadowy valley between her breasts. The realization
leaped within him that she was naked beneath the
robe.

Her fingers closed over his wrist to stop the progress
of the zipper. "You are not listening to me." She
swallowed to control the husky tremor in her voice.
"I'm trying to explain . . ."

"I am a man," Brig interrupted with careless ease.
"And you are a woman, Jordanna, with needs as basic
and old as time itself. What more is there to explain?"

His gaze slid to her lips. They opened, but no answer
came out. Brig needed no second invitation to possess
their parted softness. The instant his mouth touched
them, all gentleness left him and he bruised them with
the fierceness of his desire. He felt himself grinding
her lips against her teeth and tasted the trace of blood
in her mouth, but he was powerless to ease the brutal
pressure.

Of its own volition, his hand eased the zipper all
the way down past her navel and the hand on his wrist
made no attempt to stop him. The robe became an
irritating barrier between himself and the living alabaster form. Impatiently he pushed it off her shoulders
and down her arms, not satisfied until its encircling
heap was around her ankles.

His hands rushed over her, too excited by the contact with her flesh to take their time. They covered
the miniature mountains of her firm, thrusting breasts
and hurried on to the slender ribcage tapering to her
waist. The swell of her hips and the rounded cheeks
of her bottom filled him with a burning urgency. Brig
crushed her to himself, uncaring of his roughness as
he tried to defy the physical limitations of the flesh
and absorb her wholly into his body. Nothing less
would satisfy the raging fire that consumed him.

He scooped her into his arms and carried her to

the bed, pausing to pull back the quilted blanket before laying her on the sheets. He stepped back to strip off his clothes. As before, she watched him with unblushing interest. While Brig undressed, his gaze roamed Jordanna. Her lips were swollen from his plundering kisses. The rise and fall of her pink-tipped breasts pulled his gaze down past her slender waist to the triangular patch of curling hair and over the long length of her shapely legs.

She was in his bed. She was his, and his alone. He was going to have her, this red-haired she-demon that had possessed him, that had interfered with his sanity and affected his potency. No longer would the ghost of this fascinating creature torment him. She was here in the flesh to satisfy him. Brig moved toward the bed.

"Aren't you going to turn off the light?" she whispered.

"No." The hoarseness of his answer betrayed the hot flames of passion that seared him. "I'm not going to let darkness hide your body from my eyes. I've waited too long to see it."

The mattress dipped under his weight, rolling her against his length and into his arms. The preliminaries of lovemaking were abandoned as the need to possess her body became greater than the desire to enjoy it.

Brig struggled to control the raging fires that flamed through him. They burned hotter and hotter until he could barely withstand them. The blaze was fueled by her writhing and twisting hips grinding against his and the stifled animal sounds of wild pleasure coming from her throat. There was no holding back the explosion of desire when it came. The violence of it left him shaken and ready to enjoy the pleasures he had ignored in the heat of urgency.

When Brig had rolled from her, Jordanna found herself drained weak by the lusting demands he had made on her. She had been pulled into the white-hot center of his fiery embrace. It had sparked a combustion that had shaken her to the core.

Jordanna was still trembling when his arm snaked under her waist to draw her torso onto his chest. His mouth sought her lips, as he revitalized himself with their sweetness. She drew strength from the contact with his solidly muscled physique, lazily sensual and stimulating. Abandoning herself to the heavy oblivion of his kiss, she was filled with a gratifying ecstacy that satisfaction hadn't burned out his need for her.

His hands made a languid search for her shoulders and back, following the curve of her spine and arousing tingling gooseflesh over her skin. The soft brush of his mustache led the way as his mouth explored her face, gradually making its way to her ear. His warm breath stirred her senses and Jordanna shuddered at the erotic lick of his hard tongue.

A fire was rekindled inside her, a golden warmth spreading through her veins to heat her pulse. His mouth momentarily became entangled in the silken curls of her hair before he pushed it aside to moistly investigate her neck. Perspiration gave a slick finish to his hard flesh beneath her fingers. They clung to the sinewy cords rippling in his arms. Jordanna arched her head back to permit him more access to provocative explorations.

Spanning her waist with his hands, he tightened his grip and lifted her above him. A rivulet of perspiration trickled between her breasts. His mouth formed a dam to stop it before it climbed to the peak of her breast. Jordanna quivered at the teasing flicker of his tongue and curled her fingers into his deep brown hair to force him to end the torment. A moaning sigh slipped from her throat as his mouth encircled the whole peak. When he'd taken his pleasure to the maximum, he repeated the procedure on its twin.

A golden ache consumed her. She tried to ease it by rhythmically moving her hips against his muscled thigh. It gave only partial satisfaction. His hand curved her rounded cheek to press her hips to his hard flesh. Shifting, Brig reversed their positions, forcing her shoulders to the mattress and sliding between her legs. She whimpered breathlessly in anticipation.

Her hands and body showed him what she wanted while her lips clung to his. Brig murmured love words of praise and demand, exhorting her to please him as much as he was pleasing her. The perspiration of their bodies melted them together, fusing them as one. The rapture of this selfless giving had not been an illusion never to be repeated, Jordanna realized, as she was lifted once more to breathless heights.

It was a drifting, weightless descent into his arms. She snuggled against him, kissing the bullet-scarred shoulder that pillowed her head. His hand gripped the curve of her waist to keep her close. It was the most natural place in the world to sleep, exhausted by his lovemaking and warmed by his flesh. Jordanna wasn't conscious of the moment when he covered them both with the quilt.

Brig had never felt this fierce possessiveness, this refusal to relinquish the woman in his arms. Its newness was unsettling. He wasn't sure he liked this subtle domination. He had guessed one night wouldn't satisfy him, but he hadn't realized how powerful the desire to keep Jordanna within his reach would be. No woman had ever aroused more than surface emotions, but this one had moved him deeply. He felt raw and exposed. She had made him vulnerable. That made her dangerous, because he wasn't certain he could trust her. Why, he didn't know.

Jordanna stirred and tried to shift from her side into a more comfortable position, but an iron band around her waist held her fast. A furnace-like heat bathed her shoulders, back, hips, and the crook of her legs. Fumbling, she reached to free her waist of the confining band. Her fingers encountered the hair-roughened skin of a man's arm.

Her eyes opened, startled for a minute before the memory came rushing back. Brig was lying on his side, his enveloping length molded to her position. She had never slept with a man before. It was a new and rather pleasant experience to wake up in his arms. Outside the bedroom window, the pale gray of early dawn was lighting the sky.

Jordanna turned toward the warmth, stretching to see the dark head on the pillow beside hers. "Brig. Wake up," she said softly and reluctantly. "It's morning."

"Mmmm." His sun-bronzed features were expressionless in sleep. His rumpled hair invited fingers to smooth it and Jordanna did, feeling the scrape of his night's beard growth on her palm.

"Come on," she coaxed again. "You'd better get up before the others do."

His hand slid from her stomach to enclose her breast in its hold. Dark lashes lifted slowly to reveal eyes that were amazingly alert for a man just waking. They skimmed her face thoroughly. He bent his head to nibble at her ivory shoulder.

"There's no rush."

"It's nearly dawn." Jordanna hunched a shoulder to protect her neck and keep his sensual nibblings from going any farther.

"So?" He finished turning her so that she was flat on her back.

Her hands came up to strain against his chest when he started to lean over her. "You have to get up, Brig, before someone finds you in here."

That familiar hardness stole into his eyes. "What if they do?"

He tried to kiss her, but Jordanna eluded his descending mouth. "Not now," she protested.

"Not now?" His gaze narrowed. He had intended to do no more than indulge in a good morning kiss. Granted, it would have been a long and lingering one. Her attempt to dictate to him when they would make love angered him. She had driven him out of his mind already. He was not about to let her drive him out of his bed.

"If not now, when would you suggest?" Brig challenged coldly. "Perhaps you could check your calendar of events and let me know when next you'll be free."

"Brig, please." A wary anger flashed in her eyes.

"Please what? Be a good little boy and run along," he taunted with soft savagery.

"I didn't say that." She sounded indignant and hurt, and more than a little angry.

"But you don't want me to make love to you now."

"No, I don't."

When she tried to slip from the bed, Brig pinned her to the mattress. "We'll see about that." His mouth curved into a mocking smile.

At first she resisted him, but his weight easily kept her crushed beneath him. He let her expend her strength in useless struggles to avoid his mouth while he explored those areas her twistings exposed. He continued to tease her with his kisses and caresses even after she began to respond. She arched against him, seeking the thrust of his hips, but he held back. She writhed beneath him, animal sounds of frustrated desire coming from her throat. But Brig wouldn't ease her aching, even though his was just as great.

"I thought you didn't want to make love," he taunted.

"Damn you," Jordanna gasped in angry unfulfillment.

She attacked him, nipping and clawing and biting, demanding the satisfaction his caresses had promised. This wild aggression provoked Brig as tears and pleadings never could have. Their coupling—born in violent frenzy—continued in fiery passion, and ended in a mutual fury of satiated desire.

When it was over, Brig lay in the bed for long minutes to catch his breath and wait for his heart to stop hammering against his ribs. He didn't want to move, but a golden hue lit the gray dawn. Swinging his feet to the floor, Brig rose and began to dress. He was aware of Jordanna watching him. He wondered when he'd be able to be with her again. Damn that green-eyed vixen, he thought. His loins weren't cooled from this last time and he was already worrying about when the next would be.

Brig jammed his shirt inside his pants. Without glancing to the bed where she lay, he walked to the door and jerked it open.

"Brig."

Ready to close the door, he stopped and glanced over his shoulder, but he made no move to return to the bed. When she realized this, she slid out of bed, dragging along the patchwork quilt to cover the front of her. She hurried to the door and stopped to search his face.

"Don't be angry," she asked.

It was a simple request, spoken neither as an apology or a demand. His gaze focused on her mouth. Was she aware of the irresistible power she held over him? What did it matter? His hand cupped the back of her neck to pull her head forward and meet the hard pressure of his kiss.

There were footsteps on the stairs behind him. He abruptly broke off the kiss, recognizing that tread before he turned. As he met Fletcher Smith's narrowed look, Brig cursed himself for not exercising more caution—for Jordanna's sake if not his own. But he was equally relieved that his desire for her was out in the open. Directly behind Fletcher on the stairs stood his son. Brig noted his presence, but kept his attention directed on Jordanna's father.

"Was there something you wanted to say to me, Fletcher?" he asked in quiet challenge.

There was an instant of grim hesitation as the older man's gaze sliced to his daughter. When it returned to Brig, it was veiled. "No."

With the risk of confrontation gone, Brig glanced at Jordanna. She looked composed, if a trifle self-conscious. Brig could find no reason to linger. Inclining his head in a faint nod to Jordanna, he walked to the kitchen.

Jocko was pouring a cup of coffee when he entered. He handed it to Brig. Tandy and Frank were already seated at the table. From their knowing looks, Brig knew it was no secret where he had slept last night.

"I think you still enjoy danger, Brig," Jocko commented.

A muscle tightened in his jaw. "You do." It was a non-committal response.

"I think, too, that this Mr. Fletcher Smith is a powerful man," he continued. "I would not like to have him dislike me."

"I doubt that you would ever do anything to earn his dislike, Jocko," Brig retorted.

"But how about you, senor?"

"That becomes my problem, doesn't it, Jocko?" he challenged.

"Si, and I worry for you."

"Brig can take care of himself," Tandy inserted.

"You'd better get breakfast started, Jocko. As for you two," Brig glanced at the cowboys seated at the table, "finish your coffee and get the horses saddled and the packstring ready to be loaded."

He didn't need a discussion over the wisdom of becoming involved with Fletcher Smith's daughter. The deed was already done. Brig doubted he would change it if he could. Damn, but he was tired. He caught Jocko's grinning look. The wily Spaniard had seen his weary expression and knew the cause. The momentary flash of anger gave way to a wry smile.

"She was worth it, no?"

"I think so, yes," Brig acknowledged.

After Brig had disappeared into the kitchen, her father descended the steps. Jordanna remained in the bedroom doorway, the quilt clutched a little more tightly in front of her. She didn't know what he was thinking about her, whether he was comparing her to his wife. Jordanna hadn't been able to tell him about the stranger at the party—Brig. However close their relationship was, it didn't include intimate confidences or discussion of personal, sexual satisfaction. The parent-child barrier always got in the way.

Christopher followed him down the stairs. When he stopped in front of Jordanna, her brother touched his arm. "Come on, Dad. It isn't any of our business."

Her father shrugged away his hand. His brown eyes were disconcertingly direct as they met Jordanna's unflinching gaze. "Do you know what you are doing?" he asked simply.

"I am a grown woman," she reminded him.

"McCord . . ." He started the sentence, then changed his mind. "Don't care about him too much, Jordanna," her father advised instead. "I don't think it would be wise."

"I'm not sure that wisdom has anything to do with emotion," she replied.

"I don't want you to be hurt." There was a look of pain and indecision in his face. "But there are some things I can't change."

"I know." Jordanna felt strangely very calm and secure. "Don't worry about me, Dad."

He hesitated and rubbed his forehead. "You'd better get some clothes on and get your things ready." He turned away from her door. "I'll see you at the break-fast table."

Chapter XII

"I HOPE YOU have a nice, quiet horse for me, Brig."
Max eyed the saddled horses with misgivings.

"Ride the paint. It's the gentlest mount in the
remuda." Brig pointed to the brown-spotted horse
standing three-legged at the corral fence.

Jordanna stood to one side, watching the last minute preparations. Tandy was weighing the panniers to
evenly distribute the load on the pack horses, while
Jocko went over his checklist. Frank, who had maintained a respectful distance from her all morning, was
tightening the saddle cinches on the horses. The attitude
of all three men had changed toward her. They now
regarded her as Brig's woman and she liked the feeling it gave her.

"Jordanna." Brig was assigning the riders to their
horses.

A pleasant warmth spread through her when he
spoke her name. "Yes." She stepped forward, her
hands in the pockets of her hunting parka, her hair

swept under the crown of her wide-brimmed western hat, revealing the long, slim line of her neck.

"You'll ride the sorrel." His look was impersonal, but then it had been ever since he'd left the bedroom that morning.

"Alright." She walked toward the saddled horse Frank was untying from the fence. Looping the reins over its neck, he held the horse's bridle while she mounted. "The stirrups are too short, Frank. They need to be lengthened," Jordanna noticed.

"You'd better tell Brig," he mumbled and moved quickly away.

She stared after him for an amazed instant. His avoidance of her was almost comical. With a wry shake of her head, Jordanna started to dismount and do it herself.

"What's the problem?" Brig walked toward her.

She sat back in the saddle. "The stirrups are too short."

"I'll take care of it."

Drawing her foot out of the stirrup, she bent her leg back toward the cantle. She watched Brig lengthen the strap a notch before he walked to the other side of the saddle to do the same. When he'd finished, he stepped back.

"How is that?"

Jordanna stood in the stirrups. The scabbard containing her rifle rested familiarly under her leg. "Fine." She nodded. He held her gaze for a moment, then patted the sorrel's withers and walked away to give Tandy a hand.

Her father and brother were astride a pair of bays —tough, mountain-bred horses, their dark coats showing the thickness of winter growth. In the saddle of the pinto, Max looked more adept on a horse than he had led them to believe. All of the riders wore wide-brimmed western hats like Jordanna's to shade their eyes from the glare of the sun at the higher elevations and to protect their faces from the dust, wind, and rain.

Kit rode over to wait beside Jordanna for the last of the packs to be tied. "It won't be long now before we leave," she observed.

"You're looking forward to it, aren't you?"

"Of course." It seemed a foolish question. Jordanna couldn't help smiling at it. "This will be a hunt of a lifetime. Dad has often said that a man is entitled to only one bighorn sheep in his life." Brig was walking the packstring, double-checking to be sure all the packs were securely fastened. He'd been just as thorough in his lovemaking, Jordanna thought, and was warmed by the comparison.

"You look happy." Kit eyed her thoughtfully, an unspoken question in his expression.

"I am." Maybe mellow was a better word. For the first time, there didn't seem to be anything missing in her life.

Her brother followed the direction of her gaze, stopping when he found the object of her attention, Brig McCord. "Dad didn't have anything to do with last night, did he?"

She was startled by the question, and confused. "What do you mean?"

"I know Dad suggested you should be nice to McCord when he was so upset about having a woman along, especially you." His gaze continued to probe her expression, indifferent to the indignant anger he saw gathering.

"And you think that last night, I . . . slept with Brig because Dad wanted me to?" Jordanna raged, in a low, vibrant voice. "My God, you're my own brother. How could you think that of me? Of Dad?"

"I know you practically worship the ground Dad walks on. In your eyes, he can't do anything wrong. I don't know how far you would go to please him," Kit calmly defended his position. "I do know you are attracted to Brig McCord. It's possible you rationalized last night with the knowledge that Dad wanted you to make McCord change his mind about you."

"You're wrong. You couldn't be more wrong." She

was so angry and hurt she could hardly talk. The sorrel horse sensed the violent agitation of its rider and shifted nervously, tossing its flaxen mane. "In the first place, I would never do such a thing for that reason. And Dad would never suggest it."

"I never said you were consciously influenced by him," her brother clarified. "I don't underestimate Dad. And I don't like the idea that he might be using you to get something he wants."

"He isn't," Jordanna retorted in a hiss.

"Dad wasn't very upset when he saw McCord coming out of your room this morning."

"How could he be? I'm an adult. He has no control over what I do," she argued.

"You are his daughter," Kit reminded her. "Dad is pretty possessive about things that belong to him. He doesn't like people taking what is his . . . unless he wants them to. What I'm saying is that either he wanted you to become involved with Brig, or Brig has made himself an enemy."

"No wonder Dad dislikes you," Jordanna lashed at him with words, wanting him to feel their sting. "You aren't a son to him. You're a Judas."

A sad smile touched his mouth. "He isn't God, Jordanna." He reined his horse away from hers and walked it over to Max.

Jordanna sat rigid in the saddle, staring after him. Tears burned her eyes. How could he say those things about her—about their father? Such insidious things. She didn't hear the muffled thud of a horse and rider approaching her.

"What's the matter, Jordanna?" Her father's voice startled her. "What did Kit say to you?"

After one surprised glance, she kept her face averted from him and struggled to keep her expression of wounded outrage from showing. "Nothing unusual." Her voice was tight and husky. "We can't talk for five minutes without arguing. It's the same old thing." She couldn't risk looking at him to see if he believed her.

"Jordanna, I . . ." Whatever he had intended to say, he abruptly changed his mind. "I hope you brought plenty of lip balm this time. I don't fancy the idea of using grease for my chapped lips the way we had to on the Alaskan trip."

At high altitudes, the atmosphere was less dense, permitting the sun to quickly dry and chap lips. His reminder of that previous trip was an attempt to distract her from the unpleasant conversation with Kit and joke about a time when they had shared hardships. Jordanna tried to respond.

"I have three tubes this time," she assured and flashed him a tight smile.

"That should be enough," Fletcher returned the smile, a veil masking the piercing look he gave her— or had Jordanna only imagined the look because of Kit's accusations? Before she could decide, her father was turning away. "It looks like we're ready to leave."

Brig was mounting a big, muscled buckskin. Its coat gleamed a palomino gold in the early morning sunlight, contrasted with a black mane, tail, and stockings. Its size suited the rangy build of its rider. Brig turned the horse in a semicircle to face the hulking frame of Frank Savidge.

"You know the general area where we'll be hunting. With any luck, we'll be back in less than three weeks," he told him.

"I'll look after things here," Frank promised.

With a curt nod, Brig let his gaze encompass the hunting party. "Let's go," he said simply and started his horse forward.

Jordanna's sorrel stepped out eagerly as Brig took the lead. The pack horses were tied single file, one roped to the next one's tail with Jocko leading them and Tandy bringing up the rear. The group of riders trotted across the mountain meadow, clustered in no particular order. Moving offered release, but Jordanna continued to feel a measure of tension in the company of both her brother and her father. The broad shoulders of the rider in the lead offered an escape from it. She urged her horse to catch up with the buckskin and slowed it when she came alongside Brig.

"Do you mind if I ride with you?" she asked, meeting his sidelong look with candor. Jordanna wanted to be with him and made no secret of the fact. She had made her attraction for him much too plain in the last twenty-four hours to hide it now.

His saddle creaked as he turned to look over his shoulder at the trailing riders. His questioning glance back to her was lazy and warm. "Are you sure your father doesn't object?"

"I'm past the age of consent."

Her comment drew no reply as Brig faced the terrain ahead of them. Jordanna saw the faint curving of his mouth beneath the mustache. It was his only indication that he wanted her riding beside him. The knowledge warmed away the chilling tension Kit's words had created.

By late morning, they were miles from the ranch house and riding deeper into the mountains. The rough country had strung the riders into single file with Tandy and Jocko bringing up the rear with the pack horses. The sun was hidden by a gray cloud cover that crowded the mountain peaks around them. The nipping temperatures turned the horse's breath into white vapor. The air was sharp and invigorating to the senses.

Traversing the shoulder of the mountain, the horses walked quietly on a carpet of pine needles. They were riding the edge of a thick stand of fir trees and skirting a talus of loose rock that fell away to the canyon below.

When Brig reined the buckskin to a halt and the rest of the horses stopped automatically, Jordanna thought his intention was to give the horses a rest. It had been more than an hour since their last stop and they had been steadily climbing. Her lungs were trying to adjust to the thinning oxygen of the higher altitude, her breathing slightly labored.

She glanced behind her to see how her brother and Max were holding up. Novices were often deceived by the belief that the horse was doing all the work when, in reality, horseback riding was an exercise that, like swimming, used most of the muscles and expended a lot of energy. Both of them looked to be in good shape, although the discovery was registering that they weren't simply sitting in the saddle.

"Look." Brig's quiet order pulled her attention to the front.

Her gaze followed his pointing arm. Where a ridge joined their mountain slope to a companion peak, the trees thinned to form a rocky meadow. Her gaze swept the area once without seeing anything more than the rough terrain. On the second pass, something moved and she focused on it.

A massive bull elk stood at the edge of the clearing, his rack of antlers blending in with the limbs of the trees. Despite its heavy, square body, it appeared majestic rather than clumsy. The lift of its head gave the impression of regal power. It started forward with a lordly walk. The white circle on its rump—which earned it the Indian name of "wapiti," meaning white rump—showed up plainly against its buff-colored coat. It stopped and turned its head in their direction, as if warned by some sixth sense of their presence. The spread of its antlers from tip to tip took Jordanna's breath away. It was easily the largest rack she had ever seen, more than five feet.

"Look at that elk, Dad." She spoke in an awed breath and glanced over her shoulder to see if he had spotted the huge animal.

But he had already dismounted and pulled his .270 Winchester from its scabbard. His expression was absorbed in calculating the distance and measuring the wind currents. Absently he responded to her comment

"That's a Boone and Crockett rack if I ever saw one," he declared, referring to the trophy standards of the famous Boone and Crockett Club.

Brig reined his buckskin horse into her father's line of fire. "I thought this hunt was organized for bighorn sheep. You didn't mention you were going to take other game. Or do you normally shoot everything you see?"

"My God, man! That's a trophy head out there! Get out of my way," her father ordered harshly, an angry frown creasing his forehead.

The buckskin received no command to move as Brig rested both hands on the saddlehorn. "Just to make sure I understand you—all you are interested in is a trophy kill and you don't care what kind of animal it is, is that right?" Behind the taunting question was a silent challenge. "As your guide, I should know because we'll be spotting more game while we're looking for the bighorn. If you are going to shoot at everything that comes along and not concentrate on the bighorns, you should have mentioned it to me before."

"I want the ram," her father stated.

Jordanna knew Brig was questioning how badly he wanted a trophy bighorn—bad enough to pass up the elk? Indecision warred in his expression before Fletcher finally turned to impatiently thrust his rifle in the leather scabbard. Brig reined his buckskin back to the head of the group, not commenting on the hunter's decision to forget the elk.

With his line of sight unobstructed, Fletcher's gaze returned to the massive creature and Jordanna saw the anger and frustration written in his look—an anger that he had been deprived of something he wanted and a burning resentment of the person who had thwarted him. She glanced at the elk trotting over the ridge and out of range. It was a splendid animal and would have made a priceless trophy. She didn't understand Brig's objection to killing it.

Brig waited until her father was in the saddle before he resumed the journey. Jordanna maintained her place in line behind him. The atmosphere around the silent riders was considerably heavier than it had been.

In the middle of the afternoon, Brig called a halt to rest the horses. Three hours of crossing a solid field of rock had noticeably tired their mounts. Max swung stiffly out of the saddle, grimacing at the soreness of his muscles. No amount of conditioning had prepared him for the effects of the first day, although he was standing up well to the test.

"How much farther are we going today?" he asked Brig.

"We'll camp around four. It will take us the rest of tomorrow to reach the site of our base camp." Brig loosened the saddle cinch on his buckskin, then moved to the pinto horse to loosen Max's.

From habit, Jordanna removed her rifle and scabbard when she dismounted, in case the sorrel decided to roll on the ground. The afternoon temperature had reached its height, which was still very chilly and brisk. She joined the huddle of riders sheltering near some scrub brush from the nipping breeze. Jocko was doling out the last of the coffee from the big thermos.

Their rest stop was near the timberline with steep, rocky crags climbing to the peak. Stunted conifers and dwarf willows dotted the land around them. A cobweb of animal trails wound through a pasture of moss and lichens, following the rolling contours. Her father was sitting on his heels, warming his hands with the cup of coffee.

"This is sheep country, Max," he said when the man joined them, hunching his shoulders against the wind. He looked unimpressed by the statement. "You almost have to be a hunter to feel the excitement of it. The land where the bighorns range has a look to it—a feel—that makes it different from any other kind of country. It's part of that special glamour attached to hunting bighorns. Some people say grizzlies are the most dangerous to hunt and the elk can be more physically demanding on a hunter, but going after a bighorn ram has an aura that can't be matched by any other big game. I don't care what it is."

Jordanna saw the gleam in his brown eyes and understood the awed fascination for the bighorn sheep. They had adapted to this harsh and forbidding terrain of the mountain rooftops, an alpine world of snow-capped spires, a wild grandeur that was unmatched except by the animals themselves.

"I know what Dad means," she offered. "Bighorn sheep have a charisma, something that's rare in people and rarer still in animals. They are magnificent."

"I know what you mean," Tandy agreed. "I've been up in the mountains during their rut. One time I saw a pair of big old monarchs fighting. It was a sight." He shook his head in remembered amazement. "They'd walk all stifflegged away from each other like the other one wasn't worthy of their interest. Then they'd spin around and throw themselves at each other. It sounded like a pair of billiard balls coming together, only much louder. The mountains would echo with it. After they made a few passes at each other they quit. There was a bunch of ewes there, but they didn't seem to care who won."

"At least they don't kill each other over the females," Kit inserted.

"Some of them do die from the fights," Jocko corrected. "They come together with such force that sometimes there are internal injuries. The bighorn sheep fight more than any other hooved species."

"But only in the breeding season," Jordanna added, "which is in late November, isn't it?"

"Si. That is when the rams leave their bachelor lives behind and seek out the ewes."

"Is there any coffee left, Jocko?" Satisfied that the horses were taken care of, Brig finally joined the circle. He picked up the discussion. "The strongest rams have the breeding priorities, although they are challenged by lesser or younger rams. It is nature's way of insuring that the offspring will be strong. Weakness is bred out, instead of in."

"The ram with the largest horns is always the dominant one." Jocko poured the last of the coffee into a cup and handed it to Brig. "He rarely lives to old age, because he is always fighting and breeding. It all becomes too much for him."

"Now we know what our problem is, eh, Max?" Fletcher laughed and slapped the man on the shoulder in jest. "We're a pair of old rams that are wearing out."

"That's probably it," Max laughed in agreement. "Too many ewes instead of too many years."

Kit ignored the ribald humor of the two men. "How long does the rutting season last?"

"About a month. Late November into December," Jocko answered. "Or sooner if winter comes early to the mountains, and it is going to be a bad one. The wild animals always know. They live with nature and recognize her warning signs, while man tries to build machines to do the same thing."

"Wait until you get your first look at a ram, Kit," Tandy said. "All spring, summer, and fall, he's been grazing to get his strength for the rutting season. He's a massive, chunky animal. When you refer to them as sheep, most people think of something the size of domestic sheep. But a bighorn is about the size of a mule deer. Those big, curling horns can weigh forty pounds. Can you imagine carrying that kind of weight around on your head? It's no wonder he's got a neck like a football player."

"Yes," Jocko agreed with what his friend said. "And you should see this same ram after the rutting season. He rarely eats at all during that time. He fights and chases ewes and breeds. By the time it is over, he will be thin and scrawny. That is why when the big ones get older, they do not always make it through the severe winters in the high mountains."

"The bighorns sound like fascinating animals," Kit murmured.

"They are," Fletcher insisted.

"If they are a wild sheep, how come they don't

resemble our domestic sheep more? Or vice-versa?"
Kit asked.

Jordanna answered that question. "It's believed that
the bighorns are descended from the large Asian sheep
and migrated here to North America when the two con-
tinents were linked by a land bridge. Our domestic
sheep resemble the Middle East sheep."

"You do know something about the quarry you're
after, don't you?" Brig eyed her with grudging approval. "More than just what part of the body to hit
for a sure kill."

"Dad taught me to know all I could about whatever
I was hunting," she replied with a slight shrug that
said the knowledge was part of being a good hunter
and warranted no special acknowledgement.

"It's essential to know as much as you can about
the animal you're hunting," her father elaborated on
her statement. "What his habits are, what time he eats,
what time he rests, the type of terrain he prefers. This
is especially true with the Rocky Mountain Bighorns
because they have been hunted so hard and been
driven back by man's encroachment into some of the
roughest country there is. They have become doubly
wary, which makes them that much harder to stalk—
and that much more of a prize."

"Except during the rutting season," Tandy inserted.
"Then those rams are so wrapped up in each other
you can practically walk right up to them. Which is
why they don't schedule the hunting season during the
rut."

Brig drained his cup dry and straightened. "The
rest stop is over. It's time we were moving on." He
passed the cup to Jocko to put away while the others
pushed stiffly to their feet.

Jordanna followed Brig as he walked to her sorrel
horse to tighten the saddle cinch. The discussion about
the bighorns had eliminated the tension of the earlier
confrontation between Brig and her father.

"Brig." Jordanna watched him flip the stirrup across

the saddle seat. "Why did you object to Dad shooting that elk this morning?"

"I don't believe in killing an animal for his horns."

His answer brought a frown. "If you feel that way, why did you agree to act as a hunting guide for the bighorns?"

He jerked the cinch strap tight. "Because I needed the money." Without looking at her, he held the horse's bridle while she mounted, then walked to his own horse.

Her father had said he'd bought McCord, but somehow Jordanna hadn't believed it until Brig had said it just now. She was beginning to understand why her father had backed down from taking that trophy elk. He was allowing Brig to hold onto a fragment of his principles, rather than push him too far. Jordanna suspected it had probably been a wise decision.

"What's the frown about?" Kit had walked his bay horse up to hers.

"I was just thinking about Brig and why he objected to killing that elk," she murmured absently.

"He probably shares my contempt for killing as a sport," he supplied the same answer Brig had. "There should be a law that people have to eat whatever they kill." He urged his horse ahead of hers to follow Brig when he started his mount forward.

Shortly after four that afternoon, they stopped to camp for the night. Brig and Tandy took care of the horses, hobbling them and turning them loose to graze on the thick mountain grass. Jocko started a fire and immediately put a pot of coffee on before fixing the evening meal. A screen of bushes at the edge of camp provided nature's version of a latrine. Jordanna was just walking out from the bushes to return to the fire when her father approached. She smiled and started to walk past him, but he stopped.

"There is something I've been meaning to speak to you about, Jordanna," he began. "But I haven't had a chance to see you alone today until now."

"What is it?" She experienced only a mild curiosity for this unknown subject he wanted to discuss in private.

"It's about last night. Or, maybe I should say this morning."

Jordanna felt her cheeks growing warm.

"What about it?" She tried not to appear as insecure as she felt.

"Yesterday, when I asked you to be nice to McCord, I never meant for you to go that far." He looked embarrassed, and apologetic. "I was suggesting that . . ."

"I know what you were suggesting," Jordanna interrupted him to spare him further explanations. "It was entirely my own decision."

"Are you sure that . . ." He was skeptical, not fully convinced.

It hurt that he believed she would do it for him. It hurt and it irritated. "I am an adult, Dad," she told him stiffly. "I'm capable of doing my own reasoning. For once, will you trust me to know what I'm doing?"

"I do." His smile was apologetic and rueful. He cupped her cheek in a gentle caress. "I just wanted to be absolutely certain that you knew what you were doing."

"I do, Dad," Jordanna assured him. "I promise there is nothing for you to worry about."

Turning, her father draped an arm around her shoulder in a gesture of affection. "Let's go back to the fire and see if that coffee is ready."

Brig remained hidden in the long shadows cast by the bushes. When the horses had been rubbed down and hobbled, he had approached the screen of bushes from the opposite side. He had overheard Fletcher's request to speak privately to Jordanna. Instead of making his presence known, he had turned away, intending to permit them their privacy, until he'd heard the subject. His involvement in last night had prompted him to listen.

". . . when I asked you to be nice to him . . ." That phrase of Fletcher's was still ringing in his ears.

The clenched muscle in his jaw smoothed out as he watched the father and daughter stop at the fire, stretching out their hands to the flames to warm themselves. Jordanna's reply had confirmed that last night had been what she wanted, too.

Not that he would have settled for anything less than sleeping with her. He wouldn't have. But if the light hadn't been on in the bedroom, would he have gone to the door? She had waited up for him, invited him to come.

His mouth curved into a half-smile beneath his mustache when he remembered her claim that she wasn't promiscuous. He should have guessed that from the first time he'd made love to her and had discovered the thread of inhibition holding her back.

Last night her response to his lovemaking had been unrestrained. He had wakened her. Or was that his damned male pride talking? He almost chuckled aloud at the question.

Brig found himself wondering briefly what was so important that Fletcher had felt it necessary that Jordanna "be nice" to him? Could it be the hunt? The man seemed inordinately determined that he would have this hunt. Brig supposed that Fletcher was obsessed with the idea of bagging a trophy ram. Wealthier men than Fletcher Smith had been known to have more peculiar idiosyncracies.

Chapter XIII

THE CAMP SCENE wasn't one Brig wanted to return to immediately. The serenity of the blazing bonfire and the smell of fresh coffee didn't appeal to him. He preferred the biting chill in the air, stinging his nose and lungs, to the warmth of the golden flames. It brought all his senses to life.

And isolation was better than the voices and the atmosphere of comaraderie in the camp, nestled near a windbreak of trees. A purpling mountain stream was braided copper in a reflection of the day's sunset. Ridge after ridge marked the horizon stretching to the endless beyond. A coyote yipped from one of them.

The night's camp was crude compared to the accommodations that would be available at the base camp they'd reach tomorrow. Jocko was cooking their meal on an open fire. Only two tents had been pitched, a larger one to accommodate the majority of the party and a smaller one for Jordanna. Brig saw her carry an armload of pine needles into the small tent, where there was barely enough room to stand upright.

He was drawn to her, with the same irresistible force that pulls a moth to the flame. It was an upsetting weakness, but when had he been able to resist her since he'd met her?

Today, when she had ridden beside him, he had felt good inside. He had liked the feeling of someone riding with him, someone who didn't take his orders, who was there to share. She had aroused feelings in him that were deep and gentle. It was the way he wanted to be with her.

Scooping up half an armful of rusty pine needles, Brig walked to the small tent. One flap was fastened open to reveal Jordanna on her hands and knees spreading the pine needles for a mattress. Brig ducked under the canvas roof and stepped inside, crouching to spill the pine needles to the ground. She sat back on her heels, her look of concentration replaced by a radiant smile that knotted his insides.

"Hello." Her voice was slightly breathless, tinged with a huskiness that caressed the ear like a cat's purr. "I was trying to get my bed fixed while there was still enough light to see."

"We're only going to camp here one night. You're going to a lot of work."

His comment seemed to confuse her. She began smoothing out the pile of pine needles he'd brought, adding them to the rectangular collection of her own. Brig felt a need to conceal how very vulnerable he was with her.

"I know," she admitted. "But it doesn't seem to matter how much goosedown there is in a sleeping bag. After you lie on it for so long, the body weight packs it down and you start to feel the cold ground beneath you. I used to haul around an air mattress, but pine needles work just as well for insulation."

Brig had the impression she was talking to hide her nervousness. He disturbed her as much as she disturbed him. Or was she being self-conscious because of the conversation he'd overheard with her father?

His gaze probed her. Bundled up in that heavy parka

with a pair of corduroy jeans tucked into her boots and gloves on her hands, her body was hidden from him. All there was for his eyes to see was a slim but shapeless form. Even her sun-kissed brown hair was hidden under the wide-brimmed hat she wore. The only part of her that wasn't covered was the classic purity of her face. Brig almost resented the fresh, unspoiled beauty of her features, clear and smooth, adult and not falsely innocent. As if aware of his scrutiny, Jordanna looked at him.

He had to say something. "You look like a boy, with your hair tucked under your hat like that."

"Something must be wrong with your eyes, I hope." With a laugh, she swept the hat from her head and combed her fingers through the touseled silk of her hair, its flames hidden in the curtain of nut brown.

Her expression sobered under his narrowed look. Brig wanted to drown in the murky green depths of her eyes, never to surface and face reality.

"Are you planning to sleep here alone?" he heard himself ask.

"I . . ." She faltered and glanced through the opening of the tent flap to the cluster of men at the fire, among them her father. After another second's hesitation, her gaze touched the ground near his boots, then lifted to meet his eyes with unabashed candor. "I don't want to."

"I don't want you to."

When Jordanna swayed toward him, Brig met her halfway. Cupping a hand behind her head, he bruised her mouth. He wanted to crush those soft lips, but it didn't work that way. Her ready response to his brutal kiss revitalized the deeply rooted emotion. He broke off the kiss before his desires burned out of control.

Without a word, he left the tent and walked to the larger one. Inside, Brig took his duffle from the pile of the others and carried it back to her tent. He was aware that the men at the fire had observed his action, but no one said a word. It had been years since he had so blatantly defied convention. But his needs were primitive and uncontrollable. Jordanna was his woman and he would take her—physically, if he couldn't have her any other way.

Ducking inside the opening, he tossed his dufflebag onto the ground beside her. Brig saw her attempt to hide a sudden rush of vulnerable sensitivity.

"I'll need some more pine needles to put under your sleeping bag," she offered.

"Don't bother," he smiled stiffly. "I'll spend most of my time on the side where you are, anyway."

With fingers clasped behind the back of her head to act as a pillow, Jordanna lay inside the two sleeping bags zipped together to form one. She stared into the darkness at the roof of the tent, where the hard rain hammered at the canvas. A clap of thunder seemed to break over her head and rumbled ominously, vibrating the ground beneath her. The portent of the cloud cover that had followed them all day had finally unleashed its fury in a mountain storm.

Where was Brig? Her heart pounded as she listened for the sound of his footsteps outside her tent above the wild drumbeat of the rain and the crashing thunder. Jordanna found her eagerness to see Brig—her total lack of inhibition—vaguely frightening. She didn't seem to have any shame. She couldn't discern right from wrong anymore. But how could it be wrong when being with him made her feel so good? So right?

The tent flap lifted and Jordanna saw his silhouette outlined by a flaming bolt of lightning. The air crackled with the storm's electricity and something more. He stepped inside, dropping the tent flap. The action fanned the cold night air that slipped inside the canvas structure. Jordanna shivered as the icy, wet breeze touched her face.

Brig wasted no time in stripping out of his wet, dripping clothes down to his thermal underwear and slipping inside the pocket-like opening of the sleeping bag. His hands reached for her and Jordanna turned into his arms as thunder rumbled the ground. She felt the hesitation of his caress when his hand came in contact with the coarse material of her insulated underwear. The warmth of his breath was near her lips, mingling with hers. The feathery dampness of his mustache tickled the tip of her nose.

"What are you doing with all these clothes on?" Brig grumbled next to her mouth.

"The same thing you are," Jordanna murmured. "Keeping warm."

His mouth came down hard to part her lips as lightning flashed from the sky, illuminating the canvas walls of the tent. "I can think of a better way," he said against her teeth, and slipped a cold hand under the top of her underwear to warm it against the heat of her soft flesh. Jordanna quivered with longing when his hand surrounded her breast. A fire flamed through her veins, despite the coolness of his caressing fingers, a fire as hot and brilliant as the lightning outside.

"So can I," she agreed.

Outside, the storm raged on the mountaintop. Dark masses of clouds rammed together, raining fire from the heavens while thunder rolled, vibrating the earth and the air. The elements collided, combined, then withdrew to meet again in raw splendor, building to a crescendo.

His hands couldn't seem to get enough of her. The storm outside the flimsy tent had abated, but even now, after he'd satisfied his lust—and hers—his hands continued to roam her body, lazily caressing her hips, breasts, and shoulders. The driving rain that continued to pelt the canvas roof emphasized the need he felt. She lay inside the circle of his arm, her head resting on his shoulder, the silken texture of her hair near his chin. Her arms hugged his stomach and a knee was bent across his legs. He burned with an ache that couldn't be satisfied with physical possession.

"Tell me," Brig summoned words to quench the emotional thirst within, "do you favor all your hunting guides with this particular brand of compensation for the long, stormy nights on a mountaintop?"

Thunder rumbled distantly as she rubbed her cheeks against his chest in a feline caress. "Let's see, there was that white hunter guide in Africa and that Spaniard in Argentina . . . and a French-Canadian in Alberta." The lilt of amusement in her voice said she was teasing. She concluded the list with a mock sigh. "I just can't remember them all."

He didn't find it funny. "I'll bet you can't," he muttered.

Jordanna tipped her head back, but the unrelieved darkness hid his face. "I was only joking," she insisted.

His finger traced the smooth line of her jaw. The nagging memory of her father's admonition to "be nice" to him chose that moment to return. Not that it mattered, Brig decided. He was secure in the knowledge that he had aroused feelings in her that no other man had.

"Did I forget to laugh? Sorry," he feigned an absent apology. "It's time we got some sleep."

"I suppose," she murmured and snuggled into her former position.

The occasional flashes of lightning were growing less frequent as Brig listened to the patter of rain. Jordanna fell asleep long before he did.

The next morning, all that was left of last night's storm was drizzling rain and a few gentle rumbles of thunder. Shortly after dawn, they broke camp and started for the site of their base camp. The riders wore a variety of rain gear—yellow slickers, ponchos, rain suits. The clouds hung like a shroud on the mountain peaks, gray wisps drifting across the trail. The rough terrain was sometimes slick beneath the horses's hooves. There was little talking back and forth among the riders as they followed the wet gold rump of the buckskin leading the way.

By the middle of the afternoon, they had reached

the more substantial accommodations of the base camp. A large, lodge-pole framed tent, complete with wooden table, benches, and a shepherd's stove offered them warmth and shelter from the misting rain. The manta from the packs served a double use as the tent floor. While Jocko put a match to the kindling to start a fire, Tandy finished unpacking the horses, and Brig pitched the small tent where he and Jordanna would sleep, preferring the natural heat of her body to the artificial warmth of the stove.

The next morning, the drizzle turned into a steady downpour as Jocko started dishing up stacks of flapjacks. The hard rain continued throughout the day, confining the hunting party to the base camp. Max took advantage of the opportunity to rest his weary muscles while Fletcher, ever the hunter, checked his gear. Tandy had brought along a deck of cards and the cribbage board, and he and Kit were soon locked in a game.

Brig found plenty to keep him occupied, from checking the horses and gathering more firewood to cleaning the saddles and tack and hauling fresh water. Jordanna was beginning to discover that the only place he didn't disguise his interest in her was in the darkness of their tent. The rest of the time he held himself aloof. The way his gaze seemed to keep track of her made her think that he was trying to be discreet rather than brazenly flaunt their intimate relationship in front of her father. With that reasoning, she couldn't find fault with his withdrawn attitude when they were in the company of others.

Jordanna passed the rainy time by helping Jocko. At first, he had started to refuse her offer to help with the meals until he realized that it was a means to occupy the hours. He had graciously accepted her assistance.

On the morning of the fourth day, the sun broke through the clouds. Within an hour after first light, Jocko and Tandy were left alone in camp as the party started out on its first day of active hunting.

It was mid-morning when they sighted their first bighorns. They had stopped on the rim of a barren plateau to glass the adjoining ridges. Max and Kit had stayed with the horses, using the animals as windbreaks against the swirling mountain air currents. Fletcher, Jordanna, and Brig had taken their binoculars and moved to a vantage point on the plateau.

After twenty minutes with no success, her father had lowered his glasses to rest his eyes. "It's a natural area for bighorns," he murmured.

"Yes," Brig agreed and continued to scan the mountain basin to the right. "There's plenty of graze and water in the stream. The steep cliffs behind offer the sheep a perfect escape route." Brig sat comfortably on the ground, resting his elbows on his knees to support the arms holding the binoculars.

Jordanna detected a movement near some rocks and tried to zero her lens in on it. "I thought I saw something near that old landslide area."

Both Brig and her father concentrated their glasses on the same area. "There they are." Brig saw the brown-bodied rams first. "They've stopped grazing and have laid down to chew their cud and rest."

"They are young," her father observed. "I only see one there with more than a half curl." Glancing over his shoulder, he waved to Kit and Max. "Come have your first look at some bighorns."

As the other two joined them, Jordanna offered her binoculars to her brother. While she and her father helped the two to locate the resting bighorns, Brig continued to glass the area for more, possibly older, rams.

"What now?" Max asked.

"We'll wait," Brig said. "There might be more around that are out of our view at the moment."

They waited another hour, periodically glassing the area, but nothing larger than what they had first seen appeared. Mounting, they rode to another section where Brig had spotted some good sized rams before.

An hour before sundown, they returned to base

camp without having seen a ram either Fletcher or Jordanna were interested in trying. Max had found the experience boring. Although he tried to hide it, it showed.

"I had barely recovered from the ride up in the mountains and I'm stiff and sore all over again," he grumbled to no one in particular.

But Tandy took up the comment. "Aren't your muscles used to all that riding yet?"

"We spent more time getting in and out of the saddle and climbing ridges and embankments than we did riding. The back of my legs are killing me," he complained. "It was all a waste of time as far as I'm concerned."

"Patience and persistence, Max," Fletcher smiled across the fire and tamped down the tobacco in his pipe. "If a hunter doesn't have those two qualities, he might as well give up and go home."

The veiled criticism prompted Max to sit a little straighter. "I suppose, but I guess I'm used to a little more action."

"We'll have you participate more actively with us," Fletcher declared. "I have a spare set of binoculars. Jordanna will get them for you. Tomorrow when we go out, you can help us look for game instead of standing around."

"That's generous of you." Max smiled tightly.

"After all, this is your vacation. I wouldn't want you to be bored to death." There was a mean taunt in her father's droll tone that made Jordanna frown.

"It's late." Kit rose abruptly from his cross-legged position in front of the bonfire. "I think I'm going to call it a night."

"I suppose we all should," Fletcher straightened, too, to join the exodus to the large framed tent. "Good night, Jordanna."

"Good night, Dad," she replied and noticed that he said nothing to Brig. She had suspected that he didn't exactly approve of her behavior, but this was the first indication of it. He was placing the blame on Brig.

She stared into the dwindling flames of the fire, unaware that all of the others had retired.

"Are you planning to sit in front of that fire until you toast like a marshmallow or are you coming to bed?" Brig was standing to one side, studying her in an oddly calculating way.

Jordanna chased away her father's attitude. She was too old to need his approval of how she conducted her affairs. Besides, Brig was waiting for her and that was more important. Rising, she cast him a provocative look.

"Don't you like to eat toasted marshmallows?" she mocked.

His arm curved around her waist to pull her against him and outside the circle of firelight. That familiar, languorous warmth melted her bones as she rested against his hard length. A faintly breathless anticipation parted her lips. Tipping her head back, she gazed into his raw, virile features, bronzed by the glow from the fire. She could see the flames dancing in his hard brown eyes.

"I like my marshmallows burning on the outside and soft and creamy on the inside," he said huskily before his firm, male mouth took its first bite of her lips. Jordanna curled her arms around his neck as he lifted her off her feet to carry her to the tent.

The fifth day was as unsuccessful as the previous one. On the sixth, they spotted the first trophy class bighorn. They were near the place where they had seen the group of young rams. The large ram was grazing on a grassy ledge, its brown body and white rump as roundly stuffed as a sausage. The massive horns were thick at the base and curled close to the head, spreading out at the broomed tips. The battering of the rutting season had chipped one side of the horns, but the flaw didn't diminish the size of the prize.

"He's way over forty inches." Fletcher's statement was barely a whisper. He lowered his binoculars, excitement gleaming in his eyes.

"Look at how far back the points have been rubbed," Jordanna murmured in awe.

"That's so he can see to the side," Brig said. With his binoculars, he scanned the terrain immediately around the heavily horned ram. "He's located in a bad place."

"Yes," Fletcher agreed and glassed the area again. "Even if I was able to execute a successful stalk and got into position for a shot, look where he's likely to fall if I hit him."

Jordanna directed her attention to the area below the ram where a crevasse of jagged rocks opened the earth as if the mountain had yawned to reveal a gaping mouth of teeth.

"Even if you were able to recover its body from the crevasse, the horns are liable to be broken in the fall," she sighed.

"We'll wait." Her father stretched out, belly down on the ground. "Maybe he'll move to a more accessible location."

"I might as well get comfortable, too." Max shifted his position so that he, too, was lying on the ground.

For more than an hour, the monarch of the mountains grazed on the nutritious grass on the ledge. The tension mounted, gradually building to an excitement as the ram began wandering away from the crevasse.

"Come on," her father urged under his breath as he watched the slowly moving bighorn. "That's a good place right there. Lie down, you crafty, old bastard."

"He is," Brig said, "but I don't care much for his choice. You would have been better off if he'd kept grazing. At least you could have moved whenever his head was down. This way you aren't going to be able to get very close to him without him seeing you, not with this wind."

After exchanging opinions about which was the best route for a stalk, the two men started out. Jordanna, Kit, and Max were left on the ridge to watch. It was a long, arduous route they chose. It involved circling half of a mountain slope on foot and climbing to the backbone of a ridge in hopes of approaching the big-horn from above, not always a successful maneuver with a high-strung, suspicious wild sheep, hunted to perpetual wariness.

An hour after the two men had disappeared on the stalk, Max turned to Kit. "Is there any coffee left in that thermos Jocko sent? I sure could use a cup." He sniffed at his runny nose and beat his arms to try to warm them.

"I think so." Kit carefully slipped down from the ridge to where the horses were tied and returned with the thermos.

"Don't drink it all," Jordanna cautioned. "Dad and Brig will probably need some when they get back."

It was another hour before Jordanna glimpsed the two men through her binoculars. They had just crested the ridge above the ram, but the steepness of the slope and a ragged tangle of rocks blocked the ram from their view. She watched her father try to maneuver into a position where he could find the ram in his rifle scope.

Something went wrong. Either the wind changed or a localized air current carried their scent to the ram. In the blink of an eye, the bighorn had bounded to its feet and was racing up a craggy rock face amidst a clatter of hooves on stone. He leaped and climbed with the sureness and grace of an aerialist. Her father never had a chance to get off a shot.

"All this time," Max grumbled, "and he didn't even fire a shot."

"If you don't like it Max," Kit murmured, "you don't have to come along every day. You can stay in camp."

Max glared at him with a look that said such a suggestion was preposterous. Jordanna hugged her arms around her knees. The man was really determined to sell that stock to her father, no matter what personal discomfort it cost him.

By the time Brig and Fletcher circled back to where they were waiting, it was late afternoon. Fletcher looked exhausted and offered no argument when Brig suggested they return to camp early.

The sight of the massively horned ram had fueled Fletcher's enthusiasm. The next morning he was eager to find it again. They covered a lot of ground and sighted several respectably horned rams, but Fletcher was determined not to settle for less than the prize he had seen—at least, not yet.

It was two whole days before Brig located the big ram again.

"Is it the same one?" Jordanna was lying on the ground, her elbow nearly touching his as she propped up her binoculars.

"It's the same one," Fletcher insisted. "See that chip broken off the right horn."

"Yes."

Brig's mouth thinned into a grim line as he surveyed the possible route of a stalk. He heard Fletcher swear under his breath and guessed that the hunter had seen the same thing he had.

"There is only one way to get to him and that's too dangerous," Brig stated.

"I suppose we wait again," Max said and breathed out a disgusted sigh.

"Maybe he'll move," Fletcher muttered, but he didn't sound hopeful.

Brig glassed the area again. No matter how thoroughly he studied the area, he could find only one route where Fletcher could get within range of the bighorn resting serenely on the mountainside. The way was worse than treacherous. They would have to circle the base of a wide landslide area where the footing would be questionable. A loose rock tumbling from their feet wouldn't necessarily alert the ram to their stalk, since falling rocks were a frequent occurrence in its world. But Brig's blood ran cold at the sight of the chasm at the base of the talus. One missed step, one faulty choice of where a foot should be placed, and it would mean a five hundred foot drop.

One hour. An hour and a half. The ram hadn't budged from its spot. Brig glanced at Fletcher, prepared to suggest that they try another day, but the almost obsessive gleam in the man's eyes stopped the words. He looked back at the ram. Without the magnification of the binoculars, it was a brown lump, barely distinguishable from its background, nature's camouflage.

"I don't see why you don't just go around that loose rock and sneak up on that sheep," Max inserted, tired of the incessant waiting.

"It's too dangerous," Brig stated.

"It doesn't look it to me." Max shrugged his shoulders.

"Why don't we give it a try?" Fletcher suggested. Brig guessed that after more than an hour of studying those great, sweeping horns, Fletcher's obsessive need to bag that trophy had overpowered his reason. "Maybe when we get closer it won't look as bad as it does from here."

"That sounds like a good idea," Max agreed.

"You know it won't be any better." Brig eyed the hunter grimly.

"I think Brig is right," Jordanna gave him her support.

"It'll be dark soon and we'll lose the ram anyway. We might as well take a closer look at the route," Fletcher argued and glanced at the curly-haired man on the ground beside him. "Do you want to come, Max?"

Brig saw his cousin's startled look and knew Max hadn't bargained on that invitation. Max had been eager enough for action as long as it didn't require any effort on his part. Cynical amusement deepened the corners of his mouth at Max's hesitation.

"Sure, I'll go," he agreed unexpectedly.

"Don't be ridiculous, Max!" Brig snapped, impatient with his cousin's foolish attempt to please the man whose money he wanted. "You're in no condition to make a climb like that."

Immediately he realized that he had used the wrong tactic. He should never have criticized Max in front of Fletcher, nor implied that he was physically less of a man than one who was his senior. Now Max felt he had to prove Brig wrong. Brig silently cursed the quickness of his tongue.

"Don't worry about me, Brig," he said stubbornly. "I can make it."

"All we are going to do is take a closer look at that slide," Fletcher reasoned. "If it looks too risky, we'll simply have to forget it."

"I'll come with you," Kit volunteered and quickly rose to his feet.

"No." The denial from Fletcher was sharp and abrupt. He tempered his tone when he glanced at Jordanna. "You stay here with your sister. Three people are enough. Any more than that and we'll sound like an army and spook that ram for sure."

Brig could tell by the expression on the young man's face that he wanted to argue, but his father's reasoning was too sound. Brig understood the feeling, since Fletcher's insistence that they would turn back if it was too risky had forced him to agree to go along.

Chapter XIV

IT WAS ALMOST an hour before they reached the slide area. Brig had taken it slow for Max's sake. Glancing behind him, he saw his cousin struggling for breath in the high, thin air. His own lungs were burning from the demanding physical exertion of traversing the rough terrain on foot. But neither he nor Fletcher was suffering as badly as Max. Yet not once had his cousin begged for them to stop so he could rest. Brig had to admire his guts even if he questioned his sanity.

He stopped short of the slide area and glanced to the far ridge, where Jordanna waited with her brother. Fletcher joined him while Max collapsed against a large boulder, straining to catch his breath. Brig forced his concentration on the forbidding ground ahead of them.

"It's no good, Fletcher." His hands rested on his hips as he surveyed the perilous footing along the lip of the chasm.

"I'm not so sure." Fletcher wasn't convinced. "Look

there, where it's so narrow." He pointed. "That huge boulder will give a person something solid to hang onto."

"It's also something he has to go out and around from," Brig reminded him. "And you can't see what it's like on the other side of that boulder for about a foot or more."

"Supposing there's nothing there but empty space, so what?" Fletcher shrugged. "A foot is less than a man's stride. I think it can be crossed."

"It's suicide." Brig stared at the man with a determined look.

But Fletcher paid no attention to him. Turning, he said to Max. "How about it? Are you coming along with me?"

Max took a deep, gulping breath and pushed away from the rock supporting him. "Yeah, I'll come." He started forward.

Stunned, Brig looked from his cousin to Fletcher. But the hunter was already moving toward the narrow path at the base of the talus. Brig stopped in front of his cousin.

"Are you out of your mind, Max?" He spoke in a low, taut voice that wouldn't carry to Fletcher's hearing. "Look at you. You can hardly breathe. The muscles in your legs are probably trembling after that walk. It's insanity to go with him."

"Get out of my way, Brig." Max tried to make his breathing normal. "I didn't ask for your advice."

"Maybe you didn't ask for it, but you're getting it. Don't go."

"You can stay here if you want, but I'm following Fletcher." Max pushed him out of the way.

Brig watched the two of them. They were a pair of damn fools. He was supposed to be the guide, but neither of them were listening to him. He cursed angrily because he knew he had to go with them.

The first twenty yards presented no obstacles. Brig watched Fletcher carefully picking his way along in the lead. There was the consolation that the man was at least exhibiting some sense of caution. The path continued to narrow as the ground began to sheer away to the floor of the glacial ravine five hundred feet below. Brig didn't follow Max too closely. If the scree above them started moving, a man would be swept over the edge by the flow of rock—and anyone else who was close enough to get caught in the current would be swept along.

In the lead, Fletcher had reached the massive boulder. Hugging close to it, he began to inch his way around. Both Brig and Max slowed to watch. The strap of Fletcher's rifle sling became caught on a jagged edge. He had to stop to free it. Brig started to sweat. He didn't mind being afraid. It sharpened his senses and pumped the adrenalin into his veins. Fletcher edged around the rock and disappeared for a few seconds.

"It's all right on this side," he called softly to them.

"It's not too late to turn back, Max," Brig advised in a low voice.

All he received for an answer was a silencing glare of resentment. He waited while Max hugged around the boulder, then moved to take his place. Holding onto the solidness of the stone felt better than balancing unaided on the tightrope of the ledge. Rounding the boulder, Brig saw Fletcher pause to glance back at Max. From his angle, Brig could see the way the rim had started to crumble about a foot or more from the boulder. The area had been undermined, leaving a shaky lip. Dirt and loose pebbles trickled from the underside as Max approached it. The faulted area was no wider than a man's stride. Brig expected Max to step across it. When he saw Max's foot coming down, it was squarely in the center of the undermined area. Brig knew instinctively the thin crust would never support his cousin's weight.

"Max, don't step there."

But the warning came too late. Max was too overbalanced to change the placement of his foot. The ledge took his weight for barely a second before the crust of earth crumbled. Max yelled and grabbed for anything that would stop him from falling.

Stretching, Brig gripped a jagged edge of the boulder and grabbed for a flailing arm. By some miracle, his fingers closed around Max's forearm near the wrist. He braced himself to take Max's weight, but nothing could prepare him for the tearing pressure. Max clutched his arm with both hands as the ground vanished beneath his feet. He kicked and fought for a toehold, but a river of rock was streaming through the gap in the ledge.

"Don't let me go, Brig. Don't let me go." Max whimpered in stark panic.

There were a hundred and forty pounds dangling on his arm. Brig expected any minute that Max's weight would yank his arm out of its socket. The pain was excruciating. Max's deathlike grip on his arm made it impossible for Brig to let go. If Max fell, he'd be pulled along with him.

"Dammit, Fletcher! Where the hell are you?" Brig gritted his teeth, feeling the muscles popping in his arm. "Help us!" A savage anger raged within him for the man who had risked their lives for a bighorn ram —a pair of horns to display on the wall of his den.

"I can't reach you." Fletcher's voice sounded far away. He was making no attempt to come closer.

Brig's fingers were slipping on the rock, losing their grip. He strained with all his might to counteract the weight pulling him into the yawning jaws of the mountainside. The knowledge stabbed knife-sharp that Jordanna was watching from the ridge. Brig didn't want her to see him die. Unexpectedly, the pressure on his arm was eased. Max had found a toehold. The relief was sweet. While maintaining the precarious foothold, Max searched for another, not panicking despite the whimpering sounds coming from his throat. Finally he was able to hook a knee over the solid part of the ledge and Brig found the strength to pull him the rest of the way to safety. Brig leaned against the rock, sweating and panting, while Max sat trembling on the edge, his eyes closed against the sight of the chasm. Brig's arm was numb. He wasn't even sure whether it was still attached to his body. He waited until he'd caught his breath, then glanced at his cousin.

"Come on, Max. Let's get off this ledge."

Max's face was white, a sickly color that told of nausea, but this wasn't the time to give in to its weakness. Max swallowed and crawled shakily to his feet, clutching the stone support of the boulder. Brig started the retreat, inching back around the boulder and walking the tightrope of the ledge to the point where it widened.

When he reached the comparative gentleness of the rugged mountain slope, Brig stopped and began rubbing his shoulder, trying to get the feeling back. Max appeared to crumble onto the ground, his legs refusing to support him any longer.

"I . . ." Max lifted his gaze to the man who had saved his life. For once, he seemed at a loss for words. "Thanks, Brig."

Brig could have called him forty kinds of fool for attempting to cross the ledge in the first place. It would have been a stupid way to die, but ignorance and inexperience had killed many a man. Brig knew Max would have thought twice about walking down a dark city alley at night, but he blithely walked onto that ledge without considering the danger it held. It had nearly killed him and Brig, too.

A rattle of stone heralded Fletcher's arrival. He glanced with a show of concern at Max before he looked to Brig. Brig felt the fury boiling up within him. The hand of his good arm doubled into a fist. This had all happened because of a damned pair of horns! There would be tremendous satisfaction in busting that man's face open.

"Are both of you all right?" Fletcher asked.

"Yeah." His lip curled in a wolflike snarl. "No thanks to you."

"There was nothing I could do." Fletcher misunderstood and thought the criticism was for his lack of help rather than his attempting to cross the slide area in the first place. "Once that ledge gave way and that rock started coming down, I couldn't get into a position to reach Max."

That was probably true. Brig had been too occupied to take much notice of Fletcher's position on the ledge. It was possible there had been no way for him to safely reach them without starting a major slide, sweeping all three of them to their deaths. Brig suspected that Fletcher had been more concerned with saving his own neck than rescuing them.

"The whole thing was a damned fool stunt." Brig wasn't about to forget whose idea it was. "You should have warned Max about that undermined area before he blundered onto it."

"I . . . thought he saw it." Fletcher frowned and shrugged at his weak excuse.

"Come on, Fletcher." Brig was contemptuous of the answer. "You know that a person could write on his little finger all the information Max knows about the dangers in this kind of country."

The hunter bristled defensively. "You're the guide. You were supposed to be out in front leading the way, not me."

"And I advised you that it was suicide to try to skirt that slide, but you ignored me," Brig shot back.

"If he hadn't come after us, I would have been killed," Max stated in a voice that still carried a tremor.

Fletcher turned to him. "Believe me, I know that, Max. I can't tell you how sorry I am that it happened, but it's too late for hindsight."

"You can say that again," Brig muttered. "We were damned lucky."

Half-turning, the hunter looked up the slope. "That ram is probably clear over the next mountain ridge by now."

My God, Brig thought, he's still thinking about that damned sheep! Fletcher was a self-centered man, never concerning himself with anyone else for long. He

wouldn't tolerate anyone standing in the way of something he wanted. The only way Brig could have stopped
him from going on the ledge would have been with
physical violence. The more Brig learned about the
man, the more wary of him he became.

His shoulder was starting to hurt. Brig preferred
the pain to the paralyzing numbness. He glanced at
Max to see how he was recovering. He still looked
shaken, but more in control of his limbs.

"We'd better start back," he said.

Brig walked over and slipped a hand under Max's
arm to help him to his feet. The trio started back for
the high ridge, taking a more direct line, no longer
needing to conceal themselves from the bighorn ram
that had since fled. Neither he nor Fletcher commented
on Max's wet pants.

Halfway back, they were met by Jordanna and her
brother. Her eyes were wide with concern and alarm
when she reached Brig. The brush with death made
him want to feel the life in her body against his. But
a glance at Fletcher's grim face kept him from sweeping her into his arms. The man puzzled Brig. On the
surface Fletcher endorsed, with his silence, Brig's relationship with his daughter, yet he appeared to resent
it at the same time.

Jordanna stopped before him, only inches separating them. Alert, she noticed the way he favored his
sore arm. She touched it hesitantly, as if aware the
contact could ignite an embrace.

"Are you hurt?" she asked.

"Not seriously."

"I was . . . worried about you." The admission was
made with a hesitation, and she glanced at her father.
"You shouldn't have tried it. You could have gotten
yourselves killed."

"Why did you?" her brother demanded, searching
Fletcher's face with an intent look. "You said you
wouldn't if it was too risky."

"Because I thought we could make it," was the impatient defense. "I did."

"But Max didn't," Kit accused. "He nearly fell to his death because of you."

"But he didn't." Fletcher was barely controlling his temper. "What has happened is over. There is nothing to be gained by rehashing it."

"Except to be sure nothing else like it happens," Kit murmured in a tone that sounded like a challenge. He flashed a cold glance at his father and walked over to Max. "Are you all right?"

"Yeah. And don't worry," Max said. "Your father can stalk his own game from now on. I'm not budging off the horse."

"First we have to get to the horses," Brig reminded him, and the small party started forward again.

After the long climb back to where the horses were left, it was a welcome relief to their legs to ride the distance back to the camp. A quarter-mile from camp, the buckskin broke into a trot. Brig winced as the pace jarred his arm. As they dismounted near the picket line, the sharp-eyed Tandy Barnes noticed the careful way Brig held his arm so as not to aggravate the injury to his shoulder.

"What happened to you?" he wanted to know.

Brig explained briefly, and not too precisely, what had happened. He glossed over the accident as something that could have happened any time, and not as the result of Fletcher's foolhardy attempt to cross a dangerous slide area.

"Jocko and me will take care of the horses. You go on to camp and get some hot coffee in you," Tandy insisted. "As soon as I'm through, I'd better take a look at your shoulder."

It was paining him enough so that Brig didn't object to Tandy's examination. In the large tent, warmed by the shepherd's stove, he stripped to his pants, an action that stabbed him like a hot knife. Jordanna hovered near the table, watching as Tandy probed the shoulder with his sensitive fingers.

"It's lucky you didn't dislocate it. You should have

. . . if you was a normal man," the stocky cowboy grumped.

"I just pulled some muscles." Brig pulled away from the pushing, prodding fingers that were adding to his pain.

"Yeah, you pulled some muscles, all right, and sprained 'em, and wrenched 'em, and every other damned thing," Tandy scoffed at the light dismissal of the injury. "We'd better wrap that shoulder up some to support them muscles and give 'em a chance to rest." He turned to the Basque shepherd looking on. "Jocko, do . . ."

"Si, I will get some bandages." Jocko answered the question before it had been asked.

Jocko walked over to a corner of the tent and opened a pack containing first aid supplies. From it, he took out a wide roll of elastic bandage to give to Tandy. Tandy began wrapping the injured shoulder, but his attempt was clumsy.

"If you was a horse, I'd know how to do this," he muttered to Brig and unwound the bandage to start all over.

"Let me do it." Jordanna stepped forward to take the flesh-colored bandage from the cowboy's hand.

"Do you think you know how?" Brig taunted, not in the best of moods.

"I've had several weeks of training," she replied calmly. "It's handy knowledge to have on a hunting trip. You never know when you might need it."

Her hands were gentle and efficient. She stood close to him to secure the end of the bandage, bent at the waist, her long hair falling forward across one shoulder and glinting red in the lantern's light. Her familiar scent drifted to him. She smelled of horses and saddle leather mixed with a clean, sensual fragrance.

Despite the primitive conditions of the camp, she washed frequently, heating the water in a kettle over the open fire and sponge bathing in the privacy of the tent. He'd seen her silhouette on the canvas walls on more than one occasion. It hadn't been a provocative act on her part, but the result had been the same, the indistinct outline of her body and his own imagination firing his blood with desire. The same look was written in his stone-brown eyes now.

His shoulder was firmly bound. As Jordanna smoothed the end of the material, she glanced at him. "Is that all right?"

"It's fine." The discomfort that the injury was causing him was far from Brig's mind at the moment, and she saw it in his look.

She straightened, avoiding his eyes as her gaze flickered to Tandy and Jocko. The hint of self-consciousness seemed to be more for their sake than hers. She reached for the long-sleeved, thermal undershirt draped across the wooden bench.

"I'll help you put this on," she said.

"It looks like you're in good hands, Brig." Tandy moved to the tent flap. "I'll go get that firewood you were wanting, Jocko."

"I will come with you. I need to get some water from the stream to heat so the men can wash up." Jocko found an excuse to leave them alone.

When Jordanna turned to him with the shirt, Brig reached out to slide a hand over her thigh, clasping her hipbone to draw her close. He buried his face in the valley between her breasts, layers of clothing keeping his mouth from her bare skin. He listened to the reassuring sound of her heartbeat and pulled her down to his knee while his mouth worked its way up to hers. Her lips were creamy smooth and the kiss lingered possessively.

"Today . . ." she began and Brig knew she was wanting to talk about the accident.

"I don't want to talk about this afternoon." He didn't want to remember the way his thoughts had turned to her when he thought they wouldn't make it. Brig stood her up. "Help me with the undershirt."

After she had helped him slip his arms into the sleeves and drew the thermal shirt over his head, Brig refused her assistance with his flannel shirt, managing it on his own—if painfully. He flexed his injured shoulder. It would be a few days before there was any freedom of movement without pain.

"Would you like some coffee?" Jordanna was at the stove, a cup poured for herself.

"No."

Leaving her cup sit, Jordanna put on her heavy parka. "I think I'll go outside for a while."

Brig watched her go without raising an objection.

Max was alone by the fire when Jordanna stepped out of the tent. Tandy was just approaching with an armload of firewood. Jocko was walking from the direction of the stream, carrying a bucketful of water. Jordanna glanced around for her father and brother. Sipping her coffee, she walked to the fire.

"Where's Dad and Kit?" she asked the man huddling close to the fire.

Max looked at her blankly for an instant, then shrugged. "I don't know. They walked off somewhere. I wasn't paying much attention," he admitted.

Jocko heard the inquiry and offered the information. "I saw them down by the stream."

"Thanks." Jordanna paused by the fire for a moment, then wandered off in the direction of the mountain stream.

As she drew near, she heard the rushing sound of the stream. The water scrambled over its rock-strewn bed, polishing the stones smooth and hammering off the rough edges. It was sharply clear and cold. Jordanna followed the snaking course it took, where the mountain offered the least resistance.

The sound of voices raised in anger slowed her steps as she tried to locate the men. Some distance ahead of her, Jordanna saw her father and brother arguing. The tumbling water blotted out their words, but nothing interfered with her vision. Jordanna had never seen her father look so angry. And whatever Kit was saying to him was only making it worse.

While Jordanna watched, her father unleashed a back-handed slap that reeled Kit backwards to the ground. She gasped in shock and rushed forward. Without waiting for Kit to rise, her father stalked off in the direction of camp. When she reached him, Kit was just pushing himself to his feet and rubbing his jaw. After one glance, he avoided her eyes.

"Are you all right?" she questioned anxiously.

"Yes." He worked his jaw carefully.

"Why did he hit you? What were you arguing about?" Jordanna couldn't imagine what Kit had possibly said to him that would incite her father to violence.

Kit hesitated, met her look for a searching moment, then turned away. "You wouldn't believe me if I told you," he muttered.

"What kind of an answer is that?" she demanded.

"Just leave it, Jordanna." The set of his jaw told her as plainly as his words that he wouldn't discuss it with her.

At the sound of the tent flap being lifted, Brig turned. He had half-expected Jordanna to return, but it was Jocko who entered the tent. Disappointment flickered in his eyes before it was screened from sight, but not before the shepherd had seen it.

"She has gone to the stream to look for her father and brother," Jocko informed him.

"I don't recall asking," Brig snapped. Was he so transparent?

"No, you did not ask," Jocko admitted and laughed softly.

Brig walked to the stove and poured himself a cup of coffee, aware that he had refused it from Jordanna. It was black and strong, the way he liked it. He carried the cup to the crude, wooden table and sat down on the rough bench.

"Have you noticed her lately?" Jocko was at the stove, getting a cup for himself.

"Who? Jordanna?"

"Si. Jordanna." The Basque mocked Brig's feigned attempt at ignorance.

"What about her?" Brig stared at his cup, feeling the agitation stirring within him like a boiling caldron.

"We have been in the mountains more than a week already and she has not changed. If anything she has grown more beautiful."

"That's natural. Being the only woman, she's bound to look more beautiful," Brig dismissed the statement.

"No, you do not understand me." Jocko's reproval was gentle, as if correcting a child. "It is that she thrives on hardship. She grows stronger on the challenge of these mountains. She can saddle her own horse, hunt her own game, cook her own food, wash her own clothes, and treat injuries. She is not frightened or intimidated by the isolation. She does not long for civilization or the comforts of a soft bed."

"So?" The enumeration of all her qualities wasn't necessary. He had noticed all those things that demanded his admiration. Her self-assurance, her strength in adversity, her warm willingness in bed, and her basic capabilities were all traits he had imagined in the ideal woman. That Jordanna possessed them, he didn't need to be told.

"She is a rare woman," Jocko stated. "She is like the pioneer women who came West with their husbands and families and worked side by side with them to build a new life."

"You left out one key ingredient, Jocko. A heart." Why had he said that?

"You think your woman does not have one?" He gave Brig a quizzical look.

Brig rose from the table as Jocko was about to sit down. "I didn't say that."

"No?" The one word was more than skeptical.

"No." His was a flat denial. Something was bothering him. He couldn't put his finger on it.

"I know she is more than just a woman to you. Is it that you are afraid to admit you care?" Jocko gave him a sad look that held pity.

"She warms my sleeping bag on a cold mountain night. She bandages my shoulder. She rides beside me. Yes, I care," Brig agreed in a confused, irritated voice. "But we're here to hunt sheep, remember. And her father wants a trophy bighorn." With a passion that had nearly killed Max this afternoon—and himself.

"What does this have to do with Jordanna? You are making things sound complicated." Jocko shook his head.

"That's because you are a shepherd, Jocko. Everything to you is very simple." Brig was over-ridden by a suspicion that it wasn't. "You don't know how devious and cunning the rich and self-centered people of this world can be in order to get what they want. It's a world of coyotes, Jocko," he declared. "I should know. I used to live in it. One coyote alone will attack only something that is weaker—a newborn lamb or a crippled animal. But you know what a pack of them will do, Jocko. Working together, coyotes can bring down a full grown elk." He glanced toward the tent-flap. "We might have a hunting party of four coyotes out there. I have an uneasy feeling that we shouldn't trust them any farther than you can spit, Jocko."

"Something happened today that you did not mention?" Jocko guessed.

"Just remember what I said." Brig took a swig of his coffee and reached for his sheepskin jacket, draping it over his shoulders before walking outside to the fire.

The next day Max decided to stay in camp with Jocko and Tandy. Yesterday's experience was too vivid in his mind. Brig couldn't blame him, although he had seen the glitter of disdain in Fletcher's look.

It was just as well Max had stayed at camp. It had been one of those days that tested the patience of a hunter. Jordanna had picked out a ram from a bachelor group. Its horns hadn't been the size of the bighorn her father sought, but considerably larger than anything else they had seen. They would have run close to forty inches, only the ram had spooked at the last minute. Her shot had missed and there hadn't been time for a second. They had spotted Fletcher's ram several times, but it was always on the move, scrambling somewhere. Their attempts to second-guess where he was going had continually proved to be wrong. It was a disgruntled and disgusted Fletcher Smith who returned to the base camp at twilight.

It was Max who became the butt of his displeasure. After the evening meal, they were all sitting around the campfire. Fletcher had been discussing with Brig where they would be most likely to find his ram the next day. Since they had never seen the bighorn monarch in the same place twice, Brig had refused to hazard a guess, which didn't please Fletcher.

He turned to Max and taunted him, "What about you? Are you going with us tomorrow? Or are you staying in camp again?" There was scorn in his look.

Max went white, but attempted a different response. "I don't know. I haven't thought about it."

"If you don't have the stomach for it, you might as well stay here," Fletcher stated in a voice that said he was convinced Max didn't have it.

"As a matter of fact," Kit spoke up, "I was considering staying in camp tomorrow. Like you, Max, I think a change of pace is a good idea once in a while. We aren't after a trophy like Dad, so there isn't any reason for us to go out every day."

"That's right," Max was quick to agree with him. "Although, who knows? In the morning, I might feel like riding along with the others."

"You must suit yourself, of course," Fletcher said and leaned back against a log to puff on his pipe. "I've been thinking about that stock of yours, Max. If I decide to buy it, how would you want the transaction to be done?"

Fletcher had thrown out the lure and like a hatchery fish, Max snapped at it. The two men became embroiled in a legal and financial discussion that lasted the rest of the evening. Before they retired, Max was talking about continuing the discussion the next day—which meant he had decided to go along.

A cynical dryness was in Brig's eyes. His cousin's fear wasn't as great as his greed. He'd risk anything to get the money from Fletcher. Max had proven that. Brig walked to the small tent, kneading his sore shoulder.

Chapter XV

"THE BUCKSKIN'S GOT a loose shoe." Tandy made the explanation to Brig while he saddled a big bay pack-horse that doubled as a spare riding mount. "So you'll have to ride Jughead today."

"Jughead?" Jordanna glanced at Brig, a laughing twinkle in her eye. "What a terrible name to give a horse."

"Just be glad you don't have to ride that hard-mouthed, bull-headed, and downright stupid excuse for a horse." A lazy hint of a smile edged the corners of Brig's mouth.

"Is your shoulder bothering you this morning?" Tandy wanted to know, grunting as he tugged the cinch strap tighter. "Do you want me to top him off for you?"

Brig hesitated, then nodded. "You'd better. I might get bucked off and that would really be adding insult to injury."

He held the horse's bridle while Tandy swung aboard. Everyone, including Jordanna, had stepped to one side to watch. Tandy pulled his hat down tight on his forehead and settled deep into the saddle seat. When Brig let go of the bridle, the bay horse gave his audience a spirited bucking exhibition. With a rolling snort of defeat, the gelding smoothed out his back and swung into a trot.

"Does he always do that?" Jordanna asked, a smile still softening her mouth.

"With a rider or a pack saddle," he nodded.

Tandy rode up to them and dismounted, handing the reins to Brig. Jordanna stood beside her sorrel. She never tired of watching the way Brig stepped into the saddle. The action was smooth, one fluid motion. Astride the horse, his gaze swung to her. She moved to the side of the sorrel, but as she put her foot in the stirrup, she noticed the saddle was loose. She started to tighten the cinch.

"I'll do it." Tandy was right there. "Dandy always blows himself up. I forgot to check him."

"There's something wrong with my horse," Max stated. "He won't move."

Jordanna glanced over to the brown-spotted gelding. Max was jamming his heels into the horse's side, but it didn't even flicker an eyelash. It stood as unmoving as a statue, despite his rider's harsh proddings.

"The cinch might be too tight," Tandy suggested. "I'll be there in a minute."

"I'll do it, Tandy," Fletcher volunteered and swung down from his horse. He walked to the pinto and looked up at Max. "You'll have to get off," he told him with taunting patience.

"I didn't know."

Fletcher loosened the cinch a fraction and adjusted the saddle to be certain it was sitting squarely on the horse's back, then stepped away. "Try that, Max."

He mounted and kicked the horse. "It still won't go," Max declared in disgust.

Tandy slapped the belly of the sorrel horse and snugged Jordanna's saddle cinch tighter. "Maybe there's a crimp in the saddle blanket. That paint is a canny horse. He won't go one step if there's something wrong with the gear. He had a bad back when we got him. I guess he made up his mind it wasn't going to happen to him again."

Max dismounted again and Fletcher completely loosened the cinch. He checked under the saddle and under the saddle-pad, smoothing them out. At one point he stopped.

"I think I found it, Tandy," he said. "There was a little crease in the pad."

"That probably did it."

When Max climbed into the saddle again, the spotted horse stepped right out. "That's a smart horse, Max," Smith observed, and walked back to his own.

Within minutes they were all mounted and Brig led them away from camp. Jordanna rode behind him. It had become her place in line. She liked following his broad shoulders. She always felt especially safe and secure when he was around—not that she had ever really been frightened, because she hadn't. It was a sensation she couldn't explain.

The plan for the day's hunt was to return to the place where they had first sighted the big ram. It was close to camp. From it, they could begin a circle to the other places until they found either that ram or one for Jordanna.

She glanced back at the rest of the group. Max was directly behind her, followed by her father, and finally Kit. He had decided to come after Max changed his mind about staying in camp. Jordanna had found it slightly touching the way her brother had leaped to defend Max last night from her father's baiting. Of course, Kit hadn't understood that their father hadn't meant to be so biting. It was his frustration over that elusive ram, something which she well understood.

The thought of the two of them reminded her of the argument she had witnessed. She had hoped this trip would patch the division between them, but it seemed to be worse. Why? She couldn't find a cause.

Absorbed in her thoughts, Jordanna didn't notice

that Brig had stopped. The sorrel horse halted of its own accord alongside him. She glanced at Brig, who had directed his binoculars to the valley below them.

"What is it?" Her own binoculars were suspended around her neck, secured to her jacket front so they wouldn't bounce as she rode.

"A black bear." Brig lowered his glasses for a minute and looked again. "Near that copse of trees. See it?"

Jordanna located the movement and focused her lenses on it. The bear was some distance below them, a dark spot ambling along until the magnification of her binoculars gave him shape. He looked no bigger than an overgrown labrador retriever. The darkness of its shaggy coat made the bear smaller than it was over a long distance. It continued its rolling gait and disappeared in the trees.

"There is so much game in these mountains." Jordanna lowered her binoculars and glanced at Brig. The small cut on his jaw brought a smile to her lips.

Brig watched it form with disconcerting interest. "What brought that?"

"I was remembering what a terrible time you had shaving this morning—until I took over." The warmth of her voice was faintly teasing.

For a minute a smile played with his mouth, then disappeared. "I think I set a dangerous precedent when I trusted you with a razor," he murmured and clicked to his horse.

As he started forward, her frown was both amused and puzzled. Brig had sounded almost serious. Her sorrel horse fell back into line. A steep switchback trail was just ahead, winding through the trees to the crest of the ridge. It was a stiff, zig-zagging climb, filled with places where the horses had to scramble for footing. Jordanna gave her mountain-bred horse its head, knowing it would do better without any interference from its rider.

The first half of the morning, they didn't spot a single sheep. Close to noon, they were belly-down on a ridge glassing a natural sheep basin with a small alpine lake, good graze, and steep, craggy cliffs. The area seemed empty of bighorns.

"Look there, just entering the meadow." Her father sighted on the southerly edge of the slope.

"I see them," Jordanna answered as three rams walked warily into the meadow. "One looks good sized."

"It's hard to tell from here," he said. "They are too far away for me to tell whether that one has a chipped horn or not."

"We'll ride closer," Brig said. "We can approach them upwind by riding just below that ridgeline to the right." He scanned the area again. "It shouldn't be too difficult a stalk from that point."

Mounting, they rode along the shoulder of the ridge, its backbone hiding them from sight. At a point Brig had picked out, they stopped and edged their way up to the crest. The trio of bighorns were still there, grazing not far from the place they had first seen them. The ram with the chipped horn was not among them, but the larger of the three was almost its equal. Jordanna studied it through the spotting scope before passing it to her father.

"It's a good one," he nodded. "Are you going to try for it?"

"Yes."

After a low discussion with Brig about the possible routes for a stalk, the degree of visibility of each, and the winds, Jordanna chose the one she preferred. Together, she and Brig began the slow, delicate process of a stalk, trying to make any exposed moves when the ram's head was down grazing, or when he was looking in the opposite direction.

When Jordanna reached a large boulder within fifty yards of her target, Brig was right beside her. His look said this was as close as they could get. There was a glint of reluctant admiration in his eyes that her skilled and silent stalking had brought them this close.

She laid the barrel of the .30–06 over the boulder,

cradling the fore-end in her left hand, and snuggled down behind it. Her throat was dry and she felt shaky. Ram fever. She took a couple of silent breaths to help the fever pass. Sighting for a point low behind the brown shoulder, she gently squeezed the trigger. The rifle boomed in the mountain stillness, shattering the air and echoing through the stone walls. The ram took a rubbery step and collapsed, as if his legs had gone out from beneath him. The rifle shot had held the other younger rams paralyzed for an instant, before they bounded in a panic to the craggy heights.

The elation of success spilled through her. Jordanna rose from behind the boulder and secured her rifle. Her eyes were sparkling when her triumphant gaze swung to Brig. There was no expression in his.

"Let's go see what you've got." He started forward and she quickly followed.

Slightly winded, as much from the excitement as the short climb, Jordanna reached the lifeless body. It was a magnificent specimen, with a massive pair of broomed and battered horns. The tip of one had been broken off. The ram had been a part of many fights and, no doubt, conquered many ewes. Jordanna was proud of her trophy.

"Do you want to skin him here?" Brig wasn't giving her any time to revel in her success.

The area where the ram had fallen was relatively level, without any obstructions to interfere with the process. She glanced over her shoulder to see her father, brother, and Max cresting the ridge on their horses and riding toward them.

"Yes, this is a good place," she agreed and removed her folded knife from her belt.

Brig paused, glancing at her with startled skepticism. "Are you going to do it?" His knife was already in his hands, the blade snapped open.

"I do know how," Jordanna told him, her eyes laughing at his doubtful expression. "You're welcome to help, if you know what you're doing."

"Thanks," he offered dryly and stood back to let her begin.

Skinning for a shoulder mount, Jordanna started behind the foreleg and cut up the back. Brig helped her turn the animal over so she could continue to cut down the other side. After circling out the forelegs, she finished the cut behind the brisket. Her knifeblade sliced cleanly up the neck along the backbone and made a "T" cut at the base of the horns. Working at a comfortably steady pace, Jordanna skinned out the shoulders and neck, careful to avoid leaving any pieces of meat or fat clinging to the hide.

"You do know what you're doing," Brig commented.

"It's part of hunting." Jordanna tried to sound modest, but she was warmed by his compliment. Brig never praised unless it was earned. She had learned that much about him already.

"You do it very well; I've seen some hunters hack away at a hide until it's ruined." Brig took over to separate the head from the neck at the first joint.

The arrival of the rest of the hunting party provided Jordanna the tools to finish the job—a screwdriver to pry the skin away from the horns, a saw to cut the top of the skull, and a bag of salt to cure the hide. It was a long, tedious process that required painstaking care.

It was a heavy prize they carried back to camp, the horns alone weighing more than thirty pounds. A magenta sunset painted a spectacular rose hue across the valleys and mountaintops at twilight. There was an air of celebration in the camp that night, a sublime aura of success. The carefully folded hide was tucked in the shady cradle of a tree limb, where it would be safe from scavengers.

"Well, you've earned your first bonus, Brig. How do you feel about that?" Fletcher asked in cheerful challenge.

Brig was seated on a log stump, close to the blazing fire. Jordanna was sitting on the ground close by him, her shoulder not far from his thigh. She wished her father hadn't introduced that subject of money into the conversation, even in jest. It sounded crass.

After a hesitation, Brig answered, "Fine."

"We should have had sheep meat for supper tonight," Jocko changed the subject. "Have you ever eaten it?" He addressed the question to Jordanna as he refilled her tin mug with coffee from a speckled pot.

"No."

"I think it is the best of all wild meat, as good as corn-fed beef. There is very little wild taste to it," Jocko said.

"So speaks the shepherd," Max mocked the praise.

"It is not like mutton."

"But that bighorn sheep was old. The meat would have been tough, not worth cooking," Max continued his disparagement of sheep meat.

"Once this whole West was populated with bighorn sheep," Fletcher mused. "They were spread from the Dakotas to the Missouri River breaks, anywhere the land was rough and wild. They were more plentiful than deer. The Shoshone Indians—the Sheepeaters—hunted them the way the plains Indians hunted buffalo. Then man invaded the area with his cattle ranches and sheep. The bighorn sheep were driven out by over-grazed land and disease."

"Their scarcity and their elusiveness are what makes them such prized trophies," Brig pointed out.

"It's a shame their numbers can't come back the way the deer has," Jordanna mused.

"It could," her father insisted.

"How?" Kit asked.

"Look at Idaho. With the exception of some farming land in the south, it's basically marginal country, not good for much other than grazing a few cows or sheep. If the government stopped leasing this land to the ranchers for graze, the food supply for the bighorn and other wild game would increase. Also the dangers of infecting the wild sheep with disease from a domestic flock would be eliminated," he argued.

"In other words, you're saying, eliminate the cattle

and sheep industry in Idaho." Brig gave him a lazy look of cool challenge.

Fletcher laughed, a trifle self-consciously. "I forgot there was a rancher in our midst, but yes, that is what I'm saying. Big game hunting would do much more for the economy than the cattleman or shepherd. It would bring in money for license fees, outfitters, taxidermy costs, travel, motels, equipment, and so on. Big game hunting is big business, and would bring more cash to an area than a simple cattle ranch. Livestock and land developers are the enemies of wild animals."

"That would be something," Max gazed dreamily into the fire. "The whole State of Idaho turned into a giant game preserve, where the wealthy of the world would come to hunt."

Jordanna could see the gleam of dollar signs in his eyes. His comment didn't make her father's plan sound very altruistic.

"It wouldn't have to be confined to Idaho. There are thousands of acres in other western states that are equally suited to bighorns and other prize wild game. The bighorn, the grizzly, and the elk could all make a comeback," her father insisted, "along with the mountain goat, the cougar, and the wolf."

It sounded like a hunter's paradise—on the surface. Jordanna heard Brig's breath of disgust. He lifted his head, the flames casting light on his contemptuous expression, as his hard gaze flicked from Max to Fletcher.

"There are people in this country and millions in other parts of the world that are starving. You want to eliminate a cattle and sheep industry that can feed and clothe thousands of people so a handful of wealthy 'gentlemen' can indulge in a game of killing for sport. The little guys are around for you to step on and get a better view, aren't they?" He pushed to his feet, regarding them with scorn before cold cynicism curved his mouth. "What scares the hell out of me is that you could probably buy enough politicians to pull it off."

Brig emptied the bottom of his cup into the fire, the hot embers sizzling. "Excuse me, but I need some fresh air."

Moving with the silence of a stalker, he left the circle of the campfire and faded into the night's darkness. The moon disappeared behind a cloud bank. Tandy muttered something about checking the horses and Jocko began clattering the pots and pans to fill the heavy silence. Brushing the dust from her hands, Jordanna rose and wandered toward the tents. Her gaze drifted in the direction Brig had taken, but she didn't follow him. She glanced at the tree where the horns and hide of the bighorn were. Suddenly she didn't feel very proud of the kill.

Behind her, she could hear her father and Max talking, in much lower voices than before. Footsteps crunched on the rough ground behind her, where the pine needles had been swept away. She turned and saw her brother.

"That was quite a speech, wasn't it?" He watched her closely, his expression gentle.

"Yes." She shivered as a cold wind brushed her cheek. "I think I'm finally beginning to understand what you've been telling me all along."

"Do you?"

"Hunting for sport should have more purpose than just killing an animal to hang it on the wall and put money in someone's pockets. It should put food on the table," Jordanna said.

"I don't think I ever phrased it the way Brig did tonight, but it's what I meant," Kit nodded. "He's quite a man, Jordanna."

"Yes." She stared into the night.

There were very few details about him that she knew, but she felt she knew the essentials. He was strong enough to be gentle, cruel enough to be kind, and powerful enough to be vulnerable. He was hard, but it was the hardness of a solid rock. And she loved him. The knowledge came gently to her, warm and glowing, and burning ever brighter. It shimmered in her eyes when she turned to Kit.

"He's the best of his kind, Kit, perhaps the only one."

"You could be right."

"I . . ." Jordanna paused. There didn't seem to be anything more to say. Nothing more was necessary. ". . . I think I'll turn in. Good night, Kit."

"Good night." Her brother lingered for a minute after she turned toward the small tent, then wandered back to the campfire.

Jordanna stopped to collect the bulky sleeping bags. She had hung them out that morning to air and dry out the moisture from their bodies, before an accumulation of dampness affected the insulating capabilities. Maneuvering them inside the tent, she laid them out on the mattress of pine needles. Jordanna stripped to her longjohns and crawled inside the warmth of the double bag to brush her hair. She felt lost in the roominess of the doubled sleeping bags.

Setting her brush aside, she lay on her back to stare at a hole in the tent roof and wait for Brig. It was an hour before he entered the tent. The absence of light gave him a dark, looming shape. She wanted to talk, but she felt oddly tongue-tied. Brig, too, was silent as he undressed and slid his long frame inside the pocket opening of the sleeping bag. He made no attempt to come close to her.

"Brig?" Her voice was so low, it vibrated.

He moved, turning to her. His hand unerringly found her waist and pulled her to him. His mouth bruised her lips and Jordanna accepted his angry possession. Rough kisses chased each other over her face.

"You're a drug, Jordanna, that's been injected into my system," Brig muttered. "I get high on you . . . and damn every minute of the addiction."

"What if . . ." Her fingers trembled over his hard, lean features, memorizing them by touch. ". . . I told you that I thought I was . . . half in love with you? What would you say?"

She felt his momentary stillness. Lifting his mouth from her skin, he breathed out a silent sound. "That you might have been in the mountains too long. It might be that all we have is a physical addiction—not an emotional dependency. Let's don't be quick to confuse the two," he cautioned.

There was an ache in her throat because Jordanna knew it wasn't true for her. "Is that what you think?"

A roaming hand found its way inside the waistband of her long underwear. "It's possible," Brig murmured against her mouth.

The words to convince him died on her lips as Jordanna became lost in the seductive prowess of his touch. Her bones melted when they came in contact with his hard length. The erratic pulsing of her heart fluttered against her ribcage as his hard lips claimed hers. She held nothing back, glorifying in the blazing fires of his passion. Love ran molten-hot through her veins. Every particle of her body gave in to him, selflessly, asking nothing more in return than his possesion. Brig's answer was satisfaction—for both of them.

Afterwards they rested in each other's arms. The caress of his hands was absently gentle, no longer demanding.

"Your father promised me a bonus for a ram with a forty-inch curl," Brig said in soft mockery. "I didn't realize you were going to throw in your particular brand of reward as well."

His words indicated that he had sensed a difference in her response. He'd come up with his own reasoning. Hurt splintered through her.

"I wish I hadn't gotten that ram," Jordanna murmured.

His head turned, but he couldn't see her in the darkness. "Why?" Brig sounded amused, in a cynical way.

Jordanna hesitated to explain. But she could never convince him, because he wouldn't believe her. She rolled onto her side, away from him.

"It doesn't matter," she insisted in a husky reply. "It wouldn't change anything."

Brig stared at the dark shape of her head. His body felt cool where hers had lain against it. He resisted the impulse to pursue her earlier declaration of love, to discover if she had really meant it.

Ever since this hunt had started, all of his instincts had been warning him of some hidden danger. Yet his only vulnerability was in his feelings for Jordanna. Something warned him not to relax his guard.

Brig stared at the roof. Today she had stalked that sheep with the skill of a tigress and skinned her kill with the sureness of a hunter. Was he to be her next trophy? Why was he asking himself such a question?

He fought down the urge to curl her body to his length and turned his back to her instead.

Chapter XVI

IT WAS DARK and gray when Brig got up the next morning. Outside the tent, he could hear the whisper of a drizzling rain talking to the trees. He fastened his pants and reached for his shirt. His glance touched on the sleeping form and the gloss of dark copper hair. God, she was beautiful! The temptation was strong to crawl back in the sleeping bag to waken her. Bending down, Brig roughly shook her shoulder.

"It's time to get up."

Her lashes fluttered, then opened. Brig turned away to button his shirt. He was conscious that she didn't immediately climb out of bed. The knowledge pulsed through his loins. Brig took his time buttoning the shirt to keep his hands and part of his mind occupied.

The zip of the sleeping bag drew his glance. Her tall, slender figure was clad in white thermal underwear. Jordanna stretched away the sleep, arching her back like a cat. His heartbeat quickened at the thrusting outline of her firm breasts.

Brig looked away and began tucking his shirt inside

his Levis. "If you wore those longjohns in New York, you'd start a whole new fashion trend," he stated in a clipped voice.

"Do you think so?" she laughed and paraded in front of him in a mocking imitation of a fashion model, posturing and posing while she made an announcer's spiel. "This, ladies and gentlemen, is what the well-dressed debutante will be wearing this season. You will notice the way the material clings to the bodice and molds . . ."

If she had been doing a striptease, the fire in his veins couldn't have been any hotter. She was joking but there was sensuality in every movement. The tantalizing sight of her was more than he could stand. His arm hooked her waist to draw her to him and abruptly cut off her mocking speech. Before he could pull her completely into his arms, she was straining to reach his descending mouth. Her eagerness and ardency tightened the circle of his arms to crush her to his length. The action stabbed a sharp pain through his injured shoulder, forcing him to lessen his hold as he winced.

"Your shoulder. I forgot." Instantly Jordanna was contrite, running a hand over it in silent apology. Her hazel eyes were dark with concern. "How is it this morning?"

The fire was under control and Brig set her away from him. "It's better." He reached for his sheepskin-lined jacket. "You should get dressed before you catch cold." Brig ignored the invitation in her look. "It's misting rain today so be sure to have your poncho and plenty of warm clothes."

Without another glance, he slipped out of the tent and walked to the larger one. The air he breathed was heavy with moisture. Water dripped off the point of his hat brim. It was going to be a miserable, cold day. He ducked inside the flap of the larger tent, feeling the warmth and smelling the aroma of coffee and sizzling bacon. Brig realized he'd overslept.

A grumpy-looking Max was sitting on the bench,

hunched over the table and his cup of coffee. Kit was unzipping the sleeping bags and arranging them to dry. At the stove, Jocko was turning the bacon.

"Is Tandy still with the horses?" Brig asked.

"Si." Jocko glanced at him. "Fletcher is helping him this morning."

Brig would have liked a cup of coffee, but knowing the man who had hired him was out there in the misting rain doing his job turned Brig around. A woman's body had made his bed too soft and he'd slept longer as a result. Or so he convinced himself.

Halfway to the grassy area where the horses were picketed, he met Tandy coming back. "I see ya' finally woke up," the stocky cowboy greeted him with a faint grin.

Brig's mouth tightened at the comment. "Are the horses ready to go?" He glanced behind Tandy. "Where's Fletcher?"

"He's back with the horses." Tandy gestured over his shoulder in the direction he'd come from. "I was just comin' to see if you was awake. The pinto threw a shoe. I was wondering if you wanted me to saddle Jughead for Max or what?"

"Damn," Brig swore softly under his breath. "Why didn't you check the horses more closely?"

"I did," Tandy protested. "I didn't notice the pinto havin' any loose shoe last night. But this morning, there it was—on the ground."

"You're slowing up, Tandy. You aren't as sharp as you used to be. Age is finally catching up with you." Brig saw the older cowboy flinch then draw himself up with pride. Brig knew Tandy was sensitive about his accumulating years and he cursed himself for taking advantage of that vulnerability when he berated the cowboy's oversight. It hadn't been necessary.

"I checked that horse. I checked all the horses carefully. There wasn't no shoe loose on any of them," Tandy repeated in stiff defense. "What do you want to do about a mount for Max?"

"Saddle Jughead."

"Do you want me to top him off or do you think my bones are too brittle?" It was a sharp challenge. "They might have aged considerably since yesterday morning."

"Go ahead and bust the kinks out of him," Brig answered and hesitated. "I . . . didn't mean what I said earlier, Tandy. I was just . . . snapping. No coffee this morning."

"Well, go get some. I'll finish the horses. I don't need your help." The cowboy turned on his heel and walked back the way he had come.

Indecision made Brig hesitate. He was tempted to leave well enough alone and have the coffee as Tandy had suggested. But Fletcher was with the horses, assuming his responsibility. He took a step after Tandy.

"Brig?" Jordanna called to him and he stopped, looking back. She was hurrying toward him, a tin mug of coffee in her hand. The hood of her poncho had slipped off her head. The dark sheen of moisture hid the mahogany cast of her hair. She stopped beside him to hand him the cup.

"Jocko said you hadn't had any coffee yet." Water dripped off the tip of her nose.

"Your hair is getting wet." Ignoring the cup, he reached out to lift the rainhood over her head. Then his hands cupped her head, rainhood and all. The moistness of her lips was too much of a temptation and he kissed the rain-clean sweetness of them. Afterwards, Jordanna rubbed her cheek against the rasping stubble on his jaw.

"You haven't shaved yet," she murmured. "Shall I do it for you?"

There were at least half a hundred things he wanted her to do for him. Desire gnawed at him like a dog worrying a bone. His hands slid to her shoulders and Brig set her firmly away from him.

"I can manage on my own," he insisted and the meaning stretched to other things besides shaving.

"Your coffee." Jordanna prompted him, holding up the cup as a reminder. Brig took it, glad of the minor distraction. "You'd better drink it. The rain has probably cooled it, as well as diluted it."

The sip he took was a little hotter than lukewarm, but it was black. "I needed that," he muttered—in more ways than one.

"Where were you going?"

"To help with the horses." Brig knew he should walk away, but the rain-washed freshness of her face kept him rooted.

"Breakfast is almost ready."

"I know. I . . ." A commotion from the horses turned Brig. Tandy was on the heavy-boned bay horse in a repeat performance of yesterday morning's bucking exhibition. After a couple of minutes, the bay horse crow-hopped a few yards and quit.

"Are you riding him again today?" Jordanna asked.

"No. Max draws the unlucky number this morning. The pinto threw a shoe."

"Poor Max." She smiled, but with little genuine sympathy.

"Don't you like him much? He's a friend of your father's."

"He's your cousin," Jordanna reminded him.

"Yes. Unfortunately."

"If you feel that way about him, why did you save him? Wouldn't you be better off if he wasn't around?" The instant the words were out she appeared to regret them, as if she had blurted them out without stopping to think.

Brig found the questions curious. His gaze narrowed on her in hard appraisal. Where had she gotten her information? Not from Max, he was certain. That didn't leave many alternatives. He thought of her near declaration of love last night. At the time, some wary instinct had kept him from believing it wholly. The sensation came rushing back this morning.

"What makes you think Max has anything I want?" he challenged smoothly.

"I don't." Her answer was fast—too fast. "I didn't mean anything by it. Forget it, Brig."

"There's a lot I would like to forget." He gave her a long, considering look that mentally stripped away the layers of garments that hid her body from his eyes. "How sensual you are behind that self-possessed composure. How you quiver in my arms. What it's like to hold your breasts in my hand—and feel you under me." He saw the flush rising in her cheeks. "This moment I would like to undress you very slowly and kiss every inch of you." Brig paused deliberately to test her with his next remark. "You are very good on your back, Jordanna."

She gasped in outrage at his demeaning tone. Brig saw the arc of her hand and did nothing to stop or elude it. The stinging numbness on his cheek was oddly pleasant. Her retaliation was what he had expected, and wanted, but he wasn't totally satisfied.

"You are a bastard, Brig McCord!" she hissed at him, her eyes glittering with fury. "There is more to life than sex."

"But sex is all there is between you and me. There's nothing wrong with unadulterated lust. You can't deny it's mutually satisfying." In spite of himself, he continued to prod, needing more proof.

"Has it?" Her jaw was taut, but there was a welling of tears in her eyes.

"If it hasn't, you've been a damned good actress, but I always suspected that you were." Brig waited for her to deny it, driven by some angry need to hear the words.

"I am. The funny part is, I played the role of lover for so long I almost began to believe it," she laughed bitterly.

"Liar!" Her sudden agreement prompted his denial. "You weren't faking those responses."

"Wasn't I?" she taunted and turned away from him.

Anger flashed inside him. Brig grabbed her arm to stop her. "Don't walk away from me." It was a bitter blow to his pride to realize that he still didn't want to let her go.

"Take your hand off of me," Jordanna ordered in

a voice icy with disdain. "I don't have to pretend to like your touch any more. The game is over."

"I'll say when it's over. Remember that," Brig warned, but released her arm to let her go.

Jordanna choked back the tears. She hated him as violently as she loved him. It hadn't mattered before that his need for her was only sexual. She had lulled her pride into believing it would change in time—that she might make him fall in love with her. But he had pulled their relationship down to such a base level that what once had been beautiful became unclean.

Why had she lied to him, pretended it had all been an act? To save face. To rescue some of her self-respect. Before he touched her again, he would have to get down on his hands and knees and beg.

Avoiding the large tent, she walked to the smaller one. She zipped apart the two sleeping bags, gathered Brig's belongings together and stacked them in a pile. When it was done, much of her composure had returned, enough to permit her to go to the larger tent to eat breakfast.

There was a bad taste in his mouth when Jordanna walked away. Her erect carriage, the stiff, proud lines of her body reminded Brig of a child who had been unjustly accused of telling a lie and sent to her room without supper. He was angry with himself. But, dammit, he'd been right! He took a swallow of coffee. It had become cold and bitter. With a disgusted flick of his wrist, he emptied the contents of the mug on the ground.

"What are you doin', throwing away good coffee like that?" Tandy frowned.

Brig jerked his head around at the cowboy's silent approach. "It was cold." He looked beyond him. "Are the horses all ready?"

"Yep. And my stomach is ready for some breakfast."

"Where's Fletcher? I thought he was with you."

"He's right behind me. He was just tying Jughead up." Tandy glanced over his shoulder just as Fletcher Smith emerged from the stand of trees near the clearing.

Brig thought he saw the hunter's gaze sharpen at the sight of him. But in the next second, he decided he was mistaken as the man smiled and greeted him.

"Good morning, Brig. How's the shoulder today?"

"Much better."

"Good. Where's Jordanna? Wasn't she with you?" Fletcher glanced around curiously.

"Breakfast is ready. I think she went to eat."

"It sounds like a good idea for us, too." Fletcher seemed in an amiable, confident mood. He fell into step beside Brig. "I think we should follow the same route that we did yesterday, don't you?"

Hunting sheep wasn't exactly the foremost thought on his mind, but it was what he was getting paid for, regardless of how much that fact stuck in his throat. Brig nodded in agreement. "It might prove as successful as it did yesterday for Jordanna."

"I'm counting on it." Fletcher paused to hold back the tent flap for Brig to enter first.

Jordanna was inside, but she didn't even glance up when they entered. The expression on her face seemed to be chiseled out of cold marble. She didn't say one word to him during the entire meal. Only once did her gaze happen to encounter his and there was a frosty coolness in her look. But he noticed the way she picked at her food, instead of eating heartily the way she usually did. She wasn't as indifferent to him as she would like him to believe. It was a relief to have that belief confirmed.

When everyone was finished eating and the final cup of coffee was downed, they left the shelter of the tent and walked through the drizzle to the horses. The big bay horse acted skittish when Max climbed into its saddle. Snorting and tossing its head, it danced around.

"Maybe I should ride him," Fletcher suggested. "You might not be able to handle him, Max."

"I'll handle him," Max insisted, jerking roughly on the reins to make the horse stand.

"He'll settle down," Tandy promised.

"You can change horses if you want to," Brig said.

"I said I didn't," Max snapped.

"Okay. Let's go." Brig turned the buckskin toward the trail they had taken the past several days.

Only this time the order of the riders changed. Fletcher rode behind him instead of Jordanna. She followed Kit, with Max bringing up the rear. Brig missed having her behind him and riding alongside him where the trail permitted. It irritated that he should be bothered by such a small thing.

As they neared the steep switchback that took them over the crest of the ridge, Brig turned in his saddle. "With this rain, it will be slippery in spots. Give your horses all the rein they want. They'll find the solid footing."

His sweeping glance saw the nods of understanding —all except for Jordanna, who looked coolly in the opposite direction. Tightlipped, Brig faced the front and gave the buckskin its head as it started the climb.

The creaking of saddle leather and jangling bits was drowned out by the sharp sounds of many hooves striking stone, scraping and scrambling on slippery rock. Behind him, Brig heard a horse snorting and rumbling angry whinnies of refusal. He didn't like taking his eyes off the trail and he was unwilling to stop the lunging buckskin's momentum. It wasn't so easily regained on a wet steep trail like this.

He stole a quick glance down and over his shoulder. The bay horse Max was riding was acting up, rearing and shaking its head and trying to refuse the trail. Max was hitting at it with the reins and jamming his heels into its flanks.

"You damned, stupid Jughead!" Max cursed the horse.

Swearing to himself, Brig rode the buckskin off the trail and stopped. "Take the lead, Fletcher." He waved the man on. He'd have to let the others go by before he could go back down the narrow trail to help Max. As Kit went by him, the bay horse made a lunge forward at Max's urging. Then it reared and squealed angrily. Coming down on all fours, it lowered its head and started to buck. Jordanna slowed up. "Move out of the way," Brig ordered impatiently, the buckskin dancing beneath him. She flashed him a cold look and hurried the sorrel up the trail.

The bay horse had bucked himself off the trail. Max had abandoned his efforts to control the horse and clung to the saddlehorn with both hands, trying to stay on. His expression showed desperation and fear. As the horse attempted to pitch its rider, it lost its footing on the steep, slippery slope. After falling to its knees, the bay scrambled to its feet in panic.

Its flight had carried the horse and rider wide of the trail. The footing was treacherous, with patches of scree scattered over the entire portion of that area of the slope. Brig couldn't hurry his buckskin once it left the trail or it would begin floundering the way Max's horse was.

Loose rock slid from under the bay's hooves. The horse reared, screaming in panic. Over-balanced, without solid footing, it went over backwards. Max yelled and tried to dive off on the downhill side. He rolled down the steep grade, the bay horse, with its deadly flailing legs, only a few feet behind him. An isolated landslide of loose rock carried them along while the gravity of the sharp incline pulled them down. At the base of the slope, the mountain dropped away a hundred feet to a shoulder of rock and trees.

There wasn't any way Brig could reach them before they came to the bottom. As it was, his buckskin was covering a lot of distance sliding on its haunches and snorting nervously all the while. A lariat was tied to his saddle, but Max's headlong descent was twice as rapid as his, putting him out of reach of Brig's rope.

Twenty feet from the rim, the bay horse managed to get its legs beneath it. Lunging like a fear-crazed animal, it struggled to leap to solid ground. Its tearing, clawing hooves unleashed a new torrent of rocks that trapped Max in its current. Brig saw it and reined in his horse. He was one tight band of coiled grimness.

Jordanna had stopped her horse on the trail behind Kit's and her father's. In fascinated horror, she watched the scene unfold. There was a strange unreality to it. She wanted to believe it wasn't happening, that somehow Brig would reach Max.

"Oh, my God," she whispered when she saw it wasn't possible.

As Max was swept helplessly toward the edge, Jordanna looked away and shut her eyes tightly. A blood-curdling scream rent the air. It seemed to last for an eternity, bouncing off granite-walled canyons and echoing through the mountains. It was finally ended by a dull thud. Jordanna felt violently ill at the unearthly silence that followed.

There were voices, but they didn't penetrate her consciousness until one sharply demanded her attention. "Turn your horse, Jordanna. We must go down."

At her father's terse reminder that she was blocking the trail, Jordanna turned her sorrel mount on the narrow trail and started down. Her wide, shock-glazed eyes sought the base of the slide. Brig had dismounted and was walking down the loose rock to the edge. The bay horse was standing on the other side of the talus, its legs scraped and blooded, not moving.

They rode all the way down to where the zigzagging trail straightened out in the direction of camp. There, her father dismounted, followed by Kit, and started toward the base of the slope where Max had fallen. Jordanna hesitated. An inner force compelled her to go with them. She stepped out of the saddle onto shaky legs, accepting the churning tightness of her stomach.

Brig was standing near the rim, a few feet from the shale-like rock slide, when they reached him. His face was impassive as he looked down. He didn't glance at them, but he was aware of their presence.

"The poor, stupid bastard. I warned him the mountains would kill him," he murmured absently.

"He's dead, then," her father said in an emotionless voice.

Unwillingly, Jordanna's gaze was drawn over the edge. A hundred feet below sprawled the figure of a man, horribly contorted, lifeless like a ragdoll. Reeling, she turned away from the cliff and her brother's arm curved around her shoulders. She wanted to cry—to let tears ease the burning dryness of her eyes and the hot ache in her throat. But she was encased in a freeze-burn of shock, icy and trembling.

"We'll have to go down and get his body," Brig stated.

"I'll come with you," Fletcher volunteered quietly. "Kit, why don't you take Jordanna back to camp and tell the others what happened."

Her brother didn't respond directly to the request. He turned Jordanna toward the waiting horses. "Come on." The arm around her shoulders provided support and the impetus to walk. Jordanna started shivering with the stark, cold terror of what had happened.

"I should have done something," she whispered in an attack of guilt. "I was the closest. When he first had trouble with the horse, I should have taken hold of the bridle and led it to the top."

"Don't think things like that," her brother remonstrated gently, adding with hesitation, "I'm . . . not sure anyone's to blame."

"Oh, God." The mute prayer came out in a dry sob.

"I'll get the horse." Fletcher took a step to cross the loose rock and reach the bay horse.

"You stay here," Brig ordered. "I'll get him."

Climbing up a few feet, where the band of scree was narrower, Brig gingerly worked his way across. Miniature avalanches of stone were touched off by each careful footstep. A deadly calm robbed him of any feeling except caution.

The horse was trembling like a cowering dog when

Brig reached it. It appeared terrified to move from the solid ground beneath its feet. When Brig reached for the dangling reins, it shied, tossing its head and snorting nervously. Its rolling eyes showed the white of fear. Brig talked softly to the horse before making a second attempt for the reins. Its ears swiveled nervously at the sound of his voice, but the next time the bay didn't try to elude the hand that reached for the reins.

Brig stroked the quivering hide of its neck. The horse stood, not resisting his touch, its tremors beginning to dissipate. Assured that the horse would not suddenly panic, Brig let his gaze inspect the bay's injuries. There were scratches on its withers and flank. Patches of hide had been scraped from its legs, exposing raw flesh, blood oozing from the lacerations. But there was no sign that the horse was favoring any leg unduly, which meant no broken bones.

Gripping the reins close to the horse's chin, Brig started to lead the gelding across the loose rocks. The horse resisted, straining away from the pressure pulling him forward. Brig tugged on the reins and continued to talk to him. Reluctantly, trembling with every step, the horse submitted to the commands, snorting and whickering nervously.

"Are you going to take the horse back to camp?" Fletcher asked when Brig had led the horse across the slide.

"No. We'll tie him up along the trail and pick him up after we've recovered Max's body." Not pausing, Brig walked to where he had left his buckskin and Fletcher followed behind the slightly limping bay horse.

Fletcher had left his horse on the trail, so Brig led the buckskin as well as the bay to that point, and then mounted, leading the bay to a stand of trees farther along the trail. Fletcher hesitated, unsure about something.

"Aren't you coming with me?" Brig's question was a challenge, his expression stone-cold. "Haven't you ever seen a dead man before? It isn't much different than a bighorn or an elk—except the body once was human."

The gray-haired man flashed him an angry look. "I'm coming." He swung into his saddle and reined his horse behind the bay Brig led.

Halfway to the place where Brig intended to cut off the trail to reach the rocky shoulder where Max lay, they met Tandy. They didn't have to say anything. His expression said he knew the story from Jordanna and Kit.

"I thought you might need some help," he told them simply.

Brig gave a short nod of acceptance to the offer and Tandy turned his horse on the trail to ride along with them. Brig noticed the folded tarp tied behind the cantle of Tandy's saddle, a shroud for the body, and said nothing.

Jordanna sat on the bench at the table, unaware that her face registered no emotion. Kit sat opposite from her, his elbows on the table, his hands rubbing his forehead. Jocko set a tin cup of coffee in front of each of them, richly black and heavily sweetened.

"It happened so quickly, Jocko—yet so very slowly," Jordanna said in an absent tone.

"Drink the coffee," the Basque ordered gently, but firmly. "It will help."

Staring at the cup, Jordanna kept remembering Brig's comment. It echoed over and over in her mind. She lifted her gaze to Jocko. Her eyes were the troubled green of a storm-tossed sea.

"Brig said that he warned Max the mountains would kill him. What do you think he meant by that?"

"Probably nothing," Jocko said after a moment's hesitation. "Sometimes at the scene of death, we say things that have no meaning. They are just words spoken because we cannot express what is felt inside." He nodded to the cup in front of her. "Drink the coffee."

Obediently, she picked up the cup and brought it to her lips. The strongly sweet liquid burned its way down her throat. She glanced across the table at her brother. He looked troubled, but when he saw her looking at him, he smiled in an expression of gentle reassurance and understanding.

Chapter XVII

THE MISTING RAIN hung like a gloomy pallor over the camp as the trio of men returned. Brig was leading his buckskin. An elongated bundle wrapped in canvas was draped over his saddle, tied with a rope. The slow cadence of the horses' plodding hooves resembled a death march. Jordanna, Kit, and Jocko came out of the tent to meet them.

While Tandy and Fletcher dismounted, Brig began untying the ropes that held the body in the saddle. Jocko went forward to help them. Together, they lifted the body down and laid it on the ground near the large tent. Brig's rain poncho glistened wetly as he straightened and addressed them in an emotionless voice of calm command.

"We're breaking camp. As soon as everything is packed and loaded we'll start out of the mountains. We don't have any way of getting in touch with the authorities about the accident so we'll have to pack Max's body out."

"I have already begun the packing," Jocko told him.

Brig nodded his approval and walked back to take the buckskin's reins in his hand once more. "Let's get the horses ready, Tandy." He added the reins of Fletcher's horse to the ones in his hands.

"You aren't going to leave Max lying there . . . in the rain," Jordanna protested.

Brig gave her a stony look. "He's past the point of knowing that it's raining." He stepped into the stirrup and swung smoothly into the saddle, leading Fletcher's horse.

Tandy followed him, leading his horse and the limping bay. At the picket line, Jordanna and Kit's horses stood saddled, a blanket draped over the leather to protect it from the rain. Brig and Tandy did the same with their horses, all except the injured bay.

"We'll have to clean out these wounds and put some disinfectant on them," Brig said. "Go get some from Jocko." The saddle tree was broken. Brig un-cinched the saddle and lifted it to the ground. "I'll save the cinch straps. The rest of the saddle is worth-less now." As he pulled off the saddle blanket, he noticed the line of gouged hide beneath it. He frowned. "Look at this."

"Must have cut himself when he fell," Tandy commented. "I'll fetch that medicine."

Opening his mouth to call Tandy back, Brig hesi-tated. He turned back to the horse and re-inspected the wound and its location beneath the saddle blanket. He was suspicious of the wound. It would take a very sharp rock to cut like that. Bending down, Brig picked up the saddle blanket and looked on the underside. In a corner, corresponding to the location of the wound, he found a thorny twig imbedded in the stiff material. The thorns were savagely sharp and large.

Brig rolled it between his gloved fingers. There hadn't been any thorn bushes or berry bushes on that slope. In his mind, he went over the route of the trail. There hadn't been any along there either. Where could the twig have come from? The last place he remembered seeing bushes with thorns the size of this one was two or three days ago. It couldn't have been caught in the saddle blanket all that time. Tandy wasn't that lax.

His fingers closed into a fist, the thorns of the twig digging through the leather into his palm. It had to have been put there by someone. As a practical joke? Had someone wanted to see Max get bucked off? It was certain that the instant those thorns dug into the boy's back, the horse would start bucking. Which is exactly what it had done.

Brig studied the location of the wound again and the placement of the twig. Initially the thorns would be a minor irritant to the horse. Brig remembered how skittish the bay had been when Max had first mounted at camp. The thorns wouldn't pierce the hide until the rider's weight shifted to the back of the saddle— as it had when the bay had started to climb the switch-back trail.

Someone had killed Max—deliberately or accidentally. There wasn't anyone in camp with such a perverted sense of humor to play this kind of practical joke. That left a deliberate attempt. But why? Brig shook his head in confusion and tried another approach.

Fletcher had been the last one to handle the bay before Max got on it. He had tied the horse up after Tandy had ridden out its morning buck. That meant Fletcher had the opportunity to put the thorns under the blanket. And Fletcher had asked if they were following the same route—which meant the steep trail over the ridge. There was the other incident when Max had nearly fallen and Fletcher hadn't helped to save him. And the incident with the rattlesnake back at the ranch.

"But why?" Brig muttered tightly under his breath. Why would Fletcher want him dead? A person like Max could never be a threat to a man like him. It made no sense. A puzzled and angry frown creased his forehead.

There was Jordanna. What part did she have to play in all this? Fletcher had given orders for her to be nice to him. Why? Pain squeezed at his chest. Was it tied up with this—Max's death? Was she a diversion to keep him from becoming suspicious? This morning, she had waylaid him with coffee, and kept him talking while Fletcher helped Tandy with the horses. Brig had to clench his jaw tightly to keep the anguished groan from tearing out of his throat. The words she had said that morning came back to him like a knife slicing into his heart: *Why did you save him? Wouldn't you be better off if he wasn't around?* He forced his mind to concentrate on the lost shoe on the pinto horse, which began to take on a suspicious light.

Max's death had been murder—made to look like an accident. But how could he prove it? He couldn't. Tandy had had access to the bay. As far as that went, he had access himself. Lord knew, that of all the hunting party, he had more motive for killing his cousin than anyone else. Had that been planned, too? Brig had wondered why Fletcher had chosen him as a guide over the many professionals. His reasons had sounded so logical, if a little weak. But Brig had needed the money too badly to ask many questions. Fletcher had probably counted on that.

It had been a set-up from the beginning. And he was the patsy, the fall guy. If the accident was uncovered as a murder, he had the motive, the opportunity, and the means. Who were the witnesses? Fletcher, his son, and daughter—all supposedly innocent observers. Brig realized that if he opened his mouth, he might be putting his own neck in a noose. He had to have some kind of proof against Fletcher ... a motive.

He had never really liked or respected Max. Brig didn't pretend to feel any grief at his death. But to condone murder simply because he didn't like his cousin? No. He wasn't about to let Fletcher get by with it.

"I've got that salve from Jocko." Tandy came hurrying through the rain. "And some rags and warm water to wash the grit out of his wounds."

"Take care of him then." Brig moved away from the bay, slipping the thorned twig into his pocket.

Tandy crouched beside the horse's front feet and began gently bathing the scraped flesh. Brig walked over to the three remaining packhorses and wiped the moisture from their backs before putting on the pads and packsaddles.

"We're two horses short. What are we going to do?" Tandy asked.

"We'll have to distribute gear to the riders. Everyone will have to carry his own duffle, and anything else that the packstring can't handle. We don't have any choice."

"What about Jughead? He ain't going to be in fit enough condition to travel." The horse pulled away from the picket line as the soapy water Tandy was washing his legs with stung its raw flesh.

"We'll have to turn him loose. Pull the shoes off the pinto, too. They'll follow us for awhile. Eventually they'll make their way back to the ranch." The fate of two horses was the least of Brig's concerns at the moment. "Have you noticed any thorn bushes around?"

"Thorn bushes?" Tandy looked up with a frown.

"Yes, thorn bushes. Or berry bushes," Brig repeated with marked patience. "Have you noticed any?"

"Not that I recall, but I wasn't exactly looking for them either. Why?"

"It's not important." Brig shrugged. "Are any of those scrapes serious?"

"No, but they're gonna be sore as hell." The horse kicked at Tandy and tried to bite him. "Settle down!" Tandy yelled and hit the bay in the belly with his fist. "I'm trying to help you, you old crowbait nag! You deserve all this pain for buckin' on that slope and getting a man killed." The horse snorted and stood stock-still, intimidated by the roaring voice more than the blow. "Do you reckon the authorities will want to see Jughead, him being the horse that throwed Max and all?"

"I don't know. But we can't very well take him along. He'd slow us up too much." Brig adjusted the packsaddle on the last horse and tightened the cinch. "If they want him, they'll have to come look for him."

"I s'pose you're right." Tandy sighed. "Damn, but it's a lousy day."

Brig walked to the buckskin and stripped off its protective blanket to step into the saddle. There was a nagging doubt in his mind and he knew he wouldn't rest until it was satisfied.

The stocky cowboy glanced up. "Where are you going?"

"To check something. I won't be long."

The buckskin made little sound as Brig walked him through the trees and the rain-soaked carpet of needles. Deliberately he avoided riding through the camp, skirting it widely before picking up the trail that led to the switchback. The whispering rain continued to fall. Brig walked the horse slowly, stopping every now and then to search the trail on either side for thorn bushes. There was little undergrowth along the trail. The area around the switchback was devoid of any at all. Brig dismounted, dropping the reins to groundhitch his horse. He walked the churned earth where the bay had first started acting up, and followed its route to the patches of talus. Halfway down, he saw an object that didn't belong in its surroundings. It was a leather wallet, half-covered by the loose rock. Brig picked it up and slipped it into his jacket pocket, opposite the one that contained the briar. A last scan of the area convinced him he hadn't been wrong. There wasn't a thorn bush, a briar patch, or a clump of berry bushes to be found.

A rolling whicker came from the buckskin as Brig walked back to it. He absently rubbed the wet nose the horse thrust toward him and walked to its left side to mount. His features were grim and hard as he turned the horse toward camp.

Brig had intended to turn off the trail and skirt the camp area itself again. Before he reached that point, he saw a yellow-slickered figure at the head of the trail. It was Fletcher. Brig rode the buckskin directly toward camp. Fletcher's expression was smoothly controlled to show only mild interest.

"Where have you been?" he asked.

"I went back over the trail," Brig admitted.

"Why?"

He reached in his pocket and took out the billfold. "I remembered that Max didn't have his wallet on him. I went back to look for it." His hard expression was equally bland.

"Tandy said you were turning the bay horse loose to make his own way home."

"That's right." Brig stopped the buckskin and leaned forward to rest his forearms on the saddle horn, the rain dripping off his hat. "By tomorrow morning, that horse will be so stiff he probably won't be able to do much more than hobble. He'll come to the ranch when he's able." He looked Fletcher in the eye. "I don't think the authorities will be particularly interested in seeing him. After all, it was just an unfortunate accident."

"Yes. Yes, it was," Fletcher nodded with a show of sorrow. "I offered to ride the bay this morning. I was afraid he was more horse than Max could handle, but he wouldn't hear of it. Now . . ." he sighed. "Now, he's dead."

Brig tossed the wallet to Fletcher and the saddle creaked as he straightened in the stirrups. "Have Jocko put that with Max's things."

"I will."

Clicking to the buckskin, Brig reined the horse around the man in the path and trotted it through camp to the picket lines. The tents were already struck and two of the packhorses were being loaded.

*   *   *

Within an hour they had left. They rode until twilight before making camp that night. No one talked much, communicating only when it was necessary. The camp was crude, consisting of two lean-to's. The slanted canvas roof was supported by two poles in front and weighted to the ground in back with heavy rocks, forming a shelter from the steady drizzle. After supper, it was a somber group that sat huddled under the lean-to near the fire. Jordanna was one of the first to call it a night and crawl into her sleeping bag fully clothed. The others gradually followed her lead one by one until only Brig was left at the fire. Jordanna rolled onto her side and watched the dancing shadows cast on the canvas by the flickering fire. Her eyelids seemed heavily weighted. She closed them.

Sleep was a welcome escape. Then the dream began. She was on the slope again, watching the bay horse wildly trying to pitch its rider. It was rearing over backwards and Max was falling. Inexplicably, the dream changed. Jordanna became the one rolling down the incline. She fought the nightmarish image, telling herself she was dreaming and making the person become Max again. But it kept switching. First it was Max; then it was herself. Back and forth. Back and forth. The moment came when her mind couldn't force it back. She was tumbling to the edge, swept by the torrent of loose shale. She was going to fall to her death.

Something touched her shoulder and Jordanna grabbed for it blindly to keep from slipping over the precipice. But that something started shaking her hard, demanding that she wake up. The palm of her wildly flailing hand was stabbed by a sharp object. The pain snapped her awake.

Brig was bent over her. Jordanna was drenched in a cold sweat and shaking uncontrollably. The vividness of the nightmare clung to her. Not fully cognizant of what she was doing, Jordanna sat up and threw her arms around his neck in panic, needing the comfort of his hard arms. She wasn't aware of his hesitation before his arms circled around her wildly trembling body to hold her close. He picked her up and carried her to the fire, as if its heat could warm the cold terror within.

"I h-had this dream," Jordanna tried to explain, stammering in a frightened whisper. She had to talk about it to end its possession of her mind. "I was falling down that slope. It w-was supposed to be Max, but it . . . kept turning into me."

"It's over." The hard, flat statement offered no comfort other than the truth.

Her face was buried against his heavy parka, trimmed and lined with sheepskin. It smelled of dampness, horses, and smoke. Mixed in with the pungent combination was an elusive, musky scent of a man. Jordanna tried to control her gulping, agitated breathing, but it was hard to do when her pulse was leaping so wildly. She turned to rest a cheek against his jacket. Becoming conscious of the stinging pain in her palm, she lifted her hand. Blood was trickling from two small wounds. She wiped it on the sleeve of her heavy blouse, trying to figure out how she had hurt herself.

"You'll never be able to wipe the blood from your hands, Jordanna." Brig's voice was low, pitched at an ominous level.

It shivered down her spine. Drawing away from the support of his solid chest, Jordanna looked into his face. The wide brim of his hat cast brooding shadows on his roughly chiseled features. The dark line of his full-broomed mustache looked even darker and more forbidding. The searing dryness and contempt in his dusty brown eyes was oddly menacing. Alarm skipped through her pulse.

"W-Why would you say a thing like that?" Jordanna was confused, angry, and a little bit frightened.

"What part is yours in this, Jordanna?" he continued in the same vein.

"In what?" She shook her head in blankness.

"Max's death."

"I don't know what you're talking about!" She pushed out of his arms and rose to her feet in agitation. The cold mountain air was making vapor clouds out of her breath. Jordanna shivered from the combination of cold without and cold within. She rubbed her hands over her arms to get rid of the chill, aware that Brig was on his feet as well. His accusing attitude intimidated her because of a nagging self-guilt. She tried to deny it. "You are insane, Brig."

He caught her arm and spun her around, his grip bruising the soft flesh of her arms. "Why did you do it, Jordanna?" he demanded savagely. "Why?"

Part of her cringed from his glowering expression, but she faced him boldly. "I have absolutely no idea what you are talking about. Now, please let me go. You are hurting me."

His answer was to jerk her hard against him and enfold her in a bone-crushing hold that threatened to snap her ribs. Her lungs had no room to expand and take a breath, and his mouth smothered her lips in brutal possession. The assault exposed the ruthless core of violence in him. Shaken by it, Jordanna weakly fought the blackness swimming at the edges of her consciousness. She couldn't breathe. He was crushing the life from her and she couldn't stop him. Her mind reeled toward the black void.

Then, as violently as he had taken her, Brig released her, almost throwing her away from him. Jordanna staggered backwards, fighting for balance and breath. His eyes were hard on her whitened face.

"Go to bed," he growled through his teeth. "Get out of my sight!"

Eyeing him warily, she stumbled to her sleeping bag and hurried inside to its warmth. She was shaking as violently as after the nightmare. His brutality had turned him into a stranger—one with intimate knowledge of her. Jordanna shuddered and curled into a tight ball.

PART THREE
THE STALK

angry glance over her shoulder. But it was her mother standing there.

"What's wrong?" His darkly handsome features were drawn into a concerned frown.

Chapter XVIII

PAUSING, BRIG GLANCED at his reflection in the large-paned window of the bar front. He hadn't slept much in the last two nights. He hadn't bothered to shave that morning. He looked haggard and tired, and he damn well felt that way, too.

After he had reported Max's death, he'd made arrangements for the body to be shipped to New York. The authorities had seemed willing to accept his account of the accident with few questions. They would be talking to Fletcher, Jordanna, and Kit to corroborate it, but Brig had no doubt that they would. The thorn-covered briar was still in his pocket, needling him with its pressure as surely as if it were against his skin.

Staring at the Coors sign, Brig wondered what had prompted him to arrange to meet the three "witnesses" here Lord knew, he wanted a drink badly to burn out the savage bitterness in his throat. But it wouldn't do anything to ease the hot ache in his stomach.

With a burst of impatience, he walked to the door

and pushed it open. His long, lazy strides made scuffling thuds on the hard floor as he crossed the room to the counter bar. The place was dim and empty of customers at this hour of the day. Brig walked to the shadowed corner at the end of the bar.

The bleached blonde had laid her cigarette down when he entered, her face lighting up as she recognized him. "Brig! It's been so long since I've seen you." Her greeting came out in a sweet rush of pleasure.

"Hello, Trudie." Brig tried to sound pleasant, but the words came out terse and lacking warmth. He sat down on the last stool, hooking a heel on a metal crossbar and resting a boot on the tarnished brass footrail. Taking off his hat, he set it on the drink-stained countertop and tiredly combed his fingers through his hair.

"You look like you've been through the mill." Trudie had moved to his end of the bar. "What happened? Did you lose your razor?" she joked.

"I had other things on my mind this morning." He rubbed the dark stubble on his jaw. The stiff growth made a rasping sound against his calloused skin.

"Where have you been?"

"I just spent the last two weeks in the mountains." Brig didn't elaborate. He didn't want to talk about the hunting party or Max's death. In order to make the arrangements to have the body sent back to New York, he'd had to identify himself as a cousin. The news would spread through the small community fast. Thankfully, the notification of Max's ex-wife and children was being taken care of through legal channels and Brig hadn't needed to assume responsibility for that.

"Two weeks?" A mocking smile curved the red mouth. "It's a miracle you bothered to shave at all during that time."

Brig could have told her that for the bulk of those two weeks he'd had reason to want a smoothly shaven face. He wouldn't have wanted his rough stubble scraping the creamy smoothness of Jordanna's soft flesh. To mar that perfect body would have been a crime, especially when there had been so many ways to arouse a quivering response without inflicting pain. He'd tested nearly all of them on his willing apprentice.

"Beer?" Trudie asked.

"Scotch."

She lifted an eyebrow in surprise. "I've never known you to order the hard stuff. What are you doing? Drowning your sorrows?" She said it in a light, bantering tone, but it was too close to the truth.

"Changed my mind," he said curtly. "Make it a beer."

"Whatever you say," Trudie shrugged and looked at him oddly. She pulled him a glass of beer and set it in front of him. "How long will you be staying in town?"

Her gaze held both question and invitation. Brig rejected them both. There was a fleeting impulse to use her the way he had been used. If he went to bed with her, it would only be for sex and he wouldn't have to guard against any other emotion. But it wasn't what he wanted.

"Not long. I'm meeting some people here." He unbuttoned his heavy parka and let it hang open. Resting his elbows on the cushioned edge of the bar, he sipped at the beer and wiped the foam from his mustache with the back of his hand.

"Oh. Did Tandy and the boys come into town with you?" Trudie guessed.

"No."

The door opened and Brig turned on the swivel seat of the bar stool. Fletcher walked in, followed by Jordanna and his son. His gaze flicked from the gray-haired man to Jordanna. Her slender, high-breasted figure was no longer padded with layers of clothes to keep out the cold. She was wearing slim-fitting, biscuit-colored pants and a creamy silk blouse with a brownish-tan furred jacket that stopped at her waist. They hadn't seen him sitting at the shadowed end of the bar yet. Brig made no attempt to disguise the naked hunger in his eyes as his gaze devoured her. But he couldn't trust her an inch. Somehow she was in league with her father in all this. Brig hadn't figured out what the son's role was, but he was bound to be involved, too.

"We must be early," he heard Fletcher say, but Brig still didn't make his presence known.

Three against one. Hell, he'd been outnumbered before and had managed to come out on top. That was dangerous thinking, he cautioned himself. Just because he had survived previous dangerous situations didn't mean he'd make it through this one. He was vulnerable this time. He had a weak link in his defenses where Jordanna was concerned. True, he hadn't gone near her since that night Max had died—when his lust to kill had equaled his lust to love. Not knowing which would win out, he had spurned her. The strain of keeping his hands off her was beginning to weigh on him and he didn't know how much longer he could hold out.

"She's the one, isn't she?" Trudie asked softly, already knowing the answer. The twinge of hurt in her eyes held envy rather than jealousy. She had neither the beauty nor that touch of class needed to stand in Jordanna's shadow.

A hard stone gate rolled down to shut out his expression as Brig flashed the blonde a brief glance, irritated that she had seen what he wanted buried. He stepped down from the bar stool, a leg scraping the floor at the shifting movement. Taking his beer, he walked toward the family trio.

The sound magnetically pulled Jordanna's gaze to the darkened corner of the bar. Brig walked out of the shadows. Last night, she had slept in his bedroom, but this time alone. He'd left the ranch this morning before she was awake. He looked tired and irritable and prepared. Prepared? Why had she chosen that adjective? It fit, but prepared for what—and why? The hard thrust of his gaze started an inner tremor. Her emotions were all confused—loving him and fearing him, hating him and wanting him, feeling safe and feeling threatened.

"Hello, Brig," her father greeted him. "We didn't see you when we first came in."

Brig nodded but offered no greeting. "Let's take this table." He chose a better-lit table for four, then sat in a chair that put him in the shadows.

Her father took the chair opposite him, Jordanna felt distinctly uneasy as she sat on Brig's right, with Kit across the table from her. The barmaid approached the table, a plumply curved blonde wearing too much make-up. She eyed Jordanna with a wounded, jealous look. Jordanna darted a sharp glance at Brig. She had never assumed that he didn't have other women, but to be confronted with one of them in this bar was something she hadn't expected. He saw her look, his jaw flexing. His gaze flickered to the blonde, then returned to her with a glint of satisfaction. Was his intention to show both of them that he wouldn't be tied down to one woman? Or was he trying to tell her the newness had worn off and she bored him? Brig had certainly avoided her these last two days, except for that night when he'd raged at her and said all those crazy things that hadn't made any sense.

"Can I get you something to drink?" the barmaid asked, smiling brightly.

"I'll have a beer," Fletcher ordered.

"Nothing for me, thanks," Kit refused.

Jordanna looked up to the woman. "Would it be possible for me to have some coffee?"

"Sure. I've got a pot on the burner. Do you want something in it? Whiskey or anything?"

"No. No cream or sugar either, thank you."

"How about you, Brig?" the woman asked familiarly. "Do you want me to put a fresh head on that beer?"

"No thanks, Trudie." He smiled at her and swirled the amber liquid around in the glass.

As the blonde left, Fletcher leaned back in his chair

and took his pipe and tobacco from his pocket. Filling
the bowl with an aromatic blend of tobacco, he tamped
it down and lit it with a pipe lighter. Brig seemed to
concentrate exclusively on the man, watching his every
move. Jordanna felt uneasy. There was brittle tension
in the atmosphere around the table and she didn't
understand what was causing it.

"How did the interview go?" Brig asked.

"Fine." The one word answer was given with the
pipe stem clamped between his teeth. Puffing out a
cloud of smoke, her father removed it from his mouth
and appeared to examine the pipe bowl. "They didn't
ask us many questions. Mostly they were just confirm-
ing what you had told them."

"I've made all the arrangements to have the body
shipped to New York."

"That reminds me." Her father glanced to Kit. "You
should call your mother before the media picks up the
story and she hears it from them."

"Why should I telephone?" Kit tipped his head to
meet his father's look.

"She'll take the news better if it comes from you.
You can assure her that we are all safe and unharmed.
I know when she hears about Max's death, she'll be
worried about us." The last sentence was delivered in
a sardonic tone. Fletcher let his gaze swing to Brig.
"My wife tends to believe that I minimize things. She
will believe my son's assurances, but not my own."

Kit's mouth tightened in grim displeasure, but he
didn't attempt any further protests. "Is there a telephone in here?" he asked Brig.

"There's a pay phone back by the restrooms." Brig
nodded toward a dimly lit hall at the back of the
room.

"I'll come with you," Jordanna offered, eager to
escape this tension playing on her nerve ends and re-
group her chaotic emotions.

Her father rose courteously in his chair when she
stood up, but Brig didn't copy his action. In fact, he
didn't even glance at her. She was hurt and confused

by his indifference toward her. When she had told Brig to stay away from her the morning Max had died, she had said it in anger, not really meaning it and not expecting him to believe her. She had wanted some capitulation from him, some admission that she meant something to him other than simply a bed partner. Her love and her pride needed it. Instead, Brig was acting as if she didn't exist.

Jordanna walked with her brother to the telephone. Absently she heard him place the call, her thoughts on the man at the table. With only half an ear, she listened to Kit speak to the maid, Tessa, asking her to call their mother to the phone, and not to leave.

After an exchange of greetings and a few irrelevant remarks, Kit said, "Mother, I have some bad news for you. There has been an accident . . . No, I'm fine. Jordanna is here with me and Dad is sitting at a table. It was Max Sanger." . . . There was a flurry of questions issued by a hysterically raised voice on the other end of the line, but Jordanna paid scant attention to them. She was unaware of Kit's sharp glance at her. Her mind was filled with thoughts of Brig . . . "I'm sorry, Mother. Max was . . . killed by a fall." He hurriedly began to explain the circumstances. Jordanna had no desire to hear it again. Glancing at the restroom door marked "Ladies," she gestured to Kit that she was going in it. He nodded and smiled briefly. Jordanna pushed open the door and walked inside.

Jordanna's departure had ended his distraction. Brig didn't have to pretend any more to concentrate on his opponent, Fletcher Smith. It came naturally—as naturally as the deadly calm that settled over him. Reaching in his jacket pocket, he took out the thorny twig and laid it casually on the table.

"What's that?" There wasn't a flicker of recognition in Fletcher's expression.

"That's what I was going to ask you," Brig countered.

"I'm a hunter, not a horticulturist," the man joked. "Where did you find it?"

"The briar was lodged under Max's saddle blanket." His statement produced no reaction from Fletcher.

"I suppose it was picked up during that tumble down the slope." The tone indicated only a minor interest in where it might have come from. Trudie returned with their order and Brig kept silent until she left.

"That was my first thought. Tandy said almost the same thing when I showed it to him," Brig admitted. "Interestingly enough, there aren't any thorn bushes on that slope. I checked. As a matter of fact, there was none anywhere in the vicinity of our camp."

"That is interesting." Fletcher nodded in an absently curious fashion and took a sip of his beer. "I suppose it was picked up someplace else."

"That's a logical assumption," Brig agreed. "It has one major flaw. If the briar was in the saddle blanket a couple of days before the accident, the pinto wouldn't have taken a step until it was found and removed. Remember, that horse won't tolerate even a wrinkle in the blanket, let alone thorns."

"That's true. I had forgotten." Fletcher puffed on his pipe and frowned thoughtfully. "How do you suppose it got there?"

"I thought you might already know." His light brown eyes gleamed with hard challenge. "Obviously, it was put there."

"You can't be serious!" Fletcher declared with a scoffing laugh. "You do know what you are suggesting?"

"That Max's death wasn't an accident? I'm not suggesting it. I am stating it." This confrontation might be a reckless move, but Brig had examined the alternatives over the last couple of days and decided that the only hope of forcing Fletcher into the open was to admit his knowledge of how Max had died.

The half-smile faded from the older man's face as

his gaze narrowed on Brig. "You do realize what you are implying? That Max was murdered."

"Yes. Someone placed this . . ." Brig flicked the briar with his finger, the action moving it closer to Fletcher. ". . . under the saddle blanket that morning, aware that the bay horse had a reputation for bucking. After that, it was merely a matter of waiting until we reached an uphill grade steep enough that a rider's weight would shift back in the saddle and the thorns would dig into the hide."

"But who would do that? And why?" Fletcher frowned in a most convincing manner.

"I know who," Brig stated. "I just haven't figured out the why."

"Then who did it?"

A cold smile twitched Brig's mouth. "You did, Fletcher."

"Me?!" His handsome features were carved with incredulous surprise. "You can't be serious!"

"I am—deadly serious. You had the opportunity when you tied the bay up after Tandy had topped him off. And you knew which trail we were taking." Brig paused. "I can't help wondering if those two other incidents weren't unsuccessful attempts. Max might have died from shock if that snake had bitten him. It was sheer luck that I managed to save him from that other fall."

An indignant anger spread across Fletcher's expression. "If we are going to start pointing fingers, you had opportunity and knowledge of our route. Plus, you have one thing I don't have—a motive. The Sanger Corporation is yours with no strings attached now that Max is dead," he accused. "Men have been known to kill for a lot less than control of a multi-million dollar corporation."

Brig's gaze narrowed shrewdly. "How did you come by that piece of information? I'm sure Max never volunteered it, not when he was trying so desperately to sell out his shares to you."

Fletcher sat back for a moment, considering his answer and Brig. "Naturally, when Max offered to sell his stock, I had my people investigate the company. And later, you. I wanted to know what kind of man I was hiring to guide my hunt. The correlation of the two investigations produced that information."

"In that case, you have to be aware that the company is on the verge of bankruptcy. I'm inheriting a white elephant—hardly a motive to kill someone."

"Maybe your motive was revenge. After all, it was Max's bad investments that brought the company to the brink of ruin. Maybe you were angry with him for mismanaging the firm's assets. You could have arranged for him to die before the company went under, thinking you could save it," Fletcher reasoned. Brig saw the circumstantial evidence of guilt framing him. "You could save it—with some financial backing. That was an offer I was considering making to Max. I'll make it to you."

"In return for what? My silence?" he mocked. "Do you want me to throw this briar in the garbage and forget I ever saw it?"

"I don't know anything about this twig." Fletcher tossed it to Brig's side of the table. "You tell me that you found it under Max's saddle. I have no proof that's where it came from. For all I know, you could have picked it up anywhere." He lifted his gaze to blandly meet Brig's. "My proposition was strictly a business one."

Fletcher was a cool one. Brig realized he wasn't going to stampede him into any kind of an admission. Fletcher had denied every one of his allegations and countered them with ones more damaging to Brig. The whole scheme had been very well laid out.

"You overlooked one major thing. I don't want Sanger Corporation. I didn't want it fourteen years ago and I don't want it now. I can't be bought by your business proposition, Fletcher. There isn't enough money in the world to make me keep quiet about the fact that you murdered Max."

Fletcher shook his gray head in confused amazement. "Why do you persist in this ridiculous accusation against me? Don't forget I offered to ride the bay horse instead of Max. I wasn't likely to do that if I had put that thorn under his saddle. I could have been the one killed, instead of him."

"I haven't forgotten. It was a very clever ploy, too. You knew my cousin would never agree to it, for fear that it would make him look cowardly. You were quite safe to make the offer," Brig countered.

"There is one thing I don't understand about all this. If you are so convinced that I arranged Max's accident, why didn't you tell your story to the authorities?" Fletcher challenged.

A cold smile curved the mouth beneath the mustache. "Because I haven't got enough proof against you. But I'll get it."

"Why this righteous crusade, McCord? Max Sanger never meant anything to you. You despised him and everything he stood for. Why do you care how he died?"

"Were you counting on the fact that I would be glad to see the last of him, and not care what might have caused his death?" The question was low and taunting. "I may not have liked my cousin, but that isn't reason enough to let his murderer go unpunished. Your second mistake, Fletcher, was setting me up for the fall guy."

"You positively amaze me with your persistence of this absurd notion!" the man laughed. "Max died in a fall, caused from being bucked off a horse. As you pointed out, it was a horse that has a reputation for bucking. Or is that what you are concerned about? Are you afraid you might get charged with negligent homicide for putting an inexperienced rider on a dangerous horse?"

"Did you implant that thought in the minds of the authorities?" Brig leveled a hard gaze at his implacable opponent.

"I had no reason to be suspicious of any involvement you may have had in Max's death until this moment. Even if I had, I doubt that I would say anything without some hard proof." Fletcher admitted with an indifferent shrug. "Jordanna has become fond of you. I wouldn't want to hurt her by making possibly unfounded accusations against you."

"Yes, Jordanna," Brig agreed dryly. "She is almost as good at acting as you are. It's a pity she didn't do a better job of keeping me distracted. I might never have found that briar."

"I don't know what you are talking about." Fletcher's voice sounded weary from repeating the phrase. "Am I to understand that you aren't interested in marrying my daughter?"

"I'll bet you'd like me to marry her. As your son-in-law, you think I could be trusted to keep your secret and not spread around what I know about Max's death, is that it?" Contempt coated his words. He had little respect for a man who would sell his daughter to obtain silence.

"I could be very generous when Jordanna married. If you aren't interested in the Sanger Corporation, I'm sure you will admit there are a great many costly improvements that could be made to your ranch."

"You may find this hard to believe, but I like the place just the way it is," Brig replied. "In the second place, I wouldn't like being an accessory to murder. And thirdly, I wouldn't trust your daughter. It's very possible that if I married her, I might meet with an untimely hunting accident in a couple of years, one of those peculiar lapses of safety by an expert rifleperson."

"I do believe you are a little insane," Fletcher mused.

"Do you? Why? Because I'm turning down not only your money but the considerable attraction of your daughter as well? You could be right. Maybe I am," he conceded. "But I can promise you that I'm going to prove you killed Max—and I'm going to find out why."

"If you find a motive, I do hope you will tell me."

There was a taunt of arrogant amusement in his voice. "As you know, Max was the kind of man I could buy and sell a half-a-dozen times. If he was any sort of a problem to me, there were any number of ways I could have gotten rid of him without resorting to murder."

That was the part that troubled Brig, because he knew Fletcher was right. He couldn't visualize Max posing such a large threat that Fletcher had felt the only way to dispose of him was to kill him. He could have ruined him financially. Brig suddenly wondered if that's what Fletcher had been doing. Perhaps he was responsible for the financial problems Max was having personally, as well as with the company. That possibility only complicated things. If Max was going under in a matter of months, why had Fletcher killed him now? There was an important piece missing in the puzzle. Brig had to find it somehow.

"When I discover your reason, Fletcher, you will know." Brig concealed his confusion and uncertainty. "Although I won't promise that you will be the first."

"I wouldn't do it if I were you, McCord." For an instant, hatred burned undisguised in his brown eyes. "You might be tackling something you aren't big enough to handle."

"Is that a threat, Fletcher?" Brig jeered. "Or just more impotent words from an old man? The truth is, you might have gone too far this time. Don't think you're going to get away with murder, because *you* will be making a mistake then."

Just when Brig thought he might have goaded Fletcher into letting something slip, a smooth mask slipped over the man's expression. He was looking beyond Brig and wearing a paternally benign smile.

"Did you speak to your mother, Kit?" he asked and Brig realized that Kit and Jordanna were returning to the table. He smothered the brief flames of irritation.

"Yes, I did . . ." Kit hesitated a fraction of a second as he sat down in his chair. ". . . and assured her that all of us were fine and quite unscathed."

"Death is never pleasant, but it's always a shock

when it happens to someone you know," Fletcher commented. "I hope you asked your mother to send flowers and our condolences to Max's family."

"I . . . didn't, but I'm sure she will," Kit replied.

"What is this?" Jordanna reached for the briar lying on the table top.

For an instant, Brig was captivated by the sight of her long, slender fingers, their delicacy and their strength. Swiftly, he pushed it down and studied her face. She seemed genuinely ignorant of its significance. But, damn, he didn't believe her!

"That's my good luck piece." He reached out and took it from her fingers.

"A stick of thorns?" She gave him a curious and skeptical look.

"Yes." Brig slipped it in his jacket pocket.

"So much for rabbits' foots and pennies," Jordanna laughed in puzzlement.

Surreptitiously he glanced at the brother. Kit was wearing a frown. It quickly vanished when he saw that Brig was looking at him. He turned to his father.

"Shall I make our return reservations?"

Fletcher took a deep breath, flicking a brief glance at Brig before beginning his answer. "Yes, I . . ."

"You aren't planning to leave now, are you?" Brig interrupted smoothly. He knew he was playing a dangerous game. But he didn't want Fletcher on the other side of the continent, not yet, not when there was a chance of uncovering some incriminating evidence. "I thought you came here to hunt bighorn sheep. That monarch is still waiting up in the mountains for you. Aren't you going after him? There's a couple of weeks of the season left and I still haven't earned all of my bonus."

Fletcher considered the suggestion for a moment. "That's true."

"We've handled all the details regarding Max's accident. There is nothing to stop us from leaving tomorrow morning for the high country, is there?" Brig challenged.

"But—what about the funeral?" Jordanna protested. "He was your cousin. Aren't you going to attend?"

Brig turned to calmly meet her accusing look. "I'm not a hypocrite. The circumstances of my birth might have made Max my cousin, but I never liked him. I wouldn't have crossed the street to see him when he was alive. I'm not flying to New York to attend his funeral now that he's dead." He looked at Fletcher in silent challenge. "Well, what do you say? You claimed you wanted that bighorn."

"I do," Fletcher stated. "Like Jordanna, I was under the impression that you would be attending Max's funeral. But if you are willing to take me after that bighorn, I can leave whenever you are ready."

"That settles it, then." Brig pushed his chair away from the table and straightened. "I'll head back to the ranch and have Jocko get everything organized to leave tomorrow."

"Fine," Fletcher nodded.

But Brig noticed that neither Jordanna nor her brother looked enthused about the prospect. He guessed that they wanted to cut and run before their deed was uncovered. Fletcher wouldn't waste any time informing them that it was already too late. Brig walked to the bar to pay for the drinks.

Trudie rang the bill on the cash register and handed Brig his change. "Are you leaving now?"

"I have to get back to the ranch." He pushed the money in the side pocket of his Levis.

When he started to turn away, she said, "Brig, Jake Phelps has been talking about marriage."

Stopping, he looked at her. They'd had some good times together before Jordanna had come along. And Jake Phelps was a jealous man. Oh, well, hadn't he decided to stay out of Trudie's life? The long breath he released was a sigh of final acceptance.

"He's a good man, Trudie." It was her decision and Brig wasn't about to make a recommendation.

"Yes, I guess he is." She looked disappointed and he knew why.

There wasn't anything left to say, so Brig walked toward the door. He was aware of the trio at the table silently watching him leave, but he didn't look in their direction as he pushed open the door and stepped outside. He paused on the sidewalk, wondering if they were plotting his death. He'd have to be extra careful in those mountains. His gaze turned to the ragged edge of the horizon. The prophecy he'd made about Max might come true for himself as well.

"There you are, Brig." Tandy's stocky figure came hurrying along the sidewalk toward him. "Are the Smith's inside?"

"Yes."

"Where are you going?"

"Back to the ranch. We're heading back into the mountains first thing in the morning to resume the hunt. I want Jocko to get everything organized."

"We're going back?" Tandy looked surprised.

"Not you. Just Jocko and me. Frank is going to need some help at the ranch. I can handle the horses this trip." He'd see to them all personally. There would be no briar slipped under his saddle. "Fletcher paid for his bighorn and he wants it."

"He don't sound too concerned that we just carried the body of a friend of his out of the mountains," the cowboy sniffed.

"Max wasn't his friend," Brig corrected and walked to his truck. "I'll see you later at the ranch."

Chapter XIX

"WHY ARE YOU going back out there, Dad?" Kit demanded when the door closed behind Brig.

"I came here to get a trophy ram. I'm going back to the mountains for the same reason," he replied in a voice that said it should be obvious. "I would have mentioned it myself, but Max was Brig's cousin. I wouldn't force a man to ignore a death in the family to fulfill a contractual obligation to me. But since he volunteered, I certainly don't intend to refuse."

"But doesn't Max's death mean anything to you?" he persisted.

Jordanna's expression resembled the one on her brother's face. She, too, thought their father was being selfish and insensitive.

"What do you expect me to say?" her father shrugged. "It was a regrettable accident. But he wasn't a close friend of mine. I barely knew the man. Life goes on. Nothing comes to a stop simply because one man dies. It's like putting your thumb in a pail of water and pulling it out. There's barely a ripple, let alone a hole. That may sound callous, but it's the truth," he stated. "Brig knows that. I agree with him that it would be hyprocrisy to pretend I felt a loss for someone I only knew superficially."

"It seems to me that . . ." Kit began.

"Naturally, I don't expect you to come with me," her father interrupted. "Your place is with your mother. After the accident, she will be worried about you. You are her only son." There was an underlying tone of contempt in his voice, which was absent when he addressed Jordanna. "If you feel it's improper, I won't suggest that you accompany me either."

Improper or not, Jordanna knew she had to go. Brig was going, and—fool that she was—she had to go, too. "No, I'll go with you."

"I'm coming, too," Kit stated.

"I don't see any point in it this time, Kit," her father declared coldly. "And don't try to pretend again that it's because of some desire to be with me."

Jordanna looked from one to the other in surprise. What were they talking about? Why else had Kit come? Everyone was talking in riddles. And she seemed to be the only one who didn't know the answers.

"I'm coming. You can't stop me." Her brother's statement was issued in calm determination.

Her father glared at him, then jeered, "You've been gone quite awhile now. Aren't you worried that your roommate might have found someone else to take your place?" There was faint, caustic emphasis in the reference.

Kit's mouth whitened in anger, but just then Tandy Barnes walked into the bar. Whatever reply Kit had been going to make was checked by the appearance of the cowboy.

"Are you folks ready to head back to the ranch?" He paused beside their table.

Her father met Kit's determined look for a long second, then nodded, "Yes, I guess we are all ready to go." He made no further protest of Kit's decision to accompany them on the hunt.

The exchange between her father and brother troubled Jordanna. It wasn't until late that afternoon after they had returned to the ranch that she had an opportunity to question her brother alone about it. And then it had occurred only after he had sought her out. She was in Brig's bedroom, where she slept, repacking her duffle when he knocked at the door.

"I've been wanting to talk to you," she told him as she let him in.

But Kit didn't give her a chance to follow up on that statement. "Is there any way you can talk Dad out of leaving on this hunt?"

"Talk him out of it?" she repeated incredulously. "He has his heart set on getting a trophy ram. I couldn't talk him out of that." Immediately Jordanna leaped in with a question of her own. "Why doesn't he want you to go?"

There was a cynically amused twist of his mouth. "Maybe he thinks I'll hamper him in some way." His attempt at humor sounded grim.

"Be serious," Jordanna complained impatiently.

"I am," he smiled.

"Then why is it that you aren't making sense?" She lifted her hands in a helpless gesture. "Nobody is making sense. I feel like you are talking in some secret code that I don't understand. Take that ridiculous remark Dad made about your roommate Mike. He knows very well that the apartment lease is in your name. Mike couldn't have anyone move in while you're away, so why did he say such a silly thing? And why did you get angry when he did?"

His gaze fell from hers and he turned away. "You wouldn't understand, Jordanna."

"I wouldn't understand," she repeated angrily. "I'll never understand if someone doesn't explain. I feel like a child with some adult telling me to wait until I grow up to ask the question. I am twenty-four years old. How much older do I have to be before I am capable of understanding? Or am I supposed to just stumble blindly on in ignorance for the rest of my life?"

"You really haven't guessed, have you?" Kit looked at her sadly.

"Guessed what? Will you stop talking in questions?" Frustration rang with silent fury in her demand.

"I know we've never been close. But haven't you ever wondered why I've never brought a girlfriend home?"

His response confused her. It wasn't at all what she expected. "If I gave it any thought at all, I imagine that I supposed you didn't want to expose them to the obvious hostility between Mom and Dad." Her shoulders lifted in an uncertain shrug.

"Jordanna, there weren't any girls to bring home," he told her in a quiet and calm voice.

She gave him a blank look. "What are you trying to say?"

"Mike isn't my roommate."

Comprehension dawned in a blinding flash that reeled her backwards. Her mouth opened and closed several times before she could force anything through the stranglehold of shock in her throat.

"No," Jordanna denied in a choked voice. "I don't believe you. It isn't true."

"It is true," Kit insisted in a gentle voice. "I know it's a shock. You can imagine how Dad reacted when I told him several years ago. I thought he was going to kill me. He made me swear that you would never find out. It was a pretty easy promise to keep. You and I never really got along the way a brother and sister should, but I couldn't bear to have you look at me with the contempt and loathing that is in Dad's eyes. I was only kidding myself that you would never find out. It would have happened sooner or later. And I'd rather be the one who did it, even if it means . . ." One corner of his mouth twitched into a sad smile of acceptance. ". . . that you won't want to see me again."

"But . . . you are my brother," Jordanna protested in an anguished whisper. "How could I reject you?"

There were tears in his eyes. "So many have turned away."

"You are my brother," she repeated. There was an enormous lump in her throat; and her vision was blurred by the welling of tears.

In the next second, they were hugging each other, crying softly on the other's shoulder. Jordanna didn't think less of him for the tears. Her brother was a strong man or he would never have been able to stand up to their father. He would have run from him and hid the truth. He was her brother. She couldn't judge him.

She wiped at the tears on her cheeks. "My God, we're becoming maudlin," she laughed, sniffing at her runny nose.

"I'd offer you my handkerchief, but I need it," Kit joked.

"I'll get my own." She walked to the tissue box in her cosmetic case. After blowing her nose, she wiped away all traces of the emotional scene and turned to discover that Kit had done the same.

"I'd better let you get back to your work," he said with a warm half-smile. "Thank you for being my sister, Jordanna."

There was nothing for her to say so she just nodded and gave him a reassuring smile. He left the bedroom and, after a couple of minutes, Jordanna returned to her packing. With that secret revealed, it was inevitable that her thoughts turned to Brig. She glanced at the bed that they had once shared and where she now slept alone. Was the affair over? And was she simply too stubborn to admit it? She loved him. She refused to accept the possibility that there was no hope.

Standing at the bathroom sink, Brig stared at his reflection in the mirror. The blade of the razor cut a path through the shaving cream on his cheek. It was late to be shaving when he would only have to turn around and do it again in the morning. He turned his head as the bathroom door opened.

Jordanna started to walk in until she saw him standing at the sink. "Sorry. I didn't know anyone was in here," she apologized.

His senses leaped at the sight of her in that dressing gown. He remembered vividly the night he had taken it off her and let his hands roam her creamy smooth flesh. Turning back to the mirror, he rinsed the lather from the razor blade with the running water from the faucet.

"I must have forgotten to lock the door." His hand didn't feel very steady when he touched the blade to his jaw.

She started to leave, then hesitated for an instant to watch him. "Why do men always make such funny faces when they shave?" she wondered aloud.

In spite of himself, a faint smile touched his mouth. "To entertain the spectators." He managed to avoid cutting himself as he stroked the razor along his jaw. "I'll be through shortly. Then you can have the bathroom."

Jordanna didn't leave. Instead she took a step into the room and reached out to lightly touch her fingertips to his muscled shoulder. As they traced a diagonal line from the point of his shoulder to the shoulder blade, Brig stood motionless, the razor poised near his cheek.

"You took the bandage off. Is your shoulder better?" Her gaze sought his reflection in the mirror.

"It's much better." After briefly meeting her glance, Brig avoided and needlessly rinsed the razor again under the running tap water. His voice was low and stiffly controlled. "Do you mind leaving? I would like some privacy."

"Of course." It was a subdued reply.

Turning away, she bent her head. Her brown hair was gilded with scarlet under the light of the bare bulb above the sink. He watched her in the mirror until her reflection left its smooth surface. The door closed and Brig lowered his hands to the sink, gripping its porcelain edge and hanging his head. She was tearing his guts out. She was a willing accomplice to Fletcher's

plans, if not more than that, but Brig still felt that
gnawing desire to love and protect her. And she needed
his protection about as much as a fully clawed tigress
would.

Jordanna lay in bed and tried to sleep, but she
couldn't force her eyes to close. The only light in the
darkened bedroom came from the single window where
the dimness of a partially obscured moon made a
square patch of dark gray and gave the room's
furniture dark shape. It was late, nearly midnight, and
she needed her sleep, but it wouldn't come. Restlessly,
she turned, punching her pillow and trying to find a
more comfortable position.

After another fifteen minutes, she gave up. It was
no use. She wasn't going to sleep. Jordanna threw back
the covers and swung her feet to the floor. Reaching
for her robe, she slipped it on and zipped it closed.
When she couldn't sleep as a child, Tessa had always
brought her a glass of warm milk. As near as Jordanna
could recall, it had always worked.

Trying to be as quiet as possible, she opened her
door and carefully closed it behind her. There were
sounds of someone snoring in the living room. Not
Brig—Jordanna didn't even remember hearing him
snore. But he was in there. She hesitated, magnetically
pulled in his direction. She resisted it and glided
silently to the kitchen door. Not until the door was shut
did she reach for the light switch. The sudden flood
of light hurt her eyes. She blinked, shielding her eyes
from the glare until they adjusted to the brightness.

The milk was in the refrigerator and Jordanna found
a small pan in the bottom drawer of the stove. While
it warmed on the burner, she searched the cupboards
for a glass, trying to make as little noise as possible.
In the cupboard by the sink, Jordanna found the
glasses setting on the second shelf. Stretching on tip-
toes, she reached one of them.

Out of the silence, Brig's low voice demanded to
know, "What are you doing?"

Startled, Jordanna pivoted around. The glass slipped

through her fingers and tumbled to the floor, shattering on impact.

"Don't move!" Brig ordered harshly.

But it was too late. Instinct had already prompted her to try to catch the glass before it hit the floor. Her reflexes were way too slow and the sole of a bare foot came down on a piece of glass. Immediately Jordanna lifted her foot, gasping at the sharp stab of pain. She tried to twist her foot around so she could see whether the piece of glass was still in the bottom of her foot.

"I thought I told you not to move." Glass crunched under his boots as Brig strode impatiently toward her.

Since it was obvious she had, the comment didn't warrant a reply. It wasn't easy balancing on one foot, but she didn't dare move. Splinters of glass were all around her. She was leaning against the kitchen counter. Distracted by the sharp pain in her foot, she was only half-conscious of Brig crossing the width of the room to her side. Jordanna was forcibly reminded of it when he scooped her up in his arms. Momentarily stunned by the sudden contact, her reaction was automatic. She clasped her hands around his neck for support, suddenly realizing that he was dressed only in Levis and boots.

His torso was bare from his hair-roughened chest to the hard, flat muscles of his stomach. The easy way his arms carried her weight revealed his physical strength. An intoxicating breathlessness attacked her lungs at the warm, male scent of his flesh. She was conscious of the rippling play of his muscles as he carried her to the kitchen table. Lifting her gaze, she studied his lean, rugged features through the sweep of her lashes. The darkness of his thick hair, eyebrows, and mustache blended with his sun-browned complexion. His face was so very close to hers. The lines feathering out from the corners of his eyes drew her gaze inward to meet his look.

Her heart began regularly skipping beats when his attention shifted to her lips. In the next second, Brig was setting her down on the table top and dragging his gaze away from her mouth. Pulling a chair along-side, he concentrated on her injured foot. The rumpled thickness of his dark brown hair invited fingers to run through it and Jordanna curled her own around the edge of the table to resist the invitation.

"Is the glass still in it?" Her voice was husky and disturbed, reflecting her inner feelings.

The heel of her foot was cupped in one large hand while the other examined the small wound where the faint trickle of blood had originated.

"Yes."

An instant later, she was wincing as he pulled it out. With the piece of glass removed, the blood flowed more freely from the wound. Brig took a handkerchief from his pocket and pressed it against the bottom of her foot. His gaze sliced to her face.

"What did you think you were doing?"

Under the disconcerting directness of his look, Jordanna lifted a hand to push her touseled auburn hair away from her face, and avoided his look. "I couldn't sleep. I thought if I drank some warm milk it might help me relax." Her nose caught the tell-tale scent of scorched milk. "The milk! It's still on the stove."

"Stay right where you are," Brig ordered sternly. Tying the handkerchief around her foot, he rose and walked across the broken glass to the stove. Removing the pan of milk, he turned off the burner and carried the pan to the sink. Jordanna saw, when he poured the milk down the drain, that the bottom of the pan was coated with the black-brown scum of burnt milk. Filling the pan with water, Brig left it in the sink to soak. Instead of walking back to the table, he went to the pantry and brought out a broom.

"I never thought of you as domestic," Jordanna murmured as she watched him sweep up the fragments of glass. Domestic, but never domesticated, she thought to herself. Brig would never be tame. He was too much his own man to ever jump at the bidding of others.

"A case of necessity," was his indifferent reply.

When the glass was swept into a dustpan, Jordanna started to get down from the table. His sharp gaze swung to pin her. "I told you to stay there."

The underlying current of anger in his voice more than the order kept Jordanna from moving. When the broom and the dustpan were put away, he cast one glance at her, then walked out the door to the bathroom. Jordanna heard the sounds of the medicine cabinet being opened and explored. Then Brig was returning to the kitchen with disinfectant and a band-aid.

Again her injured foot was the prisoner of his hand. She drew in a hissing breath as the disinfectant stung the wound. The band-aid was applied next. The roughness of his calloused fingers smoothed the adhesive over the sensitive skin on the bottom of her foot. When it was done, he continued to hold her foot in his hands and lifted his gaze to her face.

"How is that?"

"It's fine. Thank you." There was a disturbed tremor in her voice. It felt oddly intimate for him to hold her foot like that, one hand resting on her arch and the other curved around her slender ankle. Her heel was supported by his solid thigh.

"It doesn't look serious, so it shouldn't give you any problems." His gaze continued to hold hers with all the appearance of total indifference to her, but Jordanna felt his fingers absently stroke the calf of her leg.

The sensation sent tingles over her skin. He must have seen her reaction to his touch because his eyes darkened to a smoldering brown. Her breath was stolen as his hand slid further up her leg to grip the side of her knee, inching toward her inner thigh, beneath her long robe. Abruptly he withdrew his hand, tearing his gaze from her face as he pushed back his chair and straightened.

"That should take care of it, then," Brig stated.

While Jordanna was still trying to recover from the sudden removal of his touch, his hands spanned her waist to lift her to the floor. She wasn't prepared for the sudden adjustment from sitting to standing. Her fingers gripped the flexed muscles of his upper arms for support as she sought her balance. The tenderness of the wound on the bottom of her foot didn't help.

"Sorry, I . . ." She tipped back her head as she started the apology, but the unmasked desire in his look stopped the words.

Jordanna shuddered with longing. His hands tightened, almost imperceptibly, on her waist to draw her closer. She spread her fingers upward to his bronzed shoulders. His mouth opened over hers, taking her lips in a hungry, demanding kiss. Jordanna gave herself willingly to the man who already owned her, heart and soul. The molding hands at her hips and back shaped her to the hard contours of his length. The ragged tempo of his heartbeat was a glorious sound, so like her own. His mouth moved to explore the curve of her neck.

"I lied to you, Brig," Jordanna whispered with aching love.

There was a momentary stillness before he lifted his head and allowed a small amount of space to come between them. She met his penetrating gaze and its hint of wariness. Her fingers traced the smoothness of his shaven jaw in a tender caress.

"When?" It was a sharp demand.

"When I told you that I only pretended to like your touch," she answered in a soft, throbbing voice. "It wasn't true. You make me come alive when you hold me in your arms and make love to me."

"I already guessed that." His look demanded that she tell him something he didn't know.

"Brig, I want to be more than just your lover. I want you to feel something more than just lust for me." Her tone became tight with the depth of her need. "I want you to care about me. Let me be your friend, your confidante, maybe even your wife and the mother of your children some day."

Grim disgust thinned his mouth. The sight of it

slashed at her heart like a knife blade. Hurt, Jordanna turned out of his arms and took a quick step away. It was a searing pain that went deep. She had thought if she explained that she truly cared, he might reciprocate with a similar admission.

"Jordanna . . ." His hands touched her shoulders. She eluded their grasp with a flinching shrug.

"No," she denied with a flash of hurt anger. "It isn't enough for me to share your bed. I guess I'm just naturally a greedy person, Brig. I want to share the boredom, the monotony of day to day routine. I want to share the good times and the bad. I want to work with you to build this ranch. I want to argue with you —and make love with you." Pivoting, Jordanna proudly lifted her trembling chin to meet his closed look. "I love you, Brig McCord. I didn't lie about that either."

"Sometimes you are very convincing," he murmured with sufficient skepticism to prove he didn't believe her. "But I can't imagine you being satisfied for long, stuck out here in these primitive surroundings."

"It's where I belong. Not just because you are here," she qualified. "This is my kind of place, not the city, but here in the outdoors where there is nothing to block out the sun but the mountains. Where it's wild and untamed. Like hunting, it's the kind of life that demands something from you—physically and mentally. Here, there is constant challenge and I . . ." There was a sudden lump in her throat. Looking away, she swallowed before tightly completing the sentence. ". . . would love to live here with you. I love you. You do love me," she accused. "I know you care. I've seen it in your eyes, felt it when you held me. Why won't you admit it?" She turned her hurt, questing eyes to him.

His look was unreadable as his hands moved to rest on either side of her neck. There was a certain grimness that seemed permanently implanted in his rugged features. Jordanna didn't resist the light grip of his hands or the pressure of his thumbs on her collarbones.

"I could love you, Jordanna," he muttered, "if I didn't know better."

Before she could question what he meant by that, he was curving her into his arms and his mouth was blotting out her token resistance. His embrace was almost cruel in its demand for gratification. Jordanna might have struggled if she hadn't felt the tremors of desperate longing that shuddered through his hard, male frame. She couldn't deny him satisfaction any more than she could deny herself.

Without another word said, Brig picked her up and carried her from the kitchen. Unerringly, he found his way to the bedroom in the darkened house. In the black velvet shadows of the bed, the fire their kisses had kindled blazed into full flame, and consumed them both with its rapture.

Hugging his arms more tightly around her, Jordanna basked in the warm glow of satisfaction. She felt almost completely content. She looked up to him and smiled, knowing he could see her expression and she couldn't see his, and that it wasn't necessary.

"We have something special, Brig," she murmured. "You can't deny it."

His reply was to slip his arm from beneath her shoulders, the one she had hugged to more fully encircle her. He rolled to the edge of the bed and sat up. In the darkness of the room, all Jordanna could make out was the black shape of his broad-shouldered frame. The bedsprings squeaked as he stood up, removing his weight from them. She frowned at the sounds of his movement that indicated he was dressing.

"Aren't you sleeping here?" The question was out before she realized how shameless it sounded.

"No." It was a flat denial that held no regret.

"Why?" She nearly choked on a sob.

For a minute, Brig didn't answer as he walked to the door. The knob clicked when he turned it. "You can keep the bed, Jordanna . . ." he told her, ". . . and your lies. I don't need them."

Lies?!! Her heart cried in anguish, but no sound

came from her throat. The door opened and closed. How could he believe that all the things she had told him were lies? She had bared her emotions, stripped away all pretense, and virtually begged him to care about her. She had humbled herself and he'd walked all over her heart when he left her alone in the bedroom.

Her fingers curled into the pillow where his head had rested. She pulled it toward her and buried her face in it, so her wracking sobs would be muffled by its thick feathers. Jordanna wished Brig had slapped her. That pain would have eased in time, but the agony his rejection brought would be slow to heal, if it ever did. She cried until the pillow was drenched with her tears and there were no more left. But the dry, hacking sobs wouldn't stop. She found no peace until mindless exhaustion swirled a black cloud over her consciousness.

Chapter XX

A COLD, BLUSTERY wind accompanied the hunting party as they returned to the mountains. They rode with shoulders hunched and collars turned up against the icy blasts. The sky was a clear, sharp blue and there was a crystalline clarity to the air.

The second day on the trail, a stand of trees offered them partial protection from the whistling wind. The group stopped and dismounted to give the horses a rest. The horses turned their backs to the wind that whipped their tails between their legs, and huddled together.

Trying to stamp some feeling into her numbed legs, Jordanna watched Jocko bring out the thermos of hot coffee. Despite the layers of clothing, she was cold. So were the others. Kitt was slapping and rubbing his arms and her father was rubbing his hands together. Only Brig and Jocko, who were occupied with other things, weren't attempting to warm some part of their body.

She felt the dryness of her lips and reached into her

jacket pocket for the lip balm. Her heavily gloved hands were shaking as she outlined her lips with the creamy stick. She, like the others, wore sunglasses to shield her eyes from the glare of the sun, which seemed doubly bright at this altitude.

Jocko brought her a cup of coffee, which she gratefully accepted. "It's cold today." She verbalized what her shaking hands told him.

His gaze surveyed the blue sky with its horizon of snow-capped peaks. "It will snow soon."

"But there isn't a cloud in the sky," she pointed out.

The Basque shrugged that it didn't make any difference. "The wind says it will snow." He moved on to fill her father's cup.

Brig had heard Jocko's prediction as he left the horses to join the circle of riders. "If it does, it might drive the sheep down to the lower elevations." Setting his rifle scabbard on the ground near Jordanna's and Fletcher's, Brig took off his gloves to warm his hands with the hot metal of his steaming cup of coffee.

Jordanna kept her gaze averted from him. Whenever it was possible, she avoided addressing any remark directly to him. Walling herself in was her only means of defense from further hurt being inflicted by Brig. It was prompted not so much by pride as by survival.

Her silence wasn't noticeable since none of the group was very talkative this time. Everyone seemed concerned with his own private thoughts and expressed few aloud. Brig's comment about the sheep had received an ambiguous response from her father. The break lasted as long as it took to drink the hot coffee; then it was time to climb in the saddle again.

Her foot was in the stirrup. She was just ready to mount the sorrel horse when she felt a hand at her waist help her into the saddle. Thinking it was Brig, Jordanna jerked away from the contact and cast an angry glance over her shoulder. But it was her brother standing there.

"What's wrong?" His darkly handsome features were drawn into a concerned frown.

"Nothing. It isn't you," she added, in case he thought it was, and swung into the saddle unassisted.

Kit moved to stand beside the front skirt of the saddle, his hand resting on her saddlehorn. "What happened between you and Brig?"

Jordanna started not to answer him at all, before she decided he deserved some kind of response. "It was wrong to think he would care about me, that's all. I'll just have to start over." And try to find a reason to go on without him, she added to herself. Beyond that, she couldn't discuss it—not even with her brother. It was much too fresh and painful . . . and ongoing.

A horse snorted beside her, drawing Jordanna's glance. The buckskin was tossing its black forelock near her leg. Her gaze darted to Brig. The mirror finish of his sunglasses kept her from seeing his eyes, but she realized that he had overheard her answer. She felt exposed. Jordanna faced the front, holding her head rigidly straight and staring directly ahead.

After a couple of seconds, she tapped a heel against the sorrel's ribs. The horse moved reluctantly away from the windbreak of trees. The buckskin trotted past her to take the lead. There was a tightness in her throat at the sight of the lean, broad-shouldered man riding so easily in the saddle. Jordanna slowed the sorrel to bring up the rear with Jocko and the packstring.

An hour before sunset, the riders reached the site of their previous camp. The wood frame for the tent was standing like a forgotten skeleton. A ring of stones encircled the blackened ash of previous campfires, and firewood was chopped and stacked in readiness for more. After the horses were taken care of, Brig and Jocko stretched the canvas over the larger tent. While Kit helped Jordanna set up her small, private tent, Fletcher started the fire. A golden sunset darkened to orange and tinted the wild country with its fiery glow.

The next day, the sky retained its cold blue shade, reminding Jordanna of polar ice. The biting wind sent the temperature plummeting to the freezing mark. On the horizon, the first tendrils of clouds warned of a weather front moving closer. As the hunting party started out from camp, Jordanna was stunned to realize that Brig was taking the route that led up the switch-back trail.

"We aren't going up that, are we?" she said in protest.

Brig half-turned in his saddle, directing the dark mirrors of his sunglasses at her. "Why not? We have to go over the ridge."

Her gaze was drawn to the point where Max had fallen. A cold chill raced through her, but she didn't argue with his decision. The sorrel horse felt her nervousness and moved restlessly beneath her. Jordanna laid a quieting hand on its neck, trying to soothe her own nerves as well. They started forward again in single file. Jordanna didn't breathe easily until they reached the top.

They sighted one band of young rams that morning. In the afternoon, they saw seven ewes with their spring lambs. The offspring were as hardy as their parents, capable of running surefootedly within two hours of birth. But they didn't have a glimpse of the monarch her father sought.

The second day was as futile as the first. The only difference was that the sky had become solidly overcast with clouds. The wind stayed and it seemed colder than before. There was a thin crust of ice on the banks of the mountain streams they crossed.

It was drizzling when Jordanna woke on the third morning. In the night, it must have sleeted. The ground outside the tent had patches of ice. Kit slipped on one of them and sprained his ankle. Her father was practically livid with anger, although he never said a word. Both Jocko and Brig examined the injury and reached the same conclusion.

"Nothing looks broken," Brig stated, sitting back on his heels. "I'm sure it's just a sprain. If you want, we'll take you back out of the mountains to a hospital where you can have it x-rayed to be certain."

"No," Kit refused. "It doesn't hurt that much. It'll be all right in a couple of days."

Brig helped him to his feet. Kit winced when he tried to put a little weight on that foot. Jordanna gave him a worried look.

"Are you sure, Kit?" Her eyes told him not to be intimidated by their father's obvious resentment that his hunt might be interrupted again.

"It's *my* ankle," he joked weakly. "I can be fairly objective about how much it hurts. I'll just sit around camp here for a couple of days and keep Jocko company."

"You can teach me how to play cribbage so I can beat Tandy this winter," Jocko suggested with a bolstering smile.

Brig stepped away when Jordanna came to her brother's aid. She noticed it and tried not to show that it mattered. She helped Kit inside the large tent, offering the support of her shoulder while he hobbled to the bench.

"I can stay with you," she said.

"No." His refusal was quick and sharp. "I want you to be with Dad." He saw her curious frown and smiled crookedly. "Besides, what would you do here? Hold my hand?"

It did sound a bit silly. "Okay, I'll go," she accepted his decision with a ghost of a smile.

The hunting party was reduced to three riders. It was wet and miserable. Occasionally Jordanna felt the sting of ice pellets on her cheeks as they rode in search of the bighorn ram. In the late morning, they left the horses tied to some chaparral and climbed a rocky slope to glass a jagged ridge of mountains.

The ground was a cold slab of rock beneath Jordanna. Her rain suit kept out the dampness and stopped the tugging wind from piercing her clothes. Cold made it impossible to find a comfortable position. She chose to lie on her stomach so that her elbows could support her arms, while she slowly scanned the wild landscape with her binoculars.

"There, at two o'clock, halfway down the slope." Her father directed their attention to a specific area. "Is that him?"

Jordanna focused her glasses on the bighorn sheep lying down, resting and chewing its cud. Brig did the same. "It's too far away," he said. "I can't tell."

"I don't want to ride all that distance to find out it isn't the one with the chipped horn," her father grumbled. "Hand me the spotting scope, Jordanna."

"It's still in the saddlebag. I forgot to bring it," she admitted and started to rise. "I'll get it."

"Never mind. I will." Her father sounded impatient.

Jordanna started to argue that she was the one who had forgotten it; therefore she was the one who should get it. But her father was already on his feet and turning to pick his way down the rocky slope to the horses. She settled back in her former position. Relatively speaking, she was alone with Brig for the first time in several days. Jordanna tried to steady her suddenly erratic heartbeat and centered her binoculars on the ram.

"Do you think it's the one with the chipped horn?" It was a stiff attempt at conversation.

"I already said I didn't know."

"I am aware of that." Jordanna flushed. "I was merely asking for a guess."

He lowered his binoculars to look at her. "I don't make guesses."

"Don't you?" Her face was wet and shiny from the misting rain. "You've made all the wrong guesses about me."

"You have tried many times to convince me that I have," Brig said wryly.

Jordanna couldn't hold that dusty look. Her hands gripped her binoculars until they hurt, as she stared at the gray rock beneath her. Tears welled in her eyes, stinging. She blinked at them.

"I don't know why I bothered," she said thickly.

His gloved fingers caught her chin and twisted her face toward him. "Tears?" One corner of his mouth curled derisively into his mustache. "What am I supposed to do now? Kiss them away?"

There was something hard and hungry about the way his gaze devoured her lips. Her senses reeled under his look. Somehow she maintained her balance and jerked her chin from his hold.

"You don't have a heart, Brig McCord," Jordanna accused. "You're made of stone. Instead of blood, you have molten lava running through your veins. All that fire is just lust. I only wish I had realized that before."

"What flows in your veins?" he taunted.

"At the moment, it's ice water," she retorted.

"How long would it take, I wonder, to turn it to steam?" he mused.

Not long. All he had to do was touch her and she would melt. Jordanna knew it and she didn't want him testing her to find out. She scrambled to her feet and looked down the slope for her father. He had just started back to them, carrying the leather case with the spotting scope.

The high magnification of the spotting scope convinced her father that, if it wasn't the ram with the chipped horn, it was its equal or better. Jordanna excluded herself from the discussion of whether they should ride around and approach the ram from the back side of the ridge above him or try the valley route and stalk up. The former was decided as being the best choice, even though it was longer.

It was a long, rough ride. Twice they had to backtrack when the trail became impassable for the horses. Finally they made it to the back shoulder of the ridge. They left the horses on the gentle slope near some trees and climbed on foot to the top.

The bighorn ram had risen to graze, but it hadn't wandered far from where they had first spotted him. At this closer distance, the chip in its curling horn was visible. Jordanna stayed on the ridge line while Brig and her father began a cautious stalk to get within rifle range. She watched, but felt no excitement. Admiration for her father's skill and care was conspicuously absent.

Jordanna realized that she had lost her enthusiasm for the sport. She wasn't repulsed by what she saw, merely indifferent to it. There was no hatred for what her father was doing. She still understood the thrill he felt and didn't condemn him for it. But she no longer felt it.

Through her binoculars, Jordanna saw her father get into position and sight his target through his rifle scope. The crack of the rifle shot ripped through the air. The ram leaped and tried to bound mightily away, but his hindlegs refused to function. The trophy bighorn managed to drag himself several yards into the rocks that had always meant safety from predators, then died.

On the slope of the ridge, her father was feeling victory, but Jordanna experienced a vague sensation of regret. The mountains had lost a monarch. A mournful wind wailed through the trees below her. Jordanna stayed on the ridgetop a while longer, and watched the two men climb into the rocks to carefully drag the ram's body out without damaging the prize set of horns.

Leaving her vantage point, she walked down the gentle slope to the horses. Brig and her father would be needing the salt and tools packed in the saddlebags. Jordanna intended to bring these to them. A long-ago avalanche had carved a wide path through the trees and opened up a panoramic vista of the mountains, unobscured by trees. The breathtaking beauty of it halted her footsteps. She stood beneath the bough of an evergreen and gazed at the gray and brown world of clouds and mountains. Granite boulders alternated with high meadows of yellow-brown grass and gave rocky birth to tenacious pine trees. Mountain spires punctured the dark threatening clouds overhead. Jordanna lifted her face to the cold, soft rain, filtering through the pine needles.

Brig topped the ridge and saw Jordanna standing farther down the slope, not far from the horses. He paused for a moment, taking in the prayer-like attitude of supplication, before he continued down the incline. A small rock tumbled ahead of him and she turned at the sound of his approach.

"We thought you were bringing the horses." Brig stopped when he was almost level with her. On the other side of him, in the trees, the horses stood three-legged with heads hanging.

"I was coming, but I saw this view." Jordanna half-turned to look again at the wild mountain scene. There were pensive lines in the profile she showed him. "Now that Dad has made his kill, we'll be going. I don't want to leave here. These mountains are so wild and virginal that they make me feel . . . clean." She seemed embarrassed by her choice of adjectives. Brig knew what she meant. Standing there, she looked as pure and fresh as a mountain wildflower pushing through the snow in springtime.

She looked back at him, a trace of proud defiance in the way she held her head. Green fire flashed in her hazel eyes. "I suppose you think I said that for your benefit, another lie to convince you I . . ." Jordanna didn't finish that sentence. Her gaze swung back to the mountains. "I can't make you believe anything I say and I'm not going to try."

"The mountains can have a profound effect on people who are open to their influence." Brig let his gaze wander to them. They had cleansed him even as they had toughened him to live among them.

"I must be one who is, then," she said quietly.

The subdued tone of her voice drew his gaze. Like the mountain wildflower, a person was first impressed with her beauty. Not always was her strength recognized, or the stamina that was required to survive in forbidding terrain like this. Here, she flourished. Elsewhere, she would probably wilt and become a shadow of her true self. Jocko had tried to explain that to him, but he hadn't wanted to see it. He didn't want to see it now.

"I wish I didn't have to leave here," Jordanna repeated again in a wistful murmur.

Shifting his rifle to his left hand, Brig let the muzzle point to the ground. "I'm not going to ask you to stay." It was a statement of self-denial that brought her gaze sharply to him.

"I wouldn't if you did!" she flashed. "You'd have to beg me!"

There was a prickling sensation between his shoulders. Brig flexed them in an uneasy shrug. Funny, he hadn't experienced that feeling since his guerrilla days when snipers . . . He dove to the right. At the same instant, something slammed into his rifle stock and a hot flame stabbed his thigh. A split second later, the crack of a rifle shot split the air.

When Brig hit the ground, he rolled. As he came to a stop on his belly, his rifle was in firing position. It was then Brig discovered the bullet that had been meant for him had struck his rifle, damaging the firing mechanism. He didn't know where the shot had come from, except that it had been from above him. He couldn't stay where he was. Trying to reach the horses meant crossing the wide clearing and exposing himself. All these decisions were made with lightning swiftness.

Brig knew he was close to the trees. He glanced to measure the distance and saw Jordanna pressed flat against a tree trunk. Her gaze was frantically searching the ridge. Savagely, Brig realized it had been a set-up from the beginning. She hadn't brought the horses because she knew Brig would come back for them if she didn't. When he did, she had distracted him, kept him talking, and kept him out in the open where her father could get a clear shot at him.

But her father had missed. Brig knew Fletcher would try again. The hunter had committed himself to the kill. The burning in his thigh told Brig that he had a flesh wound. There wasn't time to see how serious it was. Instinctively, he had already tested the muscles in that leg and knew they responded—so the bullet couldn't have done too much damage. A good hunter will track down any game he has wounded and finish it off. Fletcher Smith intended to do just that with him. Without the rifle, Brig didn't have any means to defend himself.

This minute Fletcher was probably working into a position that would give him another clear shot. Brig couldn't stay there like a sitting duck. He had to retreat, but he needed a cover—a shield. Fletcher wouldn't risk a shot that might hit his daughter, Brig realized.

Gathering himself so that his right leg would take the initial push of his weight, Brig made a low, scrambling run for the tree where Jordanna stood, offering Fletcher as poor a target as possible. He heard the whine of a bullet race by before the sound of the rifle shot reverberated through the mountains. Then Brig was safely into the trees and grabbing Jordanna's wrist.

"What's going on? Who's shooting at us?" she demanded with only a thread of fear in her voice.

As if she didn't know, he thought with absent cynicism, and didn't bother to answer her ridiculous questions. His leg wasn't bothering him yet, but Brig felt the warm moistness of blood spreading down his thigh. Shock was numbing the pain for the time being. Pausing only a second to get his bearings and choose his route of retreat, Brig started through the trees at a jogging lope, pulling Jordanna behind him as his shield.

He kept to the trees for as long as he could. Brig coud only guess the direction of Fletcher's pursuit. When they broke from the trees, he tried to keep Jordanna between himself and Fletcher's line of fire. Their flight was taking them downhill toward smoother ground and angling them further away from camp. The rain became mixed with heavy snowflakes. At the higher elevations, Brig knew the flakes would be bigger. He stopped once in some rocky cover to study their backtrail. He was breathing heavily from the demanding pace he had set. So was Jordanna.

"Why are we running?" she demanded between gulping breaths. "Nobody is chasing us."

There wasn't any sign of Fletcher. That worried

Brig more than if he had seen the hunter. Since they were on foot, Fletcher had probably guessed that he would seek the flatter, low terrain. Fletcher was staying above them, where the ground was rougher but the vantage was better. Brig cursed himself for not thinking of that before.

With a yank, he pulled Jordanna after him and started climbing. His only hope was to get to the high elevations above Fletcher and double back. The snow was beginning to stick to the ground, making the footing slippery. Wherever it was possible, Brig tried to keep Jordanna abreast of him, alternately pushing and dragging her along. She resisted him only a couple of times.

The killing pace was beginning to tell on him. Silently, Brig wondered how she managed to keep up with him—and why she wasn't trying to get away. The wound had begun to throb, the muscles weakening in his left leg. He had to favor it now. Was that what she was waiting for? Until he was too weak to overcome any escape attempt? She hadn't given any sign that she knew he was wounded. He'd kept her on his right, so maybe she hadn't seen the blood running down his left leg. Whether she did or not, Brig wasn't about to ask.

The air was getting thinner as they climbed higher. His lungs were nearly bursting from the exertion and the diminishing supply of oxygen. Brig felt the film of perspiration on his body and knew that was dangerous in this cold mountain climate. Sweat-dampened clothes lost their insulating ability. That perspiration could turn into a thin film of ice against his skin. He slowed their pace but didn't stop.

A thin coat of snow covered the ground. The big flakes were no longer mixed with rain. Brig prayed it would keep falling and cover their tracks before Fletcher crossed them. Jordanna stumbled to her knees. Brig hooked an arm around her waist, half-carrying her as she tried to keep up with him. He was still carrying his rifle even though it was useless. It was becoming an unnecessary burden, but as long as he had it, Fletcher wouldn't know that he was virtually unarmed. If Fletcher believed his wounded prey might turn and attack, his pursuit would be cautious. Brig needed that slight advantage.

They were nearing the tree line. Ahead was a fairly tall stand of trees that would offer concealment. Brig decided it would be a good place to stop and catch their breath. He urged Jordanna toward it. They couldn't stop long, he realized. There was too much risk of his leg stiffening on him. And as long as they kept moving, they would be warm.

Either Jordanna read his mind or she wasn't able to go any further. The instant they reached the trees, she clutched at a trunk for support and stopped. His breathing was hard and labored, but he didn't dare relax. His gaze skimmed their backtrail, then swung to her. She was watching him with a wide, confused look of apprehension. Brig didn't have to worry about her trying to escape from him, not for a few minutes anyway. She had staggered the last couple of yards and she needed this short rest as much as he did. He felt a sharp stab of admiration at the gutsy way she had kept up with him, but he shook it off, not daring to believe that she wanted to stay with him.

The rapidly falling snow had almost covered their tracks. Since there had been no sign of Fletcher passing, they were still ahead of him and, by now, above him. Brig looked in the direction where he expected to find the hunter, but the snow and the trees obscured his view. Lowering his head for an instant, Brig pressed a hand against his thigh, trying to stop the throbbing pain. With each beat of his heart, blood was pulsing from the wound, draining his strength. The pressure of his hand shot pain through him. He released it and glanced briefly at the darkening stain of wet blood on his glove.

At the same second that Brig heard the creak of saddle leather, Jordanna issued a croaking whisper. "Look, there's my father."

All in the same moment, Brig glanced over his shoulder to see Fletcher ride into view, leading two saddled horses about five hundred feet below them. He caught the movement Jordanna made toward the man out of the corner of his eye. Instinct guided his reaction as Brig dropped his rifle and freed his hunting knife from the scabbard on his belt. Brutally, he pushed Jordanna backwards, slamming her against the trunk of the tree, and unsnapping his knife blade. His hand covered her mouth, smothering any outcry she might have made. He laid the cold metal blade along her throat.

"Make one sound and it will be your last," he snarled. Brig had absolutely no idea whether he would carry out the threat. His action had been dictated strictly by an animal need to survive. Fletcher was too close, his rifle in his hand at the ready. If he discovered Brig's position, he could overtake them within minutes on horseback. And Fletcher would soon learn that his rifle was inoperable. After that, not even Jordanna could shield him for long.

Brig spared a look for the rider, who hadn't given any sign that he knew where they were, then glanced at Jordanna. Her wide eyes were shaded with alarm. Her hands were gripping his wrist, but she was making no struggle to remove his hand from her mouth. Brig became conscious of his length crushing her body against the trunk. Quickly he looked away, before the sight of her distracted him from the danger of her father again. An inner confusion gnawed at him. The slightest sound—even a foot kicking against the tree trunk—would be carried to Fletcher. Yet Jordanna wasn't making any attempt to gain her father's attention. Why? Fear wasn't keeping her silent. He'd swear to that.

Fletcher was nearing the place where he would cross their trail. Brig held his breath, not sure how much of it the snow had covered. The hunter's attention appeared to be focused on the mountain below him—where Brig would have been if he hadn't abruptly altered the retreat. Fletcher walked his horse past the trail, but he looked bothered. It wouldn't be long before he would start to suspect that Brig had doubled back on him. The instant he did, Brig knew the man would ride to cut him off from camp.

The snow clouds darkened the sky. There weren't too many hours left of the gray light of day. Even without the problem of eluding Fletcher, Brig would be lucky to make it back to camp on foot before nightfall. Add to that the complications of a potentially heavy snowfall and an injured leg, Brig didn't see a chance of reaching the camp. They would have to spend the night in the mountains without any shelter ... unless ...

As his gaze searched the surrounding landscape, Brig searched his mind. Somewhere out here was an old miner's cabin that had been abandoned long ago. He'd come across it this summer when he'd been scouting the area for bighorns. The walls and roof were intact, but it had been so dirty inside that Brig had chosen to sleep outside on that trip. Now, that old log shack could give them protection—if he could remember where it was.

Unless he was mistaken, it should be in the next ridge of mountains. They would have to circle this peak, go down the other side, and hope he could find that high canyon again. How far would that be? Three —four miles? Maybe more? Could he make it that far? There wasn't any choice. He had to.

The first shiver of cold trembled over his skin. They had to start moving again. He snapped the knife shut against his leg and slipped it back in its leather sheath before he took his hand away from Jordanna's mouth. She didn't say a word as Brig stepped back to remove his pinning weight and grab her wrist again. Pulling her after him, he started through the trees to circle the mountain.

"But my father went the other way with the horses," Jordanna protested.

"I know. Why do you think we are going this way?"

He shot the answer at her, impatient that she continued to pretend.

"I think you're crazy," she murmured.

"Crazy for trying, maybe," he conceded grimly. "We've got a long way to go so I suggest that you shut up and save your breath. You'll need every bit of it."

"But why are we running from my father?" she argued.

Brig didn't answer. Her perplexed expression looked so genuine. It almost made him believe that she was an innocent and unwitting accomplice in her father's scheme. But it was too unlikely—and too dangerous to believe.

Chapter XXI

HER LEGS FELT like frozen extensions of her body. Jordanna didn't know how she continued to make them function. The wind had picked up, swirling the calf-deep snow and obscuring the field of vision. Relentlessly, Brig dragged her behind him, picking her up when she fell—which was more often now—and forcing her to continue. There wasn't a part of her body that didn't scream for her to stop. But she was aware of the urgent need to find shelter from this winter storm before they collapsed. So she pushed on.

All her physical and mental efforts were concentrated on one thing—staying on her feet. Jordanna didn't know how far they had come. She only knew that it felt like a hundred miles farther than she believed she could go. Possessing no spare energy, Jordanna didn't waste any trying to puzzle out Brig's peculiar behavior toward her father. She was too tired to think about it anyway—or to care.

Brig stopped to look around, swaying on his feet.

Jordanna didn't see anything familiar. She was certain they had never been in this area before, not during any of their previous hunting forays.

"We're lost, aren't we?" she accused in a hoarse whisper. "You don't know where we're going."

"You'd better hope I do," he rasped, tugging at her wrist to drag her with him.

At his first step, his left leg buckled under him. Jordanna heard his grunt of pain as he fell heavily to the ground. She sank to her knees beside him, wondering where she would find the strength to help him up. As Brig rolled onto his side, his face twisted with pain, she saw the crimson stain of blood on the white snow. Her eyes widened.

"You are hurt." For the first time, she saw the dark moisture of blood soaking his left pantleg. Fear shattered through her at the amount of blood Brig had lost. How had he managed to get this far?

"Just shut up and help me get on my feet," he said through his teeth.

His large hand gripped her shoulder and used it to lever himself upright. He hobbled unsteadily for a moment, clutching at her for support. His face was white beneath its tan, the strength ebbing from him. Jordanna didn't misjudge the ruthlessly determined set of his jaw. Brig wasn't finished yet. Draping his arm around her neck and over her shoulder, she tried to support as much of his weight as she could. He looked down at her, the pain-glazed brown eyes hard, rejecting her help.

"I can make it," he snapped.

But Jordanna simply tightened her hold on him. "You need me. Which way do we go?"

He hesitated, then said, "Angle to the right."

Again they started off in the direction Brig had indicated. Twice more they stopped so that he could study their location. Each time he made slight adjustments in their course. More and more he relied upon her for support. Both were draining their well of reserve strength.

"Back in those trees," Brig's voice was hoarse with exhaustion and pain as he waved to a blurred wall of evergreens ahead of them. ". . . there's an old miner's shack." The next was a thought he muttered aloud. "If it's still standing."

The wet, snow-covered branches of the trees hung low. When they pushed them out of their way, miniature avalanches of snow were dumped on them. The biting wind nipped at her face until it felt raw. Both of them were covered with white flakes, living snowmen staggering clumsily through the stand of pines. Jordanna could see the flakes that had whitened Brig's eyebrows and mustache. A few were clinging to his spiky, dark lashes.

A square of brown rose ahead of them, striped with horizontal lines of white where the snow had gathered on the top ridges of the logs.

"There it is, Brig. Do you see it?" Jordanna wanted to run, but she would be lucky if her legs carried her the last few yards.

"Yes." Brig didn't alter the rhythm of his plodding limp.

The door resisted her attempts to open it; the wood was swollen and warped. Tears of frustration welled in her eyes. Brig had been leaning against the logged side of the cabin. Seeing her difficulty, he motioned her aside and put his shoulder to the door. The wood moaned a protest, then swung violently inward. Brig's impetus carried him staggering inside, fighting for balance. Jordanna followed him inside the dark, windowless interior and heard him crash into something before she could reach him.

A crude table with one broken leg had kept him from falling to the floor. The cabin smelled dank and dusty. Cobwebs grabbed at her face. Something scurried across the floor to hide in a darkened corner. A mouse or a wood rat, Jordanna thought with weary unconcern for the rodent occupants that shared their shelter.

"The fireplace." Brig reeled heavily against her.

Jordanna felt her knees buckling under his weight. She struggled to get him the couple of feet to the crude fireplace made of stone. He was losing consciousness. She saw him moving his head, trying to fight back the blackness.

"We have . . . start a fire." He lost part of the sentence as his full weight sagged on her shoulders. Jordanna let it force her down, absorbing his fall with her body. He began mumbling snatches of sentences. ". . . clothes . . . wet . . . have to . . . dry . . . fire."

Untangling herself from his weight, Jordanna stretched his limp form in front of the fireplace. She unwound the wool scarf from around her neck with difficulty, her fingers numb and clumsy. She tied it around his wound, not so tightly that it interfered with his circulation, but just enough to apply pressure and stem the flow of blood. Sitting back, she wanted to collapse beside him, but his barely coherent mumblings before he passed out forced her to move.

A stack of kindling near the fireplace had long ago tumbled free of its neat pile. Jordanna gathered part of it and arranged it in the blackened hearth. There was enough wood there to start the fire, but not enough to keep it going all night. Mounding the shavings of wood and bark, and tee-peeing the split logs above it, she fumbled in her pocket for the waterproof pack of matches. She was shaking so badly from the cold that she had trouble striking the match. It flamed and sputtered, then caught fire. Jordanna had trouble holding the match steady as she touched the flame to the kindling. It licked at the pile the first few seconds with disinterest, before jumping onto a piece of bark. As it devoured more of it, Jordanna added new shavings to feed the tiny flame.

When it grew large enough to consume the dry logs, she straightened. Her body was stiff with cold and exhaustion, but she couldn't stay by the warmth of the fire and dry her sweat-dampened clothes that had begun to freeze. There was more wood to be gathered for the fire and Brig's wound needed attention.

By necessity, the fire came first. Jordanna neatly stacked the split logs that remained and looked around the one-room cabin. In addition to the broken table, there was a crude chair. She fought her way through the cobwebs that clogged the space and picked up the broken pieces of the table leg. The leather strips that tied the chair together had rotted. Jordanna used her knife to slice them apart and add its wood to her stack.

Her teeth had started to chatter. But if she stopped now, she might not have the strength later on. She didn't hear her sobs of exhaustion as she concentrated on the shelves of rough lumber hammered to a side wall.

Using a chairleg as a bat, Jordanna knocked out the braces that supported the shelves. A mouse squeaked in panic and raced across a bottom shelf. She pounded at the shelves and tugged until she had yanked them free of the wall. A dutch oven of cast iron clattered to the floor. Out of breath, she paused. Something crawled over her cheek. A spider belonging to one of the webs had stuck to her skin, she supposed, and brushed it off with only a hint of a tired grimace.

When all the wood was stacked by the fireplace, Jordanna decided it was enough to last until morning. There was still the wooden frame of a cot with its network of rope springs, if she needed it. Brig stirred and she dragged herself upright. She had nothing to disinfect his wound with, but as much as he had bled, surely it would be alright if she could get some sort of halfway-sterile dressing on it. That meant hot water.

Jordanna staggered to the dark corner where the iron pot had fallen. She carried it outside, careful not to shut the door tightly. In the gray light of late afternoon, she scrubbed out the dusty inside of the pot with grainy chunks of gravel gathered from under the snow. Her whole body was quaking with the cold as the falling snow swirled around her, driven by a wind whipping through the trees. She wiped out the pot with handfuls of snow and began tightly packing it with snow until it was mounded. Carrying it inside, she set it by the fire to melt and come to a boil.

The warmth from the flames hurt her skin, pricking it with a thousand sharp needles. Not having the strength to stand again, she scooted on the floor to where Brig laid. His hard features were white and stiff. His poncho glistened with moisture and his hat had fallen off, the snow melting from the crown to form a brown pool of water on the dirty floor. The rest of his clothes had to be as equally damp with sweat as her own and chilling his skin instead of warming it. The fire would do neither of them any good with wet clothes on.

Pulling off her wet gloves, Jordanna laid them in front of the fire to dry and warmed her colorless hands near the flames. When she had worked some of the stiffness from her fingers, she began undressing Brig. The rain poncho and the fleece-lined jacket came off first, followed by the heavy flannel shirt and the top of his insulated underwear. It was a struggle—his limp, massive form offering her no cooperation at all.

She rubbed his chest and arms to increase his circulation, covering every inch of his torso until she knew it intimately. Next came the lower half. After untying the wool scarf that bound his wound, Jordanna considered using her knife to cut away the material of his Levis and longjohns. But they still had to walk out of this place. In this cold, he would need all the warmth of his layers of clothes, and not a gaping slash in his pantlegs.

Unbuckling his belt, she unfastened his pants and zipped them down. As carefully as she could, she eased the material down his hips, working it over the wet, bloody area of his thigh wound. Brig groaned once in sharp pain and Jordanna bit her lip anxiously before continuing. She had to stop to remove his boots. She didn't set them close to the fire, knowing that too much heat would ruin the leather. With his pants and socks removed, she gently stripped off his insulated longjohns.

Jordanna was glad he was unconscious because she knew she was hurting him terribly. A caking crust of blood had pasted the material to his skin. The wound had stopped bleeding. Amidst the messy sight, she could see the purpling entrance and exit holes of the bullet. She was relieved that it wasn't lodged inside him still.

The snow-water in the pot had just started to boil when she had finished undressing him. Starting with his right foot, she began massaging his cold skin, working up the long length of his muscled leg to the smooth skin of his hip and including the hair-roughened skin of his lower stomach. Jordanna transferred her attention to his left foot, rubbing his hard flesh to the top of his knee, not daring to go any further because of his wound.

For a fleeting moment, Jordanna found it an unsettling sensation to have so much freedom to touch his naked form. She had found scars of previous wounds, other than the one that marked his shoulder. Brig never would have permitted her to discover so much about him if he had been conscious. He would have had her flat on her back and beneath him long before now. And she wouldn't have been objecting.

But this wasn't the time for such stimulating thoughts. Turning away from the intoxicating sight of his naked, male body, Jordanna cut off a portion of the tail of his shirt with her knife. The many layers of her own clothes were becoming cumbersome. She undressed to her insulated underwear, hesitated, then stripped off the bottoms. She cut off one leg below the knee and dropped it in the angrily boiling water. Her body was one big shiver that wouldn't stop.

Dipping the piece of his shirt tail in the water, she nearly scalded her fingers trying to wring out the excess moisture. She bent over Brig's leg and began gently wiping away the blood drying on his thigh, until the area around the wound was clean. It looked ugly and sore. Jordanna turned back to the iron kettle and the thick piece of her underwear churning in the bubbling water. It hadn't boiled long enough to be sterile yet.

She added more wood to the fire and glanced at their pile of damp clothes. They needed to be dried out. The floor was gritty beneath her bare feet as she walked over to drag the table from the center of the room. It noisily scraped across the floor in resistance. Lying on its side, it rested crookedly and formed a natural lean-to over Brig's body. She draped some of the clothes over the legs, creating sides that held in the fire's warmth. With her knife, she cut away the rope mattress of the cot and used the short lengths to make a clothesline, tying one end to a hook cemented into the side of the fireplace and securing the other end to the table leg. On it, she hung out the rest of their clothes to dry, removing her top and adding it to the line.

With a short stick, Jordanna fished out the material from the boiling water and let the excess drip and sizzle on the stone hearth. Steam rose from the wet cloth in a gray vapor. She waited until the heat subsided before touching it. Maybe it was wrong to put a wet dressing on his wound, but she didn't want to leave it exposed in this dirty place and risk infection. His muscles flinched instinctively from the hot, wet compress she applied to the wound. Needing something to secure it in place, Jordanna cut off two narrow strips from the bottom of her blouse and tied them around his leg to hold the bandage.

That was it. There was nothing left to do, she thought tiredly, and exhaustion started fuzzing her vision. No, she shook herself and stood up. She had to keep the fire going. Without anything to cover them, she couldn't let it go out. They desperately needed its warmth.

Leaning against the warm stones of the fireplace for support, Jordanna tried to maintain her vigil. Several times she dozed off, so exhausted that she could sleep upright. Each time, a chill would touch the portion of her naked body that didn't face the fire and she would have to turn to warm it, toasting herself. Half-a-dozen times, she added more wood to the fire. In her exhausted state, she moved like a robot, carrying out her task without conscious motivation.

Outside, the darkness of night settled in. A light snow continued to fall while the wind howled around the tiny, one-room log cabin. The fire crackled. In the shadowy corners, rodents scurried furtively, but Jordanna was too tired to hear them.

Brig stirred and tried to shift into a more comfortable position in the hard bed. Pain splintered through his left leg, jabbing him awake. His eyes opened slowly to take in his surroundings. In the flickering light, he saw ghostly walls of cloth around him and felt the hard, bare floor beneath him. His hand moved to grip his injured thigh and stop its throbbing. His fingers closed on soft leg hairs and he realized he was naked. Turning his head, he looked in the direction of the light and the warmth.

He breathed in sharply at the sight of the nude form leaning against the stone fireplace. Firelight bathed the porcelain figure in pale gold. Perfection was in every line, from the shapely length of her legs to the rounded bottom and slim waist that tapered wide to a pair of creamy white shoulders. Dark copper hair gilded with scarlet cascaded in curls between her shoulder blades. His gaze traveled lazily down again, lingering on the soft, rounded curves of her bottom.

Then the figure moved, coming slowly to life, and turned toward him in languid motion. High, firm breasts had rosy peaks that thrushed upward. Slender hips invited a man to fit himself to them. Nothing sculpted could achieve the natural sensuality of this living form, Brig realized.

"Venus with arms," he murmured, and the figure moved toward him, kneeling at his side so the firelight would illuminate her face. There were hollow shadows of weariness beneath the hazel eyes, but he recognized her and his mouth twisted into a faint smile. "Jordanna."

"Yes," was the soft reply. His fingertips lightly stroked his forehead. "How do you feel?"

"Tired." Not quite of this world. She was close enough to touch. Brig placed his right hand on her ribcage and let it slide up to the underside of her breast, where his thumb could rub the erect nipple. He heard her indrawn breath. "Why are you here?"

"That's a ridiculous question." Her voice was softly disturbed. "Where else would I be?"

"You could have left me to die. Chances are I would have in this storm." With his left hand, he caught her wrist and pulled her down toward him. It didn't require much exertion.

"I would have, too, if you hadn't known about this place," she reminded him as the soft mountains of her breasts laid themselves on his chest. Releasing her wrist, he slid his hand to the small of her back and caressed one of the rounded cheeks of her bottom that he had so admired. "Do you have a fever? You're talking crazy."

"If I have a fever, you are the one who is affecting my temperature." For the time being, Brig didn't care why Jordanna had stayed or bandaged his wound, when it would have been so much easier for her to abandon him to the killing elements and let nature finish the job her father had started. He curved a hand around her neck to force her head down so he could chew at her lower lip.

"Brig, don't," she protested weakly. "You're hurt."

"So? Don't fight me."

The soft moan that came from her throat told him she wouldn't fight him very hard, if at all. "Please. I'm very, very tired and I have to keep the fire going,"

Jordanna murmured between his nibbles of her mouth, but she didn't make any effort to elude them. Brig felt the lethargy of her limbs and knew she spoke the truth about her exhaustion. At the moment, he only recognized the swelling hardness of his own need.

He did acquiesce to her second argument. "Put a bunch of logs on the fire. Then it will last until morning." Unwillingly, he let Jordanna leave his arms.

Her movements were fluid and unconsciously alluring. Brig propped himself up on an elbow, testing his strength and how much interference his injury might give him. As long as Jordanna cooperated, he could manage. He felt a little shaky, but it was nothing he couldn't overcome.

When the fire was stoked with extra logs, Jordanna turned hesitantly toward him and tucked a handful of hair behind her ear. His eyes darkened as he took in the sheer loveliness of her naked body.

"Come lie with me, Jordanna."

Her fingers entwined with those he extended to her. Slowly and uncertainly, she stretched out along his right side. Brig started to shift onto his side, but she pressed her hands against his shoulders to push him back.

"No. You might start bleeding again," she warned anxiously.

"In that case . . ." Brig pulled her on top of him. ". . . we'll do it this way."

"You are mad." But she shuddered as his large hands erotically kneaded her breasts.

"Yes, it's insanity," he agreed. It was the only explanation for this plaguing doubt that she had actually plotted to kill him. If she had, why was she here? It didn't matter. His only thought now was a powerful desire to make love to her. She had implanted this demon seed of desire within him. Now it was his turn to sow his own seeds.

As his hands glided downward to her hips, Jordanna distributed her weight over his torso. She brushed her moist lips near the corner of his mouth, her breath warm and stimulating as it mingled with his.

"Be careful," she asked him. "I don't want you to do any more damage to yourself."

"Then help me," he taunted, and groaned when she did.

A chill on her backside wakened Jordanna. She was draped over Brig's sleeping form, but even while she had slept, she had avoided coming in contact with his injury. Despite the radiating heat from his body, she was conscious of a coolness. It was a second before she realized the fire must have gone out. She turned her head to see a faint red glow in the darkened ashes of the fireplace.

Quietly, she slipped out of Brig's encircling arm to rekindle the fire. With the last of the wood shavings, she started a tiny flame and shivered as she added the first small log to it. Glancing at the wall of hanging clothes, she realized they were dry. She reached for her long underwear and began hurriedly pulling them on. She didn't stop until she was fully clothed and warmed by the many layers. By then, the fire was blazing cheerfully.

The woodpile had been reduced to two logs. The log frame of the cot would yield a half a dozen more. They would need more firewood. And she was thirsty, and the gnawing emptiness of her stomach reminded her she hadn't eaten since yesterday noon. Taking down Brig's jacket from the makeshift clothesline, Jordanna covered him with it, then put on her hat and gloves, and picked up the iron kettle and her knife.

It had stopped snowing, but there was six inches on the ground, drifted deeper in places by the wind. The sun glared on the white expanse of winter snow and Jordanna had to shield her eyes from it after the darkness of the windowless cabin. In the light of day, she discovered it wasn't totally windowless. The windows had been boarded shut.

After packing the iron kettle with snow, she left it by the door to do a little exploring and seek a private place to relieve herself. On the other side of the cabin, she found a wood box half-full of firewood. There was a deadfall of timber about twenty yards from the cabin if there was a need for more.

With that problem solved, Jordanna turned her attention to the growing hunger in her stomach. Several years ago, her father had taught her that the inner bark of pine trees, as well as other trees, was edible either raw or cooked. This emergency supply of food would provide them with some sustenance. There were probably some edible supplies of greens under the snow, but the bark was easier to obtain. With water from the melted snow, she could make a nourishing soup. Using her knife, Jordanna cut away strips from the tree and peeled off the bitter outer bark for the tender, inner fiber.

When she had her pockets stuffed full, she returned to the front of the cabin and picked up the kettle of snow. After the brilliance of the sunlight, she had difficulty adjusting to the gloomy interior of the cabin. A large form was blocking out the firelight. It took her a second to remember it was Brig.

"Good morning." She walked toward him, a warm smile accompanying her greeting.

He was half-dressed, most of his weight shifted to bear on his right leg. Instead of returning her smile, Brig glared at her, his features drawn in a forbidding expression. Her spirits sagged. Last night, he'd been such an ardent and demanding lover, filling her tired body with wild excitement. This morning, there was hatred and contempt in his eyes. What had she done wrong, except love him?

"Where have you been?" His tone was harsh and accusing.

"Exploring." She set the kettle of snow on the hearth near the fire. "There is a woodbox outside with more firewood and . . ." She took the pine strips from her pockets. ". . . I gathered some pine bark to make us some soup." All the while, she tried to appear calm and controlled, showing neither hurt nor anger at his demand.

"How very resourceful of you." An eyebrow quirked in cynical mockery.

"I thought so." Jordanna tried to sound flippant.

"Did you signal your father, too?"

"Actually I didn't think of it or I would have." Her answer was cool, not understanding his tone and not liking it either.

"You had the perfect opportunity and you didn't have the guts to do it, did you? Why?" His head was drawn back to an arrogant angle that both challenged and taunted. "What's the difference between a bullet and leaving me to freeze to death?"

Jordanna looked at him with a bewildered frown and shook her head. "I don't know what you're talking about." It was warm beside the fire. She took off her hat and unbuttoned her coat.

"Don't play dumb any more. I'm sick of that game," Brig jeered.

"You were talking crazy last night, too. You must have a touch of fever." She moved toward to feel his forehead and check his temperature.

But her hand never got within reach before it was seized in a bone-crushing grip that twisted Jordanna sideways in an attempt to ease the pressure. His face was darkened with rage.

"No more lies, Jordanna!"

"I'm not lying to you!" She flared indignantly. "Have you lost your mind?"

"Yes. I must have when I met you." His lip curled in self-contempt. "I know what a lying bitch you were. I even knew you were plotting with your father to kill me, but I still let myself get maneuvered into position for the kill. It's sheer luck that I managed to get away with a flesh wound in my leg."

"What?" It was a breathless word of total confusion. "How can you say such things? You must be insane," she whispered, a little frightened of him. "I don't know who shot at us, but . . ."

"You lying bitch!!" With a savage, wolflike snarl, he pushed her away from him with a violence that sent her staggering backwards. "You and I both know it was your father!"

"No!"

"Who else was there? Who else had a rifle? Who else had reason to kill me?" He hurled the questions at her with vicious accusation.

"I don't know who else it could have been, but it wasn't my father!" There was angry frustration in her repeated denial. "How could you be so crazy to think he'd want to kill you? Brig, what's wrong with you?"

"Nothing is wrong with me. Fletcher wants me dead because I told him I knew Max had been killed. Surely he mentioned it to you." His expression was jeering in its mockery of her ignorance.

"Killed? That was an accident," Jordanna protested.

"Some accident!" he scoffed and grabbed for his jacket. Out of its pocket, he took a briar. "How many horses wouldn't buck off an inexperienced rider with this under the saddle? Don't tell me you haven't seen it before?"

She stared at it, round-eyed. "I have. You said it was your good luck charm." She lifted her gaze to his face. "Are you saying that is what caused Max's accident?"

"It wasn't an accident. It was murder. But I'm sure that, as your father's accomplice, you'll never admit it."

"No, that's not true. I don't know how those thorns got under Max's saddle, but I had nothing to do with it. And neither did my father."

"Stop pretending, Jordanna," he said contemptuously. "While you so thoughtfully brought my coffee to me that morning, you made sure I never made it to the horses and gave your father ample opportunity to slip this under the saddle. Which he did."

"No."

"I should have gotten wise when your father failed to warn Max about the snake. I didn't even suspect anything when he tricked Max into crossing that ledge without warning him about the undermined area. But my mind and my senses were all twisted up with you. That was the plan all along, wasn't it? To have me so besotted with you that I wouldn't notice what was going on? It damned near worked, too. You were such an enchanting little seductress that when we weren't in bed, I was thinking about it. Even when I overheard Fletcher give you orders to be 'nice' to me, I didn't question why. I was still fool enough to believe his story about wanting a ram. And I didn't care why you were doing it as long as I could have you any time I wanted you."

"No! You've got it all wrong! I didn't go to bed with you because he told me to!" Bitter tears were in her eyes. "I did it because I wanted to—because I loved you! Dad had nothing to do with it! And he had nothing to do with Max's death and you can't prove that he did!"

"That's what he said." Brig was unmoved.

"Wh-What he said?" she repeated in shock. "Do you mean . . . he knows you think he killed Max?"

"Why else do you think he shot at me? He doesn't want me to start talking about what I know. He nearly shut me up for good, too. Another couple of seconds and . . ." He left the obvious unsaid. "You almost distracted me long enough, Jordanna."

"Liar. None of this is true! You're making this all up. Why?" she demanded, choking on a frightened sob. "Why are you doing this?"

"You know it's true. Fletcher is out there now, looking for me. He has to kill me. He can't let me get away, not after missing me once."

"Liar! Jordanna raged. She hurled herself at him, swinging and kicking wildly, sobbing and screaming over and over, "Liar! Liar! Liar!"

The hot tears were streaming down her face, blinding her vision. Few of her hysterical blows actually hit him, but it was several minutes before Brig could capture her flailing arms and twist them behind her back. The sheer uselessness of fighting someone so much stronger than herself reduced Jordanna to a trembling mass of broken sobs.

Chapter XXII

BRIG HELD HER close, absorbing her violent shudders with his body. No actress, no matter how excellent, could have worked herself into this emotional state. A frown gathered on his forehead, the lines deepening as the quaking sobs became less severe. He released her arms and stroked the tangled silk of her auburn hair. His chest was wet with her tears.

"It isn't true," he heard her murmur brokenly.

His hand trembled as it cupped her jaw and lifted her face for his inspection. Tormented anguish was in the troubled green flecks of her hazel eyes. The doubts of her guilt that had been nagging him were suddenly confirmed and relief trembled through him, relief and a swelling gentleness.

"You didn't know, did you?"

She covered her ears with her hands to block out his voice and shut her eyes tightly, squeezing out the last tears. "I don't want to hear any more of your lies about my father."

Brig gathered her stiff body into his arms and rubbed

his chin against her hair. He felt her pain and confusion, the wrenching tear of loyalty. He realized how brutal he had been to a victim as innocent as himself, but he'd had to be sure.

"It's true, Jordanna. I'm sorry." His voice was husky with regret. "Fletcher did not choose me by accident to guide this hunting party. He had me thoroughly investigated. He knew all about my association with Max and the Sanger Corporation, all the ill feelings that were between us. He killed Max and set me up as the fall guy if there was any evidence uncovered to prove it wasn't an accident. Unfortunately for him, I found the evidence and put two and two together."

"But why?" she protested, lifting her puzzled face to him and impatiently wiping away the tears trickling down her cheek. "Why would he want to kill Max?"

"I don't know. That's the one thing I haven't been able to figure out." A nerve jerked in his jaw. "Do you? What was Max to him?"

"He was . . . just a business acquaintance." Jordanna lifted her shoulders in an unknowing shrug. "He'd been bugging Dad to buy some stock in the company. Dad said he'd had the company investigated and . . ." She stopped, her widened gaze flying in comprehension to Brig. "He had you investigated, too. Dad was the one who told me you were once a mercenary, not Max. He did know all about you."

"Did he have any intentions of buying Max's stock?" Brig saw the fear and alarm that leapt into her eyes.

He watched her struggle to remember. "He said he might. The company was almost bankrupt, but he thought with financial backing and the right man in charge, it would be all right. Do you inherit it all, Brig?"

"Yes. Did he tell you that, too?"

"Yes." Jordanna lowered her head, looking away from him. "Dad wouldn't kill Max. He had no reason."

"Why did he invite Max along?"

"He didn't. You did." She paused, doubt flashing in her eyes. "Didn't you? He told us you did."

"I didn't invite Max."

"But how could that be?" Her head moved in bewildered denial. "Dad said you invited Max, and there wasn't anything he could do about it. You two were cousins and it was a long time since you'd been together. Besides which, Max wanted to sell him that stock."

"I was there when your father initially made the suggestion that Max should come on a hunting trip with him. Later, he specifically suggested this trip. Max jumped at the chance, but certainly not because of me," Brig insisted dryly. "In fact, I'm sure he wished I was on the other side of the world."

"But it doesn't make sense," she argued, stiffening in his arms. "Why would Dad lie about the invitation? Why would he say you invited him if you didn't?"

"You'll have to ask him that question. I can only guess that he didn't want anyone suspecting that he wanted Max on the hunting trip. If you and everyone else believed that I invited Max, and your father had to tolerate his presence, he would be less of a suspect if the murder was uncovered."

"No. Dad wouldn't do this." Jordanna twisted out of his arms, angry and uncertain. "You're making all of this up. All I have is your word that he has anything to do with Max's death."

"That's part of the plan. My word against his. An ex-mercenary against a very wealthy and highly respected man. That's why I didn't mention any of this to the authorities until I could get some proof. It's a pity that bullet didn't get lodged in my leg so I would have it." Brig watched her, noting the contradiction in her proudly lifted head and her hunched shoulders. "Take him down off the pedestal, Jordanna. He's out there right now, hunting me."

"Why shouldn't he be?" She pivoted around to confront him, flame-brown hair whirling about her shoulders. "He probably thinks we got lost in that storm, or that you abducted me. Kit and Jocko are probably with him."

"Believe me, Fletcher didn't go back to camp without us," Brig stated. "He can't risk a search party until he knows I'm dead. Jocko won't be worried about us until we don't show up tonight. He'll think we started back for camp too late yesterday and holed up when the snow came. Fletcher isn't going to have them help him find us. He can't risk having witnesses he can't control around when I meet with my 'hunting accident.' "

"What about me? I'm one of your witnesses," Jordanna challenged.

"You don't even want to believe he's responsible for this." Brig touched his wounded thigh. "Daddy can't do any wrong in your eyes. He can control you. He can convince you it was a tragic accident. The gun went off accidentally—or he mistook me for some wild game. I'm sure he'll come up with a good story and you'll be so anxious to believe him, you won't question it."

"No," she denied, but her gaze fell under his level regard.

"But he couldn't have Jocko along, because he might present a problem. Your father has to have guessed that he can't buy Jocko's silence any more than he could have bought mine."

"Buy your silence? What are you talking about?"

"He made me a very tempting proposition in town the other day, when I confronted him about Max's death."

"What kind of a proposition?" She looked wary and uncertain.

"First, he offered to provide the financial backing the Sanger Company needed, fully aware that I would inherit it. He didn't like it when I told him what he could do with his money and the Sanger Corporation."

"You can't condemn him for making that offer. He wasn't necessarily trying to buy you," she argued. "Dad had already said that with the right man in charge, he would be interested in investing in the company. He probably thought you were the right man."

"Maybe. But when I turned down that offer, he made me a second, more tempting one. You."

"You're lying!" she hissed, and would have slapped him if Brig hadn't caught her hand. This time he didn't seek to punish her, and his grip was firm rather than brutal.

"He suggested in a roundabout way that you would marry me if I asked you." He saw the pink of humiliation creep into her cheeks. "When I didn't react to the idea with proper enthusiasm, he indicated that his wedding gift to us would enable me to make a considerable number of costly improvements to the ranch."

"No doubt you told him what he could do with that offer, too," Jordanna murmured tightly.

"I did," Brig admitted. "When he discovered he couldn't keep Max's skeleton in the family closet, he had to resort to this."

"But why? You haven't given me a single reason. There must be some kind of mistake." Brig could see the desperation clawing at her.

"I don't know the reason, but I'm going to find out." He kept his voice calm, but it didn't mask his determination. "Whatever it is, it's been building up inside him for a long time. I think he tried to ruin Max financially first. Max was a threat to your father somehow, and he tried to crush him. When that didn't work, he killed him."

"You're mistaken. You have to be." Brig heard the doubt in her voice.

"I'm right," he said quietly. "I just hope you're not standing over my body when you finally realize it." He heard her sharp gasp of dismay and knew he had said all he could say. She had to think it over herself and decide whether to believe him or not. "The snow is melting in the pot. You said something about some soup." He reached for his shirt. "I'll bring in some of the firewood you found outside."

"Your leg . . ." she started to protest.

"It's fine."

It hurt like hell, but he couldn't let it stiffen up on

him. There wasn't much chance that Fletcher would find this cabin. The snow would have covered their tracks. They would be safe as long as they stayed here, but how long could they last, subsisting on tree bark? Without weapons, their only hope of catching wild game was with snares. Brig didn't want to rely on that. Either way, sooner or later they would have to walk out of here. It had to be sooner, while they had the strength and before they became weakened by lack of food. There was always the risk that Fletcher might see the smoke from the chimney and come to investigate. The cabin, instead of a shelter, would become a death-trap for him.

By tonight, Jocko would be worried. Tomorrow morning he would start looking for them. If they could reach Jocko or the camp . . . It bothered Brig that he didn't know where Fletcher was. The hunter had to know that he would make a try for the camp and would have found a vantage point to cover the routes in. Where would that be? Brig studied the terrain in his mind, choosing and rejecting locations and ending up with a handful of potential sites.

Shrugging into his jacket, Brig glanced at Jordanna. She was adding the bark strips to the simmering snow water. His distraction had worked. She had stopped arguing with him and had begun mulling it all over in her mind. She needed this time to think. So did he.

The circumstances had changed dramatically in the last hour. Before, he had been angry enough to use her as a shield—angry because he had believed she was a part of it—angry because he had known it and let himself get maneuvered anyway—and angry because he had continued to feel desire toward her. Only none of that was true. Jordanna hadn't been deceiving him. She, too, had unwittingly been used by her father all along.

His first step toward the door brought a stabbing protest of pain from his wound. Beads of perspiration formed on his forehead. Brig stopped and waited until the piercing fire had receded. He tried again, using his left leg much more gingerly. Outside the cabin, Brig wiped the sweat from his face and breathed deeply of the sharp, cold air. Wounded, he had walked to this cabin, and wounded he would walk away from it.

But he was worried about Jordanna and what would happen when her father found them. A ricochet, a stray bullet, and she could be seriously hurt. Brig still did not believe that Fletcher would risk hurting her, but inadvertenly he could. By bringing her with him, he had endangered her. He had to get both of them out of this alive, not just himself. If anything happened to Jordanna, it would be his fault, and Brig didn't know if he could live with that. He didn't know if he could live without her.

He scanned the wooded area around the cabin. Looking up, he studied the wisps of smoke rising from the chimney. The wood was dry and burning with little smoke. But how far away could it be seen? And how close was Fletcher?

It was time to do some scouting, whether he felt up to it or not. Keeping to the cover of the trees and rocks, Brig worked his way to the mouth of the high canyon. Caution dictated that he never expose himself for too long a period and risk being seen by a pair of high-powered binoculars. He had to take it slow as well, so that he wouldn't start bleeding again.

Near the mouth of the canyon, he crawled up a rock incline for a better view. Brig wished for a pair of binoculars as he slowly scanned the ridges and plateaus. Nothing stirred. It looked like a Christmas card painting of snow-covered mountains and trees. He glanced in the direction of the cabin. The thin trail of smoke from the chimney was just barely visible against its background of white. He waited and watched for fifteen minutes. Then his snowy chair began to numb him with the cold.

Before he started back, Brig broke off a bough of an evergreen and brushed out his tracks in the snow, following the same route back to the cabin. Anyone looking at it from a distance, and through a pair of binoculars, would never notice the brush marks in the snow. But if Fletcher got close enough to see it with a naked eye, he'd recognize it for what it was.

Outside the cabin, Brig stopped to rest, then loaded his arms with logs from the woodbox and carried them inside. The long walk had tired him considerably. He badly needed to rest, but he had worked some of the stiffness out of his leg, if not the soreness.

Jordanna was standing in front of the fireplace, facing the flames, a hand braced against the stones. Dejection showed in her slumped shoulders and her downcast eyes. She didn't turn when he entered or indicate that she knew he was back. Brig dumped the firewood in the corner and limped over to stand beside her.

"Is that soup ready?" He took off his gloves to rub his hands and hold them out to the heat of the fire. His sideways glance noted her quivering chin.

"It's ready—for all the good it does us," she answered tightly. "We don't have any spoons or cups or any way to eat it. And we certainly can't drink it out of that kettle." There was no mistaking the defeat in her voice.

"Hey," he chided her softly. She had been through hell in these last twenty-four hours. The strain was beginning to take its toll. He cupped his hand on the back of her neck and made her face him. A tired smile of reassurance curved the corners of his mouth. "The worst is over, Jordanna. You saved my life yesterday. You helped me make it to this cabin; you built the fire after I passed out; you got me out of those wet clothes and bandaged my wound; you gathered firewood and water and stayed awake to keep the fire going; and this morning, you went out and helped yourself from nature's larder. You are a helluva woman, Jordanna Smith. Don't fall apart on me now. I need you."

His gaze slid to her tremulous mouth. Brig bent his head to kiss those soft lips. At first they were passive to his touch, but gradually she submitted to his gentle persuasion. A surge of protectiveness welled within him, a sweetly fierce emotion. When he lifted his head, Brig discovered there was a lump in his throat, choking him up.

"Let's do a bit of scavenging," he suggested huskily. "Whoever built this cabin must have left some tin cans around or some broken pottery. We'll find something."

Jordanna nodded a mute acceptance of his suggestion, a liquid brilliance to her eyes. Together they searched the dark and filthy corners of the cabin. Rust had eaten holes in the tin cans they found. Brig was starting to get discouraged when Jordanna found a pottery shaving mug with a corner chipped out of the lip.

While she went outside to wash it in the snow, Brig returned to the fire and carefully lowered himself to sit on the floor, his back resting against the table. His leg was throbbing and it felt three times its normal size. But the swelling was only slight and the heat felt normal for an injury, something he remembered from previous wounds.

When Jordanna returned, she insisted that he eat first. Brig was feeling too tired to argue. He drank two cups of the soup, chewing the bits of cooked bark. It tasted good, considering, and filled the emptiness in his stomach. Handing her the mug, he took off his jacket and arranged it as a pillow, then stretched out on his back.

"Dry out that wood I brought in before you put it on the fire. I don't want any more smoke coming out of the chimney than is absolutely necessary," he cautioned before he closed his eyes to let the tiredness claim him.

Jordanna sat in front of the fireplace, her knees bent, her arms hugged around them. It was late in the afternoon by her watch and Brig was still sleeping. She bit at her lower lip, remembering all the accusations he had made. Some of them had made sense. She raked her fingers through her hair. She just couldn't believe her father had killed Max. But who had shot at Brig? Torment darkened her gaze as she looked at him.

Suddenly she realized he wasn't sleeping. How long had he been watching her through the narrow slits of his lashes? She untangled her fingers from her hair and smoothed them nervously over her thighs. Jordanna stared quickly into the flames.

"You still doubt what I told you." His voice was low, neither accusing nor condemning.

"I can't help thinking you made a mistake." She didn't turn, but she heard him sit up. "I'm sure there is a logical and rational explanation for everything that's happened."

"Naturally, one that would exonerate your father," he murmured.

"Yes." Her lips felt dry. She moistened them.

One of her hands was swallowed in the grip of his. Startled, she turned to find him sitting parallel, facing her. He was studying her hand, tracing the length of her slender fingers, caressing it in a curious fashion.

"Once you told me that you couldn't make me believe you." He didn't look at her as he spoke. "But you were wrong. I believe you meant the things you said to me. You weren't lying to me, Jordanna. And I'm not lying to you now."

Brig lifted his gaze. The intense look in the dark sheen of his eyes caught at her breath. The tension in his body communicated itself to her. A muscle worked in his lean jaw as his gaze roamed possessively over her face.

"You were my weakness, Jordanna," he continued. "Even when I believed you and your father were using me, I couldn't resist you. You ate at my heart, my mind, and my body. The hunger started that night in New York at the party. When I came back, I couldn't forget you. There were feelings that I thought had died within me, but you made them come alive. But I didn't like the idea of just being your stud, so I tried to hate you."

"My stud?!" The term hurt. Jordanna tried to pull her hand from his, but he wouldn't let her go.

"Don't forget I believed I was being used, the rich girl getting her kicks with a mountain guide, ex-soldier of fortune. If you were one of the fringe benefits for accepting Fletcher's deal, I wanted you enough to accept—no matter what it made me. I said some things, deliberately, to hurt you." He shook his head glancing to the side to swear softly. "Damn. I'm not any good at long speeches. I'm in love with you, Jordanna."

An incredulous light entered her eyes. She wanted so desperately to believe him that she was afraid. It tied her tongue and her silence made his features grim and tight, thinning his mouth to give it a ruthless look beneath the dark mustache.

"You once said you loved me. By God, you hadn't better have changed your mind." His eyes blazed suddenly as he shifted his hold on her hand to lock their thumbs together. "Because I'm not letting you go."

Jordanna didn't mind the pain in this grip. "I don't want you to let me go." Her voice wobbled.

She curled her long legs beneath her so she could sit closer to him. With her other hand, she reached out to trace and smooth the grimness from his mouth and jaw. He shuddered violently at her touch and hauled her into his arms. Crushing her against him, the pain he inflicted was a sweet sting of love. His hard, demanding kiss was almost cruel from the lack of self-control. Brig stamped his ownership on her lips before he eased the pressure to permit a response. The hammering of his heart seemed to drive itself right through her, until her heart was thundering as loudly as his. Jordanna gloried in the reason for his roughness. His declaration had exposed himself to pain and hurt. He had permitted her to see his vulnerability and given her the power to bring him to his knees. But that wasn't where she wanted him. Trembling with the beauty of his gift, she pressed light, adoring kisses over his eyelids, cheek, and jaw.

"I used to have this aching pocket of emptiness in

me," Jordanna told him in a throbbing whisper, reveling in the rasp of his cheek against her sensitive lips. "Sometimes it would get so big that I wanted to slip into its loneliness and die. Physical satisfaction never filled it. Then I met you at the party. That emptiness became filled with so many sensations, emotions, and feelings that it overflowed. You were a total stranger. I didn't even know your name. I looked all over for you afterwards, but you'd gone."

"I thought I'd just made love to my host's mistress." Brig lifted his head to let his gaze roam over her face. His hand was caressing the sleek curve of her neck, a finger following the wild throbbing of her pulse down to the hollow of her throat. "It wouldn't have made any difference, if I had known you were his daughter. It isn't the accepted thing to do in polite society to take a man's money and his daughter." His mouth twisted in self-derision. "All I intended to do was kiss you, but it got out of control. When I came to my senses, I wasn't very proud of myself. God knows, I tried to forget you."

Jordanna traced the cruel thinness of his upper lip and the sensual fullness of the lower one. A twinge of pain flickered through her.

"Did . . . that girl at the bar help you? Trudie?"

The pause became so long that she had to lift her gaze to his eyes. They regarded her steadily. "Yes." His honesty hurt, but it was a measure of his love that he didn't deceive her. "She had about as much success as a teacup of water on a forest fire. Did you find help?"

Jordanna gave a brief, negative shake of her head. "I couldn't seem to settle for second-best anymore," she admitted. "I was almost convinced I'd never see you again."

"Didn't you ever ask who I was?" There was a curious flick of one eyebrow.

"I started to ask Olivia, but . . ." Jordanna remembered the painful misconception she had made. She didn't want to go into that now. There would be other times to air the family linen. ". . . how do you say . . . there was this stranger who made love to me. Do you know who he was?"

The half-mocking smile she wore began fading as his fingers deftly eased the buttons of her blouse free of the material. Her skin began to warm in advance of his caressing hands. His mouth teased the curves of her lips, brushing over their outline, the warmth of his breath mingling with hers.

"As I recall," Brig murmured, "the stranger had a lot fewer clothes to contend with." He pushed the blouse from her shoulders, leaving Jordanna to free her arms from the sleeves.

"I think you're right." Her heart was altering in rhythm with her shallowing breath, quickening and skittering across her ribs like a stone skipping across the surface of a pond.

While his mouth continued to tantalize her lips, Brig slid one hand under the thick material of her underwear top. The roughness of his calloused palm was a pleasant rasp against the smoothness of her stomach. Soft tremors quivered through her at the evocative caress.

"Does a man who loves you get a little cooperation or does he have to struggle without help?" His mouth followed the curve of her jaw to take a sensuous bite of her earlobe in mock punishment. The action drew a gasp of pure pleasure from Jordanna.

"I'd love to have you undress me." The husky pitch of her voice revealed the havoc he was creating with her senses. "But, under the circumstances . . ." The words trailed away, the need for them gone.

By mutual consent, they drifted apart to undress themselves as they sat in front of the fire. One watched as the layers of clothing came off the other. Jordanna studied the firelight playing over Brig's face. Its flickering light seemed to soften the angles of his features. Or was it the love, she wondered, blazing in his dark eyes, that had melted the hardness?

Brig was taking longer to undress than she was, although neither hurried. As she pushed her longjohns over her knees, his gaze burned a path from her hip down the length of her thigh. He winced, gritting his teeth against the sudden shaft of pain that accompanied his attempt to ease his Levis down his hips. Brig quickly concealed it but Jordanna had caught the brief flash of white teeth against the dark of his mustache.

"Let me help." She rose on her knees, not feeling the gritty floor beneath them. "I had some practice at this the other night."

Without arguing, Brig laid back on his coat, crossing his hands beneath his head for a pillow. Her smile trembled with the exquisite intimacy of the moment. Carefully Jordanna worked his clothes over the bandaged wound. It was difficult to concentrate under the disturbing inspection of his gaze surveying the naturally graceful movements of her nude form.

When his clothes were discarded, Jordanna sat on her bare heels, poised near his knees. She sought his eyes, feeling that wonderful unsureness that only comes with love. Brig stretched out a hand toward her, his eyes warm with command. Hesitantly, she took hold of his hand, his strong fingers entwining with hers. With the ease of a big man, he pulled her to him, laying her down to stretch her length beside his.

A skillful hand began caressing her body, languidly stimulating flesh that needed little incentive to react to his touch. The fleece lining of his coat was beneath her, but Jordanna was more conscious of the warm feel of his hard body. Seeking her mouth, Brig turned on his side. Dark chest hairs tickled her sensitive breasts. The delightful torment arched her closer until the solid wall of his chest was flattening her breasts and the curling hairs brushed all the way to her stomach.

His breath quickened, like hers, as he eased his weight around her. His hands and mouth were coaxing and driving gasps of pleasure from her. Jordanna's reaction stimulated him and sent her own senses spinning. The urgent need of his thrusting male form communicated itself to her and there was an answering ache within her, exciting and overwhelming. It was a rapturous discovery, to not only love but be loved in return.

Her fingernails flexed catlike into his hard shoulders as his mouth seared a passage down her throat and followed the natural valley between her breasts to her stomach. His tongue traced a hot circle around her navel. Jordanna bit at her lower lip to hold back the moan of sheer pleasure.

"Don't hold back," Brig ordered thickly. "Scream, if it's what you feel."

His mouth brushed the tender tips of her breasts, then rolled one around his tongue. The delicious sensation curled her toes and Jordanna didn't check the wild moan of ecstacy that came from her throat. His hand glided along her inner thigh and she moved against it. Her caressing hands felt his muscles trembling under her touch. She thrilled to the sound of her name, and the murmured love words he whispered. Brig groaned with shivering longing as he shifted his weight on top of her, pinning Jordanna to his jacket. His mouth crushed onto her in hard demand and she wrapped her legs around his hips, lost to the sensual claims of the act of complete love.

Chapter XXIII

JORDANNA LAY INSIDE his arm, facing him, her fingers tracing the hard features. Her flesh had been calmed by his lovemaking, but her soul was still soaring on the wings of his love. One, rough, masculine leg was hooked over her knees to keep her near, while a hand absently roamed the curve of her waist and hip. His eyes were brown velvet, sliding over every detail of her face.

"I never understood why women always wanted to talk after they had made love." His low voice retained its seductive pitch.

"What did you want to do?" Jordanna let a fingertip follow the sensual outline of his bottom lip, liking to watch his mouth form words.

"Most of the time I listened to their comments and questions while trying to figure out a way to get the hell out of the bed," Brig admitted without remorse. "Otherwise, I either wanted to roll over and go to sleep, or make love again."

"Which do you want to do now?" Her teasing question was faintly breathless and perfectly serious.

His gaze was dark and solemn. "I just want you to know how much I enjoy making love to you, and how good it feels to me to be inside you. You can't possibly know what it's like to feel your breasts against my skin or the thrill it gives me to know you are as wildly aroused as I am."

"I'll bet there are sensations of my own that are comparable." Jordanna lightly contested his implication that the intensity was one-sided.

"It's more than that." Brig refused to make light of it. "There is quiet pleasure in having you ride beside me through the mountains, a hidden joy in sharing the grandeur of the scenery with you, and a satisfaction that can't be described sitting with you in front of a campfire. It's your company that pleases me, Jordanna. The sexual gratification your body provides has become a fringe benefit."

Love shimmered in her eyes, glistening jewel-green. "And you said you weren't any good with words."

"I'm not." His dark brows furrowed together. "If I was, I'd find some easy way to ask you to marry me without feeling like I was tripping over some stilted phrase that had become so overused that it lost its meaning."

"I would be proud to marry you, Brig McCord. You don't even have to ask." Her voice wavered on an emotionally charged note.

Brig kissed her hard, sealing the promise while holding back the passion. A crooked smile slanted his mouth as he drew back and sighed. "I guess I'll have to build a bunkhouse for the boys, so we can start filling the upstairs bedrooms with children."

Children, Jordanna thought, with dusty brown eyes and dark brown hair. She wanted to wrap the images in her arms and hug them close. She could picture a small version of Brig tagging behind his father as he walked across the ranch yard. She could even see herself standing on the porch of the log house watching the two of them.

She gazed at Brig, unaware of the serene radiance in her expression. "We might be starting a family sooner than you think, thanks to your virility and the fact that my pills are back at camp," she admitted quite happily.

His nostrils flared to take in a quick breath; then his hand slid protectively over her stomach. With a groan, he buried his face in the curve of her long neck. The grip of the hands that held her close was fiercely gentle. Jordanna remembered that a male wolf shared equally the responsibility of raising the cubs with its mate. It was several minutes before the faint tremors stopped quivering through him and he drew away.

"Listen to me, Jordanna." His hand trembled slightly as it smoothed the hair behind her ear. The sternly serious look in his eyes was vaguely frightening. "Tomorrow Jocko will be out looking for us. He'll know something is wrong when we don't come back to camp today. If I'm lucky, I'll find Jocko before your father finds me."

Reality crashed onto the untainted beauty of her love. In the midst of its enchantment, Jordanna had momentarily forgotten the suspicions Brig had about her father and her own confusion about them.

"No." She rejected the subject from their conversation, wanting nothing to spoil the precious moments they were sharing. "I don't want to talk about it." She looked away, focusing her gaze on the ivory wool of the inside lining of his jacket beneath them.

"We have to," Brig insisted and continued. "When I leave in the morning, I want you to stay here where you'll be safe."

"No!"

Brig pretended not to hear her. "I have the paper from my cigarette pack. I'll draw a map to show where the cabin is . . . in case something happens to me, then they'll be able to find you."

"Nothing is going to happen to you!" She violently denied the possibility. It was a double denial—both a belief that he was wrong about her father and a heart-felt plea that fate wouldn't be so cruel as to take Brig from her so soon.

The pitying look in his eyes at her continued disbe-lief was hard to hold. "Not if I can help it, it won't." He stroked a caressing finger across her cheek. "I've never had more reason to want to stay alive than I do now."

"Stop it!" Jordanna choked on the words. "You've made a mistake about Dad. Somehow you have things confused."

"For your sake, I wish I did." His voice was heavy.

"We'll find him tomorrow. And he'll explain it all."

"You're going to stay here in the cabin," Brig re-peated. "I don't want to risk a chance that you might be harmed."

"Dad would never hurt me. That's absurd!" she denied.

"Not deliberately, he wouldn't," he agreed. "But a quick shot, a bad aim, a bullet that goes astray, a ricochet—No, there are too many possibilities. As long as I know you are here and safe, I'll only have myself to worry about." Brig ignored the protest in her expression. "I'll make certain you have plenty of firewood and set out some snares before I leave to-morrow. If no one comes for you by the day after tomorrow, set the cabin on fire. Someone is bound to see the smoke and come to investigate."

"No!" She angrily rejected his suggestion, her eyes flashing with unshed tears of pain. "I'm not staying here without you. If you leave tomorrow, so do I."

"Dammit, listen to me, Jordanna." He gave her a hard shake. "I'm trying to do what's best."

A stillness claimed her, hardening her determination. "I'm not staying here alone, and you can't make me, Brig," Jordanna informed him. "Either I leave with you, or I'll follow you. I won't be left behind."

An eyebrow arched in sharp query, his gaze becoming narrowed and probing. "Why?" he demanded.

"Because . . ." She wasn't sure of the reason.

". . . because you aren't positive that I'm wrong about your father. That's it, isn't it?" There was grim satisfaction in his conclusion and Jordanna wavered uncertainly.

"I . . . don't know if you are or not." The admission was frightening. She had known her father all her life. Yet she loved this man. It was a situation that pulled her trust and loyalty in two different directions. She felt trapped between two equally powerful magnets. "I won't stay behind, Brig," Jordanna insisted again. "Don't ask me."

"Don't you see, Jordanna?" His mouth quirked in a rueful smile. "I don't want you to get caught in a situation where you have to choose between us."

It was a barely stifled cry that came from her throat. Immediately, she was wrapped inside his arms. She clung to him, needing his comfort and his strength. She began to cry softly and Brig kissed the tears that dampened her cheeks. From a distance she heard his words, swearing his love for her and his wish to spare her. When her face had been kissed dry, she began returning the kisses he showered on her. The response had a catalytic effect, producing a storm of passion that didn't pass until its fury had been spent.

Brig was up before Jordanna the next morning. She knew if she hadn't awakened when she did, he would have left without her, but she didn't give him the chance. He tried once more to persuade her to stay where it was safe.

She had stood before him in stubborn defiance. "I'm going with you. Whatever happens . . . if anything happens," she had hastily corrected, "I am going to be there when it does."

Brig had been angry, but without the means to force her to stay. They had set out from the cabin with a grim silence between them. He was limping, hampered by the wound. Jordanna's insistence that they should take turns breaking a path through the snow was something he accepted very grudgingly. Logic made him agree to her plan, when pride demanded that he lead the way.

Again the skies were clear and the sun bright, but the temperature was cold. The snow, which in places had drifted to more than a foot, showed no signs of meeting in the glaring sunlight. Their breaths were vapor clouds, preceding each slogging step through the white powder.

The route Brig chose was not an easy one. They stopped often to rest, never allowing perspiration to form and freeze against their skin. They had traveled several miles before Jordanna realized Brig had not set a direct course back to camp. For a split second, she thought he might have lost his bearings, that perhaps a fever might have affected his mental state. An instant later, she guessed his reason for choosing this circuitous route through the roughest terrain. Brig was avoiding her father. The rest stops were chosen to occur at vantage points where he could survey the land ahead of them. Their route was dictated by the cover it provided—trees, rocks, or shrubs. Jordanna wanted to decry the need for such caution, but she was less positive than she had ever been before.

Animal tracks were plentiful in the snow, but there wasn't a sign anywhere of any human passage except their own. They seemed alone in the mountains, with only the wind dancing over the snow and cloud shadows floating across the mountainsides. The loneliness didn't bother Jordanna, only Brig's wariness, which seemed to increase the more familiar the terrain became and the closer they came to camp. It was almost tangible. His gaze was restless, never pausing, always searching. His alertness was uncanny, as if every one of his senses were honed to a sharp edge. The sensation shivered along her nerve ends. It reminded Jordanna of an animal sensing danger without knowing in which direction it lurked.

Leaning against a cold boulder, Jordanna shielded her eyes from the sun. Frigid air filled her lungs with each breath. Her gaze traveled to Brig. They hadn't exchanged a word the last mile. Camp wasn't more than two miles away. Brig was studying the country between them, careful not to skyline himself on the ridge. Jordanna heard him swear under his breath.

"What's wrong?" She held her breath as she asked the question.

His sideways glance was impatient and sharp. "I expected Jocko to be in this area. It looks like I guessed wrong." As he turned to limp to where she stood, Jordanna saw the dark, wet patch staining his Levis.

"Your wound has opened up. You're bleeding again," she accused.

"Tell me something I don't already know—like where your father is . . . or Jocko," he snapped.

"If I knew where either of them were, I would tell you," Jordanna flashed and pivoted from him.

Her shoulders were captured by his leather-gloved hands and hauled backwards to his chest. The sudden action knocked the hat from her head. The wind blew her hair free as the hat tumbled into the snow. Jordanna resisted his iron grip for an instant. Then she felt his lean jaw against her hair.

"The sunshine is in your hair again," Brig murmured. "I wish all this was behind us and we were back in our bed at the ranch." The apology that he couldn't voice was in his loving words.

"So do I," she agreed fervently. "And we'll be laughing over this misunderstanding about Dad."

He sighed heavily at her statement and lifted his

head. "Come on." He pushed her forward. "It's time we moved out again."

"But this isn't the way to camp," Jordanna protested when she realized the direction they were taking.

"We can't go that way. There isn't any cover. We'd be too exposed to . . . We'd be too exposed." Brig didn't correct his sentence quickly enough to keep Jordanna from guessing how he had intended to finish it. They would be too exposed to a rifleman. He didn't believe for a minute that there would ever come a time that they would laugh about this. His certainty frightened her. "We'll go this way," Brig directed.

Jordanna picked up her hat and looked in the direction he indicated. The terrain was forbidding and rough. Rocks swept clean by the wind and gleaming with icy crystals. It meant climbing higher and treacherous footing.

"You'll never make it, Brig. Not with that wound." It was a flat statement.

"I'll have to make it." There was a faint shrug of his shoulders as he took a step forward, almost dragging his left leg.

"You're already bleeding," Jordanna pointed out again. "How much do you think you can lose before you pass out?"

"I'll have to find out, won't I?" Twisted humor crooked his mouth.

"No. I can make it to camp from here and it won't matter if I'm exposed," she reasoned. "There will be spare horses. You can stay here and I'll ride back for you."

She expected Brig to argue. He studied her for a minute, then nodded, "Alright. I'll wait here for you."

Instead of being relieved, Jordanna was worried by his easy acceptance of her suggestion. It had to mean his leg was bothering him a great deal more than he had let her see.

"I'll hurry," she promised.

His gaze was suddenly very intense. "Just make it safely, Jordanna." The cool leather of his gloved fingers caught her chin and lifted it to meet his bending head. His mouth was hard in its possession of her lips, claiming them fiercely, as if it might be the last time. Fear splintered through Jordanna, and she clung to him until he firmly set her away from him.

"I'll be waiting for you."

"I'll come back," she whispered, feeling close to tears.

Relief sighed through him as Jordanna crested the rimrock and started down the slope. Away from him, she would be safe. Brig limped near the crest and eased himself into a sitting position that would permit him to see over the rise. He packed his left leg with snow, the white flakes turning crimson as they became stained with his blood. Within a few minutes, the cold pack began to numb his throbbing leg and, he hoped, slow the flow of blood.

The loss of blood and hunger had weakened him more than he had expected. He desperately needed these additional minutes of rest to conserve what strength remained. He watched Jordanna work her way across the barren mountain plateau until she was out of sight. He had never felt so lonely in his life. Firmly he pushed the empty ache aside and made a searching sweep of the surrounding craggy hills.

Compelled by an urgency that ran deeper than mere concern for Brig's injury, Jordanna pushed herself onward without stopping to rest. Once a rabbit streaked madly out of her path, but it was the only living thing she saw.

The camp looked deserted when she staggered warily into it. From the picket line in the trees, a horse whickered. Gulping in a cold breath, Jordanna walked toward the large tent where the spare tack was kept. As she lifted back the tent flap, she immediately felt the warmth from the shepherd's stove tingle over her. In the shadowy dimness, something moved.

"Jordanna!"

The voice was instantly recognizable. "Kit!" She laughed his name with a crazy kind of relief.

"My God, where have you been? We've been out of our minds worrying about you," her brother accused as he hopped toward her. "Jocko went out to look for you. Did he find you? Where's Dad and Brig?"

"I forgot about your ankle. How is it?" Considering all that had happened since his accident, it wasn't surprising. Then the inanity of her question struck her, followed instantly by the realization of what he'd asked her. "Dad isn't here?" Brig had been right when he'd insisted her father wouldn't return to camp. What else was he right about?

"No." Kit frowned. "Isn't he with you?"

"No. We . . . We got separated," she explained lamely.

"That snow came down pretty thick for awhile." He looked worried. "Are you all right? There's coffee on. You must be hungry. Jocko fixed some stew. Come on over here by the stove so you can get warm. You must be half-frozen by now."

"No, not now." She resisted his attempt to curve an arm around her shoulders and escort her deeper into the tent. "I have to leave. I just came in for the bridles and a saddle if there is one. Brig's hurt. I have to go back to him."

"He's hurt?" Kit immediately changed his direction, hobbling over to where his coat and hat lay. "I'll go with you. How bad is it? What happened?"

Jordanna wished he wouldn't bombard her with questions. Exhaustion and hunger made it difficult to think clearly at the moment. Now there was the additional confusion of her father's role in all this.

"It's his leg." She hurried toward the bridles lying

neatly in one corner. There was only one saddle. She picked it up, too, swinging it onto her shoulder.

"Did he break it?" Her brother came up beside her to relieve her of the bridles.

"No." Jordanna hesitated, then admitted, "Brig was shot. He has this ridiculous notion that Dad did it." She laughed shakily and wanted Kit to join in.

"Oh, my God!" he groaned and pain flashed across his face.

His reaction scared her. "It's funny, isn't it?" she demanded. "It's really so impossible that . . ."

"Why? Does Brig know why?" her brother interrupted.

"He says . . . it's because he knows that Dad killed Max. That isn't true, of course," she added quickly and felt a curling nausea in her stomach at the sight of Kit's expression. "It isn't. You don't believe him, do you?"

"Did Brig know *how* Max was killed?" A grim sadness pulled at his features.

"He showed me a briar that he found under the saddle." A cold feeling of dread washed over her. It was all a nightmare and she wanted desperately to wake up. She pushed her way out of the tent into the bright sunlight. Her brother limped along side of her.

"I wondered . . . I hoped . . ." Kit shook his head, unable to finish either sentence. His shoulders drooped as he closed his eyes and compressed his lips tightly together.

"Why?" The word bubbled from her throat and Jordanna swallowed. "Why would Dad want to kill Max? What reason would he have? Brig couldn't give me one. Can you?"

"I was afraid something like this would happen," Kit murmured aloud. "I thought if I came along I could stop it. I wanted so much to believe it was an accident . . . mere coincidence."

"But why?" she demanded that he answer. If her brother had come along because he suspected something might happen, then he had to know why. As they neared the picket line, a horse turned its head to watch their approach.

"Can't you guess, Jordanna?" The sad, cynical look was back in his dark eyes. "It was Mother."

"Max . . . was her latest lover?" she guessed and Kit nodded. "But that doesn't explain why," she argued. "It certainly isn't Livvie's first love. And Dad hasn't k-killed any of the others. So why single Max out from a multitude?"

"Mother was leaving him for Max . . . just as soon as Max arranged to sell Dad that stock. She couldn't divorce Dad in New York, so she was flying to Mexico or Nevada or anywhere she could get her freedom. Dad wasn't supposed to know. But she lost her temper one day and told him what she was going to do. Less than a week later, this business about Max going on the hunting trip came up. Mother was upset . . . crying. She swore to me that she hadn't mentioned Max's name, but Dad has had her followed for years. He can give you names, dates, places. There wasn't any chance he didn't know Max was her lover."

"Are you trying to convince me that Dad killed Max because Livvie was going to get a divorce because of him?" Jordanna shook her head in bewilderment. "Why should Dad care? Look at what she's done to him, how she's treated him."

"Look at how he's treated her."

"Dad has tried to give her everything she's ever wanted." Setting the saddle on the ground, she smoothed the blanket pad over the back of a bay horse.

"Except himself. Do you know why they have separate bedrooms?" her brother questioned and answered it before Jordanna could. "He moved out shortly after you were born and the doctors informed her that she couldn't have any more children. Her only function came to be an ornament to decorate his house. People could touch and admire, but they couldn't take her away from him. Dad crushed anyone who tried, including Max, I imagine."

Jordanna felt herself recoiling from the picture Kit was painting. "You make Dad sound so . . . cold-blooded. He isn't like that." She lifted the saddle into place. All her movements were unconsciously automatic.

"I've tried to explain to you before," he said patiently. "You only saw what Dad wanted you to see. Look at me. You thought you knew me, but you never really knew me at all, or you would have guessed Mike was my lover, not my roommate."

"Poor Max. Dad never intended to buy that stock. He was just stringing him along," Jordanna realized, speaking the thought aloud in a soft murmur. Her brother had supplied the motive. Now the evidence was too strong against her father for Jordanna to deny his guilt any longer. The disillusionment was a bitter, painful thing. "But why wasn't he satisfied with ruining Max?"

"Max's greed far outweighed his pride. Mother had told him about the marriage contract she had signed years ago. Dad was very generous in his provisions for her in the event of a legal separation or a divorce," Kit explained dryly. "It was a case of loving Mother and her money. Dad couldn't buy Max off—or financially ruin him—so he arranged the 'accident.' I half-believed that's what it was—even knowing all this."

With the cinch tightened, she unhooked the stirrup from the saddlehorn and let it hang. When she moved to the horse's head, Kit automatically handed her a bridle. Jordanna left the halter on as she forced the metal bit between the horse's teeth and slid the headstall over its ears. They were talking about a man she had regarded all her life as her father, yet he was suddenly a total stranger, a dangerous man who frightened her.

"Mother should have left him a long time ago." Jordanna buckled the cheek strap. "Why didn't she?"

"She was afraid. She knew the extent of Dad's power. He let her see it often enough," her brother commented and moved to the packhorse tied beside the bay. "If she'd left him, Dad would have ruined her socially. Granted, she would have had money, but he would have made sure she was shut out of the world she knew and shunned by her friends. She was frightened of being alone, knowing that Dad would use every means at his disposal to ruin any happiness she might find in another man's arms. Then Max came along and convinced her that together they could face anything. Love gave her courage."

Her widened gaze sought her brother's face. "Now Max is dead." She felt pity for her mother, compassion for the ordeal of her marriage. "You've always been close to her, Kit. You should have gone to New York to be with her now."

"Probably," he conceded. "But I didn't trust Dad. I thought he might be coming back out here to cover up some evidence. I had to know whether he was responsible for Max's death. I couldn't face Mother without knowing for sure, one way or the other." He handed her the second bridle.

An icy chill ran down Jordanna's spine. "He did come back to cover up evidence. Brig. The only reason Brig didn't tell anyone what he suspected was because he couldn't find a motive. We know the motive. Dad probably thinks I told him." Fear reduced her voice to a breathless whisper. "He is going to try to kill Brig, isn't he?"

The line of Kit's mouth grimmed. After an instant's hesitation, his head moved in a short, affirmative nod. "It's the only explanation."

"He's been hunting us." Jordanna forced herself to accept the fact. ". . . Hunting Brig. Brig lost his rifle in the storm. He's hurt. He wouldn't stand a chance if Dad found him."

The weakness of exhaustion and hunger left her

with a rush. All her movements became dictated by the need for haste. She fastened the bridle on the packhorse and took the last bridle from Kit's hands.

"I'll be right back." Kit started to move away, then paused. "Meet me at the tent."

Jordanna didn't know why her brother was going back, but it was the least of her concerns at the moment. With all three horses bridled, she unsnapped the lead ropes that tied them to the picket lines and hopped bareback onto one of the packhorses. Leading the other two, she walked the horses to the tent.

When Kit came out of the tent, he had a rifle in his hand. "We might need this."

Jordanna handed him the reins to the saddled horse and didn't comment on his remark. Not waiting for him to mount, she nudged the horse forward. The heat coming from the shaggy-coated horse warmed her legs.

The longer Brig studied the tracks Jordanna had left in the snow, the more worried he became. If Fletcher came across that trail, it would lead directly back to him. He needed a place that offered more concealment, yet kept him within view of this spot, so he could signal Jordanna when she returned.

Brig looked back over the ground they had covered to reach this point. A thick stand of pine trees was behind him. Among them was a tangled deadfall. It looked more secure than the jumble of rocks that surrounded him. Ricocheting bullets could tear him to pieces, bouncing off these rocks, while the fallen timber would absorb them.

Scraping the snow from his wound, he saw it had stopped bleeding, but the numbed and sore muscles had begun to stiffen. Brig pushed painfully to his feet, laboring the first few steps. The wind blew stiffly in front of the trees. It had almost succeeded in wiping out their previous tracks. Brig moved carefully toward the deadfall, trying to walk only where the snow was thin in order to make fewer tracks for Fletcher to trail.

At the first tree, he paused to lean against it and

take some of the weight off his left leg. The bark near his head exploded, driving splinters into his cheek. Brig dropped to the snow-covered ground as the rifle shot echoed through the mountains. His heart was thundering in his chest. He crawled on his belly to the deadfall.

Chapter XXIV

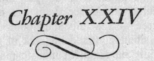

"DID YOU HEAR that?" Jordanna reined in her horse sharply and glanced worriedly at Kit.

He had stopped his horse at the sound of the rifle shot. His head was tipped at a listening angle. "Jocko said he'd fire two shots if he found you."

No second shot followed the first. The significance of that drew a sharp breath from Jordanna. She tugged once at the reins of the horse she led. When it strained in resistance, she let go and kicked the horse she rode into a canter. Kit was right behind her.

Brig waited behind the fallen timber. Sweat had broken out on his forehead as his eyes and ears strained to find his assailant. The carpet of powdery snow would silence any footsteps by one who knew how to walk on it. And he'd had plenty of opportunities to observe Fletcher's stalking skill. Brig wasn't that well concealed, but he didn't dare move. The snow hid the brittle branches in the deadfall. While trying to get into a better position, he might break one of them and he couldn't risk any noise that would draw attention to his location.

His cheek began to smart from the sweat trickling into the tiny cuts made by the splintering bark. Brig ignored it and moistened his dry lips. Out of the corner of his eye, he saw something move downhill and focused on it.

Fletcher was slowly moving toward the stand of trees. Brig guessed that the hunter probably wasn't sure whether his bullet had dropped him or not. In a moment, Fletcher would see there was no body at the base of the tree and would start combing the woods for him. Brig silently cursed his lack of a weapon. His knife would only be good for man-to-man fighting and Fletcher would never let him get that close.

As Fletcher moved onto the wide path the wind had swept free of snow, he stopped. Brig's throat was dry. He glanced at his cover. As long as he didn't move, he would be difficult to spot. He watched Fletcher search the trees with his gaze.

"McCord!" he called. "You might as well come out. I know you're wounded. I found the blood on the ground the other day. Let's make this as painless as possible. You can't travel far—not far enough to escape me. I promise you I'll end it quickly."

Brig didn't answer. The deadfall was an obvious place to hide and it would be the first place Fletcher would investigate. He looked around to see if there was someplace else. Time—he just had to buy a little time. Maybe Fletcher would make a mistake.

"Nobody is going to help you, if that's what you're hoping, McCord!" Fletcher called again, working his way slowly up the slope. "Jocko is on the other side of camp. I watched him leave this morning. Even if he heard the rifle shot, he'd never make it in time to help you. He's a long way from here. Jordanna might be leaving camp now, but she won't help you. It's just you and me, McCord. So, come on out."

There was a tree to one side of him and Brig inched toward it, moving only when he was certain Fletcher was looking in another direction. Using its wide trunk as a shield, he straightened and flattened himself against it. Each second he gained became precious.

"I know why you have to kill me, Fletcher!" he called to the hunter. "But why did you kill Max?"

"Come out where I can see you."

"No! Not yet!" Brig shouted, aware the hunter was moving, now that he had located his prey, but he didn't know in which direction. "If I'm going to die, at least give me the peace of mind of knowing all the answers!"

"The bastard thought he could take my wife and my money."

Fletcher's voice came from the left and Brig inched in the opposite direction, keeping the tree trunk between them. It mattered little that his first suspicion about Max and Fletcher's wife had been right all along.

"You are a fool, Fletcher," Brig declared.

"No, you are the fool for dragging this out! Step out here where I can see you!"

"You can still get out of this, Fletcher. You can buy yourself some attorneys and probably get off with a light charge and a couple years' probation for Max's death. But if you kill me, you are compounding everything. They'll hang you for this. It's premeditated murder and you know it."

"But you are the only one who does!" Fletcher laughed. "And you'll be dead!"

The jangle of bridle bits and laboring horses reached Brig's hearing, followed by the thudding of galloping hooves. His head jerked in the direction of the sound as Jordanna and Kit crested the rise, a loose horse galloping with them, its head held to one side to avoid the trailing reins. Jordanna slid from the bare back of the horse.

"Brig!"

He heard the panic in her voice. "Stay back, Jordanna!"

"Get out of here, Jordanna," Fletcher ordered. "This doesn't concern you."

"No!" she protested stridently. "No, you aren't going to kill him! Dad, stop this!"

"You heard me. Now do as you are told!"

"Who is next after me, Fletcher?" Brig challenged. "Jordanna is a witness. So is your son. Are you going to kill them, too? And what about Jocko? He can read signs better than you. Do you think he isn't going to know what really happened here? You kill me and you'll have to keep killing and killing. It won't stop with just me!"

A bullet whipped the tree near his head. Brig ducked to avoid the spray of bark. The man was beyond reason, driven over the edge, beyond reach of any logic.

At the shot, Jordanna whirled around and grabbed the rifle from her brother's hands. This time the tree had protected Brig, but unless she stopped her father, it might not turn out that way again. She rammed a bullet into the chamber. Before the reverberations of the first shot had died, Jordanna was firing her rifle in the air, then swinging the muzzle down to point at her father.

"I won't let you kill him," she warned.

Her father turned to look at her in surprise. Out of the corner of her eye, Jordanna saw Brig limp to a different tree, one that brought him closer to the windswept slope. But she didn't let her gaze become distracted from her father's stunned face.

"You won't kill me." He relaxed slightly, a faint smugness entering his expression.

"I don't have to kill you, Dad." There wasn't more than thirty yards between them. "At this distance, I can hit you anywhere I want . . . in the leg, the shoulder, the knee. You taught me how to shoot. You know what I can do. Drop the rifle, Dad."

"You don't understand." A frown gathered on his face. He seemed about to argue with her; then he pressed his lips tightly together and turned to take aim on the tree where Brig had been.

Jordanna fired and the bullet kicked up a patch of snow in front of him, whining into space. A handful of rocks tumbled down the slope from the rocky crags above, dislodged by the reverberating percussion of the rifle shot. "Don't make me do this." The rifle barrel wavered when she brought it to bear on him again. Despite her outward show of calm, she was crying inside. This man had once been the object of her hero-worship.

"Jordanna, he's been shot." Her father's voice was on a reasoning note. "I have to finish him, put him out of his misery. Don't you see the forgiveness in his eyes?"

"No!" She nearly screamed the word.

There was a crunching sound and Jordanna thought it was her world being stepped on. Behind her, Kit shouted, "Dad, look out!!"

Her first thought was Brig, and her gaze flew to the tree that hid him. She had a glimpse of him looking up before Kit roughly pushed her aside to run toward her father. As Jordanna stumbled backwards, she saw the huge boulders rolling silently over the snow. As they picked up speed, the earth began to rumble.

Brig heard Jordanna's scream as she realized her father was in the path of the boulders. He stepped from behind the tree and cupped his hands to this mouth to shout above the roaring avalanche of rock.

"This way, Fletcher!"

The gray-haired man was staring at the rocks rushing toward him. He didn't hear Brig call, but he saw Kit running toward him. Instead of running toward the trees, where he had a chance of escaping the slide, he started toward his son. The smaller rocks were already under his feet. The first boulder clipped his shoulder, knocking him to the ground. The rest crashed and rolled over him, dragging and rolling his limp body along with them.

It was a short, violent slide. When it subsided, Brig limped across the wide path, strewn and scraped with rocks. Kit was scrambling down the slope to where the body was wedged between two boulders. Jordanna had dropped the rifle and buried her face in her hands. When Brig reached her, she had just begun to realize it was over. She uncovered her eyes to stare down the slope.

"Daddy?" she cried brokenly and took a step toward the body Kit was uncovering.

Brig hooked an arm around her waist and pulled her back. "No. It's better if you don't look."

She lifted her tear-streaked face to stare at him. "He's . . . dead."

"Be glad the mountain took him, Jordanna. No one has to know what happened or why. Your father is dead. There isn't any reason for you, your brother, or your mother to suffer through a lot of dirty publicity. Do you understand?" he asked gently.

"Yes." She began sobbing and wrapped her arms around his neck to cling to him.

"We'll get through this." Tenderness surged through him. "We'll make it together." He held her close, absorbing her tremors.

A horse and rider crested the ridge and paused. The horse tossed its mane and chewed at the bit. Jocko took in the scene at a glance and rode down to the young man bent over the still form.